A POTION
—— *for a* ——
WIDOW

Caroline Roe

BERKLEY PRIME CRIME, NEW YORK

This is a work of fiction. Names, characters, places, and incidents either are the product of the author's imagination or are used fictitiously, and any resemblance to actual persons, living or dead, business establishments, events, or locales is entirely coincidental.

A POTION FOR A WIDOW

A Berkley Prime Crime Book / published by arrangement with the author

PRINTING HISTORY
Berkley Prime Crime mass-market edition / December 2001

All rights reserved.
Copyright © 2001 by Medora Sale.
Cover art by Jeff Barson.

This book, or parts thereof, may not be reproduced in any form without permission.
For information address: The Berkley Publishing Group,
a division of Penguin Putnam Inc.,
375 Hudson Street, New York, New York 10014.

Visit our website at
www.penguinputnam.com

ISBN: 0-425-18365-3

Berkley Prime Crime Books are published
by The Berkley Publishing Group,
a division of Penguin Putnam Inc.,
375 Hudson Street, New York, New York 10014.
The name BERKLEY PRIME CRIME and the
BERKLEY PRIME CRIME
design are trademarks belonging to Penguin Putnam Inc.

PRINTED IN THE UNITED STATES OF AMERICA

10 9 8 7 6 5 4 3 2 1

For my resourceful nieces
Emily and Alison Sale

CAST OF CHARACTERS

Clara de Finestres, a young woman from Barcelona of good family

Gil de Finestres, her father, an official of His Majesty

Serena de Finestres, his wife

Guillem, their young son

Dalmau, Serena's servant

Oliver de Centelles, a royal officer concerned with security on the Castile-Aragon border.

Mundina, his loyal nurse

*Berenguer de Cruïlle*s, Bishop of Girona

Bernat sa Frigola, his secretary

Isaac, his physician

Judith, Isaac's wife

Raquel, their daughter

Naomi, Leah, and Ibrahim, their servants

Yusuf, Isaac's assistant and student, ward to the King

Daniel, Raquel's suitor

Luis Mercer, a Girona merchant

Luis Vidal, another Girona merchant

Domingo, sergeant of the Bishop's guard

Martin from Tudela, a Castilian, a patient of Isaac

Mother Benedicta, owner of a cheap tavern just outside Girona

Bernat d'Olzinelles, minister in charge of the Royal treasury and treasurer to the King

Bernat de Relat, treasurer of the Queen's household

Crispià, a Dominican priest, a convert from Islam who befriends Yusuf

<small>WITH THE ROYAL ARMY IN SARDINIA:</small>

Pedro of Aragon, King of the Aragonese empire
Eleanora of Sicily, Queen of Aragon
Maria Lopez de Heredia, lady in waiting to the Queen
Tomasa de Sant Climent, lady in waiting to the Queen
Manuel, a nobleman
Marc, a medical attendant
Gueralt de Robau, a young squire
Asbert de Robau, a knight, his father
Lord Pere Boyll, a nobleman

Soldiers, servants, townspeople

HISTORICAL NOTE

Problems on the island of Sardinia, a part of his widespread kingdom, preoccupied the King of Aragon, Pedro (or Pere) the Ceremonious, during 1354. Old difficulties with the Catalan governors of the island had flared into open revolt. After several warnings to his subjects there, in June the King set out with his fleet to subdue the port city of Alghero.

Although Don Pedro was able to raise substantial amounts for ships and supplies, not everyone was enthusiastic about another Mediterranean campaign. A few years before, under the strategic direction of Bernat de Cabrera, one of Pedro's advisers since he became King at the age of seventeen, the Aragonese kingdoms and Venice fought a war against Genoa. Aragonese-Venetian forces won some spectacular battles at sea, but they lost a great many ships and men. As well, Cabrera's actions in settling the war led the Crown into its current difficulties with Sardinia.

Pedro decided to direct this new campaign himself. He had hoped for a lightning strike on the city of Alghero, a quick surrender on the part of its people, and a neat and orderly resolution to its problems. Shoddy equipment led to the failure of his initial attack, and the King's forces settled in for a prolonged siege. Full summer brought an epidemic of a feverish illness, which killed an indeterminate number of Aragonese troops and many officers and seriously weakened many others. Morale was low; the Sardinian air was widely believed by the Aragonese to be very unhealthy. Some of the sick were sent home to recover, and a number of officers fled with them, failing to return. Pedro's letters and other writings bear witness to the bitterness he felt at their disloyalty.

Supplies, especially for those stricken with the fever, were running low during that summer. Don Pedro wrote urgent letters back to his governing bodies in Catalonia and Valencia asking for assistance. Valencia and Barcelona responded quickly with galleys, foodstuffs, and medical supplies. With this fortification, the siege continued until the city of Alghero surrendered in November.

The Queen, Eleanora of Sicily, a fearless woman of twenty-nine, accompanied her husband to the battlefield. Long before she had married Don Pedro, those who knew her spoke in admiration of her intelligence, wit, and skill in statecraft. Certainly by this point in their lives together, Eleanora of Sicily was the King's most influential adviser, supplanting the ill-fated Bernat de Cabrera, whom she disliked and mistrusted.

Don Vidal de Blanes, abbot of Sant Feliu, the Benedictine abbey just outside the north gate of the city of Girona, was named procurator of the province of Catalonia for the duration of the campaign, with full authority to act in the King's absence. Don Vidal was soon to replace the ailing Huc de Fenollet as Archbishop of Valencia. By 1356, Vidal de Blanes held one of the most important ecclesiastical appointments in the combined Aragonese kingdoms.

During this period, however, daily life did not change much. Catalonia and Valencia were maritime nations, filled with mapmakers and boatbuilders. Their sailors and skilled navigators already traveled to every Mediterranean port, as well as to London, Brussels, and other trading cities in the Atlantic. Sea journeys were common. Ships like the Queen's galley—expensive to operate but fast—carried spices, silks, and perishables, all at risk from pirates, but high-profit goods; sturdy, capacious, slow-sailing vessels carried heavy cargo, such as wool and wine. But the line between merchant ships and war ships or between traders, naval officers, and pirates was not always as clearly drawn as it is now. Ships and their crews slipped between being one or the other with ease, and the business of the kingdom carried on as usual.

Lawyers and notaries drafted contracts and drew up wills, merchants bought and sold, craftsmen fashioned everything from armor to silk gowns, and thieves stole what they could, as they always had. Slave traders sold foreign slaves in the markets of Barcelona and raided coastal villages for adults and children to sell in North Africa and Asia. By the age of eight or nine, boys of all classes and the poorer girls were apprenticed to a trade or profession or were bound into servitude for a set period of time to gain experience and skills.

Their rulers' pursuit of foreign policy usually had little impact on their lives, unless by some unlucky chance they happened to be swept up in events that had nothing to do with them.

CANONICAL HOURS

In the fourteenth century, time was almost always expressed in what were known as the *hours*, that is, the time of regular worship in monastic life. Every three hours, starting at midnight, the bells rang, and life paused for the service appropriate to that time. The bells, however, could be heard all over the cities and the countryside and functioned as clocks to mark the hours for everyday life.

There is some variation in the names over the centuries, but the usual order, which appears in these books, is:

12:00 midnight	Matins
3:00 A.M.	Laud
6:00 A.M.	Prime
9:00 A.M.	Tierce
12:00 noon	Sext
3:00 P.M.	Nones
6:00 P.M.	Vespers
9:00 P.M.	Compline

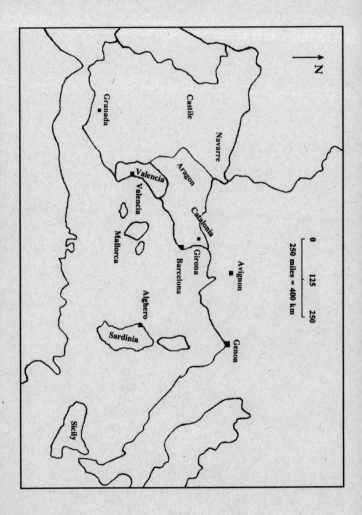

PRELUDE

Barcelona, September 1350

Clara sat sideways on the cool stone windowsill, her knees drawn up to her chest. She was staring at the hem of her dark blue gown, caked with dried mud mercilessly lit by the morning sun. She had forgotten about that mud. It had been there when she had folded the offending piece of clothing and thrust it away at the end of winter, out of sight. It was still there. The long tear in the skirt was still there as well.

Even when it was new, she had hated that gown. Its color was drab and its design ugly. She had had a hundred ideas for enlivening it, but her mother had told her firmly that until she learned to keep her perfectly serviceable clothing mended and in good repair, she could not waste any more time and silk thread on fanciful embroidery. She sighed. She would never finish her mending. Clara was lively and hard on clothes.

She threw the gown onto the floor and considered the possibility of hiding it behind the bed. Let the new owners of the house have it along with the furniture—wonderful things that for some reason they had to leave behind for them. But Mama was sure to find out. Clara's best hope was that she had grown over the summer. If the gown could no longer be made to fit her, Mama would set it aside to make a tunic for her baby brother.

As quickly as she could, she jumped down, untied and unbuttoned her new summer gown, and scrambled into the old winter one. *Please*, she prayed silently, *don't let it fit*. It had already been let out once, and there wasn't much material left in the seams. But although her eleven-year-old body had grown upward by almost a handsbreadth, she was just as thin as ever. The gown was no tighter than it had been last April, when she had put it away. Mama would take a careful look at it, tell her to sponge off the mud, mend the tear, and let down the hem. It was perfectly acceptable for everyday wear, she would say, and then ask her once more if she thought that cloth grew on the trees in the courtyard.

Papa would have bought her a length of cloth for a gown. But Papa was dead, and they had to move to the country when Mama's year of mourning was up. Now that Papa was dead, Mama said, they didn't own the house any longer. It seemed strange that someone they had never met could own a house that had always been theirs.

The door to her chamber opened, and Clara's musings on the many injustices of life were cut abruptly short. Her mother stood in the doorway. She had a big marketing basket over one arm, and Clara's two-year-old brother, Guillem, was clinging to her other hand. She came in and closed the door quietly behind her. "Clara, listen to me," she whispered, setting down the basket. "I want you to pack a few things . . . a change of linen, perhaps one other small thing. We must leave. Now."

"But, Mama. You said—" Clara fell silent. The day they brought the news that Papa was dead, her mother had looked the way she did now.

"Be quiet as a mouse, my dearest," she said, smiling as if nothing were wrong. "We mustn't let the servants hear what we're saying. I have the baby's things in the basket. I will take him and go, as if I were going marketing. Wait here. As soon as you can see me through the window, take your bundle and go to the nuns. They will know what to do."

"But, Mama, I was trying on my old gown. I must change."

"You don't understand, dear. There is no time. Go as you are. Put on an apron to hide the rip." She snatched up the girl's apron. "Here. I'll tie it for you. Give your brother a kiss, my love. As soon as it's safe, I'll come for you. I promise." She crouched down and looked into her daughter's eyes. "Let no one know you're going. Make sure no one follows you. Tell no one Papa's name. Do you understand that? For your own safety and mine and your brother's."

"Where are you going, Mama?" she said, clinging to her mother's arm.

"If anyone asks, tell them you don't know." She threw her arms tightly around her daughter. "Tell them you think I've gone to Mallorca. That I can't believe Papa is dead, and I think he's there."

"Is that true?"

"It's as true as anything in this world," she said bitterly. "You might need money for now," she added, taking a small purse out of her gown and doing up the button again. "Tuck this in your gown, under your apron tie, where no one can see it. The nuns will look after you." She picked up the boy and ran, light of step and fleet-footed, in spite of the weight of her son. Clara heard her brother's delighted giggle as they raced down the stairs. Dry-eyed with shock, she tumbled some clean linen and her summer gown into her best shawl, tied it up, paused for a moment, and stuffed another change of linen into the bodice of her gown.

She darted out the front door into the edge of a group of eight or ten people walking briskly toward the center of town. They were chatting, showing no interest in her. Reassured, she followed along behind them. At the end of her quiet little street, the ten people joined a large, noisy crowd, all moving away from the convent. Suddenly, she was caught up in the crowd, pressed on every side by people much larger than she was, and she was carried helplessly along with them.

The crowd stopped. All around her, people were shouting and jumping up and down. She tried to slip through them, stumbled against a large boy, and lost her grip on her bundle.

Before it could hit the ground, a dirty hand snaked out of the crowd and grabbed it. She caught a glimpse of a ragged skirt, bare legs, and then her bundle in the arms of a girl no bigger than she was.

She crouched down to push through the crowd in search of the girl and almost fell over into a small space between two sets of legs. Frightened and helpless, she pulled herself upright and looked despairingly around.

Tears were pouring down her cheeks. She tried to get her arm up high enough to mop them with her sleeve. Suddenly a pair of enormous hands grabbed her around the waist and hoisted her high above the crowd. She gasped, too terrified to scream. Then she was lowered onto the broad left shoulder of a man wearing the tunic of a prosperous craftsman.

"There, child," he said. "Don't cry. You can see them from up here."

"Please, sir," she whispered. "I am going to the nuns. I must get there right away."

"The sisters will forgive you if you're late, child," he said. "No one can cross through in this crowd. As soon as it's over, I'll set you back on your path."

From somewhere in front of her a trumpet fanfare blared out, startling her out of her tears and immediate predicament. A focused shout went up and there, in front of her, not two arm's lengths away, was a pair of mules bearing the King and Queen. She had glimpsed His Majesty once before, in the spring. He had just returned from Valencia after long absence, bringing his bride, a Sicilian princess. This was her first look at the Queen. Her Majesty rode easily, holding herself as straight as a poplar tree. She was tall and beautiful, like Clara's mother, and just as slender, except for her swelling belly. At the sight of it, the crowd roared again, for that belly held the hopes of the entire kingdom for an heir to the throne and an end to civil wars. She was wearing a gown of green so soft it looked to Clara as if it had been cut out of seawater.

The Queen glanced over, caught sight of Clara perched above the crowd, and smiled; she leaned over and said something to His Majesty. Don Pedro turned to look at the girl, smiled in his turn, nodded, and returned to his own thoughts.

Then they were gone. The crowd began to thin out with much jostling and pushing.

"Which convent were you heading for?" asked the man.

The magic dissolved. "Back there," said Clara, with a return of panic. She knew where the nuns were. You went to the end of her street and took the road on your right hand. Then you turned to your left at the fountain and the convent was at the end of that street. They were moving farther and farther away from it. "Please let me down. I was supposed to go straight there."

"You don't live at the convent?" She shook her head. "Do you live anywhere?"

"No, sir. Please let me down," she said, wriggling over to jump.

He clamped his hands tightly around her ankles. "Sit still for a minute. That convent back there doesn't take in little girls like you. If you've got nowhere to go, you want the one across the road," he said. "The sisters are kind and forgiving ladies." He strode through the crowd that melted like a mist before him, set her down in front of a high gate, and rang the bell. As soon as it opened, he rushed off as if ashamed of his impulse to help.

Four nuns stood in the little parlor and looked down at Clara. "Your mother told you to come here," said one in a weary voice.

"Not exactly here, Sister," said Clara. "My mother said to come to the sisters, and they would know what to do."

"The precise words do not matter, child," said the tired nun. "Do not waste our time."

"And what is your name, child?" said the nun standing closest to the window. She was evidently watching something going on outside.

"Clara, Sister."

"You will address the prioress as Reverend Mother, Clara," said the weary one.

"I'm sorry, Reverend Mother," she said, curtsying. "My name is Clara."

"Just Clara? No other name?"

Her mother's frightened "Tell no one" rang in her ears.

Never before had she seen her mother in the grip of such fear. Better the great sin of lying to the nuns than to break faith with that trembling voice. "I don't know, Reverend Mother."

"Ah, I see." She turned from the window. "How old are you?"

"Eleven."

"Are you sure? You look eight or nine, at most," said the tired nun.

"I am eleven, Sister. My mother says I am small for my age."

"What can you do?"

"Do?" asked Clara with more panic.

"What do you know how to do?" explained the prioress. "What have you been taught?"

"To read and write," said Clara, and then considered her deficiencies. "A little," she added in interests of accuracy. "I can sew, but—"

"Not very well," said the tired one impatiently.

Clara was too cowed by this time to correct her.

"You have not gone out to work?"

"Gone out to work?" she whispered. "No, Sister."

"And you have no money," said the prioress, but in a kinder voice.

"My mother gave me some before she and—before she left." Clara took out the purse and handed it to the tired nun.

"How much, Sor Domenica?" asked the prioress.

"Five sous, Reverend Mother."

"The poor soul," said the prioress. "She must have given her all she had."

Clara burst into a flood of weeping.

"There, now, my dear," said the prioress. "We are all in God's hands, and He delights in looking after us. Sor Domenica, I suspect Clara needs her dinner and a bed. We need make no decisions until tomorrow."

The next morning, right after tierce, Clara found herself back in the parlor with the prioress. She made her best curtsy and wished the prioress good morning as she had been taught.

The prioress smiled. "Well, Clara," she said, "you say you

are eleven. I think you might be mistaken, but this morning I'm going to talk to you not as if you are eleven but like a young woman of fourteen or fifteen. Look out in the garden."

Startled, Clara walked over to the window. There was a sea of children out in the morning sun: some playing, more sitting silent, a few squabbling. The older ones were trying to keep order with the assistance of the two quiet nuns she had met the day before. "Yes, Reverend Mother?"

"The plague took half of us two years ago, and another quarter of us the summer after. Another of us died just two months ago. We are now four nuns, with two postulants who are looking after the babies and a handful of the hardest-working servants in Christendom. All those children out there are like you. Father, or mother, or both, dead. Like you, they have no one to look after them. We've taken in more of them than we can look after because someone must. If I had my way, I'd try to keep you forever, Clara. You seem a clever, good girl, quick and willing. No doubt you would be a great help to us."

"I would like to be a nun," said Clara.

"What I'm saying is that it is impossible. You have no dowry, and we could not afford to feed those poor creatures or ourselves if we took in dowryless waifs as sisters. I'm sorry to sound cruel, but that is what life is. Bread costs money. And without it, our children will die."

"Then what will I do?" she asked helplessly.

"Work, as many women must. We will find you a place, although if you are eleven, you are older than most untrained serving girls. If you wish, we will put your five sous safely away in our treasury, marked with your name. Then as you earn money, it can go with the five sous and will make up your dowry. From time to time, certain charitable people leave us funds to increase dowries for girls like you. I will see that you receive some of this extra money so that by the time you are eighteen, you will have enough to settle down in happy marriage with a respectable artisan. Do you understand what I'm telling you?"

"I must leave here and work," said Clara, thinking of the pale, thin kitchen maid in her mother's house. In what used to be her mother's house.

"Don't look so frightened, my dear. It will not be right away. You can stay with us for a few months. We must find you the best position we can. While we are looking, we will teach you some skills, and you can help us look after the little ones."

ONE

"May I ask what troubles Your Excellency?" Isaac the physician stood at the doorway to the Bishop of Girona's study, his hand resting lightly on his pupil's shoulder.

"Come in, Master Isaac," said the Bishop. "Nothing troubles me. That is, my body is well, and I have no private cares, for which I most heartily thank God. Nothing troubles me but the prospect of trouble."

"Shall I wait outside until I am wanted, lord?" said Yusuf, for although the boy possessed his fair share of curiosity, he had already heard enough political and philosophical disputations between the two men to have lost interest in them.

"No, Yusuf," said Berenguer. "You are in the middle of it, and I would like you to stay. In fact, you are its origin, perhaps even its cause."

"Me, Your Excellency?" asked Yusuf, looking with alarm at the Bishop. "What have I done?"

"One moment and you shall find out," said Berenguer. "Bernat," he called. His long-time secretary, Bernat sa Frigola, appeared through another door. "Bring me those letters from Don Vidal." The little Franciscan disappeared and returned almost at once with a handful of documents. He set each one, unfolded, on His Excellency's desk. Three pieces of the best Girona-made paper lay there, covered with writing. They were from a supply that Don Vidal de Blanes, abbot of Sant Feliu and now temporary procurator for His Majesty, had taken with him to Barcelona when he went off to serve the King.

"The letters, Your Excellency," he murmured.

"Read us the part about Yusuf from the last one."

"Certainly, Your Excellency," said Bernat. " 'In regard to the Dominican who was treated for the fever by your physician and the Moorish boy, Yusuf. As I feared, the young man has spoken to Father Salvador, who is raising questions about Yusuf's status.' "

"Status?" said Isaac.

"He explains," said Berenguer. "Continue, Bernat."

" 'Father Salvador wishes to know if the lad is a slave, and if he is not, asks why is he living in the *call*.' "

"Since everyone knows that Yusuf, as a ward of the King, cannot possibly be a slave, the question is purely mischievous," said Berenguer angrily. "And he knows quite well the complications that baptism would bring."

"He could no longer live and study in our house," said Isaac. "Or anywhere in the Jewish Quarter."

"And it might create problems if he wished to return to his own family. What did you say to him to raise such fear in his bosom?" asked the Bishop, turning toward the boy. "Don Vidal also wishes to know. Otherwise, he cannot act wisely."

The two clerics, Bishop and secretary, looked at the boy; his master and teacher, unable to do so because of his blindness, bent his head to listen. Yusuf reddened under the intensity of their combined scrutiny, blinked, and then tried to concentrate on exactly what had been said some four or five months before. "To start with," he said quickly, "I think he said I was a pretty lad or something foolish like that and asked if I came from Girona." That over with, he took a deep breath and continued at a measured pace. "This was when he was recovering from his fever but was still enfeebled and restless."

"Was anyone else in the room?" asked Isaac.

"No," he said. "He waited until you, lord, had left the room."

"Go on," said the physician.

"I said no. He asked me where I came from, and I said Granada. Then he asked if I were a slave. No, I said. Then he asked when I was returning to my family. I said I didn't know. Then, something happened—I believe my master called for me—and very thankfully, I left."

"Thank you, Yusuf," said the bishop. "Now that we know what we are dealing with, we can act."

"What does Your Excellency suggest?" asked Isaac, his face and manner calm but his voice tight with tension.

"I seem to recollect that His Majesty invited the lad to spend some time in Sardinia, practicing swordsmanship and courtly manners and learning the arts of war," said Berenguer idly.

"Yes, Your Excellency," said Yusuf, looking distinctly uncomfortable. "He did. But when he asked me to accompany him, I said I would prefer not to. It was most discourteous of me to speak to His Majesty like that. To change my mind now and ask if I might come . . ." His voice trailed away helplessly. "It is not possible."

"That is nothing," said Berenguer. "Most of his courtiers cannot remain wedded to one idea for longer than ten minutes. He will be neither upset nor surprised that you have changed your mind. Consider the problem, Master Isaac. We will discuss it further after Don Vidal's secretary arrives with the noble abbot's thoughts on this and other matters."

"To Sardinia! Nonsense." The voice of the physician's wife cut through the drowsy summer heat. Everyone sitting at the table in the shaded courtyard looked up from their dinners.

"Who's going to Sardinia?" asked Nathan, one of the eight-year-old twins. "Is it near Constantinople? Will he see Daniel?"

"Yusuf," said his sister Miriam. "Why don't you listen?"

"Can I go to Sardinia, Papa? And I listen better than you do, Miriam. When I'm at school—"

"It is for his own safety," said Isaac in an attempt to cut off the twins' bickering before it started. "It won't be for long, I hope, and while he is gone, we shall all miss him."

"He isn't going," said Judith. "I won't have him sent off to fight a war that has nothing to do with him. All that distance, in a ship, alone. He's just a boy."

"He's thirteen," said Isaac. "Are you not, Yusuf?"

"I may be," said Yusuf uneasily. "I'm not sure."

"How old were you when you went to Valencia with your father?" asked Isaac.

Yusuf's face paled. "I'm not sure."

"You said you were seven," said Raquel. "Were you lying?" The twins' older sister looked accusingly at the boy.

"I don't think so," he said unhappily. "But someone told me I was seven in the year of the plague."

"We can't go by that. People will say anything," said Judith. "Do you remember losing your first milk tooth?"

"Yes," he said. "I was in the courtyard, playing."

"Which courtyard?"

"Ours," he said. "It was the day before we left for Valencia. I gave it to my mother, and she gave me a kiss and silver coin for it," said the boy, startled. "All the way to Valencia I had a strange hole between my teeth. And then I lost the silver coin. After—"

"I don't believe he's more than twelve," said Judith briskly. "I always thought he was younger than he said."

"He is old enough to follow His Majesty to Sardinia and to sail across the sea," said Isaac. "There are many younger than he at the court and in the ships of the kingdom, learning the arts of war and navigation. We have no choice, my dear."

"He's not going," said Judith.

Tuesday, July 29, 1354

"An excellent idea," said Don Vidal's secretary. The sharp-eyed young man had ridden thirty miles that morning and, in spite of fatigue, the dust of the road, and the heat of the day, he managed to look sleek and neat. "For several reasons," he added, taking a large draft of the cool drink set in front of him, his only concession to the rigors of the day.

"Indeed?" said Berenguer.

"I left Barcelona on Tuesday, Your Excellency, having

other business along the way to transact for His Excellency, Don Vidal. When I last spoke to him, Don Vidal had just heard distressing news from Sardinia. There has been an outbreak of fever among the troops; not only have many died, but supplies needed to succor the ill are running low. His Majesty urgently requires medicines, wine, poultry, and sugar. Galleys will be leaving as soon as the supplies can be loaded and the ships manned. His Majesty's ward can travel with one of them in comfort."

"When will that be?"

"The first galley might be able to leave as early as Monday; another will be going later in the week."

"I have a simple solution to this problem," said Berenguer.

"A simple solution?" asked the secretary. "Do you mean sending the boy back to Granada? Are you sure that His Majesty would approve of it at this particular time?"

"That was not in my thoughts," Berenguer said crisply. "As you and I both know, all he requires is a license to stay where he is. His Majesty will no doubt grant one. Or—"

"In the absence of Don Pedro, His Majesty's procurator can supply it," added the secretary. "Don Vidal has, of course, thought of that. But there are considerations—"

"Such as why did Father Salvador wait almost five months before speaking up against something that he found so repugnant?" said the Bishop wryly. "Does he, by the way, have an explanation for his delay?"

"He says that, since he is well acquainted with your careful scrupulousness in matters of religion, he knew that you would not act hastily but had hoped that you would have acted by now."

"That is, he was waiting—"

"Until Their Majesties had set out for Sardinia, hoping that they would be too preoccupied with the war to concern themselves with such a small matter. And in that case, His Excellency Don Vidal might very well issue a letter granting the boy permission to stay where he is."

"He knows them little if he truly believes that Don Pedro will find this a small matter," observed Berenguer. "But I understand Don Vidal's concerns. Such a letter might give malicious souls grounds for accusing him of placing the King ahead of the Church. A serious matter for a churchman with a bright future ahead of him, as I understand is the case."

"Some possibilities have been mentioned," said his secretary modestly with the pleased air of one who plans on having a bright future in his superior's wake.

"The archbishopric of Valencia is no small thing," said Berenguer. "It would be a pity if it went to a lesser man through someone's ill will or even mere incompetence."

"Since the lad is under the protection of His Majesty," said the secretary, "Don Vidal suggested that he avail himself of that protection now. If he is in Sardinia, nothing—shall we say—unfortunate can happen to him before His Majesty can intervene."

"Then he must be sent away as soon as possible," said Berenguer. "I shall speak to the physician."

"I know that he will be safe with His Majesty," said Judith, in a troubled voice. "But the journey! Traveling with all that money. He could be killed on the way to Barcelona."

"What money, Mama?" said Raquel.

"Permissions are not given away," said Judith sharply. "Yusuf will have to carry a large purse of gold with him."

"His Majesty's ward requires no gold to keep him safe," said Isaac. "No money will change hands for that letter."

"So you say," she said doubtfully. "He will travel by boat."

"He will be traveling in a swift galley, my dear, protected by armor of rawhide."

"Why rawhide, Papa?" asked Raquel in an attempt to deflect her mother's attention.

"Stout rawhide fastened over the hull protects it from the fiercest attack," said Isaac. "These days, even Daniel's ship will have it."

"Rawhide won't protect him from storms," said Judith.

"It is not the season for storms," said her husband. "And he will be traveling on Her Majesty's own personal galley."

"And how can the Queen protect him?" said Judith.

"Please, Mama," said Raquel, "must we talk about disasters happening to travelers? I find it disturbing."

"There's no use worrying about Daniel. He's already in

Constantinople," said Judith with fine disregard for logic. "He's been gone at least a fortnight."

"Three weeks and four days," said Raquel.

"And he went on a merchant ship, not a ship of war," added her mother. "Who would attack him?"

"Who?" said Raquel. "Pirates. Storms. Warships from other countries. The Genoese. The Moors. They're all looking for cargoes and slaves. Why did Master Ephraim send him away?"

"Perhaps because those few brave souls who manage to return from trading ventures—and there are cities filled with them," said Isaac dryly, "come back rich both in learning and in worldly goods. Not a bad gift for a young man about to marry, even if it does frighten my normally lion-hearted daughter out of her wits."

"Papa, you mock me and my fears."

"Not you, Raquel, only your fears. The dangers that Daniel faces are not as large as you think. Pray for his safety and then find Yusuf. I shall send some of my most efficacious compounds with him. They might be of use to Their Majesties and their troops. You two must check what is there and then gather or buy what is needed. And soon. We have little time—and none for useless weeping."

"Tomorrow there will be preparations for the Sabbath," said her mother relentlessly. "And Yusuf's clothes have still to be taken out and made ready for him."

"Must I do everything?" said Raquel.

"It won't hurt you, and we will all be busy enough," said her mother unsympathetically.

The next morning, the sun rose above the hills into a sky already silvered over with a shimmer of the heat to come. By tierce, it was hanging, copper-colored and slightly ominous, in the southeastern sky, still not high enough to penetrate the narrow, canyonlike streets of the city.

With the passing of another hour, here and there sunlight reached the pavement and found its way through ground floor windows. The stones began to warm; the heat in the city started to build. Wives out marketing early slowed from a brisk trot to an amble. Dogs found quiet corners in the shade and settled down to sleep away the day. By the time bells rang for noon, the laborers in the fields would be edging early from their toil toward their dinners, after which all work would cease until the sun began to dip to the western hills.

Berenguer de Cruilles sat in front of his unshuttered window and considered the problems that Bernat had laid on his desk early that morning. He had already done the simple things: signed letters of permission and approved arrangements for duty that had been drawn up by meticulous subordinates. Instead of working, though, he allowed his mind to wander far and randomly, drawn where it would by the scented breeze from the hills and the muted noises from the streets. His reverie was interrupted by a quick knock and the turning of the latch to his study. Bernat. Again.

"Has Your Excellency had a moment to consider Father Pau's request? He is waiting below."

"It is hot, Bernat. I cannot remember a summer here when it was so hot. How do you expect me to consider anyone's request, especially such a foolish one? Tell Pau that if he wishes an answer that is not a simple no, he should return when it is a little cooler."

"As Your Excellency wishes," said Bernat with a faint smile. Berenguer deduced from the smile that his secretary did not like Father Pau. "And, Your Excellency, there is a gentleman to see you."

"A gentleman?"

"A friend," said Bernat, "looking travel-stained and weary."

"Your Excellency," cried a voice from behind the secretary. Towering in the doorway was a big, square-shouldered man with strong features, a luxuriant head of light brown curls, and a military air, although he dressed like a man of peace in a modest station in life.

"My Lord . . . my good Oliver," said the Bishop. "What brings you here in all this heat? But first, sit and have something cool to drink. You look like a man with a dry throat."

"I would be grateful for that, Your Excellency, although my stout mule and I have already stopped to drink at your fountain. I also attempted to wash off some of the dust of travel," he added, looking ruefully down at his tunic.

"With a singular lack of success," said Berenguer. "But we will excuse you. You come alone, bailiff?"

Oliver's eyes flicked momentarily over to the Bishop's secretary.

"If you will excuse me, Your Excellency, I must make sure your guest's mule is attended to," said Bernat, moving quickly toward the door. "And refreshment is brought."

"An excellent fellow, that," said Oliver. "Very efficient, although not happy to see me interrupt you." He moved a chair so that the breeze from the window touched it and sat. "And I will be very happy to sit down before unburdening myself," he added. "I have had a long and weary ride."

"May I ask from where?"

"From some forty miles to the west," he said vaguely.

"Forty miles this morning in the heat, Oliver?" said Berenguer. "Your mule must be as strong as tempered steel."

"The moon is full, Your Excellency, and we traveled by its light for the first fifteen of them."

"A lonely ride, bailiff," observed the Bishop. "On somewhat dangerous roads."

"I was not entirely alone," said Oliver. "I had with me a companion. A man you might remember," he added casually. "Then we chose a quiet spot to rest ourselves and the beasts, but it was not a healthy choice, it seems. My companion was unable to continue the journey."

"How unable?" said Berenguer in quick alarm.

"I cannot say," said Oliver. "Because I do not know. I fell asleep. When I awoke, I was alone. I know nothing more, Your Excellency."

"When did you set out?" asked Berenguer. "After the world was asleep?"

"Most of the world. Where we lay, the bells for matins called us from our beds. We ate a crust or two with a draft of wine and water, and left, having prepared for the journey beforehand. Allowing for a few quiet words to the lad in the stable, and walking the mules down to the road, so as not awaken the house, I would say that we were in the saddle some five to ten minutes after midnight. It was the very end of night when we stopped. That is, the moon was just starting to pale with dawn."

"Did his mule disappear as well?"

"She did. But not mine. It would take a magician to drag my Neta off in the night while I slept nearby. Her braying would wake the dead, never mind me."

"Perhaps your companion had his own reasons for going off."

"It is possible. I make no hue and cry over his disappearance for that reason, Your Excellency. I come to you, instead, to beg a favor."

"You have but to ask, bailiff," said Berenguer courteously.

"I ask a bed in a quiet corner, Your Excellency, and harborage for Neta, until Monday morning. We must travel to Barcelona, but it is not necessary for us to be there before Monday at sundown. I thought to stay here as long as I could. In fact, to spend a quiet Sunday in Girona."

"You are most welcome to all that we can offer," said the Bishop. "Bernat will see that you have everything you need. And you intend to travel on Monday?"

"I do. I can wait no longer, I think."

"Then perhaps I can find another companion for you."

"If he has a quick eye and skill with a sword," said Oliver, "he will be welcome. And no small measure of courage, of course."

"I think you will find he has all that," said the Bishop. "And what he lacks in experience, he makes up in wit and quickness. For a lad of twelve or thirteen, he's coming along well."

"Twelve or thirteen!"

TWO

Monday, August 4

The square at the foot of the hill slumbered quietly in the moonlight. To the east, behind the looming blackness of the cathedral, the sky was beginning to lighten. The faint screech of a hinge signaled movement somewhere within the sleeping city; the postern gate to the *call* opened, and three dark shapes came out. As soon as they stepped into the light, they turned into the lightly cloaked figures of a tall, broad-shouldered, bearded man, a boy, and a tall, slender woman. In the man's hand was a long staff; the other two each carried a small bundle. After a brief interval, three grotesquely bulky shapes followed them and were transformed by the alchemy of moonlight into a smaller boy and two women, all heavily laden with bundles, baskets, and packages.

A single bird began to sing in the Bishop's garden.

Raquel, the tall young woman, tossed back her hood and walked over to the three late arrivals. "Mama, why are you carrying all that?" she asked, taking a basket and a bundle wrapped in a linen towel from her.

"It's some cold dinner for the road," said Judith. "I know the rubbish they feed you when you travel. I wouldn't give it to a dog. Yusuf will need something to eat."

"You brought enough to feed him until he gets back from Sardinia," Raquel observed. "Where are the others?" she added, looking around her.

"At the stables," said her father. "I hear them now."

Night still reigned in that end of the square, but the sound of shod hooves on cobbles betrayed the presence of two guards, their dark mounts almost invisible until they moved from the shadow of the walls into the growing light from the east.

"Will His Excellency come to say good-bye to Yusuf?" asked Raquel quietly.

"I believe so," said Isaac. "The lad will be disappointed if he does not," he added.

The next to appear was the captain of the Bishop's Guard, walking briskly across the square toward them. "And where is my pupil?" he asked briskly, looking and sounding as if he had slept soundly and breakfasted heartily.

"Here, sir," said Yusuf, stifling a yawn.

"I bring you your sword," he said, holding it out with a slight bow, as if presenting it to a newly made knight. "Buckle it on. Until you return, you are in His Majesty's service and must go armed, prepared for anything."

He slid the leather harness over the lad's shoulder and waited silently for him to buckle it. That accomplished, he handed him the sword and watched until it was resting properly against his side.

"Thank you, sir," said Yusuf. "I had forgotten that I would need it," he whispered in embarrassment.

"His Majesty expects to see his generous gifts in use," said the captain just as quietly. "And I know you will do me credit, lad," he added in normal tones. "I have no doubt at all of your courage. But remember what I taught you."

"I remember it all, I believe," said the boy, with just a hint of complacency.

"When is your enemy at his most dangerous?"

"When he appears to be defeated," said Yusuf quickly.

"Yes. And yet it still happens every time that we match swords, doesn't it? I pause for breath and you let your guard down. I could have killed you ten times over. Or more."

"Yes, Captain," said the boy.

"And don't stop to rejoice when you seem to be winning; move in and finish your opponent. Such behavior has been the downfall of many a cocky young warrior. Remember that your opponent is there to kill you. War is not a game of chess, Yusuf. A wily enemy will pretend weakness to lure you into a trap. Trust no one, and remember your elbows," he added, giving one of them a tap.

"I will, Captain. I promise, sir," said Yusuf.

At that moment another guard rode up, followed by stable lads leading four sturdy baggage mules and Yusuf's bay mare, her glossy coat and rich color just visible in the strengthening light. "Where is the bailiff?" asked the sergeant of the guards, who had been released from his usual duties rather reluctantly by the captain to oversee the valuable cargo and equally valuable person of the King's ward.

"Oliver? I have not seen him," said the captain. "He may be with His Excellency."

"The day gives every sign of becoming hotter than yesterday, Captain," said the sergeant. "And the mules are carrying heavy loads. If we are to be in Barcelona before nightfall, we must leave soon. Or procure more baggage animals."

"Listen, Domingo," said the captain to his sergeant, "if it cannot be done in one day, so be it. Ride as far as you can under these conditions and finish the journey tomorrow. Our first responsibility is to get these loads safely to Barcelona."

"We could leave now, Sergeant," said a younger one. "And leave Oliver Climent to catch up with us."

"His Excellency would not be pleased," said the sergeant. "He wishes us to lend our protection to his friend's bailiff."

"His friend's bailiff looks able to protect himself," muttered the second guard, an unangelic-looking Gabriel.

"Who is this Oliver?" asked Judith, who until now had stood uncharacteristically silent. "Is he trustworthy?"

"He is a dependent of a friend of our Lord Bishop," said Isaac, "and is apparently strong and handy with a weapon. His Excellency is most anxious that they travel together."

"And so they must needs fry in the sun together because Oliver likes his sleep," said Judith. "Look . . . it is quite light now. They will scarcely need the moon to light the road. Soon enough they will have the sun."

"Very true, Mistress Judith," said the sergeant. "And the lads have not finished loading those mules. Here!" he called. "What are you layabouts up to? Get to work." And he strode over to the mountainous stack of baggage that had been carried out of the palace and the strong room of the cathedral. "Do you expect these chests to climb on the animals' backs by themselves?"

When the loading was finished, two stout baskets and three bundles were still sitting on the ground. "What are those?" asked the sergeant.

"They are to go with you," said Judith.

"Mama is worried that you will starve on the road to Barcelona," said Raquel. "She has packed a little cold dinner."

"And how are we to carry it?" asked the sergeant. "The mules are already heavily loaded for this heat and distance."

"My daughter and husband will ride with you the first part of the way," said Judith. "They have no baggage with them. Their mules can carry the food and bring back the baskets."

"Coming with us?" said the sergeant faintly. "His Excellency neglected to mention that."

"My father thought it possible that Yusuf might find leaving difficult at first," said Raquel.

"He is not a baby," said the sergeant.

"No, but my father will miss him," whispered Raquel. "And so will I. Don't worry. We plan to turn back when you stop for breakfast."

"And here is His Excellency," said Judith with relief. "At last." She had been watching the sergeant's face, where exasperation had given way to disbelief that was slowly turning to anger.

As the Bishop came down the hill, two more mules were being brought to the waiting travelers.

At that moment, fortunately for his reputation, Oliver Climent arrived. He was mounted on a heavy, powerful-looking horse, leading his mule, which was piled high with baggage, and chatting with a fourth guard who rode beside him. In a flurry of activity, the last baggage was fastened on and last farewells were exchanged. There was nothing left to do but leave when His Excellency's flustered-looking secretary came running down the hill in a state of agitation, bearing a packet in his hand.

With a sigh, the sergeant dismounted to find out what was wrong this time.

Across the square to their north, a sleepy gatekeeper yawned and began to unbar and unlock the gate to Sant Feliu and the Via Augusta, that great Roman road that runs from the Moorish and Castilian lands to the south and west of Valencia to the farthest northeastern borders of Catalonia—not that the gatekeeper cared where the road came from or where it was going.

"Are we so late that the city gates are already opening?" called Oliver.

The gatekeeper turned. "I know nothing of your life, bailiff," he said. "I only know I am to open early this morning."

"But not for us, surely?" said Oliver.

"Why should I?" said the gatekeeper, spitting into the dirt on the edge of the pavement. "I haven't felt the weight of your money. There are other folk in the city with important business," he added, "and one of them is expecting such riches by cart this morning that he'll pay a steep fee for dragging me from my bed before the city awakes. Now let me get back to my work."

"Nothing could please me more," said Oliver.

At that moment, another man entered the square from the southeast, hurrying down the hill toward the north gate. "Hola," he called, "gatekeeper! Has my carter arrived yet?"

"No, Master Luis," said the gatekeeper. "It's all quiet out there." He finished fastening back the second of the great doors against the high stone archway that held them, glanced out, saw and heard no sign of a cart of any size, and retreated to his little dwelling place, ready to rush out and attempt to hold up the carter for an additional penny or two.

The square returned to the somnolent peace of early morning. The only noise—except for the murmur of conversation among the sergeant, the Bishop, and his secretary—was the sound of distant hoofbeats and the chattering of birds. The physician dismounted and joined the others in their low-voiced discussion. With nods of agreement, the four men moved apart and again only the birds and the rider, drawing closer, could be heard.

The half silence was broken by a harsh, low cry, a loud clatter of hooves, and the sickening thud of a body colliding with something hard and unyielding. For an infinite moment, everyone was shocked into immobility.

"What was that?" said Judith.

"Over there," said Yusuf, pointing to the north gate.

A man had appeared in the archway. His hood had fallen down over his eyes; in his left arm he clutched a bundle close to his chest, and with his right arm he was supporting himself against the wall.

The man took another step and then began to crumple.

"Drunk," said the youngest guard.

"I don't think so," said the sergeant, wheeling his horse around. "That is blood that he trails behind him on the pavement."

A mule followed him around the corner, her reins dragging on the cobblestones as she went.

While the others were speaking, Oliver Climent dismounted and ran toward the staggering man. He caught him around the chest as he was falling, as easily as if he had been a child. He looked at his back and roared, "Get him a surgeon. He's been stabbed. Find out who did this."

Two of the guards put spurs to their horses and were gone. After another glance at the scene, the sergeant followed.

Oliver lowered the injured man gently onto his side. "Has someone gone for the surgeon?" he called, undid his own hood, and folded it for a pillow to put beneath the man's head.

"The blind man and his daughter will do as much and more for him than the surgeon can," said the captain. "They are close behind me." He turned. "Master Isaac," he said. "You are needed."

"Papa," said Raquel. "There is a badly injured man—"

"So I hear, Raquel. Where is that wretched boy?"

"Yusuf?" said Raquel, shocked.

"No," said her father. "Little Judah, the kitchen boy. He

must start learning Yusuf's role sometime. Judah! Take me over to the injured man."

"Shall I come, too, Papa?"

"Of course," said her father with angry impatience. "Unless you think he needs washing or turning on the spit. Those are little Judah's only skills at the moment."

"Yes, Papa," said his daughter, startled at her father's anger.

Raquel knelt on the cobblestones by the wounded man's back; her father crouched across from her, bending down until his ear was pressed against the man's side to listen. "He is shivering with cold and pain," said the physician.

"I will cover him." Oliver unstrapped his cloak from behind his saddle and covered the man from the waist down.

"Papa," said Raquel, "I think the knife must be taken out."

"I agree that he cannot live with a knife like that in him. It is worth the try," said Isaac, standing up. "Although I do not think there is much possibility of saving him—but we are in the Lord's hands and must help even when it seems beyond hope."

"We will take him into the palace," said Berenguer firmly. "He should not have to suffer out here on the cobblestones like a beast." The Bishop bent over him and began to push back his hood. "Good man," he said gently, "we will take you—God help us all!" he exclaimed. "It is Pasqual. We must save him if we can."

"Yes, Your Excellency," said Isaac. "But he is sorely wounded." The physician turned back to the captain. "It's the clerk at the Exchange, is it not?" he murmured.

"It is," said the captain. "Pasqual Robert." He looked around for some sturdy arms and backs. "You two," he called to the stable lads who were standing about watching, "help us to carry him to the palace."

"Where is Yusuf?" asked Isaac.

"He has gone to the house for some things you might need," said Judith, who was standing behind her husband.

"He is a clever lad," said Isaac.

Judith refrained from mentioning that she had sent him to do just that; instead, she turned back to her self-appointed task of collecting the injured man's possessions, scattered over the pavement when he fell, and neatly bundling them up.

As soon as he had seen Pasqual carried off to the episcopal palace, Oliver whistled for his horse and set off, grim-faced and silent, to find the officers.

Yusuf arrived at the palace shortly afterward, somewhat out of breath. He was carrying a large basket filled with clean linen bandages, herbs and leaves to stanch bleeding, and tinctures for pain, as well as a few extra remedies for fever and infection that he put in on his own initiative. He set them down close to Raquel and stepped back. "May I help, lord?" he said.

"No," said Isaac. "But wait. We might need you," he added and turned back to his patient.

"Yes, lord," said the boy and wandered over to the window to look out at the sky, gone from black to gray. When he leaned out of the window and looked up, he could see the moon, her light pale and feeble against the brighter sky. On the other side of the palace, the sky would be turning pink in preparation for sunrise. Behind him, he was aware that the knife was being drawn from the wound, and working with speed that he knew he could not match, Raquel was stanching it and binding it up. He heard her murmurs as she tried to give the patient a draft to ease his pain. He knew enough about such wounds now to realize that not much more could be done for him today. Surely they would not stay any longer. It was getting late, and he was overcome with an enormous impatience to be gone.

At that moment, he heard the firm, booted tread of an officer coming along the hall. "Any news?" said someone outside the room.

"Clean away," said an unfamiliar voice. The door opened and the bailiff, Oliver, came into the room.

They were leaving. Yusuf turned to say farewell to his master and Raquel and then stopped where he was. Oliver had not come to fetch him. He had instead pulled up a chair and sat down beside Pasqual as though he intended to stay with him all day.

Baffled, Yusuf went back to the window and tried to puz-

zle out the scene from there. Oliver and Pasqual seemed to
have become uncommonly close in a very short period of
time. Odd. Pasqual Robert, in Yusuf's eyes, had been an
unimportant and uninteresting nonentity. The boy knew most
people in the city but had never heard anything of interest
about the clerk except what anyone could know. He was
quiet, of something below average height, and rather thin. A
shy man who scampered, mouselike, from his employment
to his lodgings by clinging to the safety of the walls rather
than striding across the open spaces. Not a man to inspire
this level of devotion in someone, he thought. So there had
to be something else.

He understood his master staying at a stranger's bedside
for hours or even days. The physician felt an overwhelming
obligation to any man—or woman—who, sick or injured,
placed himself or herself in his hands. And so did Raquel,
although, he thought shrewdly, some patients inspired her
with less devotion than others. But why would this stranger
from wherever, on his way to Barcelona, be concerned with
Pasqual, the clerk?

Yusuf could foresee them all standing around until sunset,
then going home, and rising once more in the middle of the
night to start on their journey tomorrow. Too restless to stand
still any longer, he slipped out of the room into the hall.

Father Bernat, the bishop's endlessly busy Franciscan secretary, was standing near the door, doing nothing. It was not
like him. Everyone, except for his master and Raquel, was
behaving very oddly.

"Why is the bailiff keeping watch over Pasqual's bedside?" asked Yusuf. He had discovered some time ago that
Bernat's greatest weakness was gossip and that he knew
everything that was going on around the palace.

"Pasqual Robert has been working for him recently," said
Bernat. "When he was here last, Oliver asked His Excellency
to recommend a reliable man, and His Excellency suggested
Pasqual. His Excellency is most upset," added Bernat, as if
this were the gravest aspect of the incident.

"Was he to ride with us?" asked Yusuf. "No one spoke of
it."

"I don't know," said the secretary, shaking his head. "But

he and his mule disappeared last week. In the middle of the night."

"I wouldn't sit by the bedside of someone who left me like that," said Yusuf, yawning. "Anyway, if we're not leaving until Oliver Climent does, I'd better go back in case I'm wanted."

When Yusuf entered the room again, the physician was bending over Pasqual, with his ear against his chest, listening, and his hand on the side of his neck. Raquel stood by the pillow, a cloth in one hand and a cup of water in the other. The patient was worsening. His face was gray and sunken; his body seemed to have shrunk on its bones. But his eyes were open and focused sharply on Oliver. He had grasped the big man's forearm and was speaking to him in a quick, low voice.

The physician straightened up and stepped back. "Raquel," he murmured.

"Yes, Papa," she said, handing the cup and the cloth to Yusuf.

"Come out in the hall for a moment. I hear His Excellency. Keep him comfortable for the moment, Yusuf, and fetch me if I am needed."

"Yes, lord," he murmured, wondering that the physician could always tell when he had entered the room. As he listened to his master, he also tried to follow what Pasqual was saying. There was a sense of great urgency in the man's speech, but he spoke so rapidly in an accent so strange to Yusuf's ears that only a few words made sense to him.

The injured man paused to draw a labored breath. Yusuf bent over him, placed the cup against his lips, and then gently sponged his face. That done, he tactfully stepped back a pace.

"I shall report that at once," said Oliver in low tones, but perfectly comprehensibly. "But can you not say who did this to you? Did you get a glimpse, anything? Clothing? Voice? Was he mounted?"

A sound at the door made Yusuf look up and see that His Excellency the Bishop had entered the room with his master and Raquel.

"I know well enough," whispered the wounded man and coughed painfully.

Yusuf moved quickly to clear away a trickle of blood from his lips. Raquel whispered rapidly to her father.

Pasqual managed to draw another breath and continued speaking in a low murmur. He stopped and smiled. Or perhaps, thought Yusuf, it was a grimace of pain. Still, it seemed to be a smile. Then he closed his eyes as if to concentrate his failing resources on breathing.

"Now, if ever, Your Excellency," said the physician, and withdrew with his daughter into the hall as two more priests entered the chamber for the administering of the last rites. Yusuf set down his cup and cloth and slipped rapidly out of the room after them.

In the short time that he had been in the sickroom, day had begun. Just as he opened his mouth to speak to his master, the clamor of the bells drowned out everything else. When it faded away, he realized that everywhere in the palace there were people who were up, dressed, and moving about in normal fashion. Everyday conversations were going on that had nothing to do with the events of the dawn.

"Which bells were those?" he asked, suddenly worried that it was even later than he had thought.

"Prime," said Bernat absently, still keeping his vigil in the corridor.

"He is going fast," said Isaac quietly. "There was nothing more we could do."

"No one doubts that," said Bernat. "Few men live long after a blade of that length has been planted in their backs."

"You saw the weapon?" asked Isaac.

"Yes," said Bernat. "It is a good knife with a blade of uncommon length. The blade is of excellent metal and ground to a keen edge."

"The man who carried it planned to use it for more than display," said Isaac.

"Without a doubt," said Bernat.

The door opened, and Oliver came out, followed by the Bishop. "He is gone," said Oliver flatly.

"We shall bury him with all honor, my friend," said the Bishop. "He was a good man. I know that you must be on your way, bailiff, but there are a few things I would like to settle first. Bernat?"

"Certainly, Your Excellency," said Oliver.

"Yes, Your Excellency," said the secretary.

"Are you ready, Yusuf?" murmured Isaac.

Yusuf moved over next to the blind man. "I am," he said, "although with all this time passing, I grow hungry."

"Fear not. Judith will not let us starve," said Isaac, laughing. He set his hand lightly on the boy's shoulder, ready to leave.

But Berenguer seemed intent on settling some things in the corridor, then and there. "As I came in the room, he was speaking, although in so low a voice I could understand nothing he said. What were his final words? Did he name his attacker?"

Oliver Climent shook his head. "It was the random disconnected muttering of one whose mind is wandering, Your Excellency. Little of what he said made any sense."

"What were his precise words?" asked Berenguer.

"As I remember, Your Excellency," said Oliver, "he said, 'the dog,' and 'a new gown,' and 'oak tree.' And a few other words that I cannot recollect. Ah, yes. He spoke of a ball and a pony."

"Wandering back to his childhood," said Bernat.

Berenguer looked skeptical. "He said nothing else?"

"At the end," said Oliver, "he said, 'God spare me, and forgive me for failing you. Pray for my soul, I beg you.' "

Yusuf looked up, startled, and was about to speak when his master's hand closed firmly over his shoulder. Oliver, he realized, was staring at him intently, and he was not sure how friendly that look was.

"This sad business has delayed you long enough," said the Bishop. "Your escort is waiting. The captain of my guard will be going with you as far as Caldes. He will return with Master Isaac and his daughter. I would not have them traveling unescorted."

"Your Excellency is very good," murmured Isaac.

"I have only a few more words to say to Oliver here. I will then be down to hasten you on your way." Berenguer headed purposefully off, with Oliver Climent and Bernat at his heels.

"You are coming with us, lord?" asked Yusuf.

Isaac turned to his apprentice. "Only for a short while in the cool of the morning. His Excellency thought it a good idea. And it enabled him to entrust me with some of his other business. Now, tell me, Yusuf. What *did* Pasqual say?" he asked.

"How did you know that Oliver was lying?" asked Yusuf.

"You told me. You jumped like a startled rabbit when the bailiff spoke. I fear even he may have noticed it."

"Well, lord, he—Pasqual—spoke in a foreign tongue. In the manner of Aragon or Castile, I think. And quickly. It was difficult for me to understand," said Yusuf. "When they spoke together, Oliver usually answered in the same manner."

"But you must have understood some of it," said Isaac, "or you would not have been startled."

"I did. But I heard nothing about ponies or dogs or gowns or oaks," said Yusuf. "I think he told him to be on his guard, but I am not sure. But at the end he spoke slowly, and I think he said, 'Be serene, my friend. It is a jest, a jest—the Lord laughs at me. Pray for me, and look after my little ones.' I may not have all the words quite right, but it was very like that."

"Laughs?" said Raquel.

"Laughs," repeated Yusuf.

The crowd waiting in the square had reorganized itself. The baggage mules had been freed of their burdens and were wandering about in search of stray mouthfuls of grass, under the sleepy care of one of the stable lads. The guards had dismounted and their horses had joined their cousins, the mules. Narcís, the youngest of the guards, was stretched out with his pack behind his head, asleep; the captain had left, promising to return.

Naomi embraced Yusuf when he reappeared and handed him a basket from which a most promising aroma wafted up to his nose. "Eat it now, young master," she said, lifting up a corner of the napkin that covered the contents. "It's a terrible journey, and you'll need something in you. Then give the basket and the napkin to that worthless boy, Judah. He'll bring it home. I must go now or the twins will be out of their beds with nothing set out for their breakfasts. And you must promise me to eat while you're away, or you'll fall ill, and the master will not be there with his potions to cure you."

He vowed he would continue to eat, even though she wasn't with him in Sardinia to make sure he did, bid her an affectionate farewell, and lifted up the napkin. The basket was filled with Naomi's spicy pastries, made of bread dough, stuffed with cheese and highly flavored mixtures of various things, and then fried. He gave one to Raquel—who had been working hard—and to Judah, the kitchen lad, who was always hungry. And suddenly he was aware of the guards, and the stable lad left with the mules. And his master and the mistress, who must also be hungry. The pastries disappeared, as did the loaf of soft bread he discovered under them. Even the bored horses and mules gathered around, nibbling on whatever crusts they could beg or steal.

"Where is His Excellency?" asked Yusuf at last.

"And Oliver Climent," pointed out the youngest guard.

"Go get one of the pages, Narcís, and ask him to find out when we are to start loading the mules again," said the sergeant. "That should move them."

After another endless interval, a small page came running down the hill from the episcopal palace and whispered something in the sergeant's ear. The stable lad whistled piercingly, and his mate came ambling slowly over to help load up the mules again. For a second time, Judith embraced Yusuf, took her husband's staff, and gave Raquel firm instructions about the return of two of her best baskets.

The captain of the guard mounted his horse, raised his arm, and three hours after their planned departure time, the little procession left the city.

THREE

By the time they reached open countryside, the party had already spread out. Raquel was in front, with the lead rein to her father's mule looped in her hand, deep in conversation with the sergeant. Her father was talking to Yusuf about his own youthful journeys by land and sea, where he had picked up some of his most useful medical lore. Oliver was in the rear with the captain, behind the baggage mules. Gabriel and Narcís rode on either side of the party, casually alert for the unexpected.

"You are called Domingo, are you not?" asked Raquel shyly, even though she had come to know the sergeant quite well on the trip to Tarragona she had made a few months before. The question still seemed rather bold.

"Since it is my name," he said smiling, "I am. By some. If those two lazy shirkers tried it to my face," he added, pointing to Gabriel and Narcís, "they wouldn't forget the occasion. But you, mistress, are welcome to call me Domingo."

"Did we set out very much later than you expected?" asked Raquel, making a quick retreat from such a personal question. "Or did you expect us to be delayed?"

"I did not expect someone to be slain under our noses, Mistress," said the sergeant dryly. "And no, I did not expect delays." He paused. "Although when traveling with His Excellency, I always prepare for them."

"Is he such a tardy person?" asked Raquel, somewhat surprised.

"His Excellency? No. He is always close to his hour. But his people crowd around him with a thousand foolish requests, making it impossible for him to depart, unless we avoid them by leaving before they awaken. But I expected no problems with this group."

"Why would we be different?"

"My men are out of their beds and ready to leave when I tell them to be. I know the lad can rise early; he's at the stable and out on that mare before sunrise most days. And I expected no problems with the bailiff back there. Judging by his behavior," he said, "he spent his youth as a soldier, although I would not presume to ask him about his past."

"Why not?" asked Raquel.

"I would guess—in spite of his easy, friendly manner— that we are not on an equal footing," he replied quietly. "If he is a bailiff, Mistress Raquel, then I must be a count. But in answer to your question, I thought we would be away by moonlight. We'll not get to Barcelona tonight," he concluded gloomily.

Raquel glanced back at the silent Oliver. "He'll be upset."

"Maybe," said Domingo. "But even so, it can't be done. We'll go as far as we can, sleep through the heat, and then ride until it's too dark to see."

"You'll never find an inn," said Raquel, remembering how large that problem had loomed on their earlier journey.

"We need no inn," said the sergeant with a grin. "We have no grand ladies to protect. We are six armed men. The nights are warm and dry, and we'll find some place quiet by the road to catch some sleep until the moon is high enough to light our way to Barcelona. Ten or fifteen miles by moonlight, and we'll be at the city gates. Before sunrise, I'll warrant. And that will be an excellent thing, Mistress Raquel."

"Excellent, Domingo?"

"It's hotter there, you know, than it is here. This time of year. Not as hot as Granada, of course," he added. "I was

there once when I was a lad, as guard to an emissary from
His Majesty. That was hot."

"How hot?" asked Raquel, loosening her veil and settling
in to enjoy the sergeant's reminiscences.

Almost two hours later, the captain rode up beside Isaac.
"Master Isaac," he said, "we are near our destination. If you
would say your farewells, we can let the party move on."

"So we are," said the sergeant, with a pretense of surprise.
"I had enjoyed fighting old campaigns with Mistress Raquel
so much that I scarcely noted where we were," he added
gallantly. "But before parting, Captain, why not stop together
and enjoy some of the food we are carrying?"

The captain had stopped them under a pair of spreading trees
that shaded a small river. The heat and drought of summer
had reduced the water to hardly more than a trickle in places,
but it was still pleasantly cool and musical as it ran over the
stones and gravel of its bed. He nodded his agreement and
set the guards to work unloading baskets and bundles of
food. In a moment or two, they were helping themselves to
soft, sweet apricots and hard early pears, cold braised beef,
and a cold roasted chicken, along with an abundance of
bread.

"We cannot take any of this back with us," said Raquel,
looking at what remained. "Mama and Naomi will be most
upset."

"Then I suggest that we empty those fine baskets," said
the sergeant, "send them back with you, and put the rest of
the food in the baggage mules' panniers. With some rear-
rangement of loads, we should have enough room. Do you
agree, Master Isaac?"

"I leave such strategic decisions to Raquel, whose wisdom
in these things greatly surpasses mine," said Isaac, smiling.

"An excellent idea. I will do it," said Raquel firmly, "to
make sure they are well packed. Eat the other dishes for your
dinner before they can spoil."

Raquel removed some items that had been in the panniers
and filled the empty spaces with food from the baskets.
"There," she said, "that is done. We are ready to leave, but

first I must say good-bye to my new little brother." She embraced Yusuf, who in the last year had become her friend and ally, and pulled her veil over her face to hide her tears. "Look after yourself," she whispered. "And keep your guard up."

"You were listening," said Yusuf indignantly.

"Of course. Now I will let Papa say good-bye," she said.

Isaac embraced the lad and stepped back. "I will give you no more advice," he said. "You have survived thus far on your wit and intelligence and will continue to do so, I know. I only ask you to pay heed to the captain's last suggestion to you."

"That I hold elbows correctly?" he said, puzzled.

"No, although it is important. Trust no one," he murmured. "Farewell, lad. If all goes well, we shall see you before long. My blessings go with you," he added quickly and turned away.

"He will be back before the High Holidays, Papa," said Raquel, forcing a cheerfulness she did not feel. "You speak as if he were to be gone for many years."

"A journey once started can lead to unexpected places, my dear," said her father and mounted his impatient mule.

Yusuf stood for a moment, his hand on the saddle, puzzling over his master's words. He glanced around at his companions on the road; Miquel, Gabriel, and Narcís, the three guards, his old friend, the sergeant Domingo, and the Bishop's apparent friend, Oliver. He shook his head, sprang up on his mare, and headed with the others on the road south.

The three who were left behind moved out from under the shade of the trees. During their brief halt the day had become heavy with heat. The dust from the departure of the others still hung in the air; there was not a breath of wind. Raquel settled herself on her mule and looked around. The young guards had gone, the captain was too intent on his own concerns to worry about her, and the countryside was otherwise deserted. She pushed her veil back a little from her face. But even the lightest touch of the cloth on her hot cheeks and forehead was more than she could bear. She tossed the veil until it hung down her back from a single pin anchored in a coil of hair on top of her head.

"The packet you were given, Master Isaac," the captain was saying, "is to be delivered to a farmhouse that sits near a narrow road slightly ahead of us. And it would be better if you and your daughter could deliver it without my assistance."

"Certainly, Captain," said Raquel with more confidence than she felt.

"Take the first road to the right and follow the river until it bends sharply. You will see a pool and a small waterfall. Just beyond that point is the entrance to the house."

"His Excellency gave me instructions from that point on," said Isaac. "It seems a simple enough mission."

"It is," said the captain. "But Master Isaac, if you do not object, I would like to follow a short distance behind you instead of waiting here. If all seems well at the house, I shall ride past and catch up with you as you leave."

"Certainly, Captain," said the physician. "We will be glad to know you are there."

The distance, as the captain had said, was not far. The road followed a stream lined with trees and was so narrow that even a small oxcart would have difficulty making its way through. But it was cool and welcoming under the shade of the trees, the fields to the far side of the stream were planted with grain, and the slopes were rich with olive trees and vines laden with unripe fruit. Instead of worrying about Yusuf and fretting over Daniel or wondering if she really wanted to be married—her usual occupations when her mind wasn't taken up with more pressing affairs—Raquel began dreaming of life in a peaceful place like this, untroubled by the rest of the world.

These dreams of an idyllic existence were abruptly shattered by a sudden burst of sound. Shouts and yelling echoed off the hills, growing louder as they approached their destination.

"What is that, Papa?"

"Someone who is annoyed?" suggested Isaac with mild irony.

Behind them, the captain put spurs to his horse and was

soon abreast of them. "That noise comes from the farm," he said. "I will go ahead to make sure that nothing is wrong."

"Yes, indeed," said the physician. "We do not wish to ride into the middle of a battle of some kind."

At a word, the captain's horse broke into a fast gallop, throwing dust and stones into their faces. The mules, spurred into action by the volley of pebbles and the sudden departure of their stable mate, speeded up to a fast trot. Raquel, newly skilled in the art of riding, was hard pressed to lead her father's mule and stay on her own. The mules broke into a canter and swerved onto a well-tended drive.

Ahead of them, the captain's horse slowed to a stately walk. The mules caught up, lost their interest in the race, and drifted toward the grass on the verge of the drive.

The bellowing issued from a tall man on a horse. Both he and his mount were covered with dust and sweating profusely, as if they had traveled a considerable distance. He was roaring at an elderly serving man who defended the door as from an army.

"I am not leaving this place until I gain admittance, you old fool," the man shouted at this desperate and unlikely hero.

"The master does not allow strangers in the house when he is not in residence," said the servant with high courage but in a quavering voice. "And whoever this person may be that you search for, there is no one like that here."

The captain dismounted, drew his sword, and approached the man on the horse. "What is going on?" he asked.

Both combatants turned to look at him, armed, booted, spurred, and in the uniform of captain of the Bishop's Guard.

"This gentlemen threatens my life if I do not produce some person who does not exist," said the old man. "Someone who does not live here and has never lived here, not in my lifetime. I am responsible for my master's possessions," he went on. "I cannot allow people into his house in his absence."

"It is no concern of the Bishop's Guard what is going on here," said the man on the horse. "Nor is it the concern of his dubious acquaintances and their even more dubious companions," he added, staring hard at Raquel long enough to bring a scarlet flush to her cheeks. "I am attempting to visit an acquaintance. That is all."

Suddenly Raquel remembered her veil and hastily reached back to pull it across her face.

"Peace and good order in the diocese are my concern," said the captain coldly. "If I cannot ride past a gentleman's estate without being drawn in by the sound of threats, it is my business. I suggest, sir, that you may be at the wrong house. I suggest that you leave and pursue your quarry elsewhere, and that you leave the physician and his daughter unmolested." A wave of his hand encompassed the old man, the physician and his daughter.

"And I suggest, villain, that you go to hell and stay there with your whore of a mother for eternity," said the angry man, digging in his spurs and galloping off before the captain could react.

"You know, Papa, I believe that was Master Luis," said Raquel. "The man has an unpleasant temper."

"It most definitely was Master Luis," said the captain. "I wonder what has come over him to behave like that."

"He does seem to be out of temper this morning," said Isaac.

"He is rarely jovial," said the captain. "But even for him, this behavior is extreme."

"Perhaps he is affected by the heat."

"That could well be the case. If you will excuse me," he said, "I will be on my way."

"Certainly, Captain," said the physician and waited until the sound of his horse's hooves faded in the distance. "Am I speaking to Dalmau?"

"You are, sir. May I be of service?"

Isaac dismounted. Deprived of his staff and on unfamiliar ground, he paused, feeling for the path beneath his feet. Raquel scrambled down from her mule to help. "I have something for you, Dalmau," said the physician. "It is from His Excellency the Bishop." He took a packet from the leather purse tucked inside his tunic and held it so that Dalmau could see the seal.

"If you will come into the house, sir," said the old servant, "you and your daughter, I have something for you, as well.

Take my arm," he added. "I will bring you in and see you safely out again."

Isaac went with the old man, with Raquel following behind. Dalmau ignored the heavy front door, leading them to a small doorway in a high stone wall. Inside was a courtyard, cool with running water and trees. "If you would wait here a moment, Mistress," said the servant, "we will return shortly." They crossed over smooth flagstones and stopped. Dalmau banged on a door. "Open, you idiot," he hissed. "It's Dalmau."

There was the thump of a bar being loosened and shifted, and then the screech of a large lock being turned; a door opened and cool air wafted out to embrace the physician. Stepping cautiously on the unfamiliar footing, he followed the servant in.

"Who is that, Dalmau?" called an apprehensive voice from above.

"It is the blind physician, Madam, sent by the Bishop. He has brought a packet for the master. The previous gentleman had come to the wrong house. He is gone."

"I see," she said in relieved tones. "Give the physician the packet on the table, Dalmau, and offer him some refreshment."

"Your mistress is most kind," said Isaac.

"Oh, she is not the mistress," said Dalmau. "She is the housekeeper."

"I am amazed," said Isaac, courteously. "She sounds—"

"Indeed, sir, if you'll excuse me for interrupting, she does, does she not? I expect she has come down in the world, like so many people these days. Will you take a cup of something, sir?"

"Thank you, but we must be on our way before the heat of the day gets worse."

"Then here is your packet, sir."

Isaac tucked it away in his tunic and allowed himself to be led back to the courtyard.

"What did you think of that, my dear?" asked Isaac, once the door in the wall had been locked and barred once more.

"It is a lovely little estate, Papa," she said. "The house is solid and secure. Very secure. The master must greatly fear thieves and marauders," she added. "The doors are locked and barred and all the windows on the ground floor are closed with heavy shutters as well."

"I expect it is because the servants worry more when the master is away," said Isaac casually. "The house is their responsibility, not his. They certainly hastened me away as quickly as they could." But neither one questioned the purposes behind the Bishop of Girona receiving and delivering mail through a small, handsome, and prospering farm.

The sun climbed higher in the cloudless sky, the temperature rose, and the brisk forward movement of the little troop on their way to Barcelona began to slow.

Then the gentle breeze died. The landscape shimmered in the heat rising from the road and the dry fields. The most heavily laden of the mules—a strong and surefooted creature—stumbled twice. The sergeant pulled up his horse and raised his arm for a halt.

"If we keep on, we will lose our best mule," he said, glaring at the others as if they had disagreed. "I told His Excellency we were carrying too much before the extra food was loaded on."

"Shall we stop here, Sergeant?" asked Miquel, in his capacity as senior of the three guards.

"Here?" said the sergeant. "With no shade and no water? Your wits must be addled by the heat," he added. "Not here. There is an excellent place no more than a mile ahead. Over that hill. But we must lighten her load at once before she pulls up lame."

"I will dismount," said Yusuf. "My mare can carry it."

"An excellent idea, lad," said the sergeant, "but it makes more sense if someone heavier, riding a heavier horse, makes the sacrifice." He glanced around and smiled. "Narcís. You'll enjoy stretching your legs awhile."

Narcís shrugged. "I knew it would be me," he muttered.

Two small but very heavy chests destined for His Majesty went from the overburdened mule to Narcís's sturdy horse, and the whole group started forward again, at walking pace, up the hill. It was higher than they expected. By the time they reached the summit, everyone was walking to lighten the loads of the overburdened mules. "I have blistered my heel," muttered Narcís as they crested the hill and stopped.

Halfway down the slope ahead was a small but thickly wooded copse. A considerable and fast-moving stream ran through it, and grassy lands surrounded it, partially shaded by the trees.

"There it is," said the sergeant. "Won't take us a minute."

It was a long minute. When they finally reached the shade of the trees, they unburdened the animals, turning them loose to drink and graze, and left them with Narcís, who had taken off his boots and was looking gloomily at his feet. Domingo and Oliver stripped and waded into the river to wash off the sweat and dust of travel. Miquel and Gabriel followed suit. Oliver found a deep pool where he rinsed himself in the cold water with careful deliberation, before shaking the water from his hair, stepping out, and throwing himself on his belly near the edge of the stream.

Yusuf stood by the stream, watching. He was not by nature or training particularly shy or prudish, but looking at Oliver, with his arms, neck, and chest like a muscular wrestler, made him feel small and insignificant. Even so, pride demanded that he not stand on the bank like a modest virgin afraid to strip. Hastily he pulled off shoes, tunic, shirt, and hose, left them in a heap, rushed into the water, and splashed vigorously about. Before he clambered out of the stream and covered himself with his shirt again, the hot sun had dried Oliver off. He stood up and put on his shirt, rinsed his hose in the water, wrung them out, and hung them on a branch to dry. "I recommend you do the same, lad," he said. "You'll thank me when the time comes to move on."

By this time, the others were dry and half dressed as well.

"Food," said the sergeant, "and then sleep. When it's cool enough to think, we'll set out again."

"When will that be?" asked Narcís, relieved from duty and just coming out of the water.

"When I say it is, guard," said the sergeant coldly.

When they piled up the baggage, they had put the panniers with the food in them to one side. Oliver and Domingo carried them to a pleasant spot near the water and lifted the lid. "They are remarkably heavy," said Oliver.

"This is one reason," said the sergeant, drawing out two tightly corked clay bottles. "And this is another." Two covered clay dishes, wrapped and tied in linen towels, were brought out, untied, and set beside them. "And underneath is dried fruit, ham, and bread sent by His Excellency's cooks."

"We can leave those for supper and breakfast," said Oliver, "since we have no hope of getting to Barcelona today."

"Agreed," said the sergeant. "Come on, you lazy louts."

The clay bottles contained wine. The sergeant drew the cork on one and sent Narcís to the river to put the other in to keep cool. When he returned, there was an impressive feast spread in front of them. One dish contained chicken and duck, cut in pieces and cooked in a thick, spicy sauce, still cool and fresh in its protective clay as it had been the night before when it was placed in the deepest cellar of the house. The other dish was of lentils and rice, cooked in broth, with onions, garlic, and savory herbs. They fell on the food with gusto.

When everyone had eaten and the wine was running low, talk—such as it was—halted. Narcís fell asleep; for a while Domingo and Oliver kept up a low-voiced conversation on the subject of horses and then dozed off; Miquel and Gabriel had been posted to keep watch; Miquel was near the baggage and Gabriel on the edge of the grove from which he could observe their surroundings. It was quiet. The heat had stilled the chirping and rustling of birds and small animals. Sensible people, Yusuf thought, would now be at home, asleep somewhere cool and comfortable.

Having concluded that he was the only living being awake in this part of the world, Yusuf noticed a flash of movement out of the corner of his eye. He glanced over without moving his head and saw a thickly growing shrub with something brown crouched under it. It blinked. Dark brown with eyes. And a fair size, he thought, but too small for a man. A dog? A fox? Something more menacing? He almost cursed out loud in his frustration. His sword was once more out of reach, in spite of all the good advice he had received this morning. Using his body as a shield from those watching eyes, he reached out very slowly and grasped a piece of wood.

He noticed that Oliver Climent was looking at him. The bailiff, his hand on his sword hilt, shook his head almost imperceptibly. Yusuf let go of the wood.

A thin, white arm snaked out from under the bush and reached for a piece of bread that one of the guards had left lying on the ground. Oliver moved just as swiftly. He clamped a large hand around the wrist and held on tight.

"Come out of there," said Oliver in a conversational tone, although his grip did not loosen. "We won't hurt you." The person behind the arm neither moved nor made a sound. "If you don't come out, I shall have to pull you out." Still nothing happened.

"If you prefer." Oliver yanked sharply and dragged out a small thin lad with long, unkempt hair, wearing a coarse brown tunic much too big for him. Tears ran through the dirt on his face. "Are you hungry?" said Oliver quietly. His grip did not loosen on the thin wrist.

The lad stared at him with huge, dark eyes. "Foolish question," he continued in his soft voice. "Of course you are. What growing lad like you isn't hungry? Here," he said, "you would be doing us and our mules a great favor if you helped us to eat some of this. What we don't eat, we must carry, and the mules are overburdened already." As he spoke, he pulled off a piece of bread with one hand, put it down on one of the linen towels, and set a piece of chicken on it. He took another piece of bread and scooped up some of the dish of lentils and rice. He put that piece of bread next to the first one.

"Now," he said, "if I let go, will you stay here and eat?"

There was still no response from the lad.

"I swear by God Almighty and by all that I hold true that no harm will come to you. We are retainers of the Bishop of Girona, and the Bishop does not permit his men to harm children. Will you stay long enough to eat?"

He nodded.

"Say it. Can you speak?"

"I will stay." The voice sounded hoarse and uncertain, as if the boy had not spoken for a long time, but Oliver judged it acceptable and let go. The boy grabbed the piece of chicken and began to eat like a starving creature.

"The lad is indeed hungry," said the sergeant. "But I question the wisdom of giving him so much at once, Oliver. Here, lad," he said, "take a mouthful of wine and pause for breath. Otherwise you will be sick."

He took the bottle that the sergeant offered and drank a little. He set it down and stared at the remaining food.

"We are on our way from Girona to Barcelona to deliver this little scamp onto a ship," said the sergeant casually, pointing at Yusuf.

The lad started to scramble to his feet.

"No, no," said the sergeant. "Calm yourself, boy. He is not a prisoner. He is a ward of His Majesty, joining him for a few months as a page in his household. Is that not true, Yusuf?"

"It is, sir," said Yusuf, trying to inject earnest sincerity in every word. "I go of my own will, I swear. And over there in the meadow—I don't know if you saw her—is my mare. She is the neat-footed bay. They will stable her in Barcelona, and I will ride her back to Girona when I return."

"Is that true?" whispered the lad, turning to Oliver.

"It is," said Oliver. "On my immortal soul, I swear it. We are innocent travelers. And I think you may eat some more now."

There was a long silence, broken only by the occasional snort and mumble from Narcís, who was still sleeping peacefully, while the boy finished off chicken, rice, and bread.

"I thank you very much, señores," he said, with an oddly formal air. "I was very hungry."

"You are most welcome," said Oliver, looking hard at him. "I am called Oliver," he said. "And the sergeant of His Excellency's guard there is known as Domingo, the boy is Yusuf, the one who snores on the ground is Narcís, and there are a couple of other useless fellows out there, Miquel and Gabriel. One was posted as guard. He evidently did not see you."

"I was on the other side of the stream," said the boy. "I crossed over hoping to ask you for a piece of bread, but when I saw how many there were of you . . ."

"We won't worry about that," said the sergeant. "Now that you know who we are, may we ask your name?"

There was a brief, panicky silence. "Certainly, sirs," said the boy at last. "My name is Gil."

"And do you travel this road with your master's consent?" asked the sergeant. "No, don't flee," he said. Oliver grabbed that wrist again, since the boy had half risen once more in panic. "We are not in the business of collecting runaways, either, unless His Excellency sends us off to do so."

"Does His Excellency?" asked Oliver, looking interested. "I wouldn't have thought him interested enough to send out his men."

"Never in my time," said the sergeant comfortably. "And I certainly don't take my orders from anyone else, lad, including your master. But why run away? You must know you are now prey for any number of thieves and malefactors. And dealers in slaves."

"But that is why I ran away," said the boy, looking back and forth from the sergeant to Oliver Climent. "The cook told me that she had heard my mistress talking to a slave dealer about selling me."

"Why would she do that?" asked the sergeant, looking at him carefully. "Are you a slave that you may be sold?"

"No," he said. "I'm not. But sometimes I am clumsy," he added, looking down at the ground, "and I break things. The last time I broke something, the mistress was so angry she beat me and locked me in the storeroom for a day and a night."

"But that's no reason to sell him," said Domingo.

"Yes, it is," said Oliver. "Consider this. If she sells him, she can get rid of him and make money at the same time. If she can find a better kitchen boy, that is."

"It's a wonder more kitchen lads aren't sold, if you think of it that way," said the sergeant.

"But how would she explain to your family that you were no longer with her? It could have been awkward," said Oliver.

"I have no family, sir. She was going to tell the—the brothers at the orphanage that I had died."

By this time, Narcís had awakened and was listening to the narrative with great interest. "But that's impossible," he said. "Even if you have no family, a Christian lad cannot be sold."

"True enough," said Oliver, "but ships sailing out of Barcelona have Christian children on them who will be sold at high prices in many markets. A quick exchange of money when the wind is right and the boy—or girl—is on a ship down the coast before he knows what's happening. If the ship's captain is questioned—and that doesn't happen very often—he can say the lad is a Moor who was captured in battle. Who is to know?"

"The lad does," objected the guard. "All he has to do is tell the first official he meets that he is a Christian."

"By then he knows that if he tried to do that, they'd cut out his tongue," said Oliver. "You live too far inland, my good Narcís. These are the ways of the sea. By the way, can you read and write, lad?"

"Yes," said the boy hesitantly. "A little."

"I suggest you learn, then," said Oliver. "There are uses in being able to write. If you can, there's no point in cutting out your tongue, for you can write down your accusation. A slave without a tongue can work, but you'll get no work from a slave with no hands, and the money the trader paid for him will have been wasted. It's a practical matter from their point of view." He turned to look at the boy. "So you ran away. Sensible lad. In that situation, I would have run away, too."

"I suppose it was, under the circumstances," said the sergeant. "Where did you run from?"

"I cannot say, señores," said the lad, looking panicky again. "I do not know exactly where the house was."

"But you were raised by the brothers in an orphanage?"

"I was," he said. "My parents are dead. And then the brothers who were looking after me placed me in a household as a kitchen lad."

"Why not put you someplace to learn a trade, lad?" asked Oliver.

"The brothers have little money for apprenticing, and what there was went for—" He paused, searching for a word. "For those who seemed more apt to learn a skill," he muttered, reddening.

"Ah, well, I'm sure they were wrong," said Oliver. "You

seem a bright enough lad to me. You're certainly very quick. Almost as fast as I am, and there are few men with faster hands than mine. It is a merciful thing that I am of an honest disposition," he added. "I would have made a successful cut-purse."

"You are perhaps too soft-hearted for it, I think, Oliver," observed the sergeant.

"I wouldn't be too sure of that," said Oliver and turned back to Gil. "Where are you going now?"

"There are other kingdoms to the west and to the north," said Gil. "I shall go there."

"There are indeed," said Oliver. "But you must tread warily as you go, for some of them are our enemies. As soon as you open that mouth of yours to speak, you will be recognized for where you come from. I could make a shrewd guess myself," he added, "but if you do not wish to speak of it, I shall not."

"Can you really?" asked Narcís.

"I am teasing the lad," said Oliver. "Of course I do not know, except that he is Catalan, from somewhere close to here, like the rest of us. But in other kingdoms they speak in strange accents. You may not be able to understand them. It is something to think about."

Gil pushed his hair out of his eyes and looked haughtily at Oliver. "I know all about foreigners, señor," he said. "And I can understand the speech of many of them. Just because I can only read and write a little does not mean that I am completely ignorant."

"I apologize," said Oliver.

"He is a clever lad," said the sergeant. "Much too good to be a kitchen boy."

"Am I free to go?" he asked abruptly, turning to Oliver.

"Of course," said Oliver. "Did you think you were my prisoner? I only wished to see who had such a small, quick hand. And to make sure you had something to eat."

"Then I thank you, sirs, for the refreshment," he said. "You saved me from starvation, and I am grateful. Now I must continue on my way." He pulled out a small bundle from under the shrub and stood up, revealing himself to be taller than they had expected.

"Just a moment," said Oliver. He took one of the linen towels, piled food in it, tied it up, and handed it to Gil. "You are welcome to this," he said, "no matter where you choose to go. But I have a suggestion. We are going to Barcelona, as we said, and I suggest you join us. I can find you a place in the city where you can advance yourself and be safe from harm," he said.

"I cannot go back to Barcelona," said Gil shrilly and made a sudden bolt for the road.

"Why did you invite him to come with us?" asked the sergeant. "I do not object," he added. "I am curious."

"It's odd, but I felt loath to think of him being taken up in slavery or murdered on the road."

"And those are his probable fates," said the sergeant.

"He has never learned to take care of himself," said Yusuf in a troubled voice. "It was foolish of him to come so close to us. We could have been anything. And when he did try to run away, it was too late."

"He was starving," said Oliver. "A starving deer will eat from your right hand even when you hold the knife in your left."

They had hardly composed themselves for rest again when a high-pitched scream interrupted them. "It's the lad," said Oliver, jumping up, his sword in his hand and moving with astonishing speed toward the road. With a look of resignation, the sergeant got to his feet and followed.

Gil was halfway up the hill on the road toward Girona. Two men, their horses waiting by the side of the road, held him in a tight grip. "You'll oblige me, sirs, if you take your hands off our horse boy," said Oliver. His sword flashed in the hot sun and one of the men let go. "Gil, you fool," he said, "get back to the horses. And you, sir, release him."

"I would suggest the same," said the sergeant, yawning as he traced a pattern in the dust with his bare sword. Even in their shirtsleeves, the two men were a menacing-looking pair.

"Didn't know he was yours, sir," said the second man, letting go. "We thought he was a runaway."

"Gil? Certainly not. Probably saw something interesting when we passed by here a little while ago. Didn't you, lad?"

"Yes, sir," said Gil. "A white horse in the field, but he's gone now."

"Sensible creature," said Oliver. "It's too hot to be out in the sun. I give you good day, gentlemen," and with one arm thrown lightly over Gil's shoulder, he escorted the boy back to the grove.

"I don't care how many more orphans or runaways come by," said the sergeant, "I'm going to sleep. Narcís," he said, giving the guard a shove with his foot, "relieve Gabriel." As soon as he saw the guard on his feet, he stretched out, his pack under his head, and in a moment fell asleep.

"I am for sleep as well," said Oliver, picking up his pack and sitting down near a large tree some distance away. "But, lad, come over here for a moment. I want to talk to you."

Gil gave him a half-suspicious, half-curious look and walked over. He sat down beside him, his knees drawn up almost to his chin, and his tunic pulled down around his calves.

"I can understand why you don't want to go back to Barcelona," he said.

"I didn't say I came from Barcelona—"

"Quiet. You were born and bred in that city and at a station somewhat higher than kitchen lad. It's in your voice. But if you don't want to talk of it, we won't. I accept that it might be unsafe for you to return. You know why better than I do."

"Yes, sir," he murmured.

"My name is Oliver Climent," he said. "Not sir. And the important thing about me—aside from the fact that I am willing to help you—is that I have a friend whom I can trust with my life. And to whom I could entrust you with equal confidence."

"Who?" asked Gil nervously.

"She is known as Auntie Mundina," said Oliver. "And she will take you in for the time being. She lives at Santa Maria; we pass by her house on our way. She can use a pair of hands to help her, I believe. And you would eat well with Auntie Mundina."

"But I must go to Girona," said Gil frantically. "It is the

only place where—" He stopped, and tears welled up in his eyes.

"Come, lad, don't weep over it. If you must go to Girona, we will stop at Auntie Mundina's for you on our way back. And we will be returning, I swear it. The Bishop would not be happy to lose four guards, their horses, and his best baggage mules."

Gil smiled very slightly. "Why are you doing this?" he asked. "I do not understand."

"It angers me that an ordinary lad could be sold as a plaything for some rich foreigner—for you are a pretty boy and that is what would happen—because some woman in the city is greedy for money."

"That is what the cook said, too," murmured Gil.

"But tell me, if you can, why Girona?"

"I believe my mother had kin there," said the boy finally.

"And do you expect to find her?" asked Oliver, looking at him narrowly. "I don't believe your mother is dead. She gave you to the brothers because she could no longer feed you. There is no shame in it," he added. "It happens too frequently for that."

Gil maintained a stubborn—or frightened—silence.

"And so you hope that she sought shelter with her kinsman. Perhaps he told her he could take one person but not two."

"No," said the boy in a flat voice. "My mother is dead. And even if she were alive, she would not be there. I mean, if she were hiding, wouldn't anyone searching for her look there first, in the house of a kinsman?"

"Why would she be hiding?" asked Oliver.

"She isn't," said the boy again. "She's dead. I know it."

"Who is this kinsman?" asked Oliver. "I know some from Girona, and the sergeant over there knows everyone, even the beggars at the gates and their dogs."

"I never heard his name," he said. "But he should know my mother's name. I will ask if anyone knew my mother."

"What about you?" asked Oliver. "Won't your mistress seek you at your kinsman's house, demanding redress?"

"She doesn't know the names of my kinsmen," said the boy. "Nor do the brothers. She can't find me through him.

No one can find me if I go there," he said, his eyes drooping. "I'd be safe there, if no one could find me...." Suddenly, like a tired puppy collapsing in a heap, the boy fell asleep. As he began to fall over, Oliver caught him and lowered him gently. His head landed on the man's thigh and stayed there.

Oliver set his pack behind him and leaned back until his head rested on it, taking great care not to move his leg and disturb the sleeping boy. But it was a long time before he, too, fell asleep, as he thought over some very odd elements in Gil's story, starting with his name.

FOUR

"A skilled physician should not have to play the messenger, I know," said Berenguer, sounding not in the least contrite.

"I was happy to be of service to Your Excellency," said Isaac.

"These exchanges must be made with discretion, Isaac," he continued blandly. "And the fewer people who know of them, the better. Bernat or the captain or my excellent sergeant usually carry them, but the captain has become too well known in the district."

"In short, you do not trust your guards as thoroughly as they might believe," said Isaac, sounding amused.

"Some of my retinue are perhaps too curious. I could certainly trust many of them with the cathedral's gold or any secret I possessed," said the Bishop. "But not with His Majesty's documents. It is for Don Pedro that you have done the favor."

"We must all assist His Majesty in any way we can," said Isaac. "And the incident was not without its interest." He told the Bishop the tale of the enraged Master Luis being held back by a lion-hearted, aged retainer.

"Master Luis is a thorn in my side," said the Bishop. "My daily trial. He strengthens my soul. Do you know him?"

"Only slightly," said Isaac. "He is not a patient of mine."

"He is always at my door, demanding that I do something about the wicked behavior of his neighbors," said Berenguer. "And as for the people of that house, I doubt he is acquainted with them. They have not lived on the estate for at least twenty years. It is managed most successfully by a bailiff and a few servants. I deduce that someone connected to it—perhaps the master of the house—must be a loyal servant of the King."

"Evidently, Your Excellency," said Isaac.

"But it is another servant of the King who concerns me more today."

"Was Pasqual Robert in His Majesty's service?" asked Isaac.

"He was," said Berenguer. "And His Majesty will not be happy to discover that he has been murdered at our very gates within earshot of us all, and that we have no idea who could have done such a thing."

"We heard something," said Isaac cautiously. "Although if it was his murder, then you are looking for an assassin who can run as swiftly and as silently as thought."

"Indeed?" said Berenguer.

"Yes, Your Excellency. How else could he have escaped pursuit by your officers?"

"How long was it before they set off?" asked Berenguer.

"Not long, Your Excellency," said the physician.

"It seemed a very long time to me—long enough for an assassin to cross the river and disappear."

"I don't believe so, Your Excellency," said the physician.

"You're wrong, Master Isaac. We heard that terrible sound and much later Pasqual appeared. And all that time we stood about like so many blocks of stone doing nothing."

"Time plays tricks on our senses, Your Excellency," murmured the physician. "Could you see if there was blood on his mule?"

"My eyesight is not keen, Master Isaac," said Berenguer. "And I was more interested in the man than in his mule. No doubt someone will know. Bernat," he called, and his secretary opened the door to the adjoining room.

"Yes, Your Excellency?" he asked.

"Was there blood on Pasqual's mule?"

"One moment, Your Excellency." And Bernat disappeared again.

"We were speaking of time that actually passed, Your Excellency," said Isaac, "rather than time that seemed to pass because you were startled."

"Were you not startled, Master Isaac?" said Berenguer.

"I can be startled, Your Excellency. But not by the sound of human violence. It is too commonplace. This morning at dawn I heard a man cry out and a clatter of hooves on paving stones. What I did not hear, Your Excellency, was the sound of a rider galloping away. Nor of running feet."

"True," said Berenguer. "Nor did I. Not that I remember."

"Then," continued the physician, "after an interval during which a man might count to two slowly, my wife cried out. Was that when Pasqual appeared?"

"It was."

"I heard several different footfalls. I am told that Pasqual took a few steps while Oliver was running to him. Oliver caught him as he fell, saw the knife, and called at once for pursuit. The guards left at once. If I count it, starting now," said the physician suddenly, beating one hand on the other, and then stopping, "at this moment the guards are outside the gate and there is no trace of an assassin."

"As short a time as that for the assassin to flee?" said the Bishop. "Are you sure?"

"Quite sure, Your Excellency. I am not distracted by my other senses."

"And one does not strike a blow like that from a distance."

"No, Your Excellency. If they had found an arrow in his back, it would be easier to believe that he cried out when he was struck," said the physician. "Of course, it is possible that the door of a nearby house was open to admit the assassin."

"Someone—you, my sharp-eared friend—would have heard it open," said Berenguer. "You did not." He paused. "And which of the citizens of Sant Feliu who live in those houses close to the gates held a deadly grudge against Pasqual Robert? I cannot believe it," said Berenguer firmly. "He led a modest, uneventful, and peaceful life here. No one in the city knew him as a man of power or riches. No one. I am sure of that."

"Therefore," said Isaac, "he was attacked earlier."

"You are right," said Berenguer. "Pasqual was attacked some distance away and rode to the gate seeking help."

The door opened, and Bernat ushered in the captain of the guard. "Your Excellency asked if the mule had blood on her?"

"Yes, Captain. Was there?"

"Yes," he replied. "On her flank and on the saddle. The lads cleaned it off, never thinking, they said, that anyone wanted to see it."

"Then Pasqual was attacked while on his mule," murmured the Bishop.

"I think so, Your Excellency," said the captain. "And he must have been on it still for some time after. With the knife in the wound there was not a great effusion of blood."

"Yes," said Isaac. "We killed him by drawing out the weapon."

"What else could you do?" asked Berenguer.

"Nothing," said the physician. "He could not live with the knife in him and the wound was too deep and too wide to be stanched by any power or skill we possess."

"My friend, I saw that weapon. No one could have survived that," said the Bishop.

"Perhaps," said the physician.

"But surely it is difficult for a mounted man to stab another so neatly in the back," observed the Bishop.

"They must have been close together and deep in conference," said the captain.

"Do you mean he was murdered by a friend?" asked Berenguer.

"Friend or not, it is hard to say. But certainly not by a known enemy. You cannot dispatch an enemy like that."

"This has given me much to think of," said the Bishop. "I thank you, Captain, for your assistance. And Bernat," he added, dismissing them both with a wave of the hand.

"Your Excellency is not pleased with what the captain has said," observed Isaac as soon as the two men had gone.

"It creates difficulties," said Berenguer. "And I am sure his death was the work of a Castilian."

"A Castilian, Your Excellency?" said Isaac. "Why?"

"Because, my discreet friend," said the Bishop, "at the time of his death he was being employed by His Majesty to watch events in Castile. It would not surprise me if someone had discovered that. Clever as he was, he pursued a calling that becomes more dangerous the longer you are in it."

"That explains much," said Isaac. "Was he himself Castilian? In my few contacts with him, I noted a slight foreignness in his speech. Very slight."

"No. From Aragon," said Berenguer. "And accomplished in many ways of speaking. His mother may have been from Castile. It is the only explanation that makes sense, Master Isaac," he added. "They discovered what he was and sent someone to get rid of him. It happens on both sides of the frontier. I am distressed that it should have happened to him, and here, where he felt relatively safe. I counted him a friend."

"I am sorry, Your Excellency."

"There is another possibility," said the Bishop. "Even more distressing."

"And that is, Your Excellency?" asked Isaac.

"That he was a traitor. If he were also spying for another country, one of His Majesty's servants might have killed him. It is preferable to arresting him for treason."

"Oliver Climent, you mean," said Isaac.

"You have discovered that, Master Isaac?"

"Since the two men worked together, Your Excellency, and spoke confidentially together, and yet seemed at pains to disguise an old acquaintance, it only makes sense that they were comrades in arms."

"If Oliver killed him, then his death is none of my concern, and Oliver will report the incident to His Majesty, who can make of it what he likes," said Berenguer. "I think it more likely that he was killed by Castilians."

"But why would a Castilian follow him through Aragon and into the city to kill him with maximum danger to himself? It doesn't seem to make sense," said his physician. "But then, many things in war and diplomacy don't," he added tactfully.

"Let us discuss this further, my friend," said the bishop. "At the moment there is much to do as a result of this terrible event. I will send for you when I am next at sufficient leisure."

"And I must return home to my dinner, Your Excellency," said Isaac and took his leave.

"Why would anyone kill Pasqual Robert?" asked Raquel, as she picked at her dinner, all appetite gone.

"I do not know, my dear," said her father wearily. They were sitting at the trestle table in the courtyard, in the shade of a green and pleasant tree. A variety of excellently prepared dishes likely to tempt the appetite on a hot day had been set out on the table: grilled sardines, brought in fresh that morning from the coast, cold, spicy vegetables, chick peas dressed with herbs and vinegar, and chicken cooked with apricots. On the table with them were wine and jugs of cool drinks flavored with mint, lemon, and bitter orange.

"He seemed to be such an inoffensive man," said Raquel. "Was he a womanizer, Papa?" she added. "Perhaps he was killed by a jealous husband."

"Not that I have heard," said Isaac, who didn't seem to have much more appetite than his daughter, or as far as that went, his wife. Only the twins had eaten hungrily of their favorite dishes, and then were allowed, to their surprise, to leave the table and do as they wished.

"Yusuf would know that," said Raquel gloomily. "I still don't know how he collected so much gossip about everyone. Why people told him things he had no business to know always astonished me," she added.

"It was because he used to go down to the kitchens and listen to the servants," said Isaac, "while you and I were in the sickroom, tending to our patients."

"Although they tell you everything, too," said Raquel, nibbling on a piece of fruit.

"But the masters and mistresses don't know as much as the servants do," said Judith.

"I suppose that's true, isn't it?" said Raquel, putting down her half-eaten peach. "It seems strange not to have Yusuf here. I miss him."

"He has not gone to Tartary, Raquel, never to return," snapped her mother. "He will be back before the High Holidays. As will Daniel. You should settle down to work on your linens and think of other things."

"But, Mama. You were the one who said—"

"His Excellency believes that an outsider killed Pasqual," said Isaac, attempting to divert the conversation. "No one from the city would have stabbed him, he says."

"By a stranger?" asked Judith skeptically. "Why?"

"It is common enough," said her husband. "And a danger if a man is traveling alone on a deserted road."

"Are you saying that a common thief stabbed him for his money and possessions?"

"No, my dear. His Excellency says that. *I* do not know," said Isaac.

"And left him half dead, capable of naming—or at least describing—his attacker," she replied. "And besides—"

"Even a common thief would know that such a thrust would kill him sooner or later," said Isaac. "And Pasqual may not have seen his face."

"Then why leave behind his pack with his money and his papers and his spare clothing, all new and of very good quality?" she asked triumphantly. "As well as that excellent mule. He must be an uncommonly foolish thief."

"What do you know of his belongings?" asked her husband curiously.

"I was there, Isaac. While you and Raquel were helping him, I did what I could. I picked up everything that fell from his pack when he collapsed, folded it, and put it back. Along with his spare linen, he had a leather purse with a considerable sum of money in it and some papers with writing on them."

"Letters? Do you know if they were letters?"

"I don't know, Isaac," said Judith. "How could I tell? They were pieces of good paper, and there was writing all over them on both sides."

"And you put them back with his clothes," said Isaac.

"Of course. They had spilled out of a silk packet and I put

them back in. Brown silk. Very heavy and lined with cream. I folded them into the clothing, did the same with the gold, and made up his bundle very tightly."

"Who took it? Did you see?"

"Took it?" said Judith indignantly. "No one. I entrusted it to the captain."

"I must let His Excellency know," said Isaac, beginning to rise to his feet.

"Not now, Isaac," said his wife. "Please. It is much too hot to go out. Every sensible person in the city is asleep now, and that includes His Excellency. I wish you would go and rest as well. You were up half the night, as we all were. Deliver the message later in the day."

"You are right, my dear," said Isaac. "I shall rest for a while."

"You, Papa?" said Raquel, as her mother left the table to collect the twins. "Mama has managed to convince you?"

"Your mother reminded me that His Excellency was up very early this morning and will certainly be asleep now. This is no time for a discussion. This news your mother brings us is interesting, but the telling of it can wait until later."

FIVE

The shadows were lengthening under the trees by the little river. The three guards had spelled each other off; Miquel was nodding drowsily by the baggage, Narcís was dozing on his feet in the meadow, and Gabriel was fast asleep. The grass stirred in the occasional breath of wind; the mules and horses grazed or slept or wandered into the river for a drink, as it pleased them. Silence reigned.

Oliver had slept soundly for an hour and was awake once more. As far as he could tell, the lad at his side had not stirred all the afternoon. How long had it been, he wondered, since Gil had eaten or slept when they came across him? Days, in all likelihood. There was no need to waken him yet, but Oliver judged that the boy might not like to discover that he had spent several hours fast asleep in a total stranger's lap. Or more accurately, on his leg, slightly above the knee. He pulled himself gradually up to a sitting position, reached back for his pack, and slipped it under Gil's head at the same time as he removed his leg.

He got to his feet, stretched luxuriously, and wandered over to the other side of the small clearing where they had set up their temporary camp. He sat down by the sergeant, somewhat apart from the others. "What do you think, Domingo?" asked Oliver.

"About what?" said the sergeant, sounding amused. "The lad found himself a soft berth for his rest."

"Is that how your mind goes?" Oliver laughed. "I've knocked about this world a good deal, my friend, as have you. I assure you, he wasn't trying street boy tricks on me."

"Good," said the sergeant. "Because it's possible that he acts under orders. Someone may be interested in knowing your weaknesses," he added speculatively, looking up at the sky.

"It's possible. Such tricks have been tried on me before," said Oliver. "With women as well as boys. But don't worry. I'm keeping a wary eye on him. I was trying to dig out his background when he fell asleep on me."

"Did you get anything?"

"He says he has kin in Girona, which may or may not be true. I was not able to wrench a name out of him. The lad was trying most earnestly to explain why he didn't need our help when his eyes closed and he crumpled in midsentence. I thought for a moment someone had struck him over the head. It was like catching a wild kitten and then having it suddenly fall asleep on your lap. I admit to having my soft-hearted side."

"Then he must feel safe here," said the sergeant. "And that means if he's an honest lad, he's not a very clever one. He cannot know we are what we call ourselves."

"Perhaps so," said Oliver. "But he won't be a problem long. I thought to leave him tomorrow with a discreet woman of my acquaintance in Santa Maria. He will be safe with her. And she will be able to get some work out of him. Later, if he doesn't run away again, I might be able to arrange for something more fitting for him than working in the scullery. I have friends who owe me favors."

"That is the trouble with helping someone," observed the sergeant. "One acquires an everlasting obligation. Shall we move on now, do you think? Or wait until the shadows grow longer?"

"In an hour or so, I would say," said Oliver. "Let all the children sleep for now," he added, with a sweep of the hand that encompassed Gabriel, Yusuf, and Gil. "I will relieve Narcís until we leave."

"I will go with you and check the animals, and then relieve Miquel, who is half asleep instead of watching the baggage."

"In that case," said Oliver, "you can help me carry my trappings out to the meadow. There is a convenient rocky mound in there in which a man can conceal such things and be reasonably sure they will still be there a week or two later. I will collect them on my way back."

The sun was beginning to develop a reddish glow when Oliver and the sergeant woke up the others. The guards grumbled and pulled themselves together fairly hastily under their sergeant's cold eye. Yusuf took a little effort to rouse out of a deep sleep; he sat up finally and looked around with a dazed eye. On the advice of the others, he went down to the river to splash his head with cold water. During all this noise, Gil didn't stir.

"Up, lad," said the sergeant. "On your feet. We're leaving."

Gil made a small burrowing movement, as if to dig himself into the ground and away from the nagging voice.

"You get him up," said the sergeant to Oliver. "He's your problem. I have to oversee the loading, or they'll pile everything on poor Swallow again. This time she will go lame."

Oliver leaned over the boy. "Gil!" he said in a loud voice. "Wake up." No reaction. "Gil!" When that failed its purpose, he reached down and shook his shoulder. "Wake up, lad. On your feet, Gil, or you'll be left behind." He shook him again, harder this time, and the boy sat bolt upright, looking terrified.

He blinked and looked around, as if uncertain where he was. "Señor," he said at last. "I'm sorry. I fell asleep."

"You certainly did," said Oliver. "Go down to the river and wash—that'll wake you up. We'll be off soon."

The sergeant, Miquel, and Yusuf had all stripped off their shirts and were washing hastily in the river. Oliver noted, with amusement, that his new protégé was either very shy or very nervous, for he hid himself in a clump of bushes to strip.

Yusuf shook the water off a little and walked over to where Gil was hiding. "I know how you feel," he whispered.

"But don't worry about the guards. They make jokes, but they won't give you any trouble. They spend their pay on women. I've seen them."

There was no reply from the bushes. Yusuf shrugged and went on with getting dressed again. When the boy came out, he had obviously changed his mind about bathing. He had taken off nothing but his tattered shoes and hose. He waited until the others clambered out, then waded barefoot into the stream, quickly washed his face and arms in the cold water, and ran back to the bank.

The process of reloading was well under way. The sergeant was looking sourly at the clay dishes and bottles. "Leave them here," he said to Miquel. "Some poor housewife will find them, I hope, and put them to good use."

"But they belong to Mistress Judith," said Yusuf, with a vision of Naomi's reaction to the disappearance of two of her cooking pots.

"I shall purchase more clay pots for Mistress Judith in Barcelona," said the sergeant. "We are, after all, bringing back the mules with little on their backs but a trifling number of things for the palace."

"Are we riding, Sergeant?" asked Miquel. "Or walking?"

"We will distribute the loads and ride," said the sergeant. "Where do we put the lad?" he asked Oliver.

"He can ride with me," said Yusuf. "He doesn't look as if he weighs much."

Oliver reached over, grasped Gil around the waist, and hoisted him up a foot or so. The boy uttered a half scream and began to tremble. "By all the saints, boy," said Oliver, "Don't take on so. Or has someone bruised your ribs for you? If so, I'm sorry. Let me look at them."

"No, no. I was only startled," he said quickly. "I'm sorry."

"Nothing to be sorry about. He weighs nothing at all, Sergeant," said Oliver briskly. "I have another suggestion. I have disposed of a good part of my baggage. Some of the rest can go on my horse. Gil can ride Neta with the rest of it; he weighs less than the things he replaces. Then Yusuf's mare can carry some of the baggage mules' load along with her master."

The sergeant looked over to the meadow. Oliver's horse,

peacefully cropping the grass with the other beasts, was heavy enough to carry a man in light armor and certainly could carry his master along with a heavy pack. "That might work," he said. "Bring the animals over here," he added to the guards, "and we'll see what we can do. Swallow can carry the two heavy chests; they fit in her panniers, which are well padded. And if we can leave that as her only load, we may do well."

"And while I was sorting through my possessions," said Oliver, "I came across something for you, lad. It's not armor, but it might protect you just as well." He threw a gray garment over to Gil. "Put that on. And can you ride?"

"I can try, señor," said Gil with that sudden look of stubborn pride that flashed from time to time over his face. He straightened out the garment and looked at it. It was a friar's habit. "Is this yours?" he asked.

"I am no priest," Oliver said, "if that is what you are asking. And at the moment, the habit belongs to me, I suppose. It was cut for a smaller man than I am, but, I fear, for someone larger than you. If you tie up the waist so it doesn't drag on the ground, it won't look too strange. And with a little practice, you'll learn to walk around in heavy skirts. Take it. It is yours."

It was made for a much larger person, but Gil managed to dispose of it around his body with sufficient skill to look quite convincingly like a youthful friar. "Well, well," said the sergeant. "His Excellency would be much amused, I think. The lad does well in that garb. Except that he is not tonsured."

Gil's hand went to his head in a gesture of alarm.

"Don't worry. If we see someone who is likely to worry about it, throw your hood over your head and look as if you are praying." The sergeant laughed heartily for the first time since early that morning.

The procession set out once more. Before they had traveled three miles, the bells from a distant church began to ring for vespers. "We're late," said Oliver.

"That may be, but we're moving at a better pace," said the sergeant. "If we can keep it up, we'll reach the coast well before we have to stop."

• • •

The road wound and climbed and descended again under the declining sun. Then the sun disappeared behind the western hills and very slowly, the light began to fade. They had just crested a small hill when a stray breeze brought the unmistakable smell of salt and fish to Yusuf's nostrils. "The sea," he said. "I can smell it."

"So it is," said the sergeant, who had just ridden up from the rear. "Right where it's supposed to be. Now we must think about where to stop. How much farther do you think we can ride?" he asked Oliver, politely deferring to the man of higher status.

"Another hour, perhaps?" said Oliver.

"No more," said the sergeant. "And we should tighten up our formation, I think," he added, gesturing back to the strung-out line of mules and guards.

"I think so," said Oliver. "Do you have bowmen?"

"Why do you think we have that fool of a Narcís with us?"

"He is good?"

"None better. And it is perhaps time for him to string his bow. And Gabriel, although he is not so expert."

"There is a village over this hill," said the sergeant nostalgically. He was riding at the back of the procession with Narcís, who was holding his bow at the ready and scanning the landscape for trouble. "Where, if we were not so heavily laden, we might find a cup of wine and good cheer before making camp for the night. The place I had in mind to stop is not far beyond it."

"Which village?"

"If it ever had a name," said the sergeant, "I don't remember it. The tavern is a ramshackle place. Nearby sit a couple of hovels that have stood in the same place for countless years by the grace of Our Lord and little else. But they keep a good fire in winter, and in summer you can sit outside under a leafy arbor and stay cool in the breeze off the sea. There was a very pretty girl living in one of the hovels, as I remember, who adds to its attractions."

Since it seemed unlikely that they were going to enjoy its delights, Narcís yawned and lost interest.

Oliver, at the head of the group, crested the little hill and checked his horse abruptly. The big animal shook his head, his bridle jangling. The mules slowed as well. "My God! Look!" said Oliver, pointing.

In an instant, Narcís had an arrow to his bow and the sergeant had drawn his sword. But Oliver renewed the pace, and instead of forming a defensive line around the mules, those at the head of the group continued in the same formation as before.

"Keep ready," said the sergeant and rode up to Oliver. "What's going on?" he asked. "I thought we were under attack—Good God," he said, catching sight of the tiny village.

"Raiders," said Oliver. The two men looked at the burnt-out shells of the hovels and the poor but cheerful inn loved by the sergeant. "They have been active this summer. A little place like this has no protection against them."

"Slavers," said the sergeant, thinking of the pretty girl.

"Yes," said Oliver. "There's no gold here. Just people."

"We should carry on to our destination for the night," said the sergeant in bleak tones. "It grows dark."

While there was still enough light to see the landscape around them, the sergeant called a halt. "Up that track," he said, "there's a good stream and shelter. If the hut's gone, there'll at least be a haystack nearby. It's safer than an inn, and we won't find a better place before dark."

They followed the track up a moderately steep hill until they came to a rough shelter built of three walls and a shed roof, at that moment protecting a haystack and nothing more.

"I could do with a pair of stout mastiffs right now," said the sergeant.

"Are you uneasy?"

"I am," he said. "I'll be glad to be off as soon as we can see the roads."

"Sergeant," said Miquel, "look."

And on the horizon, just distinguishable in the dying light, was a great mass of clouds, moving at a lively rate toward them. The sergeant sniffed the air. "Rain," he said. "This entire expedition is cursed."

"It'll be cooler if it rains," said Narcís.

"Hold your damned cheerful tongue and start piling the baggage in that corner," he said. "In an orderly manner so we can load up before the end of next week. As soon as we've eaten, bring the animals in here with us."

"We're not leaving them outside to graze?" asked Miquel.

"Do you see that stuff, man? What do you call it?"

"Hay, Sergeant," said Miquel in a subdued voice.

"Exactly. While we're sleeping, I want the animals in here. The mules will kick up a fuss if someone comes around. And we might as well all stay dry. It's going to rain."

In the distance, a flash of lightning punctuated his prediction.

In a back corner near the haystack, someone had set rough boards to make a triangular shelf at about the height of Oliver's head. He leaned on them to check their strength, nodded with satisfaction, and threw several armfuls of hay on top of them.

The evening rations—bread, cheese, wine, and cured ham—had been passed around and the animals brought in. Inside the shelter it was dark, hot, and heavy with damp; outside, thunder rumbled in the distance, with lightning slicing the blackness all around them. Oliver held up the lantern with its single candle and began to look. Everyone was inside, settling into a comfortable berth, except for the boy. He looked around for Gil's little bundle. It, too, was gone.

In spite of having predicted to the sergeant that Gil would run away as soon as he had the chance, Oliver felt both disturbed and foolish. It was nothing to him if the boy had bolted in panic. Or by design. He had waited to be fed once more and then slipped out in the confusion of bringing in the animals, perhaps to join some confederates. And that meant that they had best be on their guard tonight. Having decided this, he made his way through the animals to the entrance, where a couple of ropes and some spare lengths of wood formed a rough gate.

Then a bolt of lightning lit up the area and he saw a slight figure in bulky clothing trudging toward the shelter, a small bundle under his arm. He grabbed him by the arm as soon as he reached the makeshift door. "Where have you been?" said Oliver, his voice low so as not to disturb the others.

"At the stream. I wanted to wash," whispered the boy.

"Did you see anyone else out there?" asked Oliver, embarrassed at his overreaction but still suspicious.

"No, señor. But I was trying not to be noticed. I thought I heard some people down on the highroad."

"It occurred to me that you are the only one of us not to be armed," said Oliver. "We could have problems tonight. I have tried to arrange a safer place for you to sleep."

"Problems?" said the boy, his voice tremulous. Oliver did not answer. "Where am I to sleep? Not outside?"

"In the storm? Don't be foolish. Back here. And don't step on anyone. It's crowded," he said. "Up there," he added in a soft murmur when they had picked their way over to the back corner. "There's hay for a bed. I think you're small enough to fit, and those boards will hold one of your weight. The only other person small enough to get up there is Yusuf, and he's asleep already in that back corner."

"How do I get up?" said the boy.

"Not one for climbing trees, are you?" said Oliver. "Here," he added, holding out his hands, fingers enlaced. "I'll give you a boost up."

The lad sprang lightly onto the shelf and spent a few moments arranging himself, his bundle, and the hay. Then, leaning over the edge, he said, "Thank you, señor. And good night. Where are you sleeping?"

"Right here, under you."

"Is that to protect me or to keep me prisoner?"

A hot denial fueled by indignation and guilt rose to his lips but was cut short by laughter coming from above. "You decide," Oliver said sourly. Nonetheless, he chose his position carefully. Gil could not leave and no one could get near him without stepping on his self-appointed protector.

The storm broke in a pandemonium of lightning, pounding rain, and deafening thunder. The animals huddled together, crowding in on the exhausted men who slept, or dozed, or lay awake, according to their temperaments. The sergeant took the first watch, standing in the entrance and staring out. He was worried. Inside, as securely positioned as it could be, was a king's ransom worth of goods. Only he and Oliver Climent knew what they were carrying, since they had not wanted to stir up the greed of vultures all the way from Girona to Barcelona. The road possessed enough ordinary hazards.

And the boy bothered him. Runaway, abandoned, thieving boys were as common as mice in a barn these days, he thought, what with the orphans left from the Black Death to increase the usual numbers. Some of them—if you could catch them—could even be taught a trade and made useful. The rest were doomed to a short, hungry life and a violent death. Oliver had likened Gil to a wild kitten, and the sergeant reflected that he spoke more truly than he knew. Most of these boys were like the wild cats that lurked in the filthiest city streets. The sergeant had no illusions about boys.

But there was something wrong with this one; he wasn't like any runaway boy that the sergeant had seen, and he didn't trust anyone whose motives and behavior seemed so at odds with each other. It troubled him that Oliver, who seemed to be a levelheaded man, was taken with him. But the boy was unlikely to get up to mischief tonight. He'd have his troubles getting down from the shelf past Oliver Climent.

While he was deep in thought, the worst of the storm had passed by them. Thunder rumbled in the distance, the erratic and gusty wind settled into a steady blow, and the rain began to ease off. The animals quieted down, and his men seemed to be sleeping soundly. But his hopes of pressing on by moonlight were fading. First light was more likely, he decided, and started to work out what needed to be done.

As the candle burned low, the sergeant woke up Miquel and settled himself to sleep. The rain was now light, with no discernible break in the clouds. He was considering the state of the track down to the highroad when the steady patter of water on the roof sent him off to sleep.

When he woke up again, the rain had stopped, and the cloudy sky was turning gray. He had overslept. "Up," he roared. "What's happened to the man on guard?"

"Here, sir," said Miquel, who had been propped up against the wall, peacefully dozing while the light strengthened.

Everyone moved with speed born of practice. The sergeant handed Gil the bread. The boy pulled off a share for each person and then disappeared outside with his, keeping out from underfoot. Yusuf harnessed and loaded his mare and then turned to help with the mules. In a commendably short time, they were on the road, splashing down the muddy track toward the sea.

"Auntie Mundina lives in a tiny village up ahead," said Oliver. "We should reach it in a matter of minutes."

"The sooner we rid ourselves of the boy, the happier I will be," said the sergeant. "There is something odd about him."

"Odd? What?"

"I don't know. His sudden appearance. His tale. Something."

"I know. These lads usually come in packs. I've seen no sign that he has partners. And I've been looking."

"You, too, are suspicious?"

"Sergeant, I am always suspicious."

Auntie Mundina was a woman in her forties, handsome, clever-looking, and energetic. Her small house sat up against a hill on the landward side of the road to Barcelona. It had an air of modest prosperity about it. She seemed neither surprised nor alarmed to rise from her bed and find five men and two boys, along with a dozen animals, outside her door.

"My . . . my good Oliver!" she said. "I'm happy to see you! And your friends," she added with a shade less heartiness.

"We do not intend to fill up your house with guests, Auntie Mundina," said Oliver. "But I have here a boy—his name is Gil, and if he has any other I do not know it—who is in need of a safe place to stay for a few days at least." He took the lad by the arm and pulled him forward. "I have not stolen him from the friars. The habit is one of mine, and he has no more right to it than I do. Other than that, he comes with no guarantees as to behavior, but he tells me he is familiar with work in a kitchen. I thought he could make himself useful."

Mundina looked at him, reached out, and flipped back his hood. "My goodness," she said, taking a long look at him. "You are a pretty child. You and I will have to talk . . . boy," she added. "And you have been traveling with my clever foster child for how long?"

"Only a day, señora," said Gil, turning scarlet.

"Indeed. You must have a mouthful of bread and some cheese before you ride on, gentlemen," she said, leading them out to a tiny courtyard in which a table and benches were set up. "Sit down. Come and help me bring out the loaf, child." And the two disappeared into the house.

"A fine and generous woman," said the sergeant.

"She was my nurse," said Oliver. "And later, when I was a boy, this was my refuge from everything: my angry father, my troublesome tutor, all the ills of life."

"And being a wild boy, his life had many ills," said Mundina, who had suddenly reappeared with a jug of wine and a loaf. "Gil has the cheese. Set it down, love," she added over her shoulder. "Help yourself." And she turned back into the house, dragging the boy with her.

"She'll get his life history out of him," said Oliver, laughing. "You can't lie to Auntie Mundina."

Before they had finished their impromptu breakfast, Mundina returned alone. "Can you take him, Auntie Mundina?" asked Oliver. "I would esteem it a great favor."

"Of course," she said. "It's time someone took him in hand. I will take very good care of him."

"Then we will be on our way," said Oliver.

"Have you been troubled with raiders this summer, señora?" asked the sergeant.

"Call me Auntie Mundina. Have we had the raiders?" she said, as if they were a disease. "No. They tell me it's been terrible this year, but we have escaped them so far. Other villages on this stretch of coast have been destroyed and all their children and young men taken."

"I've said before that you should come with me to Barcelona, Auntie," said Oliver. "We have stout walls to shelter us, four towers with watchmen to warn us of their approach, and ships at the ready to pursue them."

"Are you saying that we are not so well served here?" she said in mock surprise. "We have a watch."

"Excellent," said the sergeant.

"Of course, our watch is one lad, nine years old and not too clever. And he cannot be looking all the time. Still, that's more than some places."

"He's more likely to attract them than to frighten them off," said Oliver.

"He isn't there to frighten them off," said Mundina. "He's there to warn us."

"So you can take up arms?" asked the sergeant.

"So we can flee into the hills," said Mundina. "The last few ships sent in two or three eight-man boats. We have at best three men of an age to fight, armed only with staffs. We'll leave."

"When do they attack?" asked Miquel.

"It would be now, if they were going to. Early in the morning. They lie off the coast and then swoop in before people go out in the fields. The lad said he saw two ships last night, in fact."

"Last night?" said Oliver, alarmed.

"Don't worry, Oliver. No one else saw them. The boy has his daft moments when he sees things that aren't there. Then one of us goes up to look."

"Surely that makes him a poor watchman," said Gabriel.

"He may see more than exists," said Mundina, "but he never sees less. He never misses anything."

"Not even his own visions?"

"Not even those. You should be getting away if you wish to get to Barcelona this morning," said Mundina and began to shoo them toward their beasts as if they were stray geese.

Once they had mounted, Gil ran out of the house and over to them, laying his hand on Oliver's stirrup. "Thank you, señor," he said. "You have been good to me. I will never forget it. Or you."

"Auntie Mundina will look after you, lad," he said. "You can trust her. But don't pull any tricks on her."

"Tricks?"

"Good-bye, lad. We'll see you again."

The morning was gray with cloud but cool. There was a

liveliness in most of the group as they turned onto the road. Somewhere in the hills, bells were ringing out for prime. "We are on our way in good time," said the sergeant to Oliver as they waited for the mules to go by them onto the highroad. "God willing, we'll be in the city well before midday. I can almost believe now that we will transport this cargo safely to its destination. Last night I would not have given you a bad farthing for our chances."

"Why is that, Sergeant?" asked Oliver.

But he was destined not to find out. Their conversation was suddenly cut short by a piercing cry from the hill beyond Mundina's little house. A small, barefoot boy came running down it toward them. "Ships," he cried. "Ships. Tell Auntie, there's ships, and they're sending boats."

Oliver stopped. "I must stay," he said.

"First let us look to see," said the sergeant. "Remember that the boy makes mistakes."

Narcís had already dismounted and was scrambling up the hill the boy had come down. "I can see them from here," he called. "Two galleys lying off the coast. Two boats are coming in. No, they've launched another. Three boats."

"How many men?"

"I can't tell, Sergeant. Maybe six or eight to a boat."

Gabriel was climbing the hill. He turned. "Four boats, with eight men and an officer, I would say, Sergeant."

"He has good eyes?" asked Oliver.

"Excellent. Like a hawk. The pity is that he cannot shoot as straight as Narcís. I wish there were some way to combine the two."

Mundina came rushing out, pulling Gil after her, both carrying small bundles. "We must run," she said.

"No," said Oliver. "Get on Neta, both of you. Do we stay and fight, Sergeant?"

"Five—I beg your pardon, Yusuf—six against thirty or more? I am charged with getting my cargo to Barcelona, not dying a heroic death on the shore. We ride out of here as fast as we can."

"And the houses?" said Oliver.

"We cannot fight them off," said the sergeant. "Be realistic, sir. We risk our cargo, our lives, and losing houses and people as well."

"Don't worry about our belongings," said Mundina. "They won't find anything. Our valuables will still be there when we return."

"What if they burn the house?"

"The important things will still be there."

"Don't stand there talking," snapped the sergeant. "Put the señora and the boy on your mule and let us get away."

"And the others?" asked Oliver.

"They have their bolt-holes," said Mundina. "As I have mine."

SIX

By the time the boats had reached the shore, the group was over a hill, unable to hear what was going on. "I worry about the fate of your fellow villagers," said Oliver to Mundina. "We've abandoned them, and I've known some of them since childhood."

"When the raiders reach the village, they will find it deserted," said Mundina. "They would have to search for hours before discovering a single person or item of value. We learned from others' experiences that they fire houses to drive people out. We decided to run if they came, leaving our doors ajar."

"You are very calm about this," said Oliver.

"What choice do I have?" she asked. "But tell me. How did you come upon this poor creature?" she said, impatiently dismissing the topic.

"Gil?" asked Oliver. "He came across us by the side of the road, two or three hours from Girona. We trapped him with a piece of bread, didn't we, lad?"

The mumble from under the hood could have been a yes.

"And in return for the bread and a piece of excellent cold chicken, he gave us a story. It was either fanciful or odd. Depending on whether it was true or not," he added.

"It was true, señor," said the voice from under the hood. "I do not tell lies."

"No," said Mundina. "You have told one lie, at least. One great lie."

"Señora, you promised to say nothing."

"No. I promised to help you. I cannot do that until Oliver knows the truth. You are still in danger, even in that friar's habit," said Mundina. "Tell Oliver how old you are."

"Fifteen," said Gil.

"Fifteen?" said Mundina.

"Soon I will be sixteen."

"I don't believe it," said Oliver. "He looks closer to eleven than sixteen."

"And your name? Come now," she said in forceful tones. "Your name. And don't say Gil again, by all that's holy."

"Clara," said the small voice from under the hood.

"Louder."

"Clara," she snapped angrily.

"There you have it," said Mundina. "The lie. One look at her and I knew she was a girl. And a beautiful one at that. She took her mistress's scissors and cropped her hair, borrowed a tunic, and called herself a boy. But she looks no more like a boy than I do. You are not very perceptive, Oliver."

"By Our Lady," said Oliver, staring at Clara. "All I could see was that he . . . she was shy and afraid of soldiers," said Oliver. "In all that heat yesterday, she wouldn't take off her clothes and go in the river with the rest of us. I can see why, now." A sudden thought struck him. "Were you hiding in the bushes watching us . . . me . . . drying off?" He stopped.

"I saw nothing, señor," she said quickly.

"Why should you worry if she had?" said Mundina. "You're not a man who needs clothes to look handsome." And having reduced both of them to silent confusion, she burst into laughter.

"You can be wicked, Auntie," said Oliver. "We didn't make life easier for her. Since she was nervous around men, we tried most earnestly to assure her that none of us had any interest in pretty boys." He laughed ruefully. "That can't have been very reassuring. Well, Mistress Clara," he said, turning to her, "some puzzles are now solved. But tell me honestly: Why was your mistress going to sell you? Surely not for breaking a dish. She would not take such a risk for the cost of a clay pot."

"The mistress was not a comfortable woman," said Clara.

"What does that mean?" asked Oliver.

"She made the master's life a little difficult. Of course, he deserved it," she added.

"A lecherous old man?" said Oliver.

"Not that old," said Clara. "But yes. And unpleasant."

"He made your life difficult," said Oliver gently. "And you had nowhere to go?"

"The cook tried to look after me. She even let me share her bed. And the mistress kept a close eye on him. But she felt it was my fault, which I swear to you, it wasn't. I never thought to give him any encouragement. I found him disgusting."

"And your mistress decided to get rid of you and make a good sum of money all at the same time. But surely your master would have complained. He could be in great trouble if a servant in his household, a Christian girl, were sold to slavers."

"She waited until he was out of the city," said Clara.

"And then you ran off?"

"The cook told me plainly what would happen if I waited to be sold. She said girls like me were taken to other countries and sold to men for their amusement, and when they were tired of them, they were sold to brothels for common sailors."

"The cook wasn't far wrong," said Oliver.

"So I borrowed the lad's outgrown tunic from the clothing chest while I was putting away linens, put my dress in a bundle with half a loaf the cook gave me, and left for Girona."

"And the rest of the story is true?"

"Yes," said Clara. "Except that I was with the nuns, not the brothers," she added with a ghost of a smile.

"What do I do with her now?" said Oliver, looking up at the sky. "I could place a dozen clever boys with acquaintances who owe me favors and who would gladly take on a well-spoken young apprentice. But I am not used to dealing with young women."

"What she needs is a husband," said Mundina.

"But how can I hope to have a husband?" said Clara. "I have no kin, no friends, and no dowry." At that, she burst into brokenhearted sobbing.

The rain had swept over Girona the night before as well, and that morning the courtyard of the physician's house felt clean and cool. The trees were still silvery green with rain, and the table for breakfast had been set up under the sky, where the wet leaves would not drip water on their bread and cheese and fruit.

"Have you spoken to His Excellency yet?" asked Judith. "About the dead man's things, I mean." She sounded worried.

"You know very well I have not," said her husband. "Hardly had I stretched out yesterday afternoon for a well-deserved rest, I thought, than Master Astruch's little son took so very ill. We were with them until well into the night. Is that not so, Raquel?" he asked.

"Yes, Papa," said his daughter, yawning. "And I suppose he must be doing well, since they have not sent for us again."

"What was wrong?" asked Judith.

"I believe he ate something pretty from the garden that disagreed with him," said Isaac dryly.

"If people grow poisonous plants in their gardens, Papa, they have to expect accidents like that," said his daughter, with, for one brief moment, an echo of her mother's voice.

"I don't believe they intended harm to their son," said her father mildly. "They did not realize the plants were there."

"Harm! They dote on him," said Judith. "They give him everything he desires, without ever checking him. It's very bad to indulge a child that much."

"Especially when what he wants is poison," said Raquel.

"That's enough, Raquel," said her mother. "They are our good friends and neighbors."

"Yes, Mama," she said, and returned to her breakfast.

"But what I wanted to tell you, Isaac, is that I remembered something else," said Judith. "Something that in the haste and confusion of yesterday I think I forgot to tell you."

"What could you have forgotten?" asked the physician, surprised. For his wife's memory was sharp and retentive, and although he occasionally regretted her ability to remember in detail long-past events and conversations, in general, he was most impressed by it.

"In the man's possessions," she said, "along with the money and the papers with writing on them, there was a small picture, painted on a piece of smooth wood, of a woman. A very beautiful woman," she added, giving credit where credit was due.

"That is very interesting," said Isaac. "I sometimes wish, my dear, that your papa, good and virtuous man that he was, had seen fit to teach his daughters to read. You would have made a fine and observant scholar. And you could have told me what was in the letters."

"I'm happy as I am," said Judith defensively. "My papa did as he thought best. He felt it was not fitting for women to read."

"I do not doubt that for a moment, my dear," said her husband.

"What don't you doubt?" she asked suspiciously.

"Both things, my love. But you would have made a scholar." He rose to his feet. "As soon as Judah has finished turning the spit," he said dryly, "or whatever it is that occupies him whenever I want him, I will visit His Excellency with this news."

"If you wish me to find another kitchen lad, husband, you have only to say," said Judith.

"For a month or two? No. I shall share him with the spit-turning."

"Don't you think that they will have found those things by now?" asked Raquel.

"Most probably they have," said her father. "But in this strange world, Raquel, important things are often left unregarded."

"That is interesting, Master Isaac. But if anyone has thought to look at Pasqual's things," said Berenguer, "they have not condescended to tell me about it. Bernat!" he called.

"Yes, Your Excellency?" said the secretary, appearing at once through the connecting door.

"Pasqual Robert carried a bundle with him, containing money, letters, and a small painting. Have them brought at once. They were given to the captain yesterday morning."

"Certainly, Your Excellency," he murmured.

"Your Excellency's knee is troubling you?" asked Isaac.

"You have an irritating ability, Master Isaac, to understand what is wrong with me before I begin to complain. How do you do it?" asked the Bishop.

"It's not difficult," said Isaac. "I am sure Father Bernat knows when your knee is troubling you, too. I brought a new compound that may be of service, if your attendant would prepare it." Berenguer gave a clap of his hands, and his attendant appeared through the door that led to his chamber.

"Yes, Your Excellency?"

"Steep this in hot water until it is golden in color," said Isaac, "and bring it for His Excellency, along with one of his poultices." The servant whisked away. "The pain should ease a little on its own as the weather lifts," added the physician. "But if Your Excellency permits, I will check to make sure the joint is not worse."

"For all our sakes?" said Berenguer, laughing. "No doubt Bernat will thank you for restoring my temper, so do what you will, Master Isaac. And let us return to what we spoke of yesterday."

"Yes, Your Excellency," said the physician, as he explored the offending knee with strong, skillful fingers.

"I have been considering your thoughts on the matter. Since I have always believed you to be a wise and perceptive man. I still have difficulties with them."

"What difficulties, Your Excellency?"

"He cannot have been killed by someone from the city. Who bore a grudge against him here? He was instructed to lead an unobtrusive life, and as far as I know, he did. No one knew him, except as a slight acquaintance. I was the only person he ever talked to freely and openly."

"Why was he ordered to live that way?"

"I only know that His Majesty wished it. I suggested to the counselors that he be given a position as a clerk and offered myself as guarantor of his discretion and worthiness."

"Ah, yes. They said he came from Cruïlles, that Your Excellency had known him and could vouch for him."

"Almost true. I had known him for close to twenty years, but he did not come from Cruïlles," said Berenguer.

"Could your conversations have been overheard?" asked Isaac.

"No sound but the very loudest can be heard through the door into the hallway," said the Bishop. "And the other two doors are guarded by Bernat or Francesc on one side and by my faithful Jordi on the other. Jordi has been with me all my life, and I would as soon suspect myself as Bernat or Francesc. No one else could have overheard us."

"And it was very difficult to hear what Your Excellency and Master Pasqual were saying," said Bernat, appearing once more. "You will remember that both doors were always kept closed then."

"Bernat," said Berenguer. "You see? I usually leave both doors open a little, in case I need to summon either one."

"The captain is here," added the secretary, "with Pasqual Robert's belongings. Do you wish me to stay?"

"Yes, Bernat. We are looking for letters and a picture. And his money must be put safely in the treasury for his heirs."

"I will deal with that, Your Excellency, once we have counted it and the treasurer has signed for it."

"Bernat is wonderfully careful," said the Bishop. "I often think he must have seen much crime in his youth to make him so clever at preventing his fellows from absconding with treasury funds."

"It is my duty, Your Excellency," he said, ignoring the slur on his upbringing. The Bishop had an arsenal of barbed jests, which tended to appear when his gout flared up or his knee was troubling him.

Bernat opened the bundle. Murmuring to himself, he shook out each piece of clothing, folded it, and stacked it neatly under the captain's watchful eye. When the purse fell out, the captain placed it on the Bishop's desk. Next to appear was a leather bag. It joined the purse. Then the dark brown silk packet slid out from inside a clean linen shirt.

"Let us open that," said Berenguer. "We will worry about counting the money later."

"Your Excellency," murmured the secretary and brought over the packet.

There were, as Judith had promised, three pieces of paper with writing on them. "Do you wish me to read them, Your Excellency?"

"Yes, Bernat," said Berenguer in his most long-suffering tones. "That's why you're here."

"Do you wish me to stay, Your Excellency?" asked the captain.

"I think we will do well to have witnesses to this," said the Bishop. "We need you here."

Bernat unfolded the top piece, looked at it, and hastily set it down again. "The first one, Your Excellency, is perhaps not for our eyes. It is a series of words that make no sense."

"Code. Fold it up, Bernat. We will seal it and send it on to the proper person. Carry on."

"The next is a letter. It is addressed simply to 'My dearest.' " Bernat scanned it hastily, frowning over some of the writing, and looked up. "It seems to be a domestic kind of letter, Your Excellency. If Master Pasqual had a wife, I would think it was from her."

"Then read it," said the Bishop. "It may tell us something."

"If Your Excellency wishes. It says, 'We are both well and miss you very much. All is peaceful here. I wish I knew when you might return. Old F., who owns the land on the hill to the south, is very sick and wishes to sell his vineyard. His vines bear well and would do even better with more care. If we owned both, we would have good access to another stream as well as a good, established vineyard. F. refuses to wait, and so I have decided to buy it. I assure you that we can easily afford it now. I hope you agree that this is a good decision. The notary thinks it is wise and could also save trouble in the future. I wish that you were here to talk these decisions over, but since you are not, I try to do my best. The notary also suggested that we invest in a share of a ship, but I prefer to buy the meadow on the other side of the road. I think it could be for sale if I offered the right price.

" 'Your son grows more like his papa every day, except

that in the past few weeks he has become so tall I cannot
believe it. When I look at him now and see you in his eyes,
I am torn with grief and longing for you.

" 'Sometimes he smiles just like his sister, and once more
I know endless sorrow for our daughter. It was evil enough
that we should have been torn apart in that terrible time, but
that she should have died as well is more than cruel. When
you are not here to comfort me, I think of how I could have
saved her. I know you are saying with your forgiving smile
that there is no sense in tormenting myself. And I should not
add my old griefs to your greater burdens. Most of the time
I am happy, working hard, and looking after everything. I
am safe here, my love. Rest assured that no one has disturbed
our peace. But I worry about your safety. Your son sends
his papa kisses, to which I add my own.' It is signed 'S,' "
said Bernat, and handed the paper over to Berenguer.

"It is certainly from his wife," said the Bishop. "Or I
should say, his widow. I had not realized that he was married."

"She is going to be upset when she hears of his death,"
said Bernat. "She seems to have been very attached to him."

"Indeed," said Isaac. "It is the letter of a loving wife."

"And a very hardworking, clever one," said Berenguer.
"But well hidden. Who is she? Who is to tell her of the death
of her husband if we do not know who and where she is?
Did you notice that there is not a single name in that letter?
The children, the neighbor, the notary . . . none of these is
named."

"She is a very cautious woman," said Bernat.

"Did those letters you had picked up from that estate go
to Pasqual?" asked Isaac.

"That house has no mistress," said the captain. "It is managed by a bailiff. The master lives in Roussillon, I believe."

"And the letters go to Barcelona," added Berenguer. "Is
this the picture?" he asked and opened up the leather pouch.
A smooth oval of wood slipped out onto his palm. He turned
it over. "Pasqual's wife is a woman of great beauty," he said.
"Wherever she lives, I would think she would be famous.
But she is unknown to me."

SEVEN

Yusuf, the sergeant, and Miquel were riding at the head of the group, chatting idly, when the sergeant raised his hand for silence. In the distance behind them they could hear a confusion of hoofbeats. "Ready," he called. Narcís and Gabriel put arrows to their bows. Oliver pushed Neta into the middle of the crowd of mules, and the group moved warily on.

At the top of the next rise, Domingo called a halt. They looked back. "Gabriel. What can you see?"

"Dust," he said. "A pair of horses," he added, after a while. "And a small double file of fast-marching men. Eight or ten. A dozen, at most. Wearing someone's colors, Sergeant."

"That's reassuring," said the sergeant. "Unless the highway robbers are wearing uniforms now."

"Do we ride on, Sergeant?" asked Miquel.

"I think not," said Domingo. "If they are armed, uniformed men, we might as well travel together. They may be of some help if we meet any difficulties."

"But, Sergeant," he said, "they outnumber us."

"If we don't like their looks, we'll leave. We can move faster than they do. See that stream down there?"

"Yes, sir."

"We'll stop there to water the animals and see what we think of them."

"Is something wrong, Sergeant?" asked Oliver, as the sergeant brought the group to a halt.

"I thought we would give those men behind us a chance to catch up. When they appear over the rise, Miquel," he added, "busy yourself over a hoof or some harness."

"Yes, sir," said Miquel, and having nothing else to do, started methodically checking all the mules.

"Sergeant," said Oliver, swinging down off the saddle, "since we're stopping here, there is something I should point out to you. It may be important."

"I don't like conversations that start out that way, Master Oliver," said the sergeant. "Tell me the bad news."

"It's about the boy," murmured Oliver, stepping closer.

"What about him?" Domingo lowered his voice as well.

"He isn't," said Oliver with a shrug. "Look at him carefully and you'll see. Auntie Mundina spotted it right away."

The sergeant looked over at Mundina and Clara, who were still on the mule, apparently deep in conversation. At some point that morning, the girl had stripped off her hose under the all-enveloping gray habit, leaving her bare leg, slung over Neta's back, partially visible. It was slender and shapely and not the leg of a thin boy who has not yet reached his twelfth or thirteenth birthday. "By all that's holy, Master Oliver. I take your meaning. It is a girl. No wonder I thought there was something not quite right about him. How old is she?"

"Almost sixteen," said Oliver. "And as far as I can tell, honest and respectable. Out here on the road, surrounded by soldiers."

"That explains her fright. And a few other puzzling things," he said with a laugh. "I wouldn't worry, señor. She has that Auntie Mundina of yours for protection, and I'll keep the lads away from her. Including those behind us. But it makes me even more convinced that joining up with them might be worthwhile."

The party, when it arrived, turned out to be a middle-aged knight, a young man who appeared to be his son, and ten crossbowmen. "Gentlemen," said the knight in hearty tones, as if he were greeting a long-lost brother. "Well met. Are you in difficulties?" he asked, pointing to Miquel, who was frowning intently at the hoof he held cradled in his hand.

"I'm not sure," said the sergeant, glaring at Miquel. "Are we, man?"

. "No, sir. A stone, nothing more. I see no damage to the hoof at all," he said and hastily set it down.

"Do you travel to Barcelona?" asked the knight.

"We do indeed, sir," said the sergeant. "And you?"

"We do. We have marched down the coast this morning," said the knight. His face was as bronzed from the sun as any farm laborer's, and since it was unlikely that he had ever put his hand to a plough, to the sergeant he looked reassuringly like a veteran of several military campaigns.

"If you started early, you have had a wet time of it," said the sergeant.

"We did, indeed," said the son with a smile that belied his words. "Most unpleasantly wet. But we were soon dry, although we are still somewhat disheveled," he added.

"Good morning, señores," said Oliver, leaving his horse to graze and approaching the newcomers.

"This is Oliver Climent, sirs," said the sergeant. "He is in charge of our little group."

"And my name, good sir, is Asbert de Robau," said the knight. "And this young man is my son, Gueralt."

"The name and colors are famous throughout this part of the world, sir," said Oliver and nodded slightly at the sergeant. "We are fortunate to meet up with you. What brings you out on such a morning?"

Gueralt broke in before his father had a chance to reply. "May I offer a humble suggestion? If we're going to pass the time exchanging travelers' tales," he said, "why not travel together as we do it, instead of talking here by the side of the road?"

"A most excellent idea," said Asbert de Robau cheerfully. "Let us join forces and ride together. I confess that I have seen this road many times before, and my son and I have exhausted everything we had to say to each other. I am sure the same thing is true for your party."

"Very true," said Oliver, laughing. "We shall be glad of the company."

"That is, of course, if you do not mind being slowed to the pace of marching men," said Asbert.

"Not at all," said the sergeant. "If we find that it grows too late, we will say farewell and dig in our spurs."

"Excellent," said Asbert, and the whole company moved out together.

"But what does bring you out on the road in the heat of summer?" asked Oliver.

"We come to join His Majesty's ship *Alexandria* with reinforcements," said Asbert. "Not enough men to turn the tide of war, perhaps, but they are all we had to offer."

"It is unfortunate that you were not able to leave earlier," said Oliver. "You could have joined the ships at Rosas. That would surely have been easier for you."

"True. The distance to Rosas is somewhat shorter," said Asbert. "And that was what we had planned to do. But we have been plagued with illness. I was the first to be laid low, and then my elder son, young Asbert, who was to come with me."

"I am sorry to hear that, sir," said Oliver.

"We postponed our departure for a month in hopes that we would both recover sufficiently, but although I made it from my bed in good time, he did not. I am an old soldier, sir, and very hard to kill. Youth may be lively and lusty, but it's very fragile, haven't you found?"

"I hope your son—"

"He is recovering, but he is still too weak to wield a sword," said his father. "I was prepared to go on my own—with the men, of course—when his younger brother, Gueralt, arrived home from completing his education."

"And where—"

"Exactly," said Asbert. "And no sooner did he see me preparing to join His Majesty's forces in Sardinia than he insisted that he would take his elder brother's place. Now at last we hasten to assist our sovereign lord."

"He will welcome the reinforcements, I am sure," said Oliver. "It is most commendable of the young squire," he added.

"I would die for my King," said Gueralt, suddenly serious. "And gladly. I swear by Almighty God."

"I certainly hope so," said Asbert. "Or he is no son of mine," he added, turning back to Oliver. "And why do you make for Barcelona?" he asked, looking at the laden mules. "Trade?"

"We come from Girona," said the sergeant. "We are carrying household goods to the city for the use of our lord when he is there."

"You take good care of them," said Asbert de Robau in perfunctory tones and turned to Yusuf as the next person of potential interest. "And you, young sir, what are you doing on this expedition? You look to be a military man, not a carter of goods." He laughed heartily as he said this.

"Nothing, sir. Like you, I have attached myself to pleasant companions," said Yusuf. "I prefer it to making haste on my own."

"You did well," said the knight. "I recall when I traveled once to Avignon . . ." And he launched into a long and complex tale of adventure and skulduggery.

His son, who had clearly heard this tale more than once, turned to Oliver. "Look at that," he said. "You have brought your own cook and priest, riding together on that mule."

The word that Gil was really Clara, which had been whispered so discreetly by Oliver to the sergeant, had by some magic combination of keen ears and native suspicions spread throughout the group before they had left the stopping place by the stream. They all stiffened. "Hardly a priest," said Yusuf contemptuously.

"What do you mean by that?" asked Gueralt. Oliver held his breath.

"He's just a pup," said Yusuf. "Younger than I am. They're delivering him to the fathers. He's another one of the parcels they're carrying," he added, laughing.

Asbert and Gueralt laughed, looking back at them. Oliver let out his breath.

"Handsome woman, though," said Gueralt.

"Old enough to be my mother and yours, señor," said Yusuf with a remarkably lewd grin. "One of their lord's servants."

"Another parcel?" said Gueralt.

Yusuf laughed. "For delivery—undamaged—to his lord-ship's residence."

"He is a sharp-witted lad," murmured the sergeant to Oliver.

"He is. As sharp-witted as our traveling companions are cheerful," replied Oliver.

"I could wish them less so," said Domingo. "They chatter like magpies, those two. All that chatter makes staying alert a great problem."

"I wonder," said Oliver. "Do you think them a pair of amiable fools?"

Domingo shook his head. "I have no opinion. They could be exactly what they seem."

The rest of the trip was uneventful. As they passed Badalona, the clouds began to thin and rip apart, like shreds of old linen, and the heat began to rise. It was close to midday and stifling when they finally passed through the gates to the city.

Oliver had spent the rest of the trip discarding his solutions to the "Gil problem" and considering new ones. Was Clara a frightened scullery maid in need of work? Surely no scullery maid spoke as she did. Was she then a young lady in need of protection? Or, he thought pessimistically, was she something else completely? It might be wise to find out.

After the Bishop's party turned toward the royal palace, Oliver and the two women rode to a substantial house located on the far side of the city walls, out the west gate to the city.

As soon as they were admitted, a young man came into the hall, embraced Oliver, and looked inquisitively at the two people behind him. "Are you here to stay for a while, Oliver?" he asked. "I will have rooms prepared."

"There's no time for that," he said. "Listen. We need a room and some refreshment. I must talk in private to those two," he added, pointing to Mundina and Clara, who stood several steps behind him, waiting.

"A serving woman and a baby Franciscan?" murmured the young man. "Oliver, you have the strangest friends of anyone I know. Just tell me why, please, or I shall be tormented all day with curiosity."

"I swear," said Oliver, "I will explain. I have no time now," he added as he led the two women into a small sitting room.

"Very well," said the young man.

Wine, cool water, olives, nuts, and fruit were brought in and they were left alone.

"Clara," said Oliver, "I must know something about you." He spoke in a calm, matter-of-fact voice, as if he were a physician, inquiring after her health.

"You know what there is to know," she said. "I am an orphan. I was raised by the sisters. I am penniless. That is all."

"How old were you when the sisters took you in?" he asked.

"I don't remember," she said quickly. "Not very old."

"I'll accept that," he said, not believing her but judging it best not to push her yet. "Can you remember how long you worked for that woman?"

"Oh, yes, I can remember that. Almost three years," she said. She stopped and looked down at her hands, still red and roughened with work. "And in all that time I was paid nothing. What I earned was to go with the rest of my money for a dowry. A small dowry, but enough to keep me from the streets," she added bitterly.

"You had money when you came to the convent?" said Oliver.

She paused, as if to weigh how incriminating an answer would be. "Not much. A few sous," she said. "But I can't go back to get it. My mistress will have gone directly to the convent to complain that I have run away."

"I understand that, Clara. I'm not asking you to go back there. But tell me, what were you supposed to be paid?" he asked curiously.

"Nothing for the first year. After that, three pounds a year," she said. "Scullery maids are not highly valued."

"How long were you bound to stay?"

"Seven years," she said.

"Eighteen pounds," said Oliver, shaking his head. "Will you tell me your father's name, Clara?" he added casually.

All the color drained from her face. "I cannot," she whispered. Her shoulders tensed and her hands, which sat on her lap as a good convent child's hands should, began to tremble. She thrust them hurriedly in the capacious sleeves of her borrowed habit. "I don't know it," she added in a semblance of normal tones.

"Your mother's name?" She shook her head.

All this time Mundina had been looking at her in a manner that seemed more impatient than compassionate. "It has been a bad time for families," she murmured. "Hasn't it? So many dying. Do you remember your grandfather?" She spoke softly in a voice that was deep and pleasant and flowed like a gently running river. "I was very young when mine died, but I remember him. I called him Little Papa. He was a small man, not so big as my papa."

"My grandfather?" she said and relaxed, now that the talk had moved away from parents. She turned her head to look out the window at the trees with vague, unfocused eyes. "Yes. I remember him. I called him Aimi. He brought me sweets and pretty gowns and then he died when everyone died." She looked up, tears covering her face. She mopped them up with her sleeve and pushed back her roughly cut hair. "But that was very long ago," she said harshly. "I can hardly remember him." "

"Why Aimi?" asked Mundina.

"I expect it was because I couldn't say Grandpapa Aimeric."

Oliver got to his feet and walked over to the window. He stood there, silent for a while, and then turned back with a smile. "The most obvious place to put you for a few days, you and Mundina, is with the sisters. And I don't want to make the tremendous error of dropping you off with the sisters who already know you. Will you tell me this? Were they inside the city or outside?"

"Inside," she said promptly enough.

"Then I shall lodge you with the Benedictines at Sant Pere de les Puelles. You will be safe there. Will you wait here a moment? I wish to talk to Mundina about what she will do."

"I won't leave through the window," Clara said with another flicker of a smile. "I promise."

• • •

"Auntie Mundina, you are a witch, I swear. You can make people talk more easily than all the paid torturers in the service of all the kings in the world. Sweets and pretty gowns. Her grandfather was a rich man," said Oliver triumphantly.

"Not a poor one, certainly," said Mundina.

"If her mother had been a poor creature who was seduced and left to starve with her baby, as she would have us believe, we would have little hope of finding out who she is. But I knew that could not be true."

"Yes. That voice does come out now and then," said Mundina.

"Even though she has clearly tried to lose it."

"I expect she was only trying to fit in with the other servants," said Mundina.

"Not fool us?"

"No, I would guess she's been trying to speak this way since she began working," said Mundina. "After all, she knows her old life is gone forever. And it wouldn't hurt you to remember it, my lord."

"We'll see," said Oliver. "We know her grandfather's name and the year he died. Discovering who her parents are will be easy."

"You think the grandfather died in the plague?"

" 'The year everyone died,' she said."

"She might have been lying."

"No, Auntie Mundina. I've listened to her tell the truth, and I've listened to her lie. This time she was telling the truth. She was in a trance, Mundina. She's exhausted, hungry, and frantic with worry and sorrow. For the moment, she could fight no longer. She was tame . . . too tame to lie. Like a falcon that's being gentled. It's that voice of yours."

"It lulled you to sleep many a night, my lord," she said. "That and my good milk."

"Will you stay with her?" he asked. "For now? Seven pounds from now to the nativity of Our Lord. It may mean traveling."

She thought a moment. "Will you send my son to look after my house? And pay him?"

"Done. Your son shall leave as soon as he is able. Now, off to the sisters. At once."

EIGHT

"Don Bernat, I have no time now to establish beyond doubt who she is," said Oliver. "I don't want something to happen to her while I am finding out. She would be safe with Her Majesty in Sardinia." He was seated in an apartment in the Queen's palace that was assigned to the astute and scrupulously careful Bernat de Relat, treasurer of Queen Eleanora's household. The treasurer looked as if he were regretting his impulse to invite Oliver in.

"What puzzles me, Señor Oliver," said Relat, "is that you would concern yourself with the fate of one orphaned girl." He gave Oliver a quizzical look that said more than his words. "Even if she speaks like a countess, you know well that it is a simple matter to teach a clever child to mimic her betters. Lord Oliver, she is a scullery maid. If her beauty tempts you, you can afford to establish her in a secure location without my intervention."

Oliver rose. "I am not so driven by my desires that I would seek help from Her Majesty's treasurer to seduce a serving girl, Don Bernat. It would indeed be a waste of a busy official's valuable time. I thank you for listening, and I bid you good day."

"Wait a moment, Lord Oliver," said Relat. "If I offended you, then I am heartily sorry. But you must grant me, in all justice, that when a man of your standing becomes interested in a scullery maid, it is usually not her soul that he seeks."

"In all justice, I grant you that, Don Bernat. And if I thought she were simply a scullery maid, it might be true."

"Who do you think she is?"

"Do you remember, six years ago—"

"Her Majesty's household had not been established here six years ago, my lord," said Relat dryly, "but I do know something of notable events in the kingdom."

"It was the year our former Queen and her infant son died. The first summer of the plague, Don Bernat."

"The beginning of a time of great turbulence," said the treasurer, shaking his head.

"One of the members of His Majesty's household, knowing that trouble was brewing in Zaragoza, sent his wife and daughter to stay with his cousin, the most noble viscount of Cardona."

"I have heard of that incident, my lord. Did not his entire household disappear and were never heard of again? They died on the journey, it was assumed. Perhaps of the plague."

"We do not know. It is possible. It is also possible that they were killed on the road for the gold they carried." Oliver began to pace up and down the room as he spoke. "I tracked down one of the missing servants, a miserable coward of a man, who swore they were all killed by thieves. He claimed that he escaped through the mercy of God because an attack of colic caused him to fall behind the rest of the party." Oliver stopped and looked at the treasurer with a curious expression on his face. "The child's name was Clara."

"Does the girl you found resemble the missing child? Clara is not an uncommon name, Señor Oliver."

"Not strongly, Don Bernat," said Oliver. "Although she, too, has dark hair and eyes and a fair complexion. But six years have passed. She could be little Clara, older and much changed." He rested his hands on the edge of the treasurer's desk and leaned toward him. "I helped her father search for her. I vowed I would find her if she were still alive. I think I have."

"How old was she when she disappeared?"

"Seven or eight years old, I believe."

"How could she have ended up in a convent in Barcelona?" asked the treasurer. "If they were attacked on the road, no doubt she would have been sold, not given to the nuns."

He shook his head. "Many things could have happened after her capture. She could have been taken to Barcelona to be sold and run away," said Oliver.

"It is possible," said Relat, "but not convincing. Why not believe the girl's story? There are thousands of orphans and abandoned children in the kingdom. Many of them are girls cared for by the sisters, and a sad number of them do not know who their fathers are."

"Why would a slave dealer approach a respectable citizen, offering to buy a free Christian servant girl who came to them from a convent? No matter who her forebears were. Consider how dangerous this could be for him. If she were in the care of a useless, thieving father and a sluttish mother and a slave dealer offered them money for her, I would believe it more readily."

The treasurer paused to consider. "A good point, Lord Oliver. The sisters would inquire about her. Especially since they were banking her money for her. And if they were found out, the punishments for buyer and seller are heavy. There must have been a powerful motive for such drastic action, and only her abductors could have it." Excitement began to infect his voice.

"And if she is the lost Clara, we must do something right away."

"Do you think time is that short?" asked Relat. "Because if it is—"

"When I left her with the Benedictines at Sant Pere, one of the nuns said, 'Why that's little Clara!' She vowed that she wasn't, but I know the sister was not convinced. She had been at Clara's old convent, I suppose."

"It's possible," said Relat.

"And it means that I must get her away from there as soon as I can. By this evening, at the latest."

"This evening?" said Relat, with a sudden return of caution. "Lord Oliver, stop and think of what you are doing. She could be anyone. She could be a well-trained girl placed in your path by someone who knows a great deal about you and is hoping to learn more. Her master could have named her Clara deliberately, expecting that you would assume she was Cardona's niece."

"No, Don Bernat," said Oliver. "That is impossible." And patiently he outlined the same arguments he had given the sergeant: their unforeseen late departure, the unexpectedness of their stopping place.

"I suppose you are too experienced to be easily deceived," said the treasurer thoughtfully. "And we have reason to be grateful to you. But a scullery maid!"

"She isn't—"

"She was, Oliver," he said sourly. "You say she is well-spoken. Can she sew?"

"I don't know," said Oliver. "The nuns must have taught her things like that."

"Well, ask her," said Relat irritably. "She and her companion can stay here with the rest of the Queen's household tonight. And find out if she can sew. I have much to do before that wretched ship leaves port," he added.

And murmuring expressions of gratitude, Oliver left the treasurer's study.

Oliver led the two women to the convent gate where a pair of horses waited for them.

"Why must we leave?" asked Mundina. "The girl is ill with exhaustion."

"We must, that's all," he said. "But we aren't going far. Just into the city."

"Where?" said Clara, sudden terror in her eyes.

"Nowhere near a convent or an employer," he said. "It would be easier if you would trust me for a moment. I'm taking you to someplace much, much safer."

"What do you mean?" she asked.

"I'll tell you in a minute," he said. "But first I have one more question to ask you. An important question."

"What is it?" Clara asked suspiciously.

"Can you sew?"

"Can I sew?" she said, astonished. "Of course I can sew. What kind of sewing do you mean?" she added hesitantly.

"I don't know," he said. "Sewing."

"Fine needlework? Mending? Or making clothes, like a tailor?"

"Again, I don't know. What can you do?"

"Needlework and mending, of course. And I suppose if I had the cloth, I could make myself a gown, as well. But I wouldn't be as quick or as expert as those who do it for a living."

Clara, cowed, exhausted, and still dressed as a fledgling Franciscan, found herself standing with Oliver facing the Queen's treasurer, his secretary, his secretary's assistant, and his scribe. "Can you hem linen?" asked the treasurer, glancing down at notes in front of him.

"Certainly, Don Bernat," said Clara, baffled. "It is not a difficult task."

"And embroider?"

"Yes, Don Bernat," she said. "But at the moment I have no needles or scissors or any of the other tools that are required."

"That is a very good point," he said, turning to the youthful assistant secretary, who was staring at the Franciscan in amazement. "See that our young friend has all that is required by tomorrow, please. And have it verified that the kit is complete and signed for."

"A sewing kit?" said the assistant, as if he were about to protest and then changed his mind. "Of course, Don Bernat. Does he require anything else?"

"A plain gown, I suspect," said Don Bernat de Relat, looking amused. "See what the ladies in the wardrobe have. As soon as possible. Since," he added, turning to Clara, "I would judge that you and Her Majesty are of a size, although you are somewhat shorter—"

"Considerably shorter," said the secretary, looking up suddenly.

Bernat de Relat nodded at his secretary. "I am told it is a simple change to effect. There should be no problem," he continued to Clara.

"Thank you, Don Bernat," said Clara.

"And a plain gown," said the assistant secretary as he

wrote it down. "I shall see to that immediately if Your Lordship does not require my services further."

"Do that," said Relat with a dismissive wave of the hand. He watched him escape from the room. "I should not tease your young assistant," he said when the door closed behind the young man.

"If he insists on looking like a fool, he must expect such things," said the secretary.

"He is so serious a fellow I cannot help it," said Relat and turned to Clara again. "You, Mistress Clara, and your attendant will be leaving on Her Majesty's supply ship in two days' time."

"I am most grateful, Your Lordship," said Clara, looking stunned.

"And I think that for now, at least, you will be best served when you are outside these walls by remaining as a Franciscan. Good day, Mistress Clara."

Through some mysterious agency, the door opened and, in some confusion, Clara left to join Mundina in the hallway outside.

"What will I be doing in Sardinia?" asked Clara when Oliver joined her and Mundina outside the treasurer's apartments.

"Waiting on Her Majesty," said Oliver. "That is why we needed to know if you could sew."

"But what does that involve, Señor Oliver?" asked Clara.

"I don't know," said Oliver impatiently. "You would know these things better than I do. But if I were you, I would not go about asking others to explain. Don't speak of it to anyone."

"Since I won't be leaving the palace for two days," she replied with some spirit, "who do you think I would speak to? I am little more than a prisoner here."

"Not a prisoner, Clara," he said lightly. "Safe."

"Mistress Clara?" said a high-pitched voice. A small page boy in Her Majesty's colors hastened toward them.

"I am Mistress Clara."

"You are to come with me, you and your attendant, and I will show you your rooms," he said with a bow and a tiny flourish. He turned and headed rapidly down the hallway.

"Where will you be, Señor Oliver?" asked Clara in panic.

"Someplace quiet, writing a letter," he said. "Two letters, in truth. Don't worry. I will see you Thursday morning. Hurry. The page is fast disappearing."

Oliver's first letter had been finished well before vespers. He sealed it, considered it for a moment, and rang for the page. "This is to go to Girona as soon as possible," he said, holding it up. "To the Bishop. Find me a courier, will you, lad?"

"I beg your pardon, my lord," said the boy. "But you'll pay a terrible price to send that by itself."

Oliver looked up impatiently. "If I'm willing to pay it—"

"But I happen to know, my lord, that the Bishop's courier is leaving for Avignon very soon. He'll be passing through Girona tomorrow morning, and for ten pence he'll take it for you. He's very reliable. If you wish, I'll run over to the episcopal palace with it now, but he needs to be paid in advance."

"How convenient that His Excellency the Bishop of Barcelona should prefer to live in Avignon," said Oliver with a wink and gave the lad the letter and the coins. "And there's two for you, as well," he added, and settled down to compose a second, much more difficult epistle.

The boy left at a rapid pace, before it should occur to the gentleman that he had already calculated his own fee into the original price.

The letter arrived in Girona in good time for the courier and his hardworking horse to avail themselves of palace hospitality during the heat of the day. "The bishop's courier from Barcelona has arrived, Your Excellency," said Bernat sa Frigola, his secretary.

"And what does the courier bring for us today?" said Berenguer dourly. "More toil and annoyance?"

"The usual amount, Your Excellency, but most of it can be dealt with by others. There is also a letter from Señor Oliver, written yesterday in Barcelona."

"What has he to report?"

"The journey was eventful, Your Excellency, but young

Yusuf and all the goods arrived safely and are in the royal warehouse."

"Including the gold?" asked Berenguer.

"Every coin is in the treasury, counted, acknowledged, and signed for, Your Excellency. He gives an account of coming across a child, a girl, on the road. I will read that to you in a moment. He asks you about a knight, Asbert de Robau, and his son, Gueralt, whom they met on the road as well."

"I know the family," said Berenguer. "And Asbert. A brave and loyal soldier, I believe. I have not heard of Gueralt. Is he the heir? Send for Francesc, Bernat, if you please, and tell me about the girl."

Francesc Monterranes, the Bishop's confessor, was accustomed to having such questions hurled at him without notice. This one forced him to stop and consider for a moment. "I believe," he said at last, "that Asbert's heir bore his name, Your Excellency. It is possible, of course, that young Asbert has died recently of some mischance or other, leaving a brother to inherit. If he has, the news has not reached us. Asbert was said to have married a foreign woman," he added.

"A foreign woman?" asked Bernat.

"My good Bernat," said the Bishop. "The word is relative. She could have come from here and been considered by some to be a foreign woman. If Oliver thinks it important, I will write to my cousin and find out."

"Before we start on the rest of the material in the courier's bag, Your Excellency," said Bernat, "Master Pons Manet would like to see you about a charge that a citizen wishes to bring."

"Then we better see him," said Berenguer, and a page was sent to fetch the head of the council of the city.

"Thank you for seeing me, Your Excellency," said Pons Manet. "Good morning, Father Francesc, Father Bernat. I would not have disturbed you except that I myself was so troubled."

"And what is troubling you, Master Pons?" said the Bishop, surprised, for Pons Manet was a calm and sensible man by nature.

"Luis Mercer came to me this morning and said that he

wished to lodge a complaint. He said he had seen two members of the Jewish community outside the city. The man without his cape and the woman making a lewd and public display of herself, without veil or other proper covering, riding, as he put it, Your Excellency, without license or permission about the countryside like any Christian lord."

"Have they nothing else to concern themselves with?" muttered Berenguer and looked over at Master Pons. "Who were they? The Jews, I mean."

"Your physician, Your Excellency. And my physician, too. I cannot believe the allegations."

"When was this supposed to have happened?"

"The day young Yusuf went off to Barcelona. Master Isaac and Mistress Raquel rode part of the way with him."

"They did. Who did you say brought this ridiculous complaint?"

"Master Luis. Luis Mercer, that is."

"That man begins to try my patience, Master Pons. I would be greatly obliged if you would go to Luis Mercer, Master Pons, and inform him that Master Isaac and his daughter were out of the city on a license from the Bishop of Girona, on business for the diocese, and that according to reputable witnesses, both were properly attired at all times on that brief journey. And that any further attempt to harass them will have serious consequences."

"I will do that, Your Excellency. And I thank you. I, too, find myself weary of his meddlesome ways. He can see impropriety in a grandmother widowed these twenty years walking across the square alone to attend Mass. Although to be charitable," he added, "he has not been well recently."

"Then, if you will," said the Bishop, "we will not mention this to anyone unless Mercer should stir it up again."

"An excellent idea. Will you speak to Master Isaac about it?"

"Not at the moment. If it seems necessary, I will."

"Many thanks, Your Excellency." And Pons Manet, greatly relieved, headed off to tell Luis Mercer to forget his complaint.

● ● ●

As the shadows lengthened and the city began to wake up after the blistering heat of the afternoon, Isaac's meditations were interrupted by a violent ringing at the gate and an urgent summons to the house of the same Luis Mercer.

"You say he is very ill. May I ask in what way?" he said to the servant who brought the message. "I must know what I should bring."

"He can neither sleep nor eat, Master Isaac," said the servant. "He has fallen into a terrible melancholy, and he cannot work for the pains in his head."

"That is helpful," said Isaac. "Raquel?"

"Yes, Papa," she said. "I know what to bring, I think."

"Anything else can be sent over later. Let us go now," he said. "Veil yourself," he added. "Remember who we visit."

"Yes, Papa," said Raquel and threw a light veil over her head and face. She handed the basket to Judah, and all three followed the servant to Master Luis Mercer's house.

Luis was huddled in a chair well padded with cushions, looking pale and hollow-eyed from sleeplessness. Raquel knew from common gossip that he was a widower of about thirty, had lost his young wife and their newborn child six years before, had been so devastated by her death that he had not looked with desire on another woman since. She also knew—since he was sufficiently young, handsome, and rich—that several marriageable women had wasted much time and effort trying to attract his attention.

"I have heard, Master Isaac," said Luis, "that your remedies are most efficacious, especially for those complaints that seem to haunt us endlessly." His voice rose in a most troubling manner.

Raquel guided her father to a chair near his patient. He sat down. "Which complaints haunt you endlessly, Master Luis, so that you have that desperation in your voice when you speak?"

"My head pounds so that I think it will drive me mad," he said. "I cannot sleep for it, and when I do sleep, I fall from the pain of being awake into dreams of fear and terror."

"How long has this gone on?" asked the physician, who

by now had picked up his patient's wrist and hand and then gently released it again.

"The sleeplessness has afflicted me since the death of my dear wife," he said. "Or even before. But the pain in my head started only a few weeks ago, I think. It comes and goes . . . but in the last few days it has not gone away. That foolish incident when we met out in the countryside—I am sure you remember it—will have shown you what it does to me. A laborer directed me to the wrong house, and instead of asking directions to the property I wished to visit, I fell into an ungovernable rage. It frightened me, Master Isaac. I never did such things before."

"If your servant will bring some hot water, my daughter will show him how to prepare a soothing draft that will help you. But first I must examine you." And he felt the merchant's head, face, neck, and shoulders with probing fingers.

"I saw you and your daughter earlier on that terrible morning as well," said Luis, as the physician began to manipulate the flesh under his fingers in his patient's shoulders. "The morning our poor clerk died. His death had greatly upset me."

"Was he a friend?"

"He was too shy and humble to make friends with the members of the Exchange," said Luis, "but I liked him. And his death, like my wife's, was a terrible waste of a young life."

"Young?" said the physician. "Pasqual Robert was surely not young?"

"Not very old," said Luis. "Less than forty. Have they found the persons who killed him?"

"It is possible that he was killed by a Castilian," said Isaac. "For reasons that I do not know."

"Is that what His Excellency thinks?"

"I'm not certain," said the physician. "He has not spoken of it. There," he said, taking his hands away. "Take the draft. It will relieve the pain in your head, and that will loosen your shoulders. It will also help you to sleep, and more sleep will help to cure the pain. Without as much pain, you will be able to eat. Light dishes at first," he said, turning to the servant. "In order to remedy an overabundance of choler.

Herbs," he suggested, "lightly boiled. Soup, fish, and eggs. Such things do not heat the blood and overwork the body."

"What was wrong with Master Luis Mercer?" asked Judith as she cut up a pear for her husband. "To call you out on a hot afternoon." The physician's family was sitting under the trees in the courtyard, with the remains of supper on the table in front of them. The sun had set long since, but daylight lingered still.

"He seems greatly afflicted still by his wife's death," said Isaac.

"When did she die?" asked Raquel.

"A long time ago," said her mother. "Before the plague."

"Seven years," said Isaac.

"How long had they been married?" asked Raquel.

"Not long. Perhaps a year or two," said her father, yawning.

"Imagine being so faithful to a memory," said Raquel dreamily.

"That's what has made him so strange," said Judith.

"Strange? In what way, my dear?"

"Isaac, you must know about him. He sees lewdness in women everywhere," she said. "He turned away one of his maids for it not two months ago. The poor little thing had never thought of misbehaving and she would have been on the streets if Master Pons hadn't taken her in."

"That's true," said Raquel. "And I've heard other tales like that about him. But why should a man who loved one woman so much turn to hating all others?"

"He never loved that miserable little creature," said Judith. "She had a good dowry, that was all. Everyone knew that, no matter what he may say now."

"Your mother's memory is inconvenient for those who would change history," said Isaac wryly.

"What did she die of?" asked Raquel.

"Nothing. She faded away," said Judith. "She wasn't very lively to begin with, and she only got worse. And now he treats all women the way he used to treat his wife."

"Your mother exaggerates a little," said the physician mildly. "But I will be happy to have Yusuf return to us. I do not like taking you with me to the house of a patient like that. He has a fondness for false accusations. And speaking of Yusuf, His Excellency has received a letter from Señor Oliver," said Isaac.

"How is Yusuf?" asked Judith, suspended with one-half of the pear in one hand and the knife in the other. "Is anything wrong, that Señor Oliver should write?"

"No, my love. Yusuf is well. Señor Oliver had other business to discuss with His Excellency and sent this message to us out of kindness."

"He seemed a pleasant enough man," said Raquel. "Although somewhat quiet and out of sorts."

"His assistant and friend had just died," said the physician.

"Of course," said Raquel. "When does Yusuf leave for Sardinia?"

"Tomorrow," said her father.

"I wonder if we will hear anything more of him until he returns," said Raquel, sounding depressed, irritated, and close to tears. "Or doesn't return."

"Stop thinking about such things," said Judith crossly. "I won't listen to it." Raquel's stinging retort was mercifully cut off by the arrival of a boy, who rang the bell, rattled the gates, and called for the physician.

Before Ibrahim, the porter, had walked across the courtyard, Isaac was calling for Judah.

"Master Isaac!" said the boy at the gate, when he finally succeeded in getting in. "You must come quickly. There is a man lying at our house. He raves like a madman and the mistress says that if we don't fetch the physician, he'll be dead by morning."

"What is he dying of?" asked Isaac.

"I don't know, master," said the boy. "The mistress never told me."

"I need to know what kinds of potions I should bring," he said, as patiently as he could. "Why does he rave? Has he been hit on the head? Does he have a fever?"

"It is a wound on his arm," said the boy.

"Then you should have fetched the surgeon," said Isaac.

"No, it is an old wound that festers. One that he received many days ago. He has a fever, Master Isaac, and thinks that

I am his mother, and his brother, and who knows what other people."

"Isaac, you have not yet finished your supper," said his wife in protest.

"I have eaten as much as a man needs, my dear," said Isaac. "And now I am needed. Raquel, look to the contents of the basket, replacing what we used this afternoon. Let Judah fetch a lantern, flint, and steel for our return."

"Yes, Papa," said Raquel briskly, all gloom forgotten.

The boy took them to an inn by the river, outside the north gates to the city, where he labored as potboy, stable lad, kitchen help, messenger, and whatever else required work, except for cooking and the collecting of money to pay for food, drink, and harborage of man or beast. Money was such a rare commodity in his existence that he was reckoned too inexperienced to know what to do with it.

The house had only one paying guest that night in its airless garret. "We will need light, landlady," said Raquel.

"What's a blind man want light for, mistress, I ask you? Do you know how much candles cost me?"

"I know exactly what they cost," said Raquel. "And I must be able to see. There is little point in summoning us if we cannot work. You will bring me candles. Three and at once."

Cursing and grumbling, the woman retreated, sending the boy back with three tallow candles.

"He is in bad case, Papa," said Raquel. "The festering wound is in his forearm," and she guided his hand to the affected limb.

He ran his hands over the arm, from fingers up to armpit, first lightly, then with slightly more pressure. He bent over and listened to his chest for a considerable time. "What color is the arm?" he said as he straightened up again.

"The light from these candles is not good, but the whole forearm seems to be red and swollen," said Raquel. "I would guess that the putrefaction is spreading," she added tentatively.

"It is," said her father. "I can feel it. Tonight we will drain and clean up what we can," said Isaac. "A surgeon might be able to help, at the cost of his arm, but that discussion must wait until daylight."

"You don't sound hopeful, Papa," said Raquel.

"Once these things start, they can be difficult to stop," said Isaac. "The upper arm does not feel as it should."

Raquel encircled the arm above the elbow with her finger. It felt warm and oddly resistant to the touch. "You are right, Papa. Shall we start?"

Throughout the examination, the man in the bed had seemed to be either sleeping or beyond comprehending his plight. Suddenly he struggled to sit up. "We must start," he said. "Now. We must start."

"He is not from around here," remarked Raquel, as she helped Judah set out what she would need, and to mix a pain-dulling compound.

"Of course he isn't," said her father. "If he were, he would not stay in an inn."

"True. He is from Aragon, is he not?" she asked.

"Possibly."

The patient began to toss restlessly and then raised up his afflicted arm. Raquel took it firmly in both hands and pushed it gently down to the bed. "Ssh," she said. "Quietly. We're here to look after you."

"Master," he called, "help me. Master Geraldo, come and help me. I cannot do it alone. I cannot." He subsided again, panting.

"He's been doing that all day," observed the landlady, who had appeared again at the top of the stairs. "That's why I sent for you. Couldn't stand to listen to him going on like that. Can you give him something so he'll stay quiet until he dies?" she asked. "I tried brandy, but he wouldn't drink it."

"Save me, master," cried out the man on the bed. "Help me."

"Bring us hot water, mother," said Isaac. "And we'll do what we can."

And the landlady shrieked once again for the potboy and then headed back down the stairs.

Raquel mixed wine, water, sugar, and four drops of a bitter black substance together and, holding him up, slowly coaxed it down the man's throat. After a short while, his limbs relaxed and she set him back down on the bed. With her sharp knife she cut into the abscess and released a great flow of putrid matter that little Judah valiantly mopped up. She cleaned the wound with wine, dressed it with oils and herbs to keep down the infection, bandaged it, and coaxed a little more of the pain-dulling mixture down his throat.

He opened his eyes and stared wildly around the garret. "Please," he said. "Tell my master."

"Who is your master?" asked Raquel. "Tell me who he is, and I will let him know."

"Everyone knows him," said the man. "Everyone knows my master." At that, his eyes closed, and he fell asleep.

NINE

The crowd at the harbor was large for such an early hour. The city still slumbered in darkness, but down at the water's edge, a waning moon and the approaching dawn afforded enough light for working. The eastern horizon was sharply defined already by scraps of pink cloud separating black sea from graying sky.

Most of the crowd were longshoremen trudging between heavily laden carts and flat-bottomed boats pulled up to the shore, carrying goods from cart to boat. A soberly clad clerk with a detailed list stood at each cart, checking every barrel, sack, box, and parcel as it came off. Another clerk stood at each boat, checking what was going in.

When the party from Girona arrived, the sky had already turned to blue and the sun was edging up, casting its first beams on the masts of a galley waiting out in deeper water. Oliver, dressed in fitting military garb, dismounted, told the groom to take the horses back, and sought out the person in authority.

"I did not expect to find the noble Bernat de Relat with an army of scribes, loading the boats himself," he said. "Most would have been in their beds still, leaving this work to an assistant and the ship's master." And indeed, in the center of the smoothly functioning work party was Her Majesty's treasurer. At his side, a nine-year-old boy was holding a large scroll in his hands, unrolled to the last section of a long master list.

"Do you know of another way, Lord Oliver, to ensure that every item I ordered is received by Her Majesty?" said Relat.

"There is no other way, Don Bernat," said Oliver. "Otherwise, valuable cargo falls mysteriously overboard and turns up next week on the lightermen's tables or their wives' backs."

"Should that happen to any of Her Majesty's possessions, those responsible will pay dearly for it," said Relat coldly.

"Do you accompany the ship yourself, Don Bernat?" asked Oliver. "Or are you sending your young assistant?"

"My son is fully as shrewd as some," said Relat, giving the child's shoulder a pat. "He will take the lists next time. But my proctor guards this shipment. He is not so easygoing a man as I," he added, with a foxlike smile. "You can be sure he will take great care of everything. Including your Mistress Clara."

"She is not mine, Don Bernat," said Oliver hastily. "But why did you ask about her skill with a needle?"

"Her Majesty is pressing her ladies into service with the royal wardrobe," said the treasurer. "She was lamenting the absence of skilled needlewomen in her recent letter. I thought I should make sure Mistress Clara was competent."

"I think she believes she will be made into a seamstress," said Oliver, laughing. "Thank you for the explanation. And now I wish to beg a favor from you—and your proctor."

"It will be a change to have you owe me the favors, my lord Oliver. Ask, and if it can be done, it will be."

"Thank you. Could this letter be given to Her Majesty as soon as the ship arrives? It is from me."

"That seems a modest request. Nothing else? The delivery of several wild beasts or the loan of the galley? Other letters?"

"They are in the courier's bag. But in addition, may I present someone to you, Don Bernat. His Majesty's ward, Yusuf ibn Hasan, who is to serve His Majesty in Sardinia. As a page."

"He, and Mistress Clara, and the letter will all be taken

great care of," said Relat. He nodded at Yusuf and then, with
a harassed glance, dismissed them both to respond to a possible problem between a pugnacious-looking lighterman and
a quietly insistent scribe, who was intent on keeping the
lighterman from pushing off until the tally in his boat was
made up completely.

"He appears weary and ill at ease," remarked Yusuf.

"I suspect he has been up all the night, checking arrangements," said Oliver. "If these supplies are required for Her
Majesty's health and well-being—and I hear that they are—
he has much to be responsible for."

The galley was fitted for cargo, rather than passengers, and
yet more and more people kept appearing on the strip of
shore. A group of three Dominicans and a servant carrying
a heavy-looking box slung on his back appeared next, the
snowy garments of the Order of Preachers dazzling the eye
already hurt by bright sand and glittering sea. Oliver barely
noted their presence—to see Dominican fathers traveling was
common enough—until they paused near Yusuf, who was
standing with Clara and Mundina.

The Dominicans suddenly became interesting. Oliver
headed for the carts, swerved, and stopped close by them.
He bent down as if to pick something up out of the sand.
"Good day, Fathers," he said, straightening up again. "Are
you joining the ship?"

"Not all of us," said the oldest-looking of the three. "Only
Father Crispià here. We merely accompany him to the shore,
to ensure that he embarks in safety."

"And I am most grateful to my brothers for that," said
Father Crispià. He was tall and gaunt, with a hawklike nose
and bright, dark eyes. "Are you sailing with us?" asked the
friar. His voice with its southern ring and his weathered skin
suggested distant kingdoms to Oliver. Perhaps Granada.

"I, too, am here to escort others to the ship," said Oliver.
"I trust we do not have long to wait."

"We were instructed to be here well before prime," said
the senior Dominican somewhat waspishly. "And we are."

"They are still loading cargo into the hold," said the
youngest friar, who seemed to be enthralled by the process.

As they were speaking, Oliver noticed that the crowd was growing. A throng of well-wishers and bystanders milled about, men and women for whom watching the longshoremen and lightermen, the clerks and passengers, the loading and sailing of a ship was sufficiently interesting to fill their whole morning. His three charges disappeared in the sea of taller heads and broader frames.

"Señor Oliver," interrupted a familiar voice. "You have changed your coat and your colors. Do you sail with us to Sardinia?"

Oliver half turned and saw that he was talking to young Robau, his new acquaintance from the road. He shook his head. "No, señor. But were not you and your father to leave yesterday?"

"We were, Señor Oliver," said Gueralt de Robau. "Until my father remembered that he had left a piece of urgent business undone. He asked me to take care of it and secured a passage for me on Her Majesty's ship."

"No doubt young Yusuf will be pleased to have the company," said Oliver, catching sight of his charges again and heading off toward them before they disappeared once more.

"No, Master Isaac. Most fortunately, His Excellency is very well today," said Bernat sa Frigola, the Bishop's secretary. "But he wished you to join him because the party that escorted Yusuf to Barcelona has returned. They are in the small reception room, awaiting your arrival." Isaac was taken into the cool, high-ceilinged room where Berenguer, the captain, the sergeant, Bernat, and two scribes were seated at a large table.

"Master Isaac," said the sergeant, once he had given a brief report on Yusuf's health and welfare, "I fear that we have failed in one of our duties."

"And what is that?" asked Isaac.

"Burdened as we were, we left a large clay pot belonging to your wife behind us, after finishing the contents. It has been replaced. I hope she will find the new one acceptable."

"Surely you had room for one pot," said Berenguer, amused.

"Not unless we turned the guards off their mounts and

piled baggage on the horses. As it was, I was forced to bring poor Swallow back with nothing on her back, to rest her leg. Most of the baggage on our return was light enough; silk and spices weigh little."

"Now tell me what you can about Robau, Sergeant," asked Berenguer. "Señor Oliver wrote to me about the father and son. He seemed in some way concerned."

"Asbert de Robau is a well-known and worthy knight, Your Excellency," said the sergeant.

"I am aware of that," said Berenguer.

"Yes, Your Excellency," murmured the sergeant. "I had no cause to alter my opinion of him that day. But his son caused me some uneasiness. He took too shrewd an interest in young Yusuf and his reason for being with us. And in Señor Oliver, as well. The young gentleman had so many questions one might imagine he was arranging a match for his sister rather than passing the time of day with chance acquaintances on the road."

"Perhaps he found a journey in company with his father tiresome," said the Bishop. "He may have been seeking amusement from you."

"At first, that is what I believed," said the sergeant. "But it continued, and I did not like it, Your Excellency. Not at all."

"Well, you have a good nose for villainy, Domingo," said his captain. "Should we come across Gueralt de Robau, we will watch him with interest. Did you have more to be reported on? We have already heard of Lord Oliver's young orphan." The meeting drifted to speculations about Clara and then broke up.

"Before I go, Your Excellency," said Isaac, "I must report that we attended a stranger last night at Benedicta's inn."

"A stranger?" asked the captain.

"Martin is his name. My daughter and I were summoned to treat a festering wound in his arm. He charged us with a message to his master—"

"Did he say who he was, Master Isaac?"

"One Geraldo, Captain. He bade us tell his master that he was wounded. From his ravings, I would guess he had been left alone to face an enemy stronger than himself."

"Do you have a particular reason for telling us this, Master Isaac?" asked the Bishop.

"No, Your Excellency," said the physician. "Only that the sick man speaks like one from Castile. His presence in the city may be of no significance at all."

"Is this Martin well enough to talk?" asked the captain.

"I do not know. I am going there as soon as His Excellency no longer requires me," said Isaac. "He had not the full use of his wits when I left him. But you are welcome to accompany me, Captain. He may have recovered a little."

"And what sparked your interest in my patient, Captain?" asked Isaac, as they walked over to the inn, four of them: the two men, Raquel, and little Judah, followed by two guards.

"I am interested in any wandering foreigners right now," said the captain. "Until I know why they are here."

A group of four drinkers looked up in alarm at this unusual intrusion. Raquel had pulled her veil completely over her face and stumbled, half blinded in the darkness of the inn. Judah, intimidated, huddled close to her side. The captain moved across the room as if he were planning to storm the kitchen and banged his fist down on the table. "Hola, Mother Benedicta!" he called. "We've come to see your patient."

The landlady scuttled out of the kitchen and shook her head. "He's none too good," she said. "I took him up some food, but he didn't seem to want it. If he's going to die," she added, "I wish he'd be a bit quicker about it. I can't be running up and down all day and night looking after a sick man."

"He's up there," said Raquel, pointing to the steep, narrow staircase.

"You two stay here until you're wanted," said the captain to his men and ran up the stairs.

The room was hot as only an attic room in full summer can be hot. Every fleck of dust smelled of heat; heat was a force to be battled through. In the middle of it lay the poor man, looking white and miserable. But he seemed to recognize his helpers from the previous night. "Did you tell him?" he asked in a weak voice. "He's here. Or he was here."

"If you can give us his name—his complete name—the captain will do his best to find him," said Isaac briskly.

"He calls himself Master Geraldo," he answered innocently enough. "He does not seem to claim a family."

"And where are you from, friend?" asked the captain.

"Tudela," he said. "Near Tudela."

"An honest answer," said the captain. "Your name is Martin?"

"Yes, Captain."

"I will do what I can for him now," said Raquel.

"As soon as you have finished, we will move him to more comfortable quarters," said the captain. "I wouldn't leave a sick dog in the care of Mother Benedicta," he added. "Much less a sick man, even from Tudela. This heat alone is enough to discourage life. And he may have more answers."

TEN

"Would you like your habit back, my lord?" Clara asked as Oliver helped her to climb on board the galley.

"My lord?" he said. "My name is Oliver."

"I had not known your rank, my lord, when I called you that," she said demurely.

"You can be very irritating," he said. "And you may keep the habit. I gave it to you."

"But I have no further use for it, my lord."

"Never to be Gil again, Clara?" asked Oliver. "Please, keep it for now. I have no place for it. Why don't you join Mundina in your cabin?" he added quickly, pointing at the raised structure on the afterdeck. "It is the first one to your left. I will be back in a moment." He bowed and was lost in the crowd.

When Oliver stepped inside the tiny cabin, an elegant young woman in a loosely fitting plain gown of tawny yellow light silk was standing in the center of it. Her short hair was half hidden by a sash of the same material wrapped skillfully about her head, and her dark eyes glowed in the color reflected from the silk. For a moment he thought he had walked into the wrong cabin. "You look different," he said finally. "In a dress, I mean."

"Isn't it elegant?" she said, her eyes dancing. "It once be-longed to Her Majesty and was remade for one of Her Maj-esty's ladies, and now it's in its third incarnation." She whirled about to show off the skirts.

"I see you are well settled in," he said at last.

Clara glanced around in amusement. "It is smaller than my cubbyhole off the kitchen in Barcelona," she said, and he smiled. This was the Clara he knew. He looked it over. There was a net for her belongings, a narrow bunk, and little else in it.

"You're probably turning the skipper or his first officers out of their quarters," said Oliver. "But there's room to sling a hammock. The two of you won't have to squeeze into one bunk."

"I'll take the hammock," said Clara. "I'm smaller. You take the bed," she said to Mundina. "Where will you and Yusuf be?"

"Yusuf will be with the junior officers and the crew," said Oliver. "Between decks. I will not be sailing with the ship. I have other work to do at the moment."

Clara sat down on the bunk, the glow from the tawny yellow silk suddenly extinguished. "I thought you were com-ing to Sardinia," she said bleakly. She stared at him as if he had suddenly struck her.

"I cannot," he said, crouching down in front of her. "I have written a full report for His Majesty that will be carried to him. Once you are in Sardinia, you will be safe."

"And until then?" she said.

"You will be safe here. This galley can easily withstand winter storms and summer squalls. She can also move quickly under attack. There are few ships out there that could overtake her."

Clara stared down at her hands. "Why didn't you leave me to go to my family in Girona?" she asked. "Why pick me up like a stray dog and then ship me off across the sea to make my way among strangers?"

"Because you had no chance of getting there, Clara," he said flatly. "Even as a boy. It was a miracle you got as far as you did. You didn't know who your relatives were or if they were still alive. The Black Death was not confined to

Barcelona. It hit Girona, too. Also, I knew why I was helping you."

"Did you?" asked Clara. "Because your reasons for helping me still puzzle me, Lord Oliver. Do you stop to help every ragged lad you find on the road?"

"No. In all honesty I must admit that I do not."

"Then what are they? Tell me. What are they?"

"Let me say that I knew my reasons were not evil ones."

"But you will not say what they were."

"How can I tell you if I am not sure myself?" he asked. "Will you believe me if I say you might be the child of a lord to whom I owed allegiance? I am not sure, but you could be."

"And when you discover I am not? What then? Do you strip off the gown, return it to Her Majesty, and throw me in the streets?"

"What kind of monster do you believe me to be?" he said. "If that is how you perceive me, then I am no longer surprised that you question my motives, Mistress Clara." He bowed. "I wish you a calm and speedy voyage to Sardinia. Good day," he said.

And before she could answer, he was gone.

Most of the top deck of the ship was taken up with the rowers' benches, twenty-five to a side, with a gangway between them. They were angled so that three men could sit side by side, each pulling on his own oar. When Yusuf clambered on board from the lighter that brought the passengers out, he was directed to a moderately spacious part of the area between decks that had been fitted up for them and the ship's officers. Compared to his living quarters in Master Isaac's household, the space was cramped and Spartan. Four portholes provided ventilation to the entire area; it was decidedly stuffy. Clara and Mundina had been whisked away by Lord Oliver. Gueralt de Robau had disappeared as well, and Yusuf, to his horror, was left alone with a Dominican priest. The Dominican was seated on a bench near one of the portholes, looking down at the decking under his feet, thinking or perhaps praying.

In an attempt to avoid the priest's notice, Yusuf went to

another porthole and stared at the activity in the harbor.

"Good morning, young sir," said the priest. "You seem uneasy. These are not the most spacious of accommodations, but I assure you, one can make oneself quite comfortable in a galley."

"I have not traveled on a ship before," said Yusuf, turning in spite of himself to look at the speaker. "Father," he added.

"I am told your name is Yusuf," said the priest. "I am Crispià. I also heard there are only five passengers, and that two of them are ladies. That means we will be able to go up on deck once we are out of harbor. If we are lucky in our winds."

"You mean we must stay down here?"

"While we row out of harbor, there is no room for passengers to wander at will. But when the ship is under sail, there are places to go where one is not in the way."

"You have sailed many times before, Father?"

"Many times," said Father Crispià. He turned to look out the porthole to the horizon. "I came here across the sea," he said, "many years ago, and I have traveled much since. Where are you from, if I might ask, Yusuf?"

"The south," said the boy cautiously.

"I thought as much," he said. "From a slight cast to your speech . . . very slight. I, too, grew up speaking your language. And now, thanks to Her Majesty's kindness, I travel to Sardinia."

"To join the war?" asked Yusuf, startled.

"Not at all. I go for other purposes," he said, smiling. There was a shout from above, repeated in another voice.

"What is that?" asked Yusuf.

"We are preparing to leave. The passengers, being the most troublesome of cargo, are brought on board last," said the priest. "That loud creaking noise is the scrape of the anchor coming up. We can't see it from here," he added, "but in a ship you hear everything, and once you learn what it means, you know as well as those up on deck what is happening."

"That is like my master," said Yusuf, "who is blind, and knows more of the world than most who can see."

Another cry rang out, repeated again in a second voice.

"The rowers are now ready," said his informant. "In a moment we will see the oars, and we will begin to move out of harbor."

A last cry, and oars flashed by the porthole. Yusuf knelt on the bench and stared out at them. "Why are they striking the water at different places?" he asked. "Some close in, others farther out?"

"You will have noticed that the rowers' benches are angled," said Father Crispià.

"Yes, Father," muttered Yusuf, who had not noticed at all.

"That way you can have three beside each other on one bench, and their oars don't get tangled. The rowers seated in the center have longer oars than the rowers seated closest to the water. That way, each one pulls at a different piece of the water. I am told it is faster and easier for them to work that way."

"Have you ever rowed?" asked Yusuf, becoming curious—not to say suspicious—about his companion's expertise.

"No. Fortunately, God has never demanded such hard work from me. I am neither a rower nor a warrior, not even, I am afraid, on God's battlefield. I leave that to others who are better suited for it and try to do what I can as a scholar."

"A scholar?" asked Yusuf.

"I was always very curious, even as a boy much younger than you are. It was decided that I would do best as a scholar. And in what have you been trained?"

Yusuf did his best to explain with as much vagueness as possible his dual role in life.

"I heard on the shore while waiting that you were His Majesty's ward," said Father Crispià. "And now you go to his side when you are needed. Most commendable."

"I am not sure that I can help His Majesty in battle," said Yusuf. "I am not as skilled with a sword as I could be."

"Sardinia has long been known for its unhealthy climate," said Father Crispià, "although you will get no thanks from royal officials for mentioning it. Your skills in healing will be as useful as any skill on the battlefield. His Majesty has many knights and crossbowmen."

"And do you come to Alghero to minister to the sick as well, Father?" asked Yusuf.

"Alas, no. Nothing so noble. Or perhaps even useful," he said. "Our founder's purpose was that we should dedicate ourselves to learning and preaching. I am suited well enough for learning, and even for teaching what I have learned, but I am no silver-tongued orator. Few men wish to listen to philosophical arguments on their deathbeds. Or even to talk of why three oars almost abreast should pull a ship more easily through the water than the same number of oars working in a long line. They wish for exhortations and comfort and glimpses of heaven that I can see in my heart but not spread with my tongue."

"Perhaps your parents would have been better to send you off somewhere where preaching was not so important," observed Yusuf.

"My parents," he said and stopped. "I was long out of the control of my parents when I joined the order," he went on, finally. "But my superiors recognized my strengths and forgave my weaknesses . . . and so now, in a ship with passengers who go to fight, I go to find my way to a particular library where there is a book I wish to consult."

"A book of philosophy?" asked Yusuf.

"In a manner of speaking. It is a book written by a great astronomer on the workings of heavenly bodies."

"Can't anyone there tell you what's in it? It seems a waste for you to travel all that way," said Yusuf pragmatically.

"First of all, it is better if I read it myself," said Father Crispià. "And also, this is a small library in a smaller monastery. At the moment, none of the brothers there can read or write in Arabic. In return for their hospitality, I will turn the book into a language they can understand, and for my pains, they allow me to make a copy of it for the library of my order."

"And you can read Arabic? And write it?"

"Oh, yes," he said.

"Will you teach me, Father? I know the letters, and many words, but there is so much I have forgotten and much more that I never knew," he said in such great excitement that he forgot his resolution to conceal his background from this sharp-eyed man.

●   ●   ●

For the first day and the beginning of the second, the crew bent to the oars. As soon as the sounds fell into a regular rhythm, Father Crispià and Yusuf climbed the companionway to the deck. The galley was filled with men working intently, but the other passengers, Clara, Mundina, the treasurer's proctor, and Gueralt de Robau were nowhere to be seen.

"Where are they?" asked Yusuf.

"In their cabins," said Father Crispià, pointing toward the afterdeck.

"Even that Gueralt?"

"I suppose that he talked his way into a place in the castle. I know there was a bunk free. But I felt that if others had to stay between decks, I should, too," he said apologetically, as if his diffidence was a fault that he must atone for. "But I have brought a book, and some paper to write on, if you wish to start to work on Arabic."

While Yusuf was grappling with the elements of Arabic, Don Bernat de Relat's proctor was introducing himself to the women who had been placed under his protection. "I am Eximeno, Mistress Clara," he said, giving her a shrewd glance. "Should you lack anything on the voyage, send your companion to my cabin, and I will do my best to see that you are supplied with what you need."

"Thank you, Don Eximeno," she murmured. "But our cabin has been stocked with everything we could wish for."

"I'm glad to hear that. If you would like to take the air, the deck in front of the castle here is available to you. But for your own safety, mistress, I beg of you to keep well veiled and apart from the others. Otherwise, remain in your cabin, confined though it is. If there is nothing I can do for you at the moment, then I wish you good day," he said, bowed, and left.

"Well," said Mundina. "He won't forget you in a hurry. But he seems a careful man, and that is good."

Clara fastened a long veil into her hair and covered her face with it. "Come, Mundina," she said. "Let us find out if it is cooler on the deck."

But Clara had spent too long laboring under her mistress's

command to enjoy the sight of close to two hundred men bending their backs to their oars. "Let us go in, Mundina," she said.

"They are skilled at their work," said Mundina. "Not an oar off the stroke. It is a fascinating sight."

"I cannot bear the thought that it is their ceaseless labor that will bring us to Sardinia, while we do nothing up here," she said.

"Ceaseless labor?" said Mundina. "My dear child, you don't suppose we're going to row all the way to Sardinia, do you? If we're lucky, we'll pick up a wind by afternoon, and the sailors will do nothing but tend the sails or polish wood, mend oars, and tell each other foul tales until we come close to port again. Unless we meet pirates and must row to get out of their way. But we will go in if you wish."

"Gentle ladies," said a voice from behind them. "Are you enjoying the spectacle of others laboring? I admit I find it very stimulating."

They turned and found themselves face-to-face with Master Gueralt and his mocking smile. He bowed.

"We were about to go in," said Mundina. "The sun is very bright."

"I will speak to the captain," said Gueralt, with great courtesy. "He will have the awning spread."

"Please, do not bestir yourself on our behalf," said Mundina. "The crew is too occupied at the moment."

Gueralt bowed. "Allow me to introduce myself, Mistress," he said to Clara. "My name is Gueralt de Robau."

Clara dropped a half curtsey and stared down at the deck.

"I am on my way to Sardinia to fight for the King. If the King will have me, of course," he added, with a return of the mocking smile. He waited for a reaction from Clara and got none. "They tell me he is glad of anyone he can get these days. But surely you ladies do not plan to join in battle?"

"Our travel has nothing to do with His Majesty's war," said Mundina tartly.

"May I ask where you are from? I am sure that I have met your lovely mistress before," said Gueralt. "Perhaps you live not far from our estate, madam."

"Very far," snapped Mundina. "I believe it is time you

went in, madam. You do not wish to tire yourself unduly."
She placed a capable arm around Clara's shoulders and
steered her back in the direction of the cabin. "I am sure we
will have a chance to speak to you again, señor," she said,
pushing Clara in front of her like a doll until they were
through the door.

"What must he think of me?" said Clara. "Standing like a
statue under all this cloth." She pulled off her veil and irre-
pressible laughter burst up from her belly. She stifled the
noise as best she could in a cushion from the bunk.

"Imbecile, sickly, or unable to understand the speech of
the country," said Mundina, beginning to laugh as well.

"Or all three," said Clara, as soon as she could speak.
"Good."

In late morning of the second day, they picked up a favorable
wind. The rowers shipped their oars and turned back into
sailors. But instead of the atmosphere becoming calmer and
more relaxed, it seemed to Yusuf that it was, if anything,
more frantic. And instead of having to avoid rowers to explore the ship, he would now have to avoid sails, ropes, and
heavy wood beams. He went back to the study of Arabic.

As soon as the sails went up, Mundina was set to keep a
check on the whereabouts of Gueralt. And if he were not
around, the two slipped out, and Clara measured the deck,
ten paces in her fast stride into the wind from port to starboard, and ten paces with the wind at her back from starboard
to port, while Mundina sat under the awning and watched
her walk to Sardinia.

Toward evening of the third day, as Clara paced restlessly
back and forth, the steady wind that had filled their sails so
gracefully turned fickle. A sudden gust lifted her skirts and
her veil and then the air was still. Their bright pennants
drooped. Down in front of her, the helmsman was consulting
with the first officer and the captain. He pointed to starboard;
Clara's gaze followed his hand, which was directed at a mass
of black cloud moving quickly toward them. Suddenly the
pennants snapped wildly and the sails flapped. The captain

roared; his cry was taken up by other voices, and the more than two hundred individuals who had been occupied at individual tasks rapidly stowed what they had been doing and turned into teams of concentrated activity. The first officer said, "Inside, madam, if you please." Clara and Mundina dove into their cabin.

The ship pitched and rolled; rain beat in at their porthole; a sailor burst in and fastened it down. Around them, the invisible storm raged noisily. Wind howled, rigging creaked, thunder crashed so loud it seemed they must have been hit, and all the while the water fought to break in. It pounded on the castle; it smashed against the sides; it thumped down on the deck.

"Are we going to drown?" asked Clara warily.

"I don't know," said Mundina. "I expect not, though. These summer storms are not as bad as the ones later in the year. Not many drown in them. Although I've heard tales of careless sailors going over the side."

"I don't mind very much if we do," said Clara. "If we weren't on this ship, I suppose that by now I would have been sold. I'd rather drown as a free woman than live as a slave."

"Well," said Mundina. "I'm not sure which is worse. At least slaves have a chance of being freed. It does happen sometimes. If you're dead, you're dead."

And so they passed the hours of fearful darkness arguing the merits of the question.

Toward midnight, the storm began to abate. Exhausted with fear and lack of sleep, Clara and Mundina crawled into berth and hammock in the dark and slept in spite of it in the rolling, pitching vessel. Before morning, the sky cleared, the wind steadied, and the cleanup began. The navigation officer, still at his post, wet and weary, calculated how far off course they had been blown and set a new course for Sardinia. The sun rose on brisk winds, a neatly ordered ship, and a busy crew. By midday, routine had been reestablished and a cask broached.

"I can't believe it," said Clara, when she and Mundina

emerged cautiously from their cabin. "I thought the ship had been half smashed to pieces.

"It was," said a voice beneath her. She looked down and saw Yusuf's head coming up the companionway from the lower deck. "I was in the part that was smashed to pieces."

"You don't look wet," said Clara.

"I'm not wet," he said. "Just bruised. I fell out of my hammock. How are you?"

"I'm fine," she said. "Why haven't we seen you? Aren't you allowed up on deck?"

"Certainly. I thought they'd locked you up somewhere. I come up here for fresh air and exercise, although the sailors tell me if I want exercise I should climb up the rigging and help. I would, too, but they won't let me."

"We don't come out," she said, dropping her voice to a whisper, "when Gueralt is out here. I'm afraid he'll recognize me."

"He is more curious than an old woman," said Yusuf.

"He must be bored. Ships are very boring if you haven't anything to do," said Clara. "I don't even have needlework."

"Someone might have a book you could look at," said Yusuf.

"Perhaps," she said. "If it weren't too difficult. It's been a long time since I've seen a book. What do you do when you're not falling out of hammocks?"

"There's a Dominican father down there who knows my language. He's helping me to learn to write it and teaching me more words that I need. He gave me a book to write in, with a great many blank pages in it. I am to use them to keep a journal of this voyage. I was going to start this morning, if no one wanted that little table, describing how we left port, and the ship, and then the storm. He said if I write every day, I will be as proficient as he is. But he translates learned texts from Arabic into Latin. He is very proficient."

"Then you must sit down and begin to write," said Clara. "We have no wish to sit. We have done little else but sit since we came on board this galley," she said restlessly. "But it's sit inside or have to listen to Gueralt. It's odd he isn't out now."

The most productive effect of the storm, however, was that

it had induced a case of sickness in Gueralt de Robau that left him moaning in his cabin for another day and a half.

The optimists on board had averred that the ship was a miracle of speed and could not help but reach Alghero in three to four days; the realists had said five, if the winds were mostly favorable and there were no storms. So when the ship approached the harbor of the besieged city on the sixth day as the sun was low on the western horizon, the captain looked pleased, the proctor appeared satisfied, and the sailors were jubilant.

"I discussed the matter with the captain," said Don Eximeno, who had joined the two women on the deck. "After the storm we had a choice between a roundabout, cautious course and a somewhat riskier but much quicker one. I chose the riskier one, and I'm pleased that it was successful."

"What was the risk?" asked Clara.

"Of contrary winds, nothing else. But our luck held. These supplies are important enough that I was willing to put the men to the oars if I was wrong."

"It is your decision? Not the captain's?"

"Policy is my decision; how to carry it out is his," said Don Eximeno. "But the fault would have rested entirely with me if we had arrived late with an exhausted crew."

"Did the men know they might have to row?" said Clara.

"They knew, all right," said Don Eximeno. "They are all experienced sailors and know these waters better than I do. That was my cask that was broached when we got through the storm so well, and the bonus they all get today is from my purse as well. It would have cost me twice as much if I had lost my wager with Dame Nature."

Yusuf and Father Crispià appeared on deck, each carrying a bundle. When the anchor was lowered, Master Gueralt came out of the cabin he shared with the navigator and two other officers, looking pale and sickly. Working in reverse order to the loading process, the first lighter to arrive at the ship brought some of the Queen's household to assist Don Eximeno and carried off the rest of the passengers.

The first to leave the group was the Dominican priest. Two members of his order came swiftly over to meet him as soon as he stepped out of the boat. He said good-bye to Yusuf and followed his brothers to their waiting mules. The three rode off, their pale habits showing brightly against the rock, leaving a servant to bring Father Crispià's trunk when it was unloaded.

Gueralt was gone almost as quickly. Asbert de Robau detached himself from the crowd at the shore, embraced his son hurriedly, and brought him to where two grooms stood with their horses. All the while he talked of business, lamented the difficulties of his own voyage over, and peppered his son with questions, not waiting to listen to the answers.

"There's the end of him, I hope," said Clara.

"Where are you to go?" asked Yusuf. "Do you know?"

"Don Eximeno is to take me to where Her Majesty's waiting women are. Mundina and I must wait here for him to be finished. And you?"

But before Yusuf could answer, a man in the uniform of His Majesty's Guard walked up to them. "Yusuf ibn Hasan?" he asked. "I am instructed to take you to His Majesty's encampment. I trust you had a good voyage."

"Yes," said Yusuf. "Everyone arrived in good health," he added, having decided that as far as sea voyages went, that was the most that one could ask.

ELEVEN

On Tuesday morning, Oliver had left the ship at the last possible moment in considerable disruption of spirits. He had tossed a couple of farthings at the waiting boatman, who had looked at them, glared, and rowed him sullenly back toward the city.

By the time the lighter had pulled up on the sand, the wall behind the shore was already covered with wet linen weighted down with rocks. Sheets and shifts snapped and waved cheerfully in the wind. As he walked past, a washerwoman lifted a huge pile of dripping cloth from her basket with stout arms scarlet from scrubbing. A corner slipped from her grasp and began to fall. Before it could hit the ground, he caught it with the flat of his sword and presented it to her. "Careful, mother," he said. "Or all your sheets will escape in the next puff of wind."

"Be careful yourself, you young ruffian," she said. "Cut my sheets and you'll see what happens to you. Go home with you and look after your own sheets . . . and see who's in them when you aren't," she added with a malicious cackle. "I can look after mine, thank you, sir."

"I believe you can at that, mother," he said, grinning. "That is wise advice. Many thanks." He tossed a pair of pennies into her basket and walked back toward town. The astonished washerwoman stared after him for a moment, snatched up the money from her basket, and tucked it away in her bodice.

The question is, he thought as he walked toward the palace, what is my laundry at the moment? The answer was swift and unwelcome. In spite of the fruitless labor it would entail, he had undertaken to discover why Pasqual was now dead. Did those who killed him know who he was and why he was based where he was? And if they knew that, he thought, they knew more than anyone had seen fit to tell Oliver yet.

There was no point in speculating about this while walking around the streets of Barcelona. Pasqual Robert had died in Girona, on his return from Castile. The answer was not here.

Nor did it make sense to ride for Girona at midmorning. Not on a day when the stones that paved the sunny squares were so hot he could feel them through his boots. He would leave just before vespers, ride until dark, sleep until the waning moon was high enough to light the road, and carry on, reaching Girona by tierce. He had nothing to do for the rest of the morning.

By the time he argued himself to this conclusion, he was close to the palace stables. He took out his mount, turned him straight toward the convent of Sant Pere, and expended almost an hour of skill and diplomacy discovering the name of the convent that Clara must have come from. Since it was, as he pointed out to the abbess, abundantly clear that Sor Alicia recognized her. A quarter of an hour later he was at its gate, rehearsing what he should say when they told him that his beloved niece had run away from her kind and upright mistress, no doubt in order to take to the streets.

He would be astonished, he decided, and determined in spite of her weaknesses to help her anyway. That seemed a reasonable reaction for an affectionate uncle to have, he thought, and rang the bell.

The name Clara did not seem to mean much to the abbess. "This convent was sorely hurt by the Black Death," she said calmly. "That was a troubled time, late summer of the year of the plague. But we have always kept detailed records. It is necessary when you deal with children."

"I am very happy to hear that, madam," said Oliver.

"And we will do what we can for you, Señor Oliver, to help you find your niece."

"You might remember her," said Oliver. "Clara," he repeated. "She has dark hair—"

"I won't," said the abbess. "I am new here. My noble and saintly predecessor died six months ago. She had worked like three or four women to guard her charges, raise money for their maintenance, and bring them up, in addition to looking after the sisters in her care. They said that her soul simply outwore her body," she added. "She is now with God."

"I am most sorry to hear of her death," said Oliver.

"But as rushed as she was, her records were meticulously kept," said the abbess again. She rang a bell and dispatched the nun who responded for the relevant material.

When the box arrived, she turned to a page with some confidence and began to run her finger down a column. She frowned and turned back a page, moving slowly along the column. "No," she said. "No girl named Clara over the age of two years came into the convent during the summer of 1348 . . . and I've looked from April until November. One six-year-old was brought in in September by her mother, but she was taken home again two years later when her mother's situation improved. Her name was Emilia. We had several groups of children come in during that period, a sister and two brothers, two sisters—"

"No, that couldn't be it," he said. "I find this very puzzling. I found a Sor Alicia, who said that there was a Clara here, whose description closely followed that of my niece."

"Sor Alicia. I see," said the abbess, and rang once more. "Sister," she said, "we are searching for a girl named Clara, placed here during the plague, in September, her uncle thinks."

"I remember Clara," she said. "She was placed just after I arrived. I don't know how long she'd been here, Mother, but I thought it hadn't been that long."

"I have been away from the kingdom, fighting," said Oliver quickly. "For eight years. On my return, I was given a letter from my poor dead sister. It was dated September, and it talked of the plague, saying that she had taken, or perhaps sent, little Clara to the Benedictines, and begging me to find her and make a home for her on my return."

"Ah, I understand," said the abbess. "So it wouldn't be before the first year of the plague. We will try the years after, when it still appeared, although not so fiercely."

She and her assistant took out four sheets, divided them up, and began to go through them carefully.

"Here she is," said the abbess finally. "It's no wonder we didn't know that she had an uncle, señor. She gave us very little information. Whether she didn't know much or didn't want to say anything, I can't tell you. She arrived with a purse of coins in the amount of five sous and a change of linen, all tucked into her gown. She gave her name as Clara. The abbess noted that she was surprised that they weren't expecting her, because her mother had told her to come to the nuns. We would know what to do with her." The abbess looked up, her face softening. "Poor child. She must have been in great distress and her mother had counted on us to look after her. But simple people often feel that we have the answers to all of life's impossible problems. Would that we did."

Oliver did not bother pointing out that she did not seem to come from simple people. "Is that all that you have in the records?"

"Oh no. We placed her with a good family as a kitchen maid. It seems she was already twelve years old when the placement was made, and she was completely untrained. Otherwise she might have had a better job." The abbess shook her head. "But I will give you their name. I am sure that you will be able to buy off her contract for a moderate sum. If they are difficult, please let me know. I might be able to help." And she rang her bell again with the air of a very busy woman who has done her useful best. She wrote something down on a very small piece of paper and handed it to him. "The sister portress will see you out."

"Thank you for your assistance, Madam," he said, rising with a bow. The nun who had let him in ushered him to the gate.

"Did you find who you were looking for?" asked the portress, who was evidently not averse to conversation.

"My little niece? Clara? I discovered where she is now," he said. "And I am most grateful for that."

"Clara? Are you Clara's uncle? You don't look like her," she said. "A well set up man like you."

"My sister was like Clara. Thin and pale," he said. "Like our mother. I take after our father more."

"That happens in families," she said. "Funny. The minute I laid eyes on the poor thing, I knew she came from a good family. Her clothes were fine, apart from a rip that needed mending, her speech excellent, and she was clean and well mannered. Not a little mouse from the streets at all."

"You knew her, then."

"Oh yes. We were all very fond of her. There were only four of us then, you know. All the rest had died, and she was such a help with the little ones. She said she had a baby brother and then she looked as if she'd told me some terrible secret."

"Her brother . . . ah yes. The poor thing died shortly before my sister. She told me that Clara was very attached to him."

"That was a terrible time. You'd expect her to be broken-hearted—they all were, poor babies, except for the ones too young to know—but Clara was frightened as well when she came, poor thing. So frightened. She blended in very quickly with the others, as if she were afraid of being noticed. She tried to speak like them, too, but it wasn't natural to her."

"How old was she then?"

"Eleven, almost twelve. But she looked younger. Too old, really. If she'd had a dowry of any sort, our lady abbess would have taken her in as a novice. She tried very hard to get some rich gentleman to donate the money for her dowry. She kept her here as long as she could, hoping to be successful. But she wasn't, and Clara had to be placed out."

"She must have been fond of her."

"She loved her dearly. We all did. I'm so glad her family's found her. She's too good for a place in a kitchen. I'm sorry our lady abbess couldn't have known," she added somberly. "It would have made her happy." Her eyes filmed over with tears. "Go with God, señor. And give Clara our love. Perhaps she will come to see me someday."

"She will, sister. I'll see to it."

Puzzled, he mounted his horse and rode off. The only thing that seemed clear to him was that no one from her mistress's household had gone to the convent to demand an explanation of her disappearance. And that was more than puzzling.

The morning was over when he finally reached the man to whom he reported, Bernat d'Olzinelles, treasurer of the kingdom. In that capacity, Olzinelles was surrounded by an army of busy clerks who verified, tallied, entered, and preserved for inspection a mountain of accounts, bills, payments, and expenses, all of which the treasurer seemed able to carry in his head at once.

"Given what I know," he said in a puzzled tone, "Pasqual's death—in Girona—appears to be incomprehensible."

"Much seems incomprehensible, my lord," said Oliver. "Everywhere I turn I am offered fresh confusion."

"Perhaps it will seem clearer now that your other responsibilities are over," said the treasurer sourly.

"It was not such a burden, my lord," said Oliver. "I trust it did not distract me from my primary purpose. Perhaps you have received other information that could offer an explanation?"

"Nothing," said Olzinelles. "Other than the suggestion that it was a random attack such as can happen to any man."

"I don't believe it," said Oliver.

"Nor do I. And therefore we shall proceed as if Pasqual Robert were killed because he was Pasqual Robert."

"Should I submit a report on the circumstances of his death for the Prince?" asked Oliver, referring to His Majesty's uncle, who was taking care of affairs of state for the entire kingdom in the absence of Their Majesties.

"Prince Pere?" said Olzinelles, raising a finely arched eyebrow. "The prince is too occupied with other matters to find the Castilian frontier and its problems interesting at the moment," he said. "And it is not necessary. You have orders," he added impatiently. "As do I. Mine are to ensure that you complete your mission and to sign off on your expenses. Submit them before you leave. His Majesty is following your project with great attention from Sardinia. As you know, he interests himself at all times in every corner and every aspect of his kingdom. He expects his plans regarding each to carry on, even though he is out of the country." Olzinelles sighed. His Majesty also expected his officials to work as hard as he did.

"His Majesty," said Oliver, "is famed for his attention to detail. Following his example, I start for Girona in a few hours, before vespers. I will arrive tomorrow morning," said Oliver. "If I do not discover more there, I will go farther."

"In that case, you will need to draw extra. Make an estimate and submit it to me at once. I will ensure that you get it before you leave. Pasqual's fondness for written reports may have been his undoing. Remember that. If you have something you must inform me of before you are finished with all this, send it through the bishop." At that, the treasurer turned to his secretary. "You said that someone was waiting."

"One moment, my lord," murmured his secretary, and Oliver, feeling himself dismissed, took his leave.

The bells of Girona were ringing for tierce when Oliver rode up to the Bishop's palace. Brushing aside offers of refreshment, he ran up the stairs to Berenguer's study and sat down.

"We buried him on Wednesday," said Berenguer, looking up from the documents he was signing. "With all honor."

"Thank you, Your Excellency," said Oliver. "Has anyone discovered anything of use? Because I have not."

"Some things," said the Bishop. "I have sent for my physician and his daughter, who have a small but curious incident to relate, and Bernat is bringing what was found in his pack. It might be of interest. Since it will take a moment or two for them to arrive, I suggest that you eat and drink while you have a chance." He nodded at the servant by the door to the study who opened it to let in two lads from the kitchen with platters heaped with bread, cold meats, cheese, and fruit, as well as jugs of cool mint drink, wine, and water.

"I thank you," said Oliver, as soon as he had drunk a cup of water and then placed some meat on a chunk of bread. "I broke my fast by moonlight with cold water from a brook and an unripe pear stolen from a tree. I am hungry."

"Where did you stop?" asked Berenguer.

"At the same place we found the orphan girl on our way

down," he said. "I had some weaponry and armor to rescue from a cache." He continued to eat in silence, while Berenguer helped himself to fruit and a little wine and water.

The silence was broken when Bernat sa Frigola, His Excellency's secretary, came in carrying papers, followed by his scribe, who was carrying a box. "I have the items you requested, Your Excellency," said the secretary. "I did not, however, stop to take the sum of money from the treasury—"

"I doubt the specific coins are important," said Berenguer. "If they are, Lord Oliver can see them in the treasury."

"Expense money," said Oliver. "That's all—unless it was a great amount?"

"Substantial but not unusual, my lord. It was in various coins in a mix of currencies amounting to roughly two hundred sous," said Bernat. "Otherwise, we have items of clothing, a painting on wood, and a letter. There were two letters, but one was evidently written in code. His Excellency ordered that it be sent to Barcelona, and I did so. Here is the other." Without further comment, he handed it to Oliver.

"God in heaven," murmured Oliver as he read. "My dearest? The farm? Your son?" He looked up. "Did you know of a wife, Don Berenguer?"

"No," said Berenguer. "I did not suspect he was married."

"I thought I knew everything there was to know about the man," said Oliver. "He was more discreet than I realized. Or I am more inept," he added self-consciously.

"I, too, thought I knew him well," said Berenguer.

"I could wish there was a name. Or a place. She signs it with her initial only."

"There is not a single name mentioned in the entire letter," said Bernat. "Would someone attack his wife to gain an advantage over him?"

"It is possible," said Oliver. "But if I didn't know he was married, very few others would."

"We think that the picture might be of her," said Berenguer. "Bernat. Do you have it there?"

"Yes, Your Excellency," he said and took out the leather case in which it was kept.

"Well, give it to him. He might know her. She could be a

valuable source of information. She should, in any case, be told of her husband's death."

Oliver took the case and carefully removed the oval of wood. He turned it over and carried it to the window.

"Have you ever seen her?" asked the Bishop. "If the painter knows his craft, she is a remarkable beauty." He looked up as the door opened to admit the physician and his daughter. "Welcome, Master Isaac, Mistress Raquel. We speak of the mysterious lady in the painting."

"Good day, Master Isaac, Mistress," said Oliver quickly. "I have not seen this lady, although, Your Excellency, I know someone who is kin to her. A sister, or perhaps the dead child she refers to, who yesterday morning was no more dead than I am."

"Could she be his mother?" asked Bernat.

"Whose mother, Father Bernat?" asked Raquel.

"Pasqual Robert's. The man who was killed Tuesday morning, Mistress Raquel," said Bernat. He picked up the painting from the desk and showed it to her.

"She is very young to be his mother," said Raquel.

"But we do not know, Mistress Raquel, when the likeness was done," said Berenguer in a kindly but condescending voice. "It could have been painted when he was a child. Or before he was born."

"But we do, Your Excellency," said Raquel in surprise. "The trimming on the bodice of her gown and the cut of her sleeves are very new. I saw gowns like that on great ladies while we were in Barcelona in the spring. The likeness was taken this year, I would think, or last year, at the earliest, unless she lives somewhere where the fashion is a year or two ahead of ours."

"I am properly humbled for my arrogance, Mistress Raquel," said Berenguer, laughing. "You are clearly correct."

"The opinion of an expert," said Oliver. "And I agree, although I would not have thought of it. The hair, too, seems not at all old-fashioned."

"It certainly isn't," asserted Raquel firmly.

"It is his wife, then," said Oliver. He picked up the painting, slipped it back into its leather case, and then tucked it into his tunic.

"Do we know where she lives?" asked Isaac.

"No one knows anything about her," said the Bishop. "We have her likeness, but no one has ever seen her. She may live in Aragon or even Castile as far as we know."

"I would guess that she used to live in Barcelona," said Oliver. "I shall do my best to find her."

"Master Isaac," said Berenguer. "I have not yet thanked you for obeying my summons as if you had no other thing to do but attend to my whims."

"I am always at Your Excellency's service," said Isaac.

"Excellent. Then could you tell Lord Oliver, as precisely as you can, about the man you treated at Mother Benedicta's?"

Rapidly but clearly, Isaac described the state and location of the wound, the fever, and the man's raving. "It was through that that we could hear that he was Castilian."

"Can you tell me when he had been wounded?" asked Oliver.

"For a wound like that to start putrefying would take a few days—four or five. From then it might progress rapidly enough," he added. "We visited him on Wednesday night. He might have been wounded on the previous Thursday—or a day or two before or after."

"Thursday? I must speak to this man."

"Regrettably, my lord, it is no longer possible," said Isaac. "We moved him to a healthier place—cooler, with better air—and did all we could for him, but he was already doomed before our first visit. I know that the captain visited him several times in an attempt to draw more information from him before he was beyond giving it, but I do not know what, if anything, he learned."

"Can anyone describe the man?"

Raquel did her best, pointing out that he had likely looked better when he wasn't on the point of death.

"True, mistress," said Oliver, "but that does not change his height or his hair or eye color or the shape of his nose. Usually," he added. "But I recognize him anyway. He was one of the two fellows who had been trailing after us. Pasqual was annoyed by them. The night he disappeared—which was Thursday—he remarked before I fell asleep that he intended to do something about them. That festering wound you treated could well have been caused by Pasqual's sword. Or his dagger."

"His name was Martin," said the Bishop. "And he was from Tudela, as the physician would have told you, had you given him a chance."

"My apologies, Master Isaac."

"Think nothing of it. The other man you saw was undoubtedly one Master Geraldo," said Isaac. "When Martin from Tudela called out in his raving, he begged repeatedly for his master to come and rescue him. We asked him who his master was and he said Geraldo. He did not seem to feel that he owed him discretion."

"Geraldo?" said Oliver. "I'll keep it in mind."

"How long are you staying in Girona, my lord?" asked Raquel.

"Until the day cools enough to ride in comfort," he said. "I must find the assassin first. Then I shall return and search for my friend's wife."

"That may be an irksome task," said Isaac, "but it should not be impossible."

"How would you do it, Master Isaac?" asked Oliver, somewhat amused.

"If I could see? I would search the records for transfers of property connected with dowries. You tell me that she is a lady dressed in rich and fashionable garments. Her letter speaks of land and purchasing vineyards and meadows. These things are not baskets of apples or measures of flour to be traded for a few coins at the market."

"But dowries? Why not the recent transactions?"

"The dowry will give her family name and her husband's name both. That could be useful. As well as the town where the land is located."

"Most useful," said Oliver.

"And I would start here before trying elsewhere."

"Why here?"

"Have you not asked yourself where Señor Pasqual went on Thursday night and stayed until Monday morning?"

"I have, but he had disappeared on various missions before. He would often slip away and explain himself on his return," said Oliver.

"I have always wondered why a man of Señor Pasqual's accomplishments would be content with a lowly position at the Exchange," said Isaac. "But if it gave him a chance to live in hiding and to visit his wife from time to time, it would make great sense."

"You could be right. But still she must wait, I'm afraid," said Oliver. "When I visit her, I would like to bring her the head of the villain who killed her husband," he added coolly.

"That would not surprise me, my lord," said Isaac.

"I must take my leave of you, gentlemen, Mistress Raquel," he said, rising and bowing. "I am off to the west to find an assassin."

"We wish you a safe journey," said Isaac.

"And good hunting," said Raquel, to everyone's surprise.

Leah and Naomi had hastily cleared away the plates and cloths from their simple dinner. It was Friday, and they had much to finish off in the kitchen before the sun dipped below the horizon. Isaac was alone in the courtyard, seated by the fountain, listening to the gentle dropping of the water and lost in thought.

When the bell rang, he suppressed a flash of annoyance and called to Ibrahim to answer it.

"It's no use, Papa," said Raquel, coming down the stairs. "He'll be fast asleep by now. I'll answer for you."

"Thank you, my dear," said her father. There was no point in disputing a truth as self-evident as that one.

"Mistress Benedicta would like to speak to you, Papa," said Raquel.

"Is she ill?"

"No, Papa."

"Bring her in."

Mother Benedicta crossed the courtyard with a firm, quick tread and an impatient rustling of skirts. "I won't beg your pardon for interrupting you, Master Isaac, because I believe that you might be glad to have what I bring," she said. "And if not you, then your lord, the Bishop, will be, and that's almost the same thing, is it not?" She spoke fiercely, as if the physician had been contradicting her every word.

"Please, mistress," said the physician, "be seated. Would you like something to refresh yourself? It is a hot day, and I suspect you have walked quickly through the afternoon sun to visit me here. Raquel?" he called.

"Yes, Papa," she said. "I have brought something cool to drink for you both." Raquel poured a drink of tart orange and mint into two cups from the large pitcher in her hand. She left the pitcher on the table and retreated into her father's study from where she could listen to their conversation.

"When the captain of the Bishop's Guard took away my guest, without so much as a farewell and how much did he owe me," said Benedicta, "I gathered together all his things. I thought he'd send someone back for them, see, but no one ever came, and I still have them. And I'll let you know that some of that is money, and I've counted it and haven't touched a penny, even though by my reckoning he cost me ten pence before he died, and more than that if you counted the number of times I had to go up those stairs to make sure the poor gentleman wasn't dead."

"Did you bring it all with you today?" asked Isaac.

"I did that."

"Excellent," said Isaac. "Raquel? Could you come out and help me with this? And bring paper, pen, and ink. We will give you a receipt for what you have brought, so that no one can accuse you of taking anything of his."

"And what will you do with it?" said Benedicta.

"I will take it to His Excellency and let him decide what should be done."

Raquel sat down at the table with a small piece of paper in front of her and turned to the innkeeper. "If you would like to set out what you have brought, I will make a list of it for you."

Mistress Benedicta picked up a bundle from the ground and set it down on the table. "There," she said. "I wrapped it in his cloak. That's one thing," she said, looking at Raquel. "Write it down."

Raquel wrote, "1 cloak."

Benedicta looked narrowly at it, as if she suspected her of attempting some sort of trick, then undid the bundle, and laid out the contents one by one, calling each one out.

It was not a great or wealthy store. A second shirt, another pair of hose, a wineskin, and a hood. "That hood is almost new," she said. "And inside it, I found his purse . . . not his regular one. That had fivepence in it, and the Captain took that, and never gave me a paper for it, either. This is special. It has a gold piece. See, mistress?"

"Quite right, Mistress Benedicta. It is a gold piece. And three silver pieces, as well as—"

"Fifteen pence and two farthings," said Benedicta. "And if you look inside, you'll see his map."

"What is that, Raquel?" asked Isaac.

"It is a map, Papa. I'm not sure what it's of, but it's clearly a map." And she carefully set out the quantities and kinds of coins, showed the list to Mistress Benedicta, who had no trouble reading numbers, and added to it in her neat script, "1 map, place unknown." She looked at it, puzzled for a moment, and signed it Raquel, daughter of Isaac the physician of Girona. Below, she wrote "Benedicta, innkeeper of Sant Feliu," and pushed the list over to her. "Make your mark by your name, mistress," she said, "and keep that list safe."

Isaac took his purse from his tunic, felt in it carefully, took out a coin and handed it to the innkeeper. "You have assisted His Excellency greatly by taking such good care of Martin's belongings. Consider this to have come from him."

Benedicta looked at the coin, raised an eyebrow, scattered thanks around, and left before anyone could change a mind and ask for it back.

TWELVE

Sardinia, Alghero, August 1354

Soldiers swarmed everywhere over the plain outside the city. Soldiers standing or sprawled on the ground; soldiers in groups, talking, laughing, quarreling; soldiers clustered around fires, watching messes cooking in pots, or alone, lost in melancholy thought. The only ones engaged in activity were throwing dice. Several highly charged games were going on, and it was evident as Yusuf and his escort rode by that the tempers of the participants were frayed.

"The troops are falling apart," said the officer gloomily. "And their officers. You might as well know that."

"What happened?" asked Yusuf.

"Nothing," he said. "The problem is what didn't happen. We stormed the city and almost took it. Almost. We marched on Alghero in strength, fit and ready. We had support on the seaward side from the galleys. Then Her Majesty's galley came in, flying her standard, with Her Majesty on board, and the city almost gave up in despair at the sight of it."

"Why?" asked Yusuf.

"You weren't there to see it," he said, shaking his head. "The galley of a warrior queen rowing bravely into port to chastise the citizens for their wicked behavior. It was a splendid and terrifying sight," said the officer. "Our Queen is a clever and fearless lady."

"But you didn't break through their defenses?"

"It was the accursed siege engines. We couldn't knock down a straw house with them, they were so badly made," he said. "We shook the inhabitants a trifle, but we didn't breach the walls. And nothing else matters. Now we must starve them out. It's a terrible, dispiriting business. And very slow. Then the fever struck. The officers are too sick to keep the healthy men in condition. When there's nothing to do, it's hard to stay alert."

"Have many died?" asked Yusuf. "Do you know? The way people talk it sounds like a return of the plague," he added cautiously.

"No, nothing like that," said the officer vaguely. "Only the fever. Most who get it recover after a while. The number of the afflicted," he began and then stopped suddenly. "His Majesty is over by his tent," he said. "He does not like this constant talk of disease and death. We will dismount and approach."

"Here comes our page at last, armed and reporting for duty," said Don Pedro of Aragon. "Had you been with us, Yusuf, you and a dozen well-made siege engines, we would have prevailed a month or so ago."

"Your Majesty," said Yusuf, bowing low. "I am desolate that I was not."

"Do not sound so downcast," said the King. "You are in time to attend us at our council. Remember," he added, "nothing said in that tent is to be spoken of except to us in person."

"Your Majesty," murmured Yusuf, "may my tongue be torn from my head if I speak of these things to any man or woman else." He bowed again and followed him into a large, well-appointed tent containing a table around which a dozen or more men could sit with ease.

Don Pedro took his place at the table with a genial look at the assembled group. "Let us hear your reports," he said without further formalities.

"The noble Lord Felip de Castre has died of the fever,

Your Majesty," said the man on his right. "And the Lords Otich de Muncada and Pere Galceran de Pinos lie gravely ill."

"We cannot spare such men," said the King.

"Many more are ill, Your Majesty," said the first speaker. "I have drawn a list, if you wish to see it."

"How many?"

"Of nobles, Your Majesty, at present, five. Of knights and gentlemen, forty-two, some of whom appear to be recovering. Of soldiers, so many that we are still counting. We will have the figures for Your Majesty in the morning."

"Not until then?"

"By compline, Your Majesty."

"Good. And supplies for treating the sick?"

The man seated beside the first speaker took out a roll of paper and consulted it. "In wine, sugar, and foodstuffs for the very ill, Your Majesty, we are in a better position now. If the contagion does not last into the autumn, we shall do well enough," he added grudgingly. "As for medicines, the first ship brought enough to treat those now afflicted. But if the disease continues to spread, we are in difficulties. The second ship may have more. My assistants are going over the lists brought by Her Majesty's household at this moment. I need more trained men to care for the sick," he added in the tone of one who has said that same thing too frequently already.

"We fear that after doing without our page for all these weeks, that we will be forced to give him to you immediately," said the King. "This lad has been learning the physician's arts as well as the arts of war in the past year or two. Yusuf, we must turn you over to where you can be the most use. Do you have any objection?"

"Whatever pleases Your Majesty," said Yusuf. "And I bring with me from my master and from the noble Berenguer, Bishop of Girona, several boxes full of medicines that might be useful."

"Good. We must now consider," said Don Pedro, "given the great length of time it takes for a man to recover from this fever, whether it would be better to send some of the sick back to the mainland. They can be well cared for until they are recovered enough to return. I speak of those whom we value most on the battlefield and in their persons. We would be pleased to be advised."

"The question is a difficult one," said the first man. "If we send a galley back with the sickest, we have more for the rest. If the contagion continues to spread, we may be forced to do so. But if no more soldiers fall ill, we have no need for the extra supplies that would release."

"They will receive better care at home than they can in the camp," said one of the other nobles.

"True, but the voyage will be difficult for them," said the first man.

"Then we must take careful note of the numbers in the next few days and consult again on this question," said the King. "The ship that brought our ward is fast and commodious. Let it be fitted to carry at least two dozen sick men. It will need to stay in harbor another week until we are able to make the decision."

"To Barcelona, Your Majesty?" said one of the men to his left.

"No. To Valencia. Those of the sick dearest to our heart should be returned to Valencia. We shall await your further reports," he said and rose. And noticing his ward again, he added, "And you will consider yourself to be under this gentleman's orders, Yusuf." He pointed to the man who had given the first report.

Yusuf, finding himself so summarily handed over, accompanied the gentleman who turned out to be chief physician of the camp.

"How much do you know?" asked the physician as they headed back to the tent they would share with four others of his staff.

"Well, señor," said Yusuf, "I have studied with my master, a physician, for a full year now, and assisted him."

"In what ways?"

Yusuf spent the rest of the time along the way trying to give him an answer.

"That is," said the physician, "he has taught you some useful things. I would also like to see what is in your box. When it arrives, you will take out and name each item, explain its uses, and tell me how it should be administered. Then I will know how far you have traveled along the road to knowledge. Prepare yourself for much work and little rest. You will find that we, the cooks, and His Majesty himself are the only people in the camp who do more than amuse themselves right now."

Those who were ill were very ill. The tent that Yusuf was escorted into was filled with the powerful odors of fever and dehydration. There were men burning with fever and shaking violently with chills; they raved and cried out in their heat-crazed delusions. Some clutched pain-racked foreheads or beat on them with weak fists in hopeless attempts to ease the throbbing.

"What would you do with these men right now?" asked the physician.

"I would give them drafts to cool their fevers and assuage their pain, try to induce them to drink, and sponge their heads and shoulders," he said promptly, having observed Raquel at these tasks and even taken them over himself with greater frequency in the last few months.

"Why?"

"Because they smell of fever and lack of water, señor," he said, "and seem to suffer from violent headache."

"Good," he said. "And if we had a hundred of you, we could do what should be done. You will look after the men in this tent with a servant to assist you. Send for more help if it is needed. Marc," he called, and someone immediately raised the flap of the tent, held it open for the physician to leave, and then came in.

The servant was a grizzled man with the sun- and wind-roughened skin of a sailor and a pronounced limp. He cast an experienced eye over Yusuf and grinned. "Good day, master," he said. "I am Marc."

"And I am Yusuf. Are you injured?" he asked, looking at the somewhat crooked leg.

"Not what you'd call injured," he said. "I took a bolt from a crossbow just above the knee. That was some time ago," he added. "In Valencia. Then they retired me from the bat-tlefield into the sick tent. I count myself lucky that I wasn't

sent home. This has always been my life," he added, favoring
Yusuf with a barely veiled look of contempt.

"If you have looked after the sick and wounded all this
time, then I, too, count myself lucky," said Yusuf.

"I am at your command," replied Marc, his voice flat and
expressionless.

Yusuf looked at the older man and realized that he was
waiting for orders. He looked at the men lying on neatly
arranged cots and pallets. As far as he could tell, they were
all desperately ill. "What do you suggest I do now?" he asked
in a panicked whisper.

"That is not for me to say, master," said Marc coolly.
"What were you thinking to do?"

"Who are the sickest? I would like to start with them," he
said uncertainly.

"Can't you tell?"

"Not as well as you," said Yusuf. "I do not know them,
and I lack your experience."

"Well, at least you know that," said Marc. "Those two,"
he added, pointing at two men who shivered and muttered
and tossed their heads. "In my opinion, for what it's worth.
Did you bring anything with you for them?" And the two,
man and boy, went to a table in a curtained-off alcove and
rummaged through the box of supplies that had been set aside
for this group. Then Marc looked into Yusuf's compact medical kit. "What is this?" he asked, holding up a small, tightly
corked bottle, sealed with wax.

"It is for the severest pain," said Yusuf. "One drop in wine
mixed with water will calm almost any agony. My master
gives three before the surgeon comes with his knife."

"And if you give four?" asked Marc.

"I'm not sure," said Yusuf. "Five can kill a man. Six will,
definitely."

"Do you have something else for pain?"

"Yes. I have bark and herbs to make an infusion for fever
and pain."

"Then lock that vial away, young master, until the fighting
starts. It might tempt some, including me, and it must not be
wasted. It will be needed then." On that rather ambiguous

note he picked up a container and sniffed it. "This should be for the fever," he said.

"It is," said Yusuf. "It is my master's mix of herbs and bark for fever."

"The amount there won't last us long," said Marc.

"I'm sure I can find the herbs in the meadows outside the camp. I know how to prepare and mix them."

Marc gave a noncommittal grunt that could have been approval or skepticism. "I have water on the boil outside. We can steep enough for a day or two for all the tent."

And with that, a temporary truce was established between the hardened veteran and the terrified novice. Together, they set about making the twenty or so men in the tent as comfortable as possible for the night.

By the beginning of his third day in Sardinia, and his second day in the sick tent, Yusuf was so accustomed to the routine that he felt that his entire life had been circumscribed by this tent. One of the two sickest men had died during the first night, but the other was showing signs of improvement. The physician had moved two men out of the tent on the first morning and two more had just been moved in.

"That is a great lord," whispered Marc, as the second man was carried in, followed almost at once by the chief physician. "Lord Pere Boyll. He should be with his servants in his own tent, but they, too, have fallen ill. He himself said when he fell ill that he preferred to be in a tent with the others, and we have the smallest number of the sick here."

"Who are the rest of the men we are looking after?" asked Yusuf, also in a whisper. "I had no time yesterday to ask."

"Rest assured, young master, they are not common men," murmured his assistant. "His Majesty's ward would not be watching over them," he added dryly. "The common men who are sick are stacked nose to tail in a couple of tents over there, the lucky ones are, and if they can think for the fever at all, they are happy enough to be inside, out of the wind and the rain. These are knights except for Lord Pere, who is a great fighter and close to His Majesty. I suspect that we will have more help and even more supplies now."

Lord Pere was gray with the sickness, with shaking limbs

and chattering teeth from the chills. His clenched fists and the tautness of his face spoke eloquently of his pain. Yusuf approached nervously, carrying a cup of infusion of willow and other herbs for fever.

The chief physician took the cup, sniffed it, and handed it back to Yusuf. "See if you can make him drink it," he said. "It won't be easy."

But between observation and practice, Yusuf had become fairly adept at this, having learned a sort of patient determination from Raquel. He crouched beside the sick lord and coaxed almost half the cup of liquid down his throat. Then he took a damp, cool cloth and mopped his forehead and cheeks with it. "I will stay with him, señor," he said, looking up, "until he is able to drink it all."

"You do well at nursing the sick, Yusuf. His Majesty will be impressed, I am sure."

The lord's shivering fit ceased for the moment, and he focused his eyes on Yusuf's face. "Where is my man?" he whispered hoarsely. "Who are you?"

"Your servant is ill, my lord," said Yusuf. "I am Yusuf."

"And who is Yusuf?" asked Lord Pere.

"His Majesty's page," said Yusuf, "but I have a little experience in tending the sick, and have been called into service to help."

"I have heard of you, Yusuf the page," said Lord Pere. "You are Don Pedro's ward, are you not?"

"I am, my lord," he said.

"Your father died at Valencia, in the uprising. An astute man, your father was. And valorous. You are very like him." And before Yusuf could reply, he closed his eyes and drifted off into sleep.

"Do you want me to wake him?" asked Marc.

"Shouldn't he be allowed to sleep for a little while?" asked Yusuf uncertainly, trying to remember what his master did most often.

"It is your decision, young master," said Marc. "I am only an attendant." He looked at the boy and relented. "But perhaps you could let him sleep until he begins to stir again. It won't be that long, I expect."

• • •

The early evening brought a summons from His Majesty.

"We have had good reports of you, Yusuf," he said, "and now you look after a man most dear to us. Do not hesitate to seek help if he appears to worsen."

"I shall, Your Majesty. Until then, I shall stay by his side and give him every attention."

"Are you not wanted with your other patients?" asked the King.

"I have been given a most experienced and skilled attendant," said Yusuf. "And a few of the knights I care for are now much improved, Your Majesty," said Yusuf. "But they say they are not yet ready to go back to their regiments."

"A childish subterfuge," said Don Pedro in a way that boded ill for someone.

"I do not cast doubts on their honor, Your Majesty," said Yusuf. "They are weak from the fever but not mortally ill."

"No doubt. If there were a battle to be fought, we are confident they would not continue to take their ease in the comforts of your tent, Yusuf," said the King dismissively. "Now, what is this difficulty that brings you to Sardinia?"

Yusuf was braced for the question. He spoke quickly in a voice devoid of expression, for the Bishop had warned him that His Majesty would require a report and that he expected brevity. "In the winter, Your Majesty, I assisted my master to treat a Dominican priest at the Bishop's palace. He discovered that I was from Granada and on his return to Barcelona asked his superior to register a complaint about my situation—living as I do in the *call,* but being a free man— and to insist that I be returned to Granada or converted."

"And that is all, Yusuf?"

"Yes, Your Majesty."

"And for that you come here looking as if you were bearing your own death warrant. Draft a letter of permission for our signature before tierce tomorrow," he said to his secretary.

The secretary bowed and murmured appropriate instructions to his assistant.

"And Yusuf, see that our friend Lord Pere Boyll is made as comfortable as possible. Not only is he a brave and loyal warrior, but he is the nephew of the man who guarded us and our rights during the last fighting here in Sardinia. We owe his family much. You may return for your letter tomorrow."

"Thank you, Your Majesty. And I will sit by Lord Pere's bed night and day." He bowed deeply and left the tent.

In His Majesty's tent, Don Pedro turned to his secretary. "Assign a lad to help in that tent, if one can be found."

As Yusuf approached his tent, he saw Gueralt de Robau leaning lazily against a tree. "Yusuf," he called softly. "A word with you."

"Yes, señor?" asked the boy.

"My friend here has a question he wishes to ask. Don Manuel, this is His Majesty's ward, Yusuf."

His friend was thin, pale, and lethargic-looking. A most unconvincing soldier, thought Yusuf, although appearances were often deceptive. "If it is not confidential," Don Manuel said in a low voice, "may I ask if it's true that my friend Pere Boyll is dying?"

"That question is in the hands of God, Don Manuel," said Yusuf. "I do not know."

Don Manuel sat down on a flattish piece of rock, looking stricken. "I was afraid of that. I had heard that he was very ill."

"You were close to him, señor?" asked Yusuf.

"Were you ever alone and friendless when you were a small child, Yusuf?" he asked, staring down at a patch of rough grass. "I was. I was sent from my nurse's arms, so to speak, to be a page at his father's castle."

"In Valencia?"

"Yes. Lord Pere is older than I am, but he was kind to an unhappy little boy. I doubt if he even remembers who I am, but I shall never forget him. Never."

When Yusuf returned to the tent, he was as good as his word. He went around to each patient with Marc, administering drafts for the fever and sponging hot foreheads, arms, and hands with cool water into which he had placed crushed herbs that he picked during the day.

"What are those for?" asked Marc. "Their complexions?"

"My mother sometimes crushed these herbs and added them to the water we bathed in. They have a pleasant odor, and I think they are soothing to the skin."

"They also keep away biting flies and other such insects," said Marc. "I've seen them used before for that."

"Then the sick will sleep better, being unbitten," said Yusuf.

When they had finished, Yusuf settled by the couch that had been set up for Lord Pere Boyll and took a small, bound book from his tunic.

Marc brought him a candle. "If you are going to study, you will need some light," he said. "I can't see the use of book learning for a soldier, myself, but I suppose a physician needs such things."

But the day had started early, and Yusuf had been working hard. He puzzled his way through five lines of the written-through part of the book Father Crispià had given him, and then the words of the text started to form the words of a dream. His head nodded, the book fell into his lap, and he slumped forward onto the edge of his patient's bed.

When he awoke, he was conscious that someone was looking at him. He sat bolt upright, blinked, and focused on the face in front of him.

"What do you study so assiduously?" asked his patient in a weak voice.

"I am learning to read in my own language," said Yusuf, "but it is hard when there is no one to help me. I must write something every day, Father Crispià said, but I was looking in the other part of the book to find more words."

"What words do you need?" said Lord Pere.

"I need the words that have to do with illness," said Yusuf. "But this book speaks of love and war and fighting and hunting. Nothing of everyday life."

"Perhaps I can tell you," said Lord Pere. "I, too, know how to read and speak your language."

"This evening your lordship should drink this draft I have prepared for you and then sleep. Tomorrow is soon enough to help others," said Yusuf.

THIRTEEN

Clara and Mundina had been met at the shore by a small contingent of Her Majesty's Guard.

"Wait here," said one of the soldiers when they came near a tent gaily decorated with the banners of the Sicilian royal house and those of Aragon, Catalonia, and Valencia. "I will announce your arrival," he added. "Her Majesty may wish to see you." The two women dismounted and straightened their clothing.

There were men guarding the perimeter of the area they had now reached, but they had left the crowds of idle soldiers behind them. Clara pushed aside her veil so that her face could feel the breeze. "I feel sick," she said.

"All this way on the ship, tossing in the waves, and you were not sick," said Mundina. "Now that we are safely here and you are no longer in danger, you feel sick. I don't understand you."

"What if she does not like me?" asked Clara. "What will happen?"

"I doubt if she will order your head taken off because she does not like the color of your hair," said Mundina. "Her worst enemy has never accused her of such behavior. And as far as your life is concerned, I would have said that things can't be worse than they were."

"Then I had no time to think of what was happening," said Clara. "Now I am reminded every moment of what could have happened. And I am not such a fool as to think that the danger has passed."

"Her Majesty is not going to sell you into slavery, either. A young lady like you? It would not happen."

"I'm not a young lady, Mundina," said Clara, looking down at her hands. "I'm a kitchen maid."

"Lord Oliver said that you are not to mention the word *kitchen* while you are here," said Mundina.

"That is the same as telling a lie," said Clara.

"That may be," said Mundina. "I only tell you what my instructions are. I don't feel sick, but I am hungry," she added. "I wonder if they feed us here, or if we have to beg for a piece of a loaf and some soup from the soldiers."

"Surely they wouldn't make us do that," said Clara, turning to her protector with a look of horror on her face.

"No, my little pet, they wouldn't," said Mundina. "So you see, there is nothing to worry about."

The soldier came out of the tent suddenly and beckoned. "Her Majesty wishes to see you at once."

Mundina looked at her charge, picked up the cloth of her skirt, and shook it vigorously to dislodge the dust. "Off you go," she said, and gave her a push toward the tent.

Clara caught one glimpse of Eleanora of Sicily, Queen of the widespread Aragonese domains, sitting tall and composed in a regal-looking chair, before she sank in a profound curtsy.

"I am told your name is Clara," said Doña Eleanora, looking at Clara's shiny black, oddly short hair.

"Yes, Your Majesty," said Clara, remaining where she was.

"And it seems that you lay claim to no other name, but we will talk of that later. You may rise, Clara."

Clara rose gracefully enough in spite of her trembling knees and stood straight again, with her eyes downcast.

"I received a most mysterious letter concerning you, my child," said the Queen, looking quizzically at her. "But the man who wrote it is a trusted servant to whom we owe many favors. He begs us to look after you, and for his sake, we will. You and your attendant must be weary and hungry after your voyage."

Clara, too covered with confusion to respond, curtsied again.

The Queen stood up and took a step forward as if to inspect her new recruit more closely. Doña Eleanora was as tall and slender as a greyhound, standing there in a loose, comfortable gown of bright silk. When in thought, as she was at that moment, her face looked grave, serene, and very beautiful, like the marble statue of a saint, thought Clara, looking solemnly down at you at Mass. Suddenly the grave face lit up with mischief and amusement. "If you are indeed a spy or an assassin," she said, "as they say, sent here to aid the Sardinians or destroy His Majesty, you look somewhat small and undernourished for the part. But when people look oddly at you, Doña Clara, my new lady-in-waiting, that will be the reason why. Your reputation has preceded you."

Clara looked up at the Queen for an unseemly length of time, white-faced with shock.

Her Majesty laughed and sank onto a comfortable couch. "You have a most speaking face, my child," she said. "I find that reassuring." A young girl with large, dark eyes and the dusky olive complexion of the south darted over to arrange her skirts and place a small table by her side. "Bring me something cool," she murmured, and the little slave disappeared behind a curtain. "Maria," she said, "look after this poor child."

A grand-looking, elegant woman came forward and curtsied. "Certainly, Your Majesty," she said, and held out a hand to Clara.

"Is that true?" asked Clara, of Doña Maria López de Herèdia as they walked over to the second tent.

"That people have said you were likely to be an assassin?" said Doña Maria. "Yes. I don't think Her Majesty believes it, but the rumors intrigue and interest her. She is a clever woman and knows much about affairs of state," Doña Maria added. "She is not easily misled."

"But I was told I was to sew," said Clara, as they entered another large tent.

"How else would you occupy yourself?" asked Doña Maria and suddenly began to laugh in a most unstately manner. "Did you believe you were sent here to be a seamstress? Poor child. What must you think of Her Majesty, to believe she would turn a young lady into a seamstress. Next she'd be sending us into the kitchens to help. You will want to wash, I would think," she said, her voice becoming businesslike again, "and have some supper. Tomorrow is time enough to worry about your duties."

The next day, Doña Maria's maid brought Clara to the second tent, where a group of Her Majesty's ladies were sitting, engrossed in needlework and chatter. Clara slipped in quietly and took an empty place near the entrance. There were six women of various ages sitting on benches and chairs, and three or four more standing or looking over the table. They were all elegantly dressed in light, summer gowns, and she was hard put to decide which were the mistresses and which the maids. She attracted her share of quick, curious glances, nods, and smiles, but no one spoke.

Apparently, Doña Eleanora was not inclined to continue her inquiry into how Clara came to be where she was. The only other person the newcomer knew, Doña Maria, was with the Queen. And so she sat, with nothing to do, and watched the others gossiping and laughing at their needles. Finally, in an act of desperation, she turned to the lady seated next to her. "Do let me sort those silks for you," she said timidly.

The lady looked up in surprise. "There is no reason why you should do that," she said.

"But I have nothing else to do," said Clara, blushing nervously. "I brought no work with me. And when Mama's silks were hopelessly tangled—"

"Blanquina, Doña Clara has a sharp eye," said one of the others, laughing. "I heard you weren't able to bring much of anything, Doña Clara."

"My departure was somewhat hasty," she said and stopped in confusion again.

"What about the dress?" asked a bright-eyed young woman with a luxuriant head of light brown curls. "Until we can find Doña Clara some linen and such for her own wardrobe? Sancha, bring me the dress," she called over her shoulder.

Another attendant came in with a heavy silk gown, trimmed in ermine at the neck and the sleeves and along the bodice. The hem was trimmed in vair, and the silk was the soft green of the sea in a sandy cove. Doña Eleanora had been wearing that same color all those years ago when Clara had first seen her.

"If you would like something to do," said the curly-headed lady-in-waiting, "Her Majesty wants the trim changed on this gown. You can help me with it. Do come and sit by me."

"What is to be done?" asked Clara, crossing over to take the proffered chair. Sancha laid the gown across the two laps and disappeared back to where she had come from.

"It must be stripped of its ermine, Doña Clara, and the trim replaced with more vair," she answered.

"That should not be too difficult," said Clara, "But may I ask whom I have the honor of addressing?" she added in a voice so low it was almost a whisper.

"Of course," said the curly-headed one, clasping Clara's hand. "You poor child. Out in this encampment we forget our manners. No one has presented you. But you see, we know your name, and now you must learn ours. I am Tomasa, Doña Clara, Tomasa de Sant Climent."

"Climent?" said Clara.

"Yes. Do you know any of our family?"

"No," said Clara quickly, "I don't believe so."

"It does not surprise me. I have a half brother and sister, but their name isn't Climent," said Tomasa. "And there's no reason why you should have heard of them. The lady you were sitting beside is Blanquina, that is Antonia, and Elvira beside her, with Beatriu next to her."

"Thank you, Doña Tomasa. Are all Her Majesty's ladies here?"

"Oh, no. Most of the household is still at the palace. Our lady Queen brought us, her little slave, Cathalineta—she cannot do without Cathalineta—some musicians and a few servants. She even left her dwarfs behind and so there is no one to amuse us. Are you a wonderful reader? Because then if you were tired of sewing you could read to us as we work. We have a book of tales of adventure."

"I'm afraid I'm a very indifferent reader," said Clara.

"I'm terrible," said Tomasa. "Perhaps Beatriu will read. Or we must work to amuse each other in some other way. How old are you? I'm seventeen and not even betrothed. I am the despair of my mama who is hoping for a very grand marriage for me."

"I'm almost sixteen," said Clara.

"You don't look it," said Tomasa. "I thought you were twelve or thirteen. But I wish I had a face like yours and such thick, shiny hair. Why is it so short?"

Clara stopped, took her scissors out of her pocket, and looked over at Tomasa innocently. "It was tangled in something, and they cut it rather roughly to free me," said Clara. "Then Mundina trimmed it to make it even and—"

"I know. She had to take more off. That happened to my sister once. She fell from a horse and got caught in some thorns. Do you really think you would like to help with the trim on the gown? Doña Maria said you were clever with a needle. Otherwise we could leave it for one of the servants."

"I would like to help with it. It is a lovely gown," said Clara. "But don't you think that without the ermine tails falling down like that the sleeves and bodice will be very plain? Is that how Her Majesty would like it?"

"I wouldn't think so. She likes beautiful colors and striking designs, but she may have decided to give this dress to His Majesty's daughter, who has plainer tastes. What would you do with it?" she asked.

"If it were mine, Doña Tomasa?" asked Clara. She looked at it, spread out on their laps as it was, and closed her eyes. "Since it is the green of the sea," she said, opening them again, "I would fashion dolphins playing on it. It would look beautiful with silver embroidery here and here," she said, suddenly fired with excitement. "And perhaps on the sleeves."

"I'll find out," said Tomasa. "But we shouldn't do anything but take off the ermine until we know what Her Majesty wants."

And with great care, the two young ladies began to pick

out the stitches that held the ermine to the gown. By the end of that day, Clara had learned a great deal about Doña Tomasa's family and upbringing, had told her a very little of hers, and had settled into a routine that seemed at once foreign and yet very familiar.

On the fourth day of her stay in Sardinia, she entered the tent to find that no one was seated, breaking their fast, taking up their work, or even walking outside in the cool of the morning. Everyone was crowded around in the center of the tent, talking at once. Tomasa saw her come in and left the throng. She looked pale with anxiety.

"What is going on? Are we being attacked?" asked Clara.

"Worse than that," said Tomasa. "Her Majesty left in the middle of the night, taking Maria López and Cathalineta with her."

"Where?"

"To His Majesty's tent. They say His Majesty is dying of the fever."

"Dying!"

"Yes, and the Infant Johan is not yet four years old. Her Majesty could rule as regent in his stead—she is clever enough and knows as much about affairs of state as any prince, I assure you—but there are still many who want to put his uncle on the throne. Dearest Doña Clara," she said, grasping her arm, "if His Majesty dies, there will be civil war again. I know it."

The previous evening, Yusuf had gone to His Majesty's tent in the evening to report on the state of Lord Pere Boyll's health. The evening before, he had passed the message to an aide, who thanked him and sent him away. Tonight he was expecting the same and had devised several plans for spending the rest of the evening.

"His Majesty would like to hear your report from your own lips," said the aide, holding back the covering of the doorway to the tent.

Pedro of Aragon was sitting in his chair at the head of the conference table, listening to one of his generals and frowning with concentration. He was pale and perspiration shone on his forehead, although the breeze that blew through the tent opening was cool. "That does not help us," he said irritably. "We must decide soon—this evening, if possible, whether to send a ship with the sick back to Valencia. A handful of knights who complain that they are ill and bored and have nothing useful to do will not cause us to disrupt our arrangements for their convenience. Have you heard talk of it?" he asked suddenly, turning and looking directly at Yusuf. "You are in the center of those who are ill."

"The knights that I have heard complaining are not the sick in my tent, who are too ill to worry where they are. They are the idle who are bored."

"Precisely. And several of them now feign illness. Who suggested this course of action to them? And does he create trouble for us deliberately? If so, why? How is Lord Pere?"

"Very ill, Your Majesty, but he fights gallantly."

"Could he travel?" Yusuf noticed that His Majesty's voice had hoarsened and that the sweat was gathering on his forehead.

"Yes, Your Majesty, if an attendant went with him," said Yusuf. "And a sufficient quantity of medicine for the length of the journey. He would need an airy, comfortable cabin. I believe he is much worse than many who wish to leave."

"Is the boy right?" asked His Majesty.

The question was evidently directed at the chief physician, for he was the one to respond. "Yes, Your Majesty. And those knights are well enough to travel. But would it harm the cause if they were not to return?"

"Is that likely?"

"Possible, Your Majesty. In some cases. I hesitate to say likely."

"Unless we learn something that causes us to change our mind tomorrow, the ship will leave the following day with the sick men on board. Those whom we have noted, as well as any whom you wish to add, will go. If space remains, those who are better may go with them." He raised a hand for his attendant, who came forward. "Our cloak," he said. "The wind is cold."

Yusuf looked at the King with a sinking heart. He glanced

at the physician and realized that he was not the only one to realize that His Majesty, too, had fallen ill.

He had hurried back to the tent, as though the King's illness had reminded him that he had sick men to care for as well. Lord Pere was sleeping, more quietly than earlier in the day, and his forehead seemed cooler. Marc had left the tent as soon as Yusuf arrived, saying that all was well, and Yusuf wandered up and down the rows, checking his patients.

"Lad," said one of them, a gaunt and battle-scarred veteran who had been too sick to say much until that evening. "Can you fetch me something to drink? I'm parched with thirst."

Yusuf brought him a draft of water mixed with a little wine.

"I needed that," he said by way of thanks. "They say that in this tent you get the best care in the camp. If that is true, it is no wonder so many of the sick want to go home."

"Which of them want to go home?" asked Yusuf, looking around. "No one here has spoken of home, unless in his raving he thought I was his mother or his nurse."

"It is the talk of the camp everywhere but here. Or so they say. But then it is known that you have the ear of the King."

"Those who know that know very little," said Yusuf with a grin. "And most of it must be wrong. I have His Majesty's ear exactly as much as his mule does." He bent over and straightened the sick warrior's bedclothes. "But if people believe that, then they are not likely to speak of it to me. If I had the time to explore the camp, I might pick up gossip on my own. But I don't."

"I would rather be home," said the man he was talking to. "I didn't come here to die of the fever while my mates watch the enemy laugh at us from behind their walls. I came here to fight, win glory, and gain modest riches. My family is longer in name and breeding than it is in gold," he said ruefully. "And our lands are richer in rock and pebbles than in grass or trees."

"You want to desert His Majesty?" said Yusuf.

"Don't worry, lad. I would not think of it. But of all the things a soldier is asked to do, laying siege is beyond doubt the worst. And there are others out there who feel even more strongly than I do. I was talking to one who told me that he escaped the plague when everyone around him was dying, only to come over here and lie on a straw pallet, wrapped in his cloak, tormented with pain and shaking with fever. Two weeks he'd been like that, that close to death," he said, holding up his thumb and forefinger a hair's breadth apart, "and he wanted to be at home, in a feather bed with linen sheets, being fussed over by his womenfolk."

"But it takes days to get home," said Yusuf. "I wouldn't like to be deathly ill with fever and be tossed up and down by the wind and the sea as well."

"Nor I, lad. Nor can I imagine feeling better at home," he said. "You and Marc have looked after us well enough. I would rather be up and fighting. Now is the time to attack again. They won't be expecting it, and they'll be weaker now."

And so are we, thought Yusuf, remembering His Majesty's gray face and sweat-drenched forehead. "I have much to learn about military strategy, señor," said Yusuf tactfully. "I am glad the decision is not mine to make. But where do you hear all this gossip?"

"That bright-eyed jester and his friend—the one who claims friendship with Lord Pere over there—were in this evening. His Lordship was sleeping, but they were wandering about bringing tidbits of news."

"Were they?" said Yusuf. "Gueralt de Robau and Don Manuel are interesting men. Can I bring you anything else?"

"No, lad," said the knight with a sly grin. "I feel as if I could sleep. Perhaps I am recovering."

It was time to replenish their stock of herbs. The next morning, before the dew was dry on the grass, Yusuf was on the closest likely hillside with Marc's basket, searching for what he could find. When the basket was full, he flung himself down on the grass and watched the white clouds flying above him.

He could almost believe he was back in Girona for the moment. The grass under him felt like the grass on the slopes where he went with Raquel to look for herbs. Suddenly he, too, wanted to go home and was shocked to realize that by home he meant the northern fastness where he lived now.

"So His Majesty's page has been sneaking off to doze in the sun," said a voice, and suddenly a shadow fell over him.

Yusuf sat up and then rose to his feet. "Good morning, señor," he said. It was Gueralt, son of Asbert de Robau.

"This is a pleasant spot," said Gueralt. "Why did you seek it out?"

"I have been gathering herbs," said Yusuf. "And you, señor?"

"You shame me, lad. I'm here because I'm bored. Bored. I have not the old soldier's acceptance of things, and so I wander everywhere. I feel the need for exercise, and there aren't even any war games to keep us fit. It would be charitable of you to stay and talk to me. But let us sit. It is more comfortable." Gueralt flopped down on the grass and rolled over, propping himself on one elbow. "I envy you, lad."

"Why, Don Gueralt?" he said, sitting down again.

"Because you have something to do. And something that makes a difference to people when you do it. What herbs do you gather?"

"Herbs to treat the sick. To replenish our stock," he said.

"I would rather do that than nothing," said Gueralt. "Perhaps I can help you. Picking herbs should not be beyond someone schooled in fencing, horsemanship, and the arts of war," he added in his mocking tones.

"I am afraid you would not know which ones to pick."

"You could find them for me."

"By then, it would be easier to pick them myself. And I have finished for the day," he added.

"Alas, still useless," said Gueralt. "Don Manuel. Join us, please." They waited for Gueralt's friend to come panting up the hill and sit down before resuming their conversation.

Yusuf smiled politely and turned to Gueralt. "Perhaps you have no war games because the participants are ill," he said.

"True enough. Including His Majesty," said Don Manuel, once he caught his breath. "They say he is near death. The Queen rushed to his bedside last night to hear his last words."

"Really?" said Yusuf. "I have heard nothing of it."

"You are an indifferent page, then," said Gueralt in his

mocking tones. "In my day, we knew everything and every-one."

"I am helping with the sick," said Yusuf. "His Majesty has other pages."

"Then you haven't seen him," said Don Manuel sharply.

"I have seen him," said Yusuf. "But not as his page. I saw him last night."

"Was he in his bed?" asked Don Manuel.

"No, he was meeting with his council."

"He was?" said Don Manuel. "Not ill at all? I am glad. I will never learn not to listen to gossip." He laughed uneasily.

"Well," said Yusuf, "he yawned when I came in. Either he was tired or the report was wearisome. I don't know. It was late and the meeting was over then."

"Why were you there?" asked Gueralt.

"To ask if he had any commands. I am still his page and His Majesty likes me to report at the end of each day."

"And how is my friend Pere Boyll?" asked Don Manuel. "I have been most concerned."

"So I have noticed," said Yusuf. "He is doing well."

"Physicians have an odd notion of doing well," said Gueralt. "He looked at death's door to me."

That evening, Pedro of Aragon lay in his bed in the royal tent and shivered, burning with fever. The Queen sat by him, observant of every detail, but for the moment quiet.

"You must return to your royal palace, Your Majesty," said the chief physician. "The ship can sail as early as tomorrow."

"Yes, Your Majesty, you must return. It is too dangerous for your health to stay here," said the man beside him. "Leave the generals to pursue the war."

"We must stay here," said the King. His voice was weak and hoarse, but the words were clear and audible.

"Your Majesty could die if you stay here," said another.

"We could die anywhere," said Don Pedro. "We do not intend to die in a galley, running from a war."

"The air is better in a galley, Your Majesty. The air here in Sardinia is poisonous."

"Nonsense," said the King. "We find the air excellent here. Surely our generals do not wish us to go."

"No, they don't, Your Majesty. But they are only concerned with the progress of the campaign."

"And our Queen?" he whispered. "What does she think?"

"My lord King," said Eleanora, "I fear that if you leave the island, our troops will decide that you brought them to Sardinia to fight an unimportant war. They will be sadly disheartened." She leaned forward to be closer to him. "And the moment our enemies hear that Your Majesty is on a galley leaving the harbor, they will be filled with courage."

"It is to be expected," murmured Don Pedro.

"Even if we tried to keep your departure a secret, Your Majesty, they will know quickly, since among the ten thousand loyal subjects we have here the enemy can always find a few traitors." She laid her hand on her breast and looked intently at her husband. "I swear by all the holy saints that Your Majesty's life means everything to me. I would die to protect it, and I will fight to preserve it. But I prefer to do it here."

"You have heard our Queen. We must stay," said Don Pedro. With the ghost of a smile, he turned his head toward her and drifted off into uneasy sleep.

The next morning, Yusuf had scarcely finished washing his face and drinking a cup of water when the chief physician, his eyelids drooping and skin pale with lack of sleep, approached the tent. "Come over here, lad," he said.

They walked to one side and stopped. "I came to speak to you about . . ." said the physician.

"Yes, señor?" said Yusuf and waited politely.

"Those preparations for fever that your master compounded," he said at last, and it cost him dearly to say it.

"Yes, señor?" said Yusuf.

"Someone has spoken of them to Her Majesty, and she insists that they be tried, at least. They seem to have done much good with the sick in your tent—or with some of them, at least."

"His Majesty has the fever?" asked Yusuf.

"I think not," said his physician. "It is a recurrence of the ague. His fever and the headache were very bad, and then eased for a day. That is the ague, if you didn't know it."

"I have seen these symptoms before, señor."

"During his attacks, His Majesty's fever becomes rapidly frightening. If he dies . . ." He didn't bother finishing the thought. "I believe your master sent a compound for the ague."

"He did, and you are most welcome to it," said Yusuf. "I will give you the mixture. And I most earnestly hope and pray that it will help. If His Majesty can be induced to drink a whole cupful . . ."

"We will try," said the physician. "I will send my man to fetch the compound."

"And I have herbs to steep in the water that is used for cooling the head and shoulders. They, too, seem to be helpful."

The physician nodded brusquely and left.

For two days, little more happened around the camp. By the second morning, word had spread through the camp that His Majesty had come down with the fever, and rumormongers stated positively that his physicians despaired of him, and that Her Majesty was making secret preparations to return to Sicily, abandoning the heir, the Infant Johan, to his fate and leaving the country to face another civil war.

Gueralt de Robau lifted the flap of the tent halfway through the second morning and raised a friendly hand in Yusuf's direction. "Hola, Yusuf," he called. "I wondered if you would like a morning stroll. Manuel and I have discovered someone who makes wonderful little cakes. We bring her the flour, and her hens supply the eggs. Those who are recovering might enjoy them."

"I thank you, señor," said Yusuf, stepping outside and noticing Don Manuel sitting on a rock nearby. "But I have duties that I must attend to here."

"Then I shall bring you a basket of them," said Gueralt. "Are you coming, Don Manuel?"

"Later," he said. "You must be the only person in the camp who isn't ignoring his duties. Everyone is out in the sunshine."

"But surely the sentries and lookouts—"

"Not these days." He shook his head. "Don Pedro should order his ships to sit a few leagues out, or the men will be swimming to climb aboard and go home. But forgive me for disturbing you. Do you have better word on His Majesty's health?" he asked.

"I know nothing of His Majesty," said Yusuf.

"And how is my friend under your care?" said Don Manuel.

"Your friend does well. He is teaching me to read in the Moorish tongue."

"He does well indeed, then," said Manuel. "That is gratifying to hear."

After supper on the following day, Yusuf was ushered into His Majesty's bedchamber, where the King, looking pale and tired but alert, lay propped up on cushions, surrounded by attendants.

"Our Queen has confessed that the vile-tasting liquid I was convinced to drink when at my worst came from your master's hand, Yusuf," said Don Pedro. "Whether it was her prayers that went with it or your master's compound, I am now better."

"I thank the Lord for that, Your Majesty," said Yusuf.

"The ship that was to take the sick to Valencia has not yet left. It will go tomorrow. How is the noble Pere Boyll?"

"Somewhat better, Your Majesty. Weak, but not feverish."

"Will he live?"

"I think so," said the boy hesitantly.

"Our surgeon and chief physician agree with you, Yusuf. Lord Pere will be on the ship tomorrow, and you will go with him. Should you hear anything on board the ship that we need to know, give it to the noble Arnau Johan, governor of Valencia, or the Archbishop, the noble Huc de Fenollet. To no one else. The same galley will then take you to Barcelona. Our secretary will supply you with the means."

"I pray that Your Majesty will be completely recovered soon," said Yusuf and went into another part of the tent with the secretary.

"His Majesty has ordered that you be supplied with a purse

for any expenses you might incur," said the secretary, setting
a leather purse filled with coins on the table. "Guard it well."

"Yes, señor," said Yusuf.

"And these letters will give you access to the Governor
and the Archbishop in Valencia," he said, pushing across two
that were neatly folded and sealed with the royal seal. "And
this one to the Prince, his uncle, lest it be needed. I have one
piece of very important advice. Commit nothing to writing."

"I understand, señor."

"Excellent. I wish you a speedy voyage and good winds."

Yusuf was moving quietly along the familiar path back to
his tent through the velvet-black night when he heard low-
voiced murmurs from the hill to his right. The sound of his
name in a familiar voice stopped him where he was.

"But my dear Don Manuel," said Gueralt. "I fail to com-
prehend what is upsetting you."

"I tell you, I spoke to another in His Majesty's tent—not
the boy, Yusuf—and he, too, claims that His Majesty is well
again. That he is far from being near death."

"Have you considered that all of them might be lying?"
said Gueralt. "Through fear or loyalty. Her Majesty does not
wish it known that she will soon be a widow and that our
new King will be more of an age to play with toys than
statecraft. And what will happen to us then?"

"But Gueralt—"

Yusuf shifted weight from one foot to the other and a twig
cracked.

"There seems to be someone about," said Gueralt casually.

"A curse on His noble bastard drunkard of a Lordship for
sending me out in the middle of the night," said Yusuf, pitching his voice as high as he could. He kicked a stone. When
it hit the ground, he swore again, crept silently behind a
shrub, and sat down to wait.

"Someone's lad," said Gueralt. "Let us go back to the
camp."

Yusuf waited where he was until all was quiet. By the
time he reached the tent again, everyone in it was asleep.

• • • •

Excitement drew Yusuf from his bed long before the hour appointed for going down to the ship. His gear had already been taken, and the tent was in order. He checked the neat row of supplies and, last of all, he walked silently past every bed to see how his patients were faring. He stopped by Lord Pere.

"Hola, lad," said the nobleman.

"Hola, my lord," whispered Yusuf. "You should sleep. May I prepare a draft for you?"

"I grow tired of your excellent drafts, Yusuf. I long to return to a cup of rich red wine."

"You must be improving, my lord."

"Your sly friends were creeping about here last night while you were out," said Lord Pere. "I feigned sleep to avoid them."

"One of them is your friend, my lord, not mine. Do you not recognize him?"

"Recognize him? Only as an infernal nuisance."

"Don Manuel was a page in your father's household when he was seven years old," said Yusuf. "He said that you were very kind to him in his loneliness and misery."

"A page! In my father's house? Nonsense," said Pere.

"Are you sure, my lord?"

"No," he said. "Tell me. Where is he from?"

"Empuries, he said."

"Empuries! My father never had a page from the north," said Lord Pere. "Not in my lifetime. We are not kings to trade pages in games of intrigue and shifting alliances. He lies, Yusuf."

"Why lie about something like that?"

"That is not our business. Go to His Majesty's tent and let someone reliable know about this. But wake Marc before you leave. I do not wish to have my throat cut as I lie here."

"Can we trust Marc?" said Yusuf.

"We must trust someone," said Lord Pere. "Marc seems safer than most. And you, Yusuf—mind that you walk softly and carefully over to the royal tents."

Yusuf delivered a tactfully worded request to the guard outside the royal tent. To his astonishment, when the tent flap was raised, His Majesty himself came out. "You wished to tell us something more than farewell, Yusuf?" he asked. "If so, let us walk some way along this path. Out of the way of curious ears." Four soldiers fanned out discreetly to surround them at a distance, and Yusuf delivered his message as briefly as he could.

Don Pedro shook his head. "The little Don Manuel. I am surprised he has the wit to scheme against us. He is a bungler even in treachery. Such a lie is too easily checked."

"Perhaps, Your Majesty, he thought Lord Pere was soon to die."

"No doubt he did. As he evidently thought we were, as well. But Lord Pere did not. Nor did we. An experienced man does not count on what is known only to God. Have you heard anything else from the lips of his friend, Gueralt de Robau? Beyond what was said last night?"

"No, Your Majesty. He helps me, sometimes, claiming he is bored, but he jests, not liking his good deeds to be noticed. I would be distressed if two of Your Majesty's knights should have turned out to be traitors," said Yusuf.

"He may be as loyal as our hunting dogs," said the King. "I would think that Gueralt's father and elder brother are most likely to be faithful knights. Disloyalty, Yusuf, is bred by Envy out of Greed and is often the younger son's portion." He walked slowly along, silently noting everything. "Loyal or not, he is leaving for Valencia with a box full of dispatches to deliver and will no longer be a problem here."

"For Valencia, Your Majesty?" said Yusuf, startled.

"The most useful way to eliminate a possible problem is to occupy him elsewhere. But I have learned to accept these things as they happen, Yusuf. For a man is lucky if he has one or two loyal comrades. Men he can trust with his life, or what is more difficult to find, his thoughts," added Don Pedro. "I have been the most fortunate of princes. In my youth, God surrounded me with enemies who taught me much, and then gave me a few men whom I could trust with the secrets of my heart. In His mercy, He has since given me a loyal queen whose statecraft excels that of most princes and a few more men whose advice is worth listening to." He paused and looked around him at the sleeping camp. "Your ship brought me the heavy news that one of the loyal companions of my youth was killed in my service."

"Perhaps, someday, I shall be worthy of your trust, Your Majesty," said Yusuf.

"I believe you will, Yusuf," said the King. "May God protect you on your voyage."

Marc was waiting outside the tent with Yusuf's bundle when he returned. "Someone has been rummaging about in the medicines," he said softly.

"When?" asked Yusuf. "And how?" For at least one of them had slept each night in the entrance to the little storeroom.

"The night we were both out, I think," he said. "The new boy they sent us was sleeping soundly when I returned. The last trump would not have wakened him."

"Is anything gone?"

"That vial of yours," said Marc. "Was it full?"

"It was," said Yusuf.

"It isn't any longer," said Marc. "I said it would be a temptation."

"But no one knew of it," said Yusuf. "Only you and I."

"We talked about it," said Marc. "When you first arrived."

"But they were all too ill . . ." said Yusuf.

"Except for the two who were discharged the next morning," said Marc.

"I don't even know who they were," said Yusuf miserably. "I didn't take note of them."

"One of them was Lord Pere Boyll's good friend, Don Manuel," said Marc. "You had better leave, young master. Your ship is about to sail."

When the guards arrived to bring Don Manuel to His Majesty, they found him collapsed in a chair. A silver wine cup had dropped from his hand onto the ground. One of the men bent over and touched his cheek. "I think we're too late, sir," he said to his captain. "He's cold as mutton and stiff as a tree. Dead since last night, I'd guess."

"That spares us some trouble," said the captain.

When His Majesty heard, he raised an eyebrow. "Good. Where is his friend?"

"He left on the ship to Valencia, Your Majesty," said the captain. "As ordered."

"Good," said Don Pedro.

FOURTEEN

Five nights passed before Her Majesty returned to their encampment on the hill. By then, the dress had been denuded of its brave and expensive display of ermine; the ermine had been put away with great care—a count was made of the number of skins and the size and condition of each recorded for the accounts book—and the dress returned to those in charge of Her Majesty's wardrobe.

Almost immediately, Doña Tomasa disappeared to her own quarters and returned with an armful of fine linen. She collected her new protégée and dragged her over to the table where she spread it out. "There," she said. "You need a shift, and more things than that, I would think, if you came with no possessions of your own."

"Where did that come from?" asked Clara, feeling the cloth. "It's wonderful."

"My mother keeps giving me linen for wedding shifts," whispered Tomasa. "And I dutifully make them. I already have six. I think it's enough. She forgets."

"Six!" said Clara. "And you've never worn them?"

"No," said Tomasa. "I have plenty of shifts for now."

"All that plain stitching," said Clara. "How can you stand it? Or does your maid do it for you?"

"Certainly not. I'm very good. Come and look."

And in Tomasa's box, at the bottom, were two shifts made of the finest heavy silk. "There," she said, taking one out, "isn't it beautifully made?"

"Why did you bring it all the way over here?" asked Clara. "Or are you planning to marry in Sardinia?"

Tomasa giggled. "No, although I'd be ready, wouldn't I? I'm supposed to be embroidering them while I'm here. But I'm not very good at it. I don't seem to be able to think of designs, or to work without making terrible knots in the thread. Look at this. I did a scallop around the neckline, and that's bad enough."

"Let me," said Clara, taking the shift. "And if you don't like it, I'll take it out again, very carefully."

And so, while Tomasa stitched up a shift for Clara out of the fine linen, Clara turned the simple scallop pattern into sinuous wild animals looking out from among clusters of flowers. When she had finished the first one, on the right front panel of the shift, she held it up for Tomasa to see.

Tomasa's shriek brought everyone over. "Look at it," she said. "It's a lion, surrounded by flowers. It's smiling."

"That's because it's a wedding shift," said Clara.

And from then on, Clara's wardrobe became a matter of general concern. Such a clever, talented, well-spoken young lady, no matter how mysterious her background, must, it was agreed, come from a good family and was deeply to be pitied.

"Her entire family butchered by foreigners and the castle set aflame. Only Doña Clara and her maid escaped and threw themselves on the mercy of Her Majesty, who knows the family well," murmured Doña Tomasa to one of the other ladies. "She dares not say her family name, for there are brutes out there who seek to destroy her as well, in hope of seizing everything the family possessed. But Her Majesty knows who she is, of course. A kinsman of mine wrote to me about her, asking me to show her some kindness . . . but not saying who she is."

"Whatever did you tell people about me, if I may ask?" asked Clara, as the offers of assistance came pouring in.

Tomasa giggled and told her. "It's because of the design on my shift. It is so elegant and so witty that they have decided you must be from the highest of nobility . . . and where that leaves me," she added, "I do not know."

As the days passed, the smiling lion was joined on the left panel by an elegant lioness with a curly tail, lying on a bed of flowers and shyly stretching out a paw in the direction of the lion. Clara was busy adding more flowers, and between them, the heads of little animals, discernible as mice, a hare, a cat, a ferret, and a very curly-headed lamb.

Clara was still working on Doña Tomasa's silk wedding shift when the Queen returned to her ladies. She looked even thinner and more fragile, her eyes hollow from lack of sleep, but she laughed merrily at some jest, and everyone relaxed. All was well. The news had spread earlier that His Majesty was recovering, and with the Queen with them again, it was possible to believe it.

When Her Majesty retired to the privacy of her own quarters to rest, Clara went outside to escape the heat of the tent. A group of ladies was sitting in the shade, but their shrill voices hurt her ears, and their high-pitched laughter tormented her. She would rather listen to the cook complain about the mistress's meanness over expenses than to worthless gossip about who might marry which distant relative of someone's cousin. She was weary to her soul, too weary to smile and nod.

Then Tomasa bent closer to her and patted her knee. Clara jumped as if she had been touched with a sword point. "Dear Clara," said Doña Tomasa. "Calm yourself. All will be well, I assure you. Now that Her Majesty is back with us, she will quickly settle your difficulties. While the Queen was away," she added, "nothing could happen. No changes could be made. I do not wonder that you have been fretting."

"But Tomasa," she whispered, "now that Her Majesty is back, she will make decisions about what should be done with me. And who knows what will happen? This island of calm could be snatched away from me."

"An island of calm?" said Tomasa. "The court, seated on the edge of a battlefield? You are a strange and charming thing, but that you should have to come to a battlefield to find peace is the strangest part of you." Tomasa poured a cup of cool mint infusion and gave it to Clara. "Drink this," she said, "and we will return to our work. I will see you in a moment," she murmured and disappeared into the tent.

Clara could not bear to go inside again. She walked to the
path that defined the edge of Her Majesty's well-patrolled
temporary quarters; from there she could catch a glimpse of
the sea. She stared blankly at it and tried to think. Her mind
was filled with nonsensical images that refused to form into
coherent pictures. What was the worst thing that could happen? Being sent back to Barcelona. If that was Her Majesty's
decision, what would follow? She could imagine nothing but
chaos and, panic-stricken, turned back to the tent.

When she bent to pick up her work, it was gone. Tomasa's
shift was gone. She looked around wildly. All that heavy
silk, she thought. They would believe she had stolen it. "I
can't find my work," she said at last in desperation.

"Tomasa took it," said Doña Elvira. "She wanted to show
it to Doña Maria López. She's so proud of it she declared
she was going to wear it at court with nothing else on but
shoes and hose and jewels."

Everyone laughed and settled back to what they were doing. Clara picked up the neglected book, and in a very soft
voice, stumbling here and there as she went, began to read.

Suddenly, Doña Maria was at her elbow. "Her Majesty
would like to see you," she said, "if the ladies can spare you."

There was only one answer to that summons. Clara set
down the book and jumped to her feet. She curtsied to Doña
Maria and set out after her into the Queen's tent.

"My much-loved Tomasa brought me a piece of silk that she
tells me has been embroidered by you, Clara."

Her Majesty was addressing a bowed head and curtsying
form, for Clara had not yet been able to force herself to stand
upright. She looked up for an instant, caught a signal to rise,
and straightened up.

"Yes, Your Majesty," she murmured.

"It is both skillful and charming," said the Queen. "From
whose head did those ideas come?"

"From mine, Your Majesty," said Clara, subsiding into
curtsy once more.

"If that is so, it would please me if you could exercise
your fancy on the gown you and the noble Tomasa were

working on. We have a quantity of gold and silver thread with us, I believe. Doña Maria will see that you have it to work with."

Lord Pere Boyll and the Viscount of Cardona had been given the master's cabin, by right of rank; crowded in with them on hammocks were Yusuf, the viscount's manservant, and Lord Pere's surviving man, although given his state, it was more as a patient than a helper that the latter was there. Where the captain was to sleep Yusuf did not know nor did he care to inquire. There were five more lords, with their attendants, filling the other three cabins in the castle. One of them, the noble Ramon de Ruisech, was being sent to organize a small fleet of galleys in Valencia and to return with them. He was to have shared the smallest cabin with the captain, but one look at him as he climbed painfully on board and everyone agreed that he and his attendant should have it to themselves. He was very ill indeed.

The sick knights were between decks, in hammocks.

It was a grim company that rowed out from the harbor at Alghero looking for a wind to carry them to Valencia.

The Viscount was too ill for chatter. Yusuf steeped a large jug of herbal mixture, their only weapon against the fever at the moment, sweetened it with a little of their precious stock of sugar, and instructed his servant to coax him into drinking it, no matter how much he objected. He left them to survey the rest of the men on the ship. Except for Ramon de Ruisech, the other nobles were beginning to recover and had attendants with them.

Between decks there were close to twenty-five knights. Most of them were in hammocks, many asleep. He had seen only a few of them before and moved steadily from one to another in hopes of finding out who were the sickest. When he finished his tour, he pulled his book from his tunic and climbed up to the deck.

Back on deck, Yusuf discovered Lord Pere Boyll, wrapped in his cloak, sitting on the deck in conversation with a man whose back was toward the boy. "All is quiet in the cabin, lad," said Lord Pere. "I could not stand another minute of the company of sick men. And that includes my own."

The other man turned and smiled lazily. "It is the incurious page," he said. "I am delighted to find you on the galley."

"Señor Gueralt," said Yusuf. "Have you fallen ill?"

"It seems that Don Gueralt de Robau has other reasons for coming with us," said Lord Pere.

"I do. But why are you sailing to Valencia, Yusuf? Is it your native land?"

"I was sent by His Majesty," he said. "And no, it is not. But I have not been in Valencia since—"

"Since when, Yusuf?" asked Lord Pere.

"Since the war," said Yusuf hastily.

"I see," said Lord Pere. "It is time you went back to look at it. You must let me show you the city."

On Tuesday, ten days after he had left Girona, Oliver rode back into the city, looking dustier, hotter, and thirstier than ever. "Your Excellency," he said as he flung his sizable frame into a sturdy chair, "the road to Lleida at this time of year is to be avoided. My horse and I are now the color of the road, which is the same color as the fields we traveled between. This time I will not turn down a jug of water and a cask of wine to slake my thirst."

"They are on their way, Your Excellency," murmured Bernat.

"And what have you discovered, except that the road west is hot and dusty in August?" said Berenguer wryly.

"I found an inn not far from here where one Martin from Tudela—a man filled with lively jokes and pranks if you can but understand his speech, according to the chambermaid—and his master, the great Lord Geraldo, were staying."

The Bishop's man and a page entered silently. They placed wine, water, a plate of fruit, and one of cold meats and bread down on a table and disappeared again.

"This looks most inviting," said Oliver, pouring himself wine and water. "We were talking of the inn where Martin and his lord were staying. One night—it could have been a Thursday, says the chambermaid—the two of them went out. An hour or so later, Geraldo came back in considerable perturbation, bundled up everything he could carry, and rode off. Several hours later, Martin came back, discovered his master had taken most of his possessions, had begged a bandage for his wounded arm and a loaf to keep him going, and rode off himself. She hopes Martin is well. I didn't tell her he had died," said Oliver. "But I warned her against trusting great lords."

"They went off, got in a scrap—"

"With Pasqual, Your Excellency," said Oliver. "That was the night he disappeared.

"And as soon as the fighting started, this mysterious Geraldo disappeared, leaving his man to deal with Pasqual."

"Pasqual may have collected some interesting information from Martin," said Oliver. "And gone off to report on it."

"Without telling you, my lord Oliver?"

"Certainly without telling me." He cut up a pear and took a bite. "Or he may have ridden off to see his wife. That could account for the four days. I think it is time to find his wife."

"And how do we do that?" asked the Bishop.

"We search for a Doña—"

"Precisely. Doña who?"

"We take the excellent idea of your physician," said Oliver, "and look for a marriage contract between Pasqual Robert and . . . someone else."

"Do we know that his name really was Pasqual Robert?"

"Of course, Your Excellency. I've known him most of my life. Since I was a young page at the palace in Zaragoza."

"But not all his life, Lord Oliver," said Berenguer. "Pasqual was at least fifteen years older than you are. When you met him, he was in his twenties. What had he been doing before then?"

"Then we look for Señora Robert," said Oliver. "Or perhaps Señora Gil."

"Why?"

"Because the child I spoke of—the one who looks the picture of Pasqual's wife—called herself Gil. I suspect she took her father's name as her own, since she would answer to it more readily than to a completely strange name."

"You think his name may have been Pasqual Gil?"

"It's possible."

"Or Gil something else?"

"Everyone called him Pasqual. If that were not his name, he would not have answered to it so readily," said Oliver. "I think," he added doubtfully.

Bernat leaned over his master and whispered something.

"Indeed. Bernat has reminded me that among Martin of Tudela's possessions was a map. He thinks you might wish to see it, my lord. His landlady brought it to the physician and was well paid for her pains."

Bernat laid the map in front of Oliver. He looked at it, turned it from one direction to another, frowned, and set it down. "Before anything else, I want to speak to this landlady."

The inn's only customers at the time Oliver arrived were several flies, enjoying themselves in the puddles of spilled wine left by the morning's paying drinkers. Mother Benedicta appeared from the kitchen at the sound of his heavy rap on the counter, looked him up and down, and pointed her long wooden spoon at his chest. "You're Pasqual's friend," she said. "What do you want from me?"

Oliver stacked five pennies on the counter. "A few words. Nothing else. About this Martin of Tudela, the one you looked after."

"I know who he was," she said. "But I know nothing about him."

Oliver added another stack of five to the first one. "You know what he was like when he arrived," said Oliver. "If he was near death then—"

"As if I'd give a bed in my attic to a customer who looked near death," said Benedicta contemptuously. "Wasn't until Sunday night he began to look poorly. By Monday he couldn't leave his bed."

"I see," said Oliver. "He seemed in good health on Friday?"

"Lively as a sparrow," said Benedicta. "Came in here and asked for a bed, soup, cold meat, and bread. Ate two plates of soup, he did, talking all the while. He was looking for a Señor Luis, he said. Owed him money, a hundred sous, and did I know anyone of the name. Everyone in the room answered at once. It isn't hard to find someone named Luis, but most of them have never seen a hundred sous in their lives, so unless he'd given it to one of them and hoped to get it back, we didn't know who he was talking about." The innkeeper cackled with laughter.

"There are some named Luis in the city who are worth much more than a hundred," observed Oliver.

"Gentlemen," said Benedicta dismissively. "This Martin was a good-hearted sort, but he wouldn't be looking for one of them in my establishment, would he?"

"Tell me, Mother Benedicta. Did he ever find Señor Luis?"

"He must have, mustn't he?"

"Why do you say that?"

"He had money when he died," said the innkeeper. "If he had any when he rode into town, he wouldn't have stayed in my attic, would he? He'd be someplace grander. So someone gave it to him after he came into town. Luis, probably. On Sunday, since he was going to leave Monday morning. Then he sickened."

Oliver smiled and dropped a few more coins. "You are an observant and clever woman," he said. "Thank you."

Berenguer was playing chess with the physician when Oliver returned to the palace. "Study that map while we finish this game, my friend, and then we talk of what you have discovered."

The blind man captured a knight, placing Berenguer's queen in jeopardy.

"And now my concentration is destroyed," said the Bishop, moving his queen.

Isaac captured the queen, placing the king in check.

"I shall concede defeat now," said Berenguer, "before it becomes inevitable and ignominious."

"You could save your king," said Oliver, leaning over the table, "if you moved—"

"No, Lord Oliver, my friend. Having destroyed my game, you may not then rescue it for me. Let us turn to his problem, shall we, Master Isaac?"

"As Your Excellency wishes," said the physician.

"Did you learn anything from the innkeeper?"

"One or two interesting morsels," said Oliver, and told them of the conversation.

"Someone named Luis," said the Bishop. "Luis Mercer claimed some friendship with Pasqual. He attended his funeral and had masses said for his soul."

"Does that make him an assassin?" asked Oliver.

"Certainly not," said the Bishop. "He wearies me with his righteousness."

"But there must have been others at the funeral who had masses said, Your Excellency," observed Isaac. "All the merchants who deal through the Exchange thought highly of Pasqual Robert."

"Of course," said the Bishop. "There were others."

"But were they also called Luis?" asked Oliver.

"Luis Vidal was at the funeral," said Berenguer. "He is also an unlikely assassin. A man of substance and good sense."

"I shall speak to these men," said Oliver doggedly. "And to every other Luis I can find in the city and its outlying houses."

"You will have a long hunt," said Berenguer. "How do you plan to set about it?"

"I hope to induce each parish clerk to make me a list of the Luises in his parish," said Oliver. "All those who were born more than fifteen years ago. And every one will be visited."

"And have you decided how to find the beautiful woman of the painting?" asked Isaac.

"I shall visit each notary and look through dower records," declared Oliver. "As soon as I have eaten my dinner. Even if I must drag them from their couches."

"Before you trouble the parish clerks, my lord," said Isaac, "I have several Luises among my patients. I could ask if anyone has tried to collect a hundred sous from one of them. That would cut down your task somewhat."

"An excellent idea," said Berenguer. "Although I suggest that Lord Oliver take Luis Mercer. His attitude toward women can be strange," he added mildly. "I would not like to expose your excellent Raquel to difficulties."

• • •

Oliver started with Luis Mercer, who greeted him as if they were old friends. "Señor Oliver," he said. "I am delighted to see you." He rang for refreshment and, until it arrived, chatted about the weather, the heat, and the chances that a shipment of English cloth that he was expecting might arrive before the winter. He poured Oliver a cup of wine, his little servant took it to him with a curtsy, and on a signal from her master, left them alone. "Now," he said, leaning back, "what may I do for you?"

"I must apologize if I appear discourteous, Master Luis," said Oliver. "But I had not remembered our meeting before this."

"That is not to be wondered at," said Luis, shaking his head. "It was the day our loyal and efficient Pasqual Robert died. I had a shipment of goods coming in and had paid exorbitantly to have the gates opened before prime. As you can imagine, I was up early and in the square when the terrible event occurred. But a few moments before our well-loved friend came into the city, someone—I can't remember who—was about to present me to you, señor. And I have no doubt that the incident was wiped from the tablets of your memory at once."

"It is odd the tricks memory can play," said Oliver lightly. "Your face is familiar, but the incident . . . well, that is gone."

"I am not surprised. That peaceful morning! The sudden and horrifying manner of his death!" He shook his head. "I have seen death many times, but Pasqual Robert's death afflicted me most strangely. It disturbed my sleep for days afterward."

"It is about my friend's death that I come to speak."

"To me?" said Luis Mercer.

"You and many other people," said Oliver. "Has a man come to you recently to collect a debt or a payment of a hundred sous?"

"A hundred sous? What has this to do with Pasqual's death?"

"I only know that it does, señor. Perhaps you would not remember it."

"I assure you, Señor Oliver, I would not forget a demand

for an amount like that," said Mercer, laughing.

"Do you ever owe sums of that nature?"

"Certainly," said Luis. "Each time I receive a shipment, I owe that and often much more. But I am always expecting it. I do not often receive demands for large amounts from strangers wandering in off the street."

"Has any stranger asked for such a sum from you recently?"

"No," he said, shaking his head thoughtfully. "Although a curious thing did happen to me some time ago. A stranger, with a foreign manner of speaking, insisted on seeing me. When Catarina showed him in, he looked at me very carefully, shook his head, apologized for disturbing me, and left without another word."

"What did this man look like?" asked Oliver.

"Look like?" asked Luis. "Well . . . disheveled. Dressed in a fashionable tunic and hose, like a rich man's servant, but one who has fallen on evil times. His tunic was torn and dirty. So were his hose, too, I think."

"Was he a tall man? A fat man?"

"Not tall. On the thin side. I believe he had a scar on his forehead, so perhaps he had been a soldier."

"Was he wounded in the arm?" asked Oliver.

"You know, I think he was. How odd that you should know that, señor. May I offer you more wine?"

"I must not keep you from your business any longer, Master Luis," said Oliver.

On his way home, Isaac stopped at the house of Luis Vidal, a cloth merchant, who specialized in silks and fine linens. "Master Isaac," said the merchant, "I am pleased to see you. I was about to send for you on a most trivial matter, and here you are. A little wine," he said jovially, pouring it out and adding water. "It is a hot and thirsty day."

"It is," said Isaac. "I thank you. And what is the trivial matter that troubles you?"

"A rash that burns and itches here on my arm," he said.

"I have no one with me but my little Judah," said Isaac, "who as yet cannot tell the difference between a rash and a dog bite. Tell me what it looks like, and if necessary, I will return with Raquel."

After assuring the merchant that he would send over some salts to make a soothing cool-water bath for the arm, Isaac turned to his own business with Luis Vidal.

"Has someone come here to collect a hundred sous?" asked Vidal. "The short answer to that is yes, Master Isaac."

"Can you tell me anything about him? Why he wanted the money? His name? What he looked like?"

"He did not give his name, Master Isaac. But he was a thin man, with long limbs and a face like a weasel. You know, strong, pointed nose, sunken cheeks, low forehead and little, sharp eyes, but merry ones. I was inclined to like the man. He asked me if I were interested in maps."

"Maps?" said the physician.

"Yes. He was a mapmaker, he said, and could make me a map to somewhere I was longing to go. I told him I had no need of maps. I am no traveler, and the roads I do travel, I know."

"What was his reaction?"

"He thanked me most politely, said he had been misinformed, and apologized for taking up my time. A pleasant man. A foreigner, I think."

"Castilian?"

"Yes."

Since Master Luis Mercer lived not far from Rodrigue's tavern, Oliver bent his steps in that direction. Judging by the amount of noise issuing from the open door, trade was brisk among workers fortifying themselves for another three or four hours of labor in the cool of the evening. He mounted the staircase and found himself a place at the end of a long trestle table. "What do you want?" said a big, handsome woman who had appeared so silently from the kitchen that he had not noticed her entrance.

"Are you the owner of this establishment?"

"I am Ana, wife of Rodrigue."

"A plate of soup, mistress," said Oliver quietly, "a cup of wine, and a minute of your time."

"The soup and wine will be here in a moment," she replied

in a voice just as soft. "My time is my own. I don't give it away, and I certainly don't sell it to lords from the palace." She left and was back in a moment with soup fragrant with spices, some bread, and a cup of wine.

"I beg, then, instead of asking, for that moment. As a pious act for a friend who is dead," murmured Oliver.

"My friend or yours?" she asked.

"Mine. Pasqual Robert. A man named Martin, now dead from a festering wound, was looking for someone named Luis. I know Martin was following Pasqual. He had been following him all the way from Castile. I also know he didn't kill him. This Luis may know who killed Pasqual and why."

"I will sell you the information you want," said Mistress Ana.

"Excellent," murmured Oliver. "For how much?"

"A candle," said Ana. "When you light a candle for Pasqual, who was a good man, light one for a sinner named Baptista."

"I swear it," said Oliver.

"Then come into the kitchen when you have finished your soup."

"Martin came in on a Saturday. Business was brisk, and everyone very cheerful. He stood in the middle of the room and said he was looking for a Luis—he didn't know which one—but this Luis was a man who wanted a piece of merchandise and could afford to pay him a hundred sous for it. Well, there were two men named Luis in the room. He had a long conversation with each. One of them is here now. He has red hair, thin on top, and is a big man, although not as big as you, señor. Is that worth a candle for Baptista?" Her bold eyes challenged him to ask a question, but he merely nodded.

"It is well worth the candle I shall light for him and the mass I shall have said for Baptista's soul, mistress. Thank you." He slipped out of the kitchen and found himself a space beside the redheaded Luis.

• • •

"Well, it's an odd thing," said Luis, "since you ask. This Martin takes me to one side and asks if I am the man named Luis who is willing to pay a hundred sous for what has been written down on a small piece of paper. And I say there's writing I'd pay that for, but I'd expect the words to be on parchment."

"What did he say?"

"He says it doesn't matter what it's written on. It's more like information. Information that will lead me to something I really want. Now, sir," he said, "what you likely don't know is that I'm a butcher. A good butcher. And since my master died, leaving no heirs, I'm seeking a license to open my own shop on the premises. His license is available now, you see. I would pay any man a hundred sous who could get me that license," he added, leaning back and shaking his head.

"And very naturally, since you had your mind on your license, you believed that was what he was talking about," said Oliver. "I can understand that."

"I did, sir. That's me, I says. And he reaches into his tunic and takes out a piece of paper with lines drawn all over it. He puts it down and says, this is half of it. I says, half of what? 'Half of the map,' he says, 'give me the hundred sous, and I'll give you both halves. I followed him all the way from Zaragoza right to the place you're looking for, and I know how to follow people, even tricky ones like him.' So instead of giving this information to his master, he says, he's willing to sell it to me. I tell him he has the wrong Luis—I want a license for a butcher's shop—he apologizes and off he goes."

"Thank you," said Oliver. "And I wish you success with your license."

"We have three versions of Martin of Tudela's behavior," said Oliver the next morning. "At least one of them is full of lies."

"Was that because Martin's approach to each man was so different?" asked Berenguer, frowning. His physician was seated on a stool in from of him, manipulating his knee and massaging the sore muscles around it.

"Yes. One man said Martin was looking for a man with

a certain appearance, another that Martin was a craftsman, a mapmaker, and the third said he was selling information."

"All three could be telling the truth," said the physician suddenly. "A shrewd man tailors his approach to suit his audience. For instance, I explain carefully to His Excellency the importance of a balanced amount of rest and exercise in dealing with his troublesome knee, but I merely scold Caterina, the sweetmeat seller, and tell her to get off her lazy bottom for a similar condition."

"Which approach works better?" asked Oliver, laughing.

"Neither, my lord," said Isaac. "They both ignore me."

"But I appreciate knowing why my troubles recur," said Berenguer. "In knowledge there is power. Did you learn anything else?"

"Having had fair success with Benedicta and Mistress Ana at the taverns, and with Luis Mercer, I went on to my lists, which the parish clerks had prepared with commendable haste."

"And?" asked the Bishop.

"Confusion," said Oliver. "Some had been approached; some had heard about it from others; each one had a different reason for Martin's approaching him. Not even the sum remained the same. But at least half of the Luises had not been seen by Martin of Tudela at all. And there could be several reasons for that."

"He became too ill to carry on with his search," murmured Isaac.

"That's possible," conceded Oliver. "But Mother Benedicta insisted that he had acquired a good sum of money since he arrived in the city."

"So I heard," said Isaac.

"That leaves the possibility that he found his customer."

"For what?" asked Isaac. "What was he selling?"

"That map," said Oliver. "What else?"

"The first difficulty is that he did not sell it," said Isaac. "Mother Benedicta found it among his possessions. Although he could have made a copy. The other and greater difficulty is what is it a map of?"

"I shall study it with great care," said Oliver, rising to his feet. "I bid you both good morning."

"Where are you going, my friend?" asked the Bishop.

"To find six or seven notaries," replied Oliver. "And should Your Excellency need a butcher to take up that license, I would like to recommend one Luis, of this city." He bowed and left.

FIFTEEN

The day the galley left, the Queen's ladies were abuzz over the death of Don Manuel. "Was he ill?" asked Doña Tomasa.

Doña Elvira de Vilafranca looked up from her embroidery. "Don Manuel? No. He had recovered long since from the fever. My maid says he had been with a friend who left this morning for Valencia. They drank a good deal of wine and were very cheerful. But when his servant went in this morning to wake his master, there he was, in his chair, cold and stiff." She lowered her voice. "There was something in his wine, and it is thought he did away with himself, but his servant doesn't believe it, my maid says. His servant thinks his companion poisoned him."

"Who was his companion?" asked Clara idly.

"Gueralt de Robau. Handsome. A second son, no prospects," summed up Doña Elvira. "My cousin's niece sighed over him once. Her father quickly married her to someone with more to offer. Do you know him?"

"No," said Clara. "We passed him on the road to Barcelona, traveling with his father."

"What did you think of him?" asked Doña Elvira. "I'm curious after the fuss in my family. Is he that handsome?"

"Handsome enough, but too full of jests and questions,"

she said, picking up her work. "And he didn't recognize His Excellency the Bishop of Girona's colors," she added.

"Very odd," said Doña Elvira. "Your guardian's colors are so well known."

Having discovered their first real information about Doña Clara, the ladies turned to Doña Elvira with a rustle of satisfaction. "What else did you hear about Don Gueralt?"

"Do you think I should repeat this wheel on the other panel of the skirt?" asked Clara. "Or do another of the same size in gold, with different animals?"

Their attention caught again, the ladies spent the next twenty minutes in earnest contemplation of the trim on Her Majesty's gown. When a decision was made, they had forgotten Don Manuel and Gueralt de Robau.

"You are a clever woman, Doña Clara," murmured Tomasa, picking up her work. "But someday I'd like to hear what that was about. I have excellent reasons for wishing to be your friend."

By daybreak of the third day of the voyage, Yusuf felt like an experienced physician and traveler, with two dozen patients doing well under difficult conditions. By tierce, his confidence began to feel misplaced. Crosswinds set the galley rolling and pitching, and he clung to a railing, queasily aware of breakfast. "Are we heading into storms?" Yusuf asked the nearest sailor.

"No, sir," said the sailor. "Fine weather as far as you can see. As we near the islands, the winds get a bit contrary. But don't worry. We'll make it into port in fine form, I'd say."

The steersman grinned. "Don't believe him. But you'll get used to that roll, about the time it stops happening." And bursting into laughter, he went back to his steering.

At that moment, Don Ramon de Ruisech's manservant appeared at his elbow. "Young master," he said. "It's my lord. He's very bad this morning. I can't get him to take that mixture, sir."

"It's the weather. It affects everyone," said Yusuf.

"I don't think it's that, sir. You must come and see him."

"I'm coming now," said Yusuf. "Let me get my basket."

He lurched to the cabin for his basket and headed toward Don Ramon.

He was desperately ill.

Yusuf sat with him, sponging him to lower the fever; he coaxed sweetened herbal drink and a little broth down his throat. But Don Ramon kept nothing on his stomach, and time and again, Yusuf started with water and then the mixture and was unsuccessful. Remembering his master's practice, he put a drop of painkiller from his own supply in water and sponged it on his dry, cracked lips. Don Ramon slept so long that Yusuf feared he had killed him. But when he awoke, he was no better.

While Don Ramon was sleeping, Yusuf fetched pen and ink, and in spite of the movement of the galley, sat outside to write down everything he had done for his patient.

"It astonishes me that you can write in this," said a familiar voice. It was Gueralt de Robau, smiling down at him.

"The writing is not neat, but my patient is sleeping now. Why are you on deck in this weather?"

"I have been helping the poor souls down there," he said. "I needed fresh air. Is that the sad tale of my friend Don Manuel?"

"No," said Yusuf, closing the book. "This is notes on the journey and how I treated the sick so far. What sad tale?"

"I pride myself on my discrimination," he said, with a sardonic grin. "And Don Manuel has just dealt it a powerful blow. Do you know that he was never a page in Lord Pere's household? I admire a man who can tell a tale," he added lightly, "but I think he went too far. I used to ask him about life there. I finally realized he knew less about Valencia than I did."

"What did you do when you found out?"

"Do?" he said. "Nothing. He was a friend, Yusuf. Fortunately, I was to leave the camp the next day, and so I swallowed my lesson and boarded the galley. It has been painful."

"Why leave?" asked Yusuf. "You don't seem at all sick."

"Orders," he said carelessly. "I will be returning when—"

But the manservant called before he could finish. "He's stirring, sir."

Yusuf wedged book and pen under a pile of rope, corked the ink, and shoved it in as well. "Until later, señor," he said.

Don Ramon moved restlessly but did not respond to attempts to wake him. "Keep his face and hands cool," said Yusuf at last. "And his lips moistened with water. I'll be back."

"And then, Lord Pere," he said, "when I came out, I could not find my book. The ink was there, and the pen, but not the book."

The two, man and boy, were seated on the deck in a sheltered spot near the companionway. "What was in the book?" asked Lord Pere, leaning back and letting the sun play on his face.

"Tales . . . deeds of knights in faraway places and stories of love and magic. I have been keeping a diary on the blank pages."

"What do you talk about in your diary?"

"My patients, their treatment, and the outcome. And weather and events on the voyage."

"Do you repeat what you have heard in His Majesty's tent?"

"Certainly not. He said that no word I heard in that tent was to be repeated."

"Even in another tongue?"

"Many men are more skilled than I in reading it," he said.

"Do you repeat what you hear men say on the ship?"

"Only a few things the sailors tell me about boats," said Yusuf. "They are not as easy to remember. Everything else is in my head only. So there is no reason for anyone to steal the book. Perhaps I put it away carelessly and it went over the side."

"Not if your ink and pen are still there," said Lord Pere. "Everyone on board, of course, thinks His Majesty placed you here to spy on us. I expect that once someone has read your account of our voyage, the book will be returned to you." He yawned.

"Do you think I am a spy?" asked Yusuf.

"Aren't we all, one way or another? I shall walk from the boat to the shore," he said. "I grow stronger by the day."

SIXTEEN

On Saturday morning, the twenty-third of August, the galley sped into the harbor at Valencia under sunny skies. As Lord Pere Boyll had predicted, Yusuf's book had turned up the morning before, shoved carelessly under an oar that was being repaired. And as he had also predicted, he was able to step onto land as nimbly as if he had never been ill, although the pallor of his face made Yusuf wish that he had allowed himself to be helped.

Unloading the rest of the passengers was a slow and difficult business. In the middle of them all, Don Gueralt de Robau went from one to another, helping here, jesting lightly there. "Are you staying long in Valencia, Yusuf?" he asked, as the sailors lowered the last sick man over the side.

"No, señor," he said. "I return to Barcelona as soon as I can. And you?"

"I go back with the fleet," he said. "Until it sails, I will stay here. It will be a welcome change. But it is time for us to disembark now. Take care."

"You are to come with me, Yusuf," said Lord Pere, who had been waiting for him with grooms and two horses. "And I am to take care that you are on a galley for Barcelona as soon as possible."

"Where are we going?" asked Yusuf, as they rode through the shady streets.

"To the palace," said Pere. "We are to report there."

"I am not certain that I have anything important enough to report," said Yusuf.

"Even that should be mentioned," said his guide. They rode on in silence until they reached the palace steps. "We will go into the Great Hall," he said. "Do you remember it?"

"No," said Yusuf, as the doors to the Great Hall opened in front of them and he stopped dead. "I cannot go into that place," he said, turning deadly pale.

"Of course you can," said Lord Pere, grasping him by both shoulders and pushing him inside. "Look at it. It is just a room. What do you see?"

"They have changed it. It used to be bigger," said Yusuf. "Every sound echoed in here before."

"It has not changed, Yusuf, you have."

He looked at the end of the room, under the great windows through which the summer sun was dancing. His eyes followed the sun down to the tiles. They were covered in a huge pool of bright red blood and the stench of blood and death invaded his nostrils. "It is still there, Lord Pere," he whispered. "The blood is still there," and was overcome with blackness.

When he opened his eyes, he was being held upright by a pair of strong hands. "There is nothing on that floor," said Lord Pere. "Your father's blood has been cleaned long since from the tiles. Look at them."

He looked again. The blue and white tiles sparkled with cleanliness; a summer breeze scented with flowers drifted through the high-ceilinged room. "It's gone. What happened?"

"It's been gone for many years," said Lord Pere. "I think he can stand by himself now," he said to the servant who was supporting Yusuf. "Come with me, and we will sit in the courtyard." He murmured something further to the servant and ushered the boy into a space graceful with fountains and orange trees and green shrubs. "I was quite young in His Majesty's service that year—long graduated from the position of page, but still skimpy in the beard—when your father arrived with you. You charmed everyone, especially our late Queen Leonor. You were a beautiful child with the manners of an accomplished courtier."

"I often wonder why my father brought me," said Yusuf. "I must have been a burden to him."

"You were one of the reasons that he came," said Lord Pere. "You were to be a page in His Majesty's household."

"A page? To His Majesty?"

"Yes. That is why His Majesty feels such responsibility for you," said Lord Pere. "You were a small pledge in an accord between Granada and Aragon, part of an attempt to bring peace to the border lands as a hedge against Castilian power."

"A hostage," said Yusuf.

"No. Not a hostage. You would not have lost your head if the Emir had disappointed His Majesty. Your father was caught in the uprising and killed before you joined the household. We believed that you, too, were dead, although your body was not found. It is a miracle you survived the blood-bath. You must have been quick."

"I remember running. And hiding, again and again, until I was in the countryside," said Yusuf. "I was found by a traveling entertainer. He taught me the language of the country."

"Your father was a gracious man and a great warrior," said Lord Pere. "I was much saddened by his death and filled with joy when I heard his son had been found. Now we will refresh ourselves with food and drink and then report to the secretary of His Majesty's procurator."

When Lord Pere Boyll and Yusuf were ushered into the study, His Excellency, Huc de Fenollet, Archbishop of Valencia and His Majesty's procurator for the kingdom of Valencia, was seated with his secretary and several assistants. He was gaunt and exhausted looking, but greeted them with a courteous smile.

"My lord," said the Archbishop. "You are the last person I had expected to see here at the palace. I was told that you were more dead than alive when you left the ship this morning."

"Happily, Your Excellency," said Boyll, "that report was exaggerated. But I hope that we find you in better health."

Fenollet gave a slight shake to his head. "My health is of little consequence. What news do you bring of His Majesty? We have had reports . . ." His voice faded and stopped.

"His Majesty is recovered. His illness was an attack of his old enemy, the ague," said Boyll. "He is once more directing the affairs of the war."

"I am most relieved to hear you confirm that. The kingdom has joined in prayers for his health. But Ramon de Ruisech?"

"Very grave, Your Excellency. We carried him to shore."

"He was to return at once to Sardinia with six galleys, fully armed and stocked," said the Archbishop wearily. "We have been laboring ceaselessly to prepare and man them."

"Are they ready?" asked Lord Pere, turning to the secretary.

"They will be, my lord," he said, "by the time he recovers."

"Will he recover, lad, do you think?" asked Lord Pere.

"My lord," said Yusuf. "Those who are now dead were this ill. I regret I am not skilled enough to say more."

"Who is this, my lord, who speaks like a physician?" asked Fenollet. "Your page?"

"His Majesty's page, Your Excellency, Yusuf ibn Hasan."

"Young Hasan," said the Archbishop. "There were rumors that you had been found." He studied the boy intently for a moment. "I am delighted to discover that they were true. You are the mirror of your noble and valorous father," he added with courtly grace. "But the news you bring about Don Ramon is most unsettling."

"It is," said Boyll. "He has other unsettling news he heard on Sardinia if it will not weary Your Excellency."

"Let us hear it."

"Many men of rank are ill, but His Majesty's forces have been weakened by others who are fleeing the island," said Yusuf, "or attempting to."

"Why?"

"Some said that we had not the means to pursue a prolonged siege and therefore the war was useless. Some said they had not escaped the plague only to die of the fever.

Some argued that there was no profit to be made, even if they did take the city. And some said that His Majesty was too weak to rule and that the kingdom would be better off in other hands."

"Treason," said the Archbishop quietly. "On all counts, but especially the last."

"I would not take off a man's head for grumbling about the boredom of sieges or even about dying of fever," said Boyll. "Not if he is willing to follow His Majesty into battle."

"True, it is not a capital offense to grumble, but their private discontents should be kept to themselves," said Fenollet. "What more can you tell us?"

"Only that His Majesty believes someone is spreading the discontent, Your Excellency. In the morning, gentlemen in a section of the camp would be occupied in passing the time, and by dinner they would be talking of ways and means to leave and return home. I heard someone suggest—in a half-jesting manner—that they should sham illness, because he had heard that those who were ill would, if they desired it, be sent home. Some of those in the galley were shamming illness."

"They were, Your Excellency," said Boyll. "I would be tempted to have them watched, except that I think you would find them living comfortably in the arms of wife and family, having decided they did not enjoy war."

"Who was behind this, stirring up discontent?"

"His Majesty suspected Don Manuel de—"

"In that case, the problem is solved," said the Archbishop. "Don Manuel was poisoned the night before you left. Perhaps by his own hand. It was in yesterday's dispatches."

"Don Gueralt de Robau told me on shipboard he had discovered that his friend had deceived him," said Yusuf. "He seemed distressed about it. But he did not know of his death."

"His body was not discovered until after the galley left," said the secretary. "A faster ship than yours brought the news."

"We will need a report on that conversation," said Fenollet. "But now—" His words were cut off by a prolonged fit of coughing. His attendant came in, and everyone rose.

"His Excellency must rest now," said the secretary. "Is it

young Hasan's passage to Barcelona that I am asked to arrange?"

"It is, Father," said Boyll. "The lad is to be returned to Girona, to Don Berenguer de Cruïlles, as soon as possible."

"It shall be arranged."

SEVENTEEN

Oliver spent a week of monotony and frustration before returning empty-handed to Berenguer the following Monday. He had visited every notary in Girona. He had waited while each one had searched for records of a marriage contract between a woman whose name started in *S* and Pasqual, or Robert, or Gil in the ten years before Clara's birth.

He found Robert, married to Sibilla, and Pasqual, married to Salvadora. Pasqual was a joiner, said to be an excellent cabinetmaker. He had lived in the city all his life and had recently done work for the notary. Robert and his wife had both died in the plague. It was time to take his leave of the Bishop. "It is possible, Your Excellency," he said, "that Pasqual married or was betrothed before he was fourteen years old. Or that they married after Clara was born. But I think it unlikely."

"Both these things happen," observed Berenguer. "More frequently than you might think."

"I will try searching in Barcelona. If I discover nothing there, Your Excellency will see me again quite soon."

"Then I will be in the unhappy situation of finding joy in your failure," said Berenguer, laughing. "I do not know whether to wish you success or not."

Tuesday morning, Oliver hired four young and temporarily

idle clerks to ask the same questions of the notaries of Barcelona. He would attack the problem of Clara himself.

Her ex-employers' house was on a quiet street near the edge of town. It was no palace, but it was substantial; the family was doing well, thought Oliver. The street was deserted except for two boys playing a game that involved throwing stones into circles drawn in the dry dust. "Who lives in that house?" Oliver asked them, as he studied its massive, gray gloominess.

"Which one, señor?" asked one of the boys.

Oliver pointed.

"Señora Vicent," he said. "She's a witch," he added with relish. "She comes out and screams at us, and then sends someone to chase us away. But we like the cook."

"I'm looking for Clara," he said. "I was told I would find her here."

"Gone," said the other boy. "The señora sold her. That's what everyone says. Ask her," he added, with a snort of laughter. "That's her." He pointed to a sturdy-looking woman walking quickly along the street, followed by a maid with a basket.

"She looks fierce enough," said Oliver, winking at them. "I'll try the cook instead," he added, tossing a pair of pennies to the boys and going to the gate that led to the kitchen.

His big frame blocked the open door and cast a shadow across the kitchen. The cook whirled around, her face scarlet. "What do you want?" she snapped.

"Clara," said Oliver, stepping aside to let the light fall on his face. "They told me at the convent she was here." He smiled disarmingly. "Your mistress is out, and so I came this way. May I ask what is in that *olla* with the heavenly scent?" he said, pointing at the substantial pot simmering on the fire.

"Just what you'd expect, if you knew anything," she said. The words squeaked out through clenched teeth. "Shoulder of mutton, sausages, garlic, onions, and herbs."

"There's more than that," said Oliver firmly. "Anyone can put those in."

"A few spices," she admitted. "Ginger and other things."

She was alone in the large kitchen, surrounded by dishes

in various stages of preparation. She was turning the spit as she talked, leaving it to check the *olla* and stir a sauce.

Oliver took over the spit. "A haunch of young goat," he said, sniffing in admiration. "How do you prepare it?"

"At prime I rub it with oil, salt, spices, and herbs. At sext I put it on the spit," she said, and since Oliver was still turning, she went over to the table and began cutting up greens. "But if you really came for Clara and aren't just trying for a taste of dinner, you're too late," she said. "She's gone."

"Gone?" he said. "I don't understand. Where to?"

"Run off, the mistress says. I wouldn't know, myself."

"Is that why you're alone in the kitchen, doing everything?" he asked. "In a grand house like this, you'd expect the cook would have at least two or three to help her."

"Well, that's the problem, isn't it?" said the cook, putting down the knife and turning to look at him. "That haunch of goat you're turning is for dinner. The master is particularly fond of kid," she added. "And it doesn't bother me since he gives me extra to buy it." She started chopping a great pile of freshly picked herbs. "The price of goat on the market these days is beyond belief, but what he pays for, he gets. As everyone knows, she won't even spend what he gives her. I don't know what she's saving it up for."

"I had heard something of her," admitted Oliver.

"She's famous for her pinchpenny ways. The *olla* is for supper and for tomorrow, since it's laundry day, and I won't be able to cook." She picked up her knife again and began to chop as if her mistress were lying on the board, being turned into a fine mince. "How we're to manage laundry day without an extra person in the house, I don't know."

"If such an excellent cook is expected to do everything, I am surprised your mistress does not fear to lose you."

She looked faintly pleased. "I am a trained cook, and I expect to work hard. I'm strong, and I don't mind it. But when I came here, I thought I'd be cooking, not doing laundry. I don't mind giving a hand here and there when I can, yes, but the mistress expects . . ." She shook her head, as if what the mistress expected was too terrible to reveal.

"Why did Clara run off?" asked Oliver.

"I didn't say she did. Why do you want to know?"

And once again, Oliver presented himself as her long-lost, seafaring cousin. "The nuns sent me here, hoping that you would be able to help me find her."

"Well," said the cook, "first of all, it wasn't what you think. I mean, when a girl runs away, tongues wag, but here there were problems." And she told him again with gusto the story of the master and his sudden passion for the girl. "The mistress knew about it and wasn't pleased. And to tell the truth, although she's a sweet girl, and I'm fond of her, she wasn't the best kitchen maid in Barcelona. Willing and clever, but it's heavy work, and she wasn't used to it."

"So she ran away? Because the master pressed her and the work was too hard?"

"It wasn't that. She's a brave thing, you know. But someone offered the mistress five hundred sous to buy the girl. I heard him. Something had to be done. I didn't want her carried off to a heathen land to become the plaything of some rich man with a dozen wives who might do the lord knows what to her. She's a good child," she added, "for all she couldn't build a kitchen fire or boil a pot of water when she arrived here. But the mistress hated her, and she told the man he could have her, but he'd have to wait a few days until the master left for Mallorca."

All this Oliver had heard before, although from Clara's point of view, and not so freely spoken. But the cook continued, and when he heard what she was saying, he stopped turning the spit and turned to look at her.

"She *is* a good girl, you know. The master wanted to set her up as his mistress, in a house of her own, with clothes and jewels and servants, and she would have none of it. I heard him saying that, too, and her answer. Then she came to me in tears, and I told her he wasn't such a bad man, and I didn't think he'd try to force her, but you never knew, and she shouldn't stay anywhere alone with him. From then on, she shared my bed. She was safe there, with me on the outside between the door and her."

One glance at the cook's powerful arms would convince anyone of that, thought Oliver. "I am sure she would be safe with you, mistress."

"You probably haven't seen your cousin since she was a child, but she's turned into quite a beauty."

"Her mother was a beauty," said Oliver. "I'm not surprised she's taken after her."

The goat began to smoke. The cook shrieked, "Boy!"

A loutish lad who seemed to be about fourteen came into the kitchen. "I've got a name," he grumbled.

"Do you?" the cook asked. "Can you remember it? Can you remember what you were hired for?"

"Don't shout at me," he said sullenly and began turning the spit. "Everyone shouts at me. You, and the mistress. Everyone. And I heard you talking about that Clara. I want to know what's being done about my tunic that she stole. It was my second-best tunic, and it was worth something."

"Shut your mouth," said the cook. "That tunic is so small you couldn't use it to keep your idle tongue covered, much less the rest of you."

"But it was mine—"

"It belongs to the mistress," said the cook. "Go and tell her you want another—"

Since this argument seemed likely to carry on until dinner, Oliver put a small purse filled with coins into the cook's hand. "To thank you for looking after my cousin," he said and slipped out the door.

The cook pulled open the purse strings and looked inside. "See that," she said to the boy, holding up the purse. "If you'd ever been kind to the girl, I would give you some of it. But you weren't. Ever. And God knows that's the truth."

Oliver learned nothing from the cook but that Clara was truthful—a useful piece of information, but no help in his search for Pasqual's elusive wife.

With a sigh for that exquisitely roasted kid on the spit, Oliver ignored those houses with equally inspired cooks where he knew he would be welcomed and turned toward a commonplace tavern and eating house. He had invited his small force of clerks to join him there to let him know how their searches were progressing.

Their meeting place had two virtues. For one, it was centrally located. In addition, its soup was flavorless, its bread

damp, and its wine raw. Because of this, those who knew it
avoided it, and it was quiet and uncrowded. The soup disappeared, and his hungry employees had downed a good
third of a dish of lentils, garlic, and tough mutton tasting
unpleasantly of rancid fat before Oliver asked them about
their researches.

"I have seen four notaries in my district already," said the
first through a mouthful of bread, lentils, and mutton.

"Four?" said Oliver. "How is that possible? In Girona I
was lucky to deal with two in a day, much less four in a
morning. Are they looking, or are you allowing yourselves
to be chased away?"

"Certainly not," said the one sitting next to him. "But
someone else has asked for records of dower property in the
Girona area. My notaries knew what existed and were most
suspicious at having two such searches. They were particularly unhappy because I knew less than my predecessor."

"You were in a part of the city where the rich and discreet
notaries live," said the first. "They are paid to be suspicious.
From what I heard, this stranger was searching for the same
settlement. If I had had a full purse, I almost certainly could
have found out more," he said meaningfully.

"I got some of it," said the one sitting across from them.
"But you know what part of town I drew. It cost me fourpence from the boy who does the sweeping and makes up
the fire."

"What did you find out?"

"The *S* is for Serena or Sereneta, and the property lies
somewhere between Hostalric and Girona. That was all the
boy heard before he was sent out."

"Did you find out who came around asking these questions? What reason he gave? What he looked like?"

They looked at each other. "I didn't even find out there
was another person," said the second clerk. "But I realized
quickly that they had recently gone through their records.
Everything was where it could be found, and they were prepared to tell me the answer to my question right away. I
deduced the existence of another person. The notary himself
was suspicious."

"I can imagine that," said Oliver. And after reimbursing

the one who had spent his own fourpence and supplying them
all with sufficient coins to oil the tongues of apprentices, he
sent them out again.

He walked through the heat of midday to the house outside
Barcelona where he had first taken Clara. Avoiding the main
entrance, he went in through a narrow gate, around the house,
and straight into the kitchen.

"My lord," said the cook. "We didn't expect you. Have
you eaten?"

"Food has been poured onto a plate and put in front of
me," he said, "but I have not eaten. Anything will do, as long
as it is not soup made from water, a dried-out onion, and
mutton that has died from old age, having run from Perpi-
gnan to here."

She shook her head and set a plate of cold baked fish with
sauce in front of him. Beside it was an array of fruits,
cheeses, and cold meats, along with a freshly baked loaf. "If
you had come earlier," she said meaningfully. "Or I had
known . . ."

"Yes, Gabriela," he said, dipping a piece of fish into the
sauce. "But I swear to you this is honey dripping from the
comb and the finest wines of the earth compared to what I
didn't dine on. Who is home at the moment?"

"No one," she said, "but for your cousin. I baked the fish
for him, but he hardly eats enough to feed a sardine."

"I may be here for a few days, but don't make it into a
great event. I'll just slip up to my room through the kitchen
door."

"Of course, my lord."

"Wake me before vespers," he added.

The day before, he had left Girona before dawn, stopping at
various places and talking to a variety of people before reaching Barcelona just as most of its citizens were finishing late
suppers. He spent a good part of the night at the palace talking over what he had and had not found during his absence,
slept briefly at the palace, and set out on the morning's mission.

Now he slipped up the back stairs of his cousin's house

to a chamber that was kept for him, fell on the commodious and comfortable bed, and was asleep almost before he landed.

As the bells rang for vespers, he emerged from the side of the building washed, changed, and looking like a respectable gentleman. In his head was a list of the notaries that his searchers were sure had been visited before.

"No, my lord," said the first. "You are certainly not the first to inquire about Doña Serena's dowry provisions. Even today some raggedy clerk came in asking my apprentice what he knew of it. But a notary does not make common gossip of his client's affairs. This is not something that I would discuss with anyone, even if I knew what they were."

Since Oliver had known many a notary who had done just that, he was not impressed. "I only seek information about this mysterious other person who interests himself in my family's affairs. Was this ragged clerk the first to come in?"

"No. Another clerk was in three or four weeks ago, perhaps, asking the same kinds of questions. But the answer was the same. I did not have the honor of drawing up a marriage settlement for a Doña Serena and—I cannot remember the name he gave for the other party to the settlement."

"But you remember that her name was Serena?"

"My late and beloved wife bore that name," said the notary stiffly. "I am not likely to forget it."

"I regret bringing such an unhappy recollection into your mind, sir," said Oliver. "Would you remember what that first clerk looked like?"

"Nothing to describe. He looked like a clerk. Very ordinary. He said he was employed by a notary in Girona, who had sent him to find out if the document existed. His master had been informed that I had drawn it up. He was misinformed."

The second notary had disappeared since that morning, no doubt having decided that a hot day in August was no time to return to his labors in the evening.

The third notary had been approached by a different person. "No, my lord," he said, "it was not a clerk who came to see me. It was a gentleman. This Doña Serena was his cousin. She died several years ago, and the documents relating to her dowry have been lost. There is a considerable property at stake, it seems. He was searching for the names of witnesses to the documents or any other information I might have."

"Were you able to supply these?"

"Certainly not, my lord. I asked him if the lady had left a will, and he said that when the plague first came to Girona, she prudently made a will, fearing that she might die. Not only did she succumb to the plague, but her notary did as well, and the document disappeared. A more distant relative, he said, claimed to have found witnesses to the will who said all her property went to him, but that seems hardly likely."

"He told you all that?" said Oliver.

"Poor man," said the notary. "It is a difficult business, and I suppose he felt better for having explained it to me. He was hoping that I had drawn up the dower settlement, since the lady came from Barcelona, and might have had a record of the terms. If I had drawn it up," he added, "I would have had a record, but I didn't. You would no doubt be surprised, my lord, at the number of people whose affairs are in this same state as a result of the plague. It continues to complicate our lives even now, after the first devastation, we pray, has ended."

"I had not thought of it that way, sir," said Oliver.

"And what is your interest, my lord, in the case?"

"I am troubling you in the interests of the lady's only child," said Oliver. "I would imagine that the property, once we establish Doña Serena's right to it, will be the child's without question."

The notary chuckled. "And so both sets of grasping cousins will be left in the cold," he said. "My visitor did not seem to know of the existence of the child. A son?"

"Yes," said Oliver. "A son of the marriage."

The last notary for that evening had his dwelling place a little too close to the harbor to be a likely candidate to hold documents relating to a substantial marriage settlement, but the young spy Oliver had sent there had said that the office had been visited, and that he thought the apprentice might be amenable to the clink of silver into his palm.

The room in which he pursued his occupation was small, dark, hot, and stuffy. The notary himself was not there, and the apprentice looked as if he'd rather not be. "The master's gone for the evening," he said. "And I'm leaving now. Come back tomorrow."

"Very well," said Oliver cheerfully. "But the night is hot, and I am dry as dust. Can you show me a place where we can get a jug of wine? Something better than the vinegar I had at dinner."

"You're buying the wine and inviting me?" he said.

"And supper," said Oliver. "So remember the quality of the food as you choose a place." He pulled out his purse and allowed it to jingle with the heavy, satisfactory sound of one that is full.

"Certainly, señor," he said. "My master is not so generous that I will turn down good food and drink when it's offered."

"Excellent. It's a perfect evening for a stroll."

Once the young man had grasped that Oliver was not looking for an establishment that also offered young women on the menu, he took him to a pleasant spot where the smell of fresh sardines grilling boded well for the evening. Oliver called for a jug of the best wine, ordered a large plate of sardines and various other dishes, raised a cup to his guest, and drank. "Now," he said, pushing two silver groats a third of the way across the table toward him, "let's talk."

The apprentice looked at the money and then at Oliver. "What about?" he asked cautiously.

"About the man who came to visit your master some two or three weeks ago, looking for documentary evidence of a marriage settlement, or of dowry provisions, in the matter of the marriage of one Doña Serena of Barcelona."

"What do you want? A description?"

"We'll start with that."

The apprentice described an ordinary-looking man, dressed well enough, "Like a merchant," said the young man, "who was careless about his clothes. Maybe he didn't have much money. It's hard to tell sometimes."

"His name?"

"Wasn't his," said the apprentice. "He called himself Robert de Finestres, but when I addressed him as Don Robert, he didn't answer. He didn't even notice."

"That's interesting."

"Well, he had to, I think," said the lad. "He wanted all that we knew about Serena de Finestres. He said he was close kin to her, and so what else could he call himself? The master told him he had done a settlement for a lady named Serena. He couldn't remember her family name but he thought it might have been de Finestres. By then, of course, the master had had a few too many cups of wine—not as good as this one, señor—and his memory was uncertain. It seemed he had drawn up a settlement two years ago for another Serena. It wasn't the marriage this Robert was interested in."

Oliver pushed a silver groat over until it slipped under the young man's plate. "Would you know where the property is? The one he was searching for," he said, moving the second groat closer.

"He knew it was between Hostalric and Girona," said the youth. "Off the highroad, he thought, on one of the smaller roads. It would take a long time to inspect every farm along there," he added. "He was hoping that we could tell him exactly where it is. He claims it's his, by right and the lady's will."

"He's wrong," said Oliver, pushing the second groat under his plate. "Should you see him again," he added, "there will be this and more for you. Go to the palace door near the chapel and tell the guard that Lord Oliver sent you. Someone will see you. Tell him what you know." He pushed the third groat across the table. "Otherwise, maintain a discreet silence on the subject."

"Thank you, my lord," he said, scooping up the money.

"Over there are two young men who seem to know you. Perhaps they can help you finish the supper and the wine. Good night."

The crowded streets were alternately bright with moonlight and black as the pits of hell. Dizzy with lack of sleep and a sense of grim foreboding, Oliver's tired brain conjured up images of blood and death; Clara's fragile form, lost in a

ragged brown tunic, became Pasqual's bloodied corpse.
Through his waking nightmare he heard a raw voice with
country vowels. "Hola, señor," said a thin creature in a
skimpy gown. "Come with me. I'll cure your unhappiness."
A passing torch lit up her features, and with a sick feeling
in his belly, he saw that she was only a girl, no more than
thirteen or fourteen.

"Here," he said roughly. "Take this and get off the street."
He thrust money in her hand and strode rapidly through the
drunken seamen and importunate women of the night, taut
with anger at the impotence of his gesture.

His progress was stopped by the balustrade. He had
reached the harbor. Out in the deep water, a galley was still
unloading its cargo, and its passengers were milling around
on the shore. Below him a clear, boyish voice called out his
name. There, outlined in the bright moonlight, he saw a familiar form.

"Yusuf," he called. "Where in the devil's name did you
come from?"

"From Valencia, señor."

"Wait," he said. "I'm coming down."

They sent Yusuf's box and bundle off to the palace and
strolled through the moonlit night.

"His Majesty is well again," said Yusuf. "He tried one of
my master's potions and said that it was helpful," he added
shyly. "But I was not able to discover anything about Mistress Clara. Her Majesty's quarters are most strictly guarded.
I judged it wise not to attempt to get inside."

"Very wise," said Oliver. "As it happens, I have a spy in
their midst who informs me that Doña Clara is well and
happily occupied with her needle. I cannot imagine it, but it
is, no doubt, better than being a kitchen maid. And is that
all that happened to you? Come," he said, "I am weary and
full of useless forebodings. Amuse me with travelers' tales."

Yusuf told him about the tent, and Marc, and treating the
sick. "And Gueralt de Robau came over on the galley with
us. Is that not strange?"

"No," said Oliver. "How many galleys do you think leave
for Sardinia in a day?"

"I saw him often at the camp ... and his strange friend, Don Manuel. Don Gueralt went with us to Valencia. He was pleasant, señor. He helped me in many ways, refusing thanks, saying it relieved his boredom. He is often bored. He was to return here with us, but he was late, and the boat left without him."

"And was Don Gueralt the sum of your adventures? You did not draw your sword in defense of His Majesty?" said Oliver, teasing.

"There were no more of importance," he said, offended.

"Come now, tell me what else happened. I will not laugh."

"Only something that His Excellency the Archbishop said was not important."

"Tell me," said Oliver, stopping and grasping his arm.

Yusuf described the loss of his book and its return again. "They said it must have been a jest, nothing else."

"And Gueralt has disappeared. Watch out for him, Yusuf."

"He is no danger. It is his friend, Don Manuel, who was the danger. But he is dead. How goes your search, señor?"

"Slowly," he said, summing up the clerk's revelations.

"Have you spoken to the nuns who took her in?" asked Yusuf.

"Yes," said Oliver. "They know less than we do. Clara believed she was expected. The sisters said she was not."

"It's odd, señor," said Yusuf, "for a woman of property to send her child off alone, hoping she would be looked after."

"Perhaps her nurse was supposed to take her but didn't."

"Perhaps she went to the wrong nuns," said Yusuf. "It's easy if you're not used to making your own way about a city. I did that once. My old master sent me to deliver a letter to the butcher and collect payment for his work in writing it."

"Yusuf," Oliver began. "What are you talking about?"

"One moment, señor. When the butcher called the officers to throw me out of town, I found out that I'd gone to the wrong butcher. We must find the convent that was expecting Clara."

"Why?" said Oliver. "What good will it do us?"

"They might know more about her mother."

"It pains me deeply to say it, but you may be right, Yusuf," said Oliver with a deep sigh. "We will start on the convents."

"I have learned some skills from Master Isaac," he replied. "Ordering one's thoughts and proceeding with logical arguments."

With the sisters who sheltered Clara as a starting point, Oliver plotted the locations of nearby convents. "If she was sent out alone to find them, they must have been close," said Oliver.

"Close to where, señor? We don't know where she lived."

"Where she ended up," snapped Oliver. It was exasperating, he found, to be goaded into thinking, however usefully, by a lad of twelve or thirteen.

The wide circle surrounding their starting point contained three convents Oliver had not visited and two more where he had asked the wrong questions. At each he talked his way past the portress and inside to seek permission to look at their records. No record existed at ony one of them of a child named Clara. Nor was there a hint that she had been expected.

"Perhaps she went to the right convent," said Yusuf, discouraged.

"There are two farther out," said Oliver, whose ill humor disappeared as the day advanced. "When both deny knowledge of her, I will consider other possibilities."

The portress at the closer of the two gave them a suspicious look, leaving them in the street, and going to seek guidance.

"If she was supposed to come here, her mother had a high opinion of her endurance and her skills," said Yusuf. "This is a long way from where she ended up."

"She may have lived closer to this one," said Oliver.

"Our lady prioress would like to talk to you," said a voice from behind the gate, not the sister portress.

"Is she in your records, Sister?" asked Oliver.

"Follow me," was her response.

"Before I answer any questions, my lord," said the prioress, "tell me what your connection is with Clara de Finestres."

The shrewd inquiring eyes of the lady prioress gave him

fair warning. "To others, Lady Violant," said Oliver, "I have been describing myself as an uncle or a cousin, seeking to settle her mother's estate for Clara's benefit. This is not true. I am here because I am in charge of a destitute fifteen-year-old girl, whose speech and manners lead me to believe that she has a family who might be looking for her." He paused. "I wished to find that family and return her to them."

"Yes," she said. "Go on."

"While searching for her family," he said, choosing his words with care, "and in the course of my duties at court, I came across a painting of a woman so like her that I concluded that she might be her mother. That picture—and other evidence—led me to believe that the woman, her mother, is still alive and living in hiding, for reasons of state having to do with His Majesty's affairs. If she is who I firmly believe her to be, her husband is now dead, and with him dies the need for her to conceal her identity."

"You seek a woman whose existence you can only postulate."

"Yes, my lady. But Clara believes herself to be bereft of family, except for a distant cousin. Her mother believes that her beloved daughter is dead because of her negligence."

"How can you know that, if you have only postulated her existence?"

"I have a letter as well as a painting, both of which I found in my friend's effects. The letter was signed *S*. In it she talks of the death of their daughter. The painting I have here. The child looks so like this woman that they must be closely related." He took out the leather bag that held the portrait, opened it, and handed the smooth piece of wood to the prioress.

She looked at it for a long, long time. "She is very beautiful," she said at last. She handed it back and walked across her study to the window. She stared out into the garden, seemed to make up her mind, and turned briskly back toward him. "But then she always has been beautiful, even when we were children. I do not think I can help you find her, however. I believe she has gone to Mallorca."

"No, Lady Violant. Mallorca was her second line of defense, and the first place I checked. She is too striking in appearance. There is no woman like that anywhere on the island, as far as I can tell. Unless she is working as a housemaid."

The prioress's face broke into a slight smile. "Not likely," she said. "I do have a piece of information that might mean something to you; it means nothing to me. If your boy would wait here with the sister bursar, I will show you the entry."

"Did she tell you anything useful?" asked Yusuf when Oliver joined him again.

"I'm not sure," said Oliver. "But she gave me something."

"What do we do now?"

"Now? We go back to Girona."

EIGHTEEN

When Oliver came down the passage to the Bishop's study late the next morning, he saw a woman, modestly dressed in a dark gown and light veil, seated outside the door. She rose in greeting and curtsied. "Lord Oliver," she said. "Welcome back to Girona."

"Mistress Raquel, is it not?" he said. "The physician's capable daughter."

"I am, my lord. May I ask if you have had word of Yusuf? We miss him sorely, I admit."

"I have better than a word of him," he said. "When you return home, you will find him there able to deliver his own words. I have just left his horse with one of His Excellency's grooms. But why are you haunting the corridors of the palace?"

"I await my father," she said, "who is with his patient."

The door to the study opened, and Bernat came out. "His Excellency begs you to come in, Lord Oliver," he said.

"And what else have you to report of interest, Lord Oliver?" asked Berenguer. "In addition to the most satisfactory news of Yusuf's return to the city and His Majesty's return to health? Have you discovered anything of note concerning the death of Pasqual?"

"I am engaged in a search for a piece of property in your diocese," said Oliver. "If I can find it, I may learn more . . . much more. But I am afraid my search must be done discreetly and quietly. I ask only if I might have the use of one of your excellent mules, since Neta is in Barcelona and my horse's endurance has been harshly tested in the past week."

"Most certainly," said Berenguer.

"If Your Excellency will excuse me," said the physician, "I am most anxious to welcome my wandering apprentice home."

"I will walk out with you, Master Isaac," said Oliver. "I wish to see how my horse is faring."

"Do you need assistance in your search?" asked Isaac politely. "The district contains an abundance of pathways dignified by the name of roads, enough to become confusing. I could recommend—or His Excellency could as well, no doubt—some discreet man who knows these byways well. To assist you."

"I doubt if the most discreet of men could help me," said Oliver. "Unless he were also the cleverest at solving a conundrum."

"A conundrum, my lord?" asked Isaac.

"Yes. I look for property near Girona where one may fall asleep to the sound of the water."

"That sounds more like land near the sea," said Raquel.

"It could be near a fountain, Raquel," said her father. "There are many fountains in the vicinity."

"But the property must also have a beautiful pool with fish and pear trees," said Oliver.

"That sounds like a monastery," said Isaac.

"And what do you know of monasteries, Papa?"

"I have been in more than one, my dear. Even abbots fall ill. Certainly one monastery I visited while I could still see had a large fish pond and many fruit trees. And a fountain. The fountain was a thing of great beauty, although I could not say the same for the fish pond."

"I don't think this is a monastery or even a convent," said Oliver. "I believe it is a farm."

"It could almost be the farm we visited, Papa," said Raquel

dreamily. "The one that was so beautiful. With the little river and the vineyards. And the olives."

"Lacking only a pool or fountain?" said Oliver, amused. "Or pear trees?"

"There was a deep pool where a little waterfall ended," said Raquel. "It made a lovely sound. The water fell onto rocks and then into a pool."

"But no pears."

"There were fruit trees," said Raquel. "Some of them looked like pear trees. On the other hand, it was not that close to Girona, and not at all like the place you described. But it was beautiful," she added, with a sigh. "Except for the house. It was all shuttered as if the owners expected to be attacked."

"That is because the owners do not live there," said Isaac. "A housekeeper and an old man look after it," he added.

"Where is it?" asked Oliver casually.

"Just beyond the place where we stopped to eat and then parted with you on the day Yusuf left," said Raquel. "If you had looked back, you would have seen us turning."

Lord Oliver left Girona before dawn the next day, Friday, and rode south under a waning moon. When he reached the track a few paces beyond where the road crossed the river, he let his mule pick her own way carefully around ruts and potholes up to the bend in the river. When he saw the pool and the waterfall, he dismounted, leaving the mule where she was.

He walked along the road until he could see the house through its shield of trees. It was silent, shuttered, closed to the world. He left it to slumber peacefully and continued along the far side of the riverbank, away from the house. He meandered with it until he reached a vineyard and a small footbridge that led to it. There he could clearly see footprints angling across the dew-covered grasses of the meadow. Someone had walked over to the bridge and headed for the vineyard. He paused to listen and then followed the line of prints into the vineyard.

A dog barked once, a deep-throated, short, warning bark.

"Hush, Blanqueta," said a soft voice in the vineyard.

Another step and he saw a tall woman with her back to him, inspecting clusters of half-ripened grapes. She was dressed in a simple, dull brown gown of the sort that could be seen on most of the peasant women in the district. Her hair was covered and held back with a kerchief tied over it, and the strings of her apron dangled down the back of her skirt.

He stopped in disgust. He had succeeded in the perilous task of stalking an early-rising farm wife, out on a day that promised heat, starting her work before the sun rose. Cursing himself for becoming enamored with a tale of farms of magical beauty told by a fanciful young woman, he took a step backward, stepped in a hole, and stumbled. The dog began to bark in earnest.

"What is it, Blanqueta?" said the woman, turning around.

The face stunned him, but only for a moment. "Señora," he said very rapidly. "Do not be afraid. Please. My name is Oliver de Centelles. I worked with your husband, whom I knew only as Pasqual Robert, but I knew him and loved him from the time I was eight years of age in His Majesty's Service and he was kind to me when few people were."

"You knew him," she said, the color draining from her face. "Why do you say 'knew'?"

"I do not know a kind or gentle way to say this, señora."

"Then he is dead," she said, grasping an upright around which the grape vines twisted in their climb to the sun. She stared ahead, her eyes focused on nothing. "Over and over I imagined this day, when a man would come and tell me that Gil was dead. He promised he would be back to see me in a week. He didn't come. I should have known then." She walked over to a bench between the rows of vines and sat down, staring at her hands clenched together in her lap. Finally, she looked up. "How did he die?" she asked in a very controlled voice.

"He was murdered, señora. More than three weeks ago."

"What day?" she said.

"Monday. Early in the morning. Monday, the fourth day of August."

"Early in the morning? He had just left my bed," she said.

"It must have made him careless." Her face was frozen and tearless. "Who killed him? The Castilians who were following you?"

"I have been searching for the answer to that question, back and forth from Castile to Barcelona, since the moment he died in my arms. He spoke of you before he died, señora. He said what I believed to be something about serenity, but I now realize was, 'I beg you to tell Serena, my friend.' Then he said, 'It is a jest, a jest . . . the Lord laughs at me. Pray for me, and look after my little ones.' "

"Then he wasn't killed by the Castilians," she said in a flat voice. "He would not have considered that a jest, he would have thought it a failure. He was killed by someone he considered harmless."

"He was stabbed in the back, señora," said Oliver, "clearly by someone he thought posed no threat to him."

"With a dagger?"

"Yes."

"Where was it placed?" she said. "You must tell me exactly."

Oliver pointed to his own back.

"O God in Heaven," she said and dropped her head into her hands as if she could no longer bear the strengthening light of day.

"You are the son of Gilabert de Centelles," she said, looking up at last.

"Yes. My father lived near here, in disgrace, and died when I was eight."

"My husband often spoke of you," she said. "He trusted you as he trusted few other men."

"But he did not trust me enough to reveal your existence, señora," said Oliver. "I had to search long and hard before I found you."

"Who sent you here?" she asked. "I did not think that anyone knew of this place except for our notary, and I would hate to think that he would betray a secret such as that."

"It was certainly not your notary. I visited many notaries, and if one of them was yours, he swore most convincingly with all the rest that he had never heard of you."

"I have no doubt that I will be hearing of this from him, then," she said. "Although it no longer matters," she added in a low voice. "Nothing matters now."

"Señora, the person who inadvertently revealed the existence of this place was one of your oldest friends, prioress of the convent that was to receive your daughter."

"Violant did that?" she whispered and turned her head to one side to shield her face. "I beg you, my lord, do not remind me of more sorrows, not now."

He paid no attention. "And I visited Lady Violant because I was searching for the mother of a fifteen-year-old girl named Clara." Serena began to rise to her feet. He placed a hand on her shoulder and firmly pushed her down again. "Please, señora. Allow me to tell you about her. It is for the moment unimportant how I came across her, but I found myself in the strange role of being her only protector. I placed her immediately in the care of my own childhood nurse, a reliable and honest woman. This Clara claimed to have no family, and no other name, but I assure you her manners and speech betrayed her careful upbringing."

"Must you force me to sit here and endure—"

"I must, señora. I was still searching for her parents when a portrait came into my hands—a portrait of a beautiful woman I had never seen before, but whose true likeness existed in the youthful face of the girl Clara. This is the portrait, señora, and it is of you, is it not? And your child Clara looks very like you, except that she has not your height."

"My lord, are you trying to tell me that she is not dead? Do not torment me. I know she is. I have put flowers on her grave. Clara is dead."

He grasped Serena de Finestres by the shoulders and gave them a shake. "She is alive, señora," he said loudly and vehemently. "Alive and well."

"Clara is?" And suddenly she began to cry, brokenheartedly and helplessly.

"Where is she now?" asked Serena when she was once more in command of herself. "This girl you say is Clara."

"That is rather complicated," said Oliver. "She is at the moment in Sardinia—"

"Sardinia!" said Serena.

"Where she is living among Her Majesty's ladies, as safe and as well protected as if she were in a castle keep guarded by a thousand knights and five thousand bowmen."

"Why is she there?"

"It is a long tale, señora, and I will tell it to you, every word, but now it is enough to say that I feared she might need protection, and I could not think of a better way to bring it about."

"You do not take half measures, señor. Where did you come across her?"

"She was traveling to Girona, hoping to seek help from a kinsman she had been told lived there, if she could find him."

"Fine help he would have been," said Serena contemptuously. "But she would not have found him. He is dead. Long since. He died in the second summer of the plague."

"Are you certain of this?" asked Oliver.

"I am," she said. "I learned of it in a recent letter from my notary. It seems that with his usual stupidity, my cousin fled from his house—where no one died that summer—to a town that was rife with disease."

"You were his only relative?"

"I believe he had married. And certainly he had other cousins. His notary wrote my notary to ask if he knew of family with claims to the estate. He was trying to clear it up at last. I told my notary to deny any knowledge of the connection. But since I received it long after Clara disappeared, she wouldn't have known he was dead."

"She seemed not even to know his name," said Oliver.

"That is possible," said Serena.

Oliver studied the face. The lines that worry and suffering had etched on her forehead were clearly visible in the direct rays of the low sun. She was pale, and her eyes were filled with unshed tears. But in spite of all, she was one of the most beautiful women he had ever seen. She sat very quietly, apparently lost in thought.

At last she raised her eyes. "But if she is alive, as you claim, then tell me what happened to her the day she disappeared," she said.

"I will tell you all the details that I know later, señora," he said. "But as I see it—from what she told me—she became caught up in a large crowd and must have been so confused by the experience that she went to the wrong convent. The sisters were most kind and looked after her," he added.

"The wrong convent!" said Serena. "I cannot believe it. She knew the way to the convent as well as I did. One of our favorite walks was to visit Violant." She stared off into the distance with unseeing eyes for a long time. Oliver stood quietly, not wishing to break into her thoughts. "I went back five days later to get her," she said, looking at him again. "Violant said that she had not come. We inquired everywhere and discovered that a child had died in the streets that day, trampled by a horse. When they gathered up her body, her arms were wrapped tightly around a bundle. They showed it to me, to see if I recognized it."

"Was it hers?"

"Oh, yes. There was no doubt of that. I have it still. Her poor little body had already been given a pauper's grave, but as soon as it was safe for me to do so, I had it moved. What else could I think but that Clara was dead?"

"And so you ceased looking for her," said Oliver. "I can understand now how it happened. I think you should go back to the house, señora," said Oliver. "You look very pale and ill. Do you have a servant who looks after you here?"

She gave him the beginnings of a smile. "Here I have several loyal servants," she said, rising slowly to her feet. "But I forget myself. You must have ridden early and far, Lord Oliver. The kitchen fire was lit when I came out, and my cook should be able to offer you refreshment."

"Señora, please. Do not concern yourself over me. You must look after yourself."

"I cannot think why," said Serena de Finestres, and straightened her back with visible effort. "Let us, in any case, return to the house."

"Of course," said Oliver. He gave her his arm, and they walked slowly back to the house. "I have one thing to say, señora, before you go in. There are questions that only you can answer, and until they are answered, it is possible that neither you nor your daughter nor your son will be safe.

Before I leave, will you try to speak to me of these things I must know?"

She nodded and left Oliver in the care of Dalmau, the elderly manservant.

"Sit down, Dalmau," said Oliver, once he had eaten, "and tell me. Have you been much bothered by visitors seeking your mistress? Or your master?"

"We have, my lord," said Dalmau, pulling over a stool and sitting down. "From time to time. Perhaps three or four times a year. People turn up, alone or in pairs, seeking the master of the house, or the mistress."

"By name?"

"Never the master by name," said Dalmau. "One man came not long ago asking for the mistress by name. We always say the same thing. They are not in residence and we do not know when they will be. We have Blanqueta, but the master insists—insisted, I must say now," he said, crossing himself. "May he rest in peace, for he was a good man, the master was. He insisted that she stay with the mistress, to protect her and the boy."

"He was careful of her safety," said Oliver.

"He was, my lord. The mistress will be hard hit by his death. She loved him dearly."

"That is very true," said Oliver.

"What is very true?" said a voice behind him, and Dalmau rose to his feet.

Oliver turned and rose as well. "Señora. We were talking of what has happened."

"You may go, Dalmau," said Serena. "I fear you won't learn much from Dalmau."

"Enough to convince me that your life could still be in danger. After all, if someone had a personal reason for bringing about your husband's death, and if that person now knows where you live, as he may—"

"Oh no, my lord," said Serena, interrupting him. "You are mistaken. It is not my life that is in danger. It is *his* life. Let the coward come here once more to find me. Just once more, that is all that I ask, and he will discover what it is to die with a knife in his back." Scarlet patches of intense emotion were splashed across the gray pallor of her face and rose up from her neck. Her tear-laden eyes glittered with hostility.

"Señora, listen to me. When I set out to find your husband's assassin, I vowed before leaving Girona that I would present his wife with that man's head. I intend to do that. But first you must hear what I have to say."

That afternoon, Oliver de Centelles arrived at the Bishop's palace in Girona, accompanied by Serena de Finestres, her son Guillem, six years old, and a maid.

"I have sent for the physician," said Berenguer. "Señora de Finestres looks very ill."

"I hope that he can do something to help her," said Oliver. "It would be a sad thing if I had found the child's mother only to have her die of grief before she sees her child."

"But surely you have told her that her daughter is alive, Oliver?"

"I have. She admits that it could be true, but she does not believe it. Not in her heart. She grieves for her husband, whose name was Gil, Your Excellency. Gil de Finestres."

"He must have been the son of Don Francesc de Finestres," said the Bishop. "Ships and shipping."

"You knew him, Your Excellency?"

"I did," said Berenguer. "He was in Mallorca in '43 on His Majesty's side—the man who challenged King Jaume and made him back down. I recollect that one of his sons went into His Majesty's service as a lad, but I had the impression that he had died young."

"No doubt a carefully created impression, Your Excellency. Because when I went off to Zaragoza, his name was Pasqual Robert, and he had been with His Majesty since he was a boy." He walked over to the window and looked out. "The first lesson I learned at the palace was to consider all men—and women—as possible enemies. His Majesty's upbringing was harsher than that of a street urchin."

"His stepmother would have been well pleased if her husband's eldest son had died of some little ailment or other," observed the Bishop.

"But why His Majesty did not exile me from the court when my father turned out to be another rebellious noble has always puzzled me."

"He trusted you," said Berenguer. "His Majesty is prepared to forgive his enemies—most of the time. And rewards loyalty liberally. Your father was contrite and proved it for the rest of his life. He forgave him. You have been loyal. It is very simple."

Oliver suddenly whirled around in a frenzy of impatience. "Enough of this," he said. "Why is it taking the physician so long to get here?"

"My dear lord Oliver," said Berenguer. "He has been here for some time. Let us go and see how our guests are faring."

"She is perfectly healthy," said the physician. "The intensity of her grief prevents her from eating or drinking. That is, at least partially, the reason for her swoon. Raquel is with her and has convinced her to drink some broth and eat a morsel of bread. She needs to sleep, but she tells me that she must speak to you first about what she knows of her husband's deeds."

"If we are to find his slayer," said Oliver. "It is true we must speak to her if she is capable of it."

"She is strong-willed and determined," said Isaac, "and wishes to speak to you. But she is weaker than she believes. I would prefer to stay close while you question her."

"Certainly, my friend," said Berenguer.

"And the lad," said Oliver. "Since she still believes that her daughter is a phantom of my mind. He can reassure her."

Serena was propped up on pillows in a guest apartment in the palace. Her deathly pallor was gone, but her eyes were red with weeping and her face blank with hopelessness. "Señora," said the Bishop, "have you the strength and courage to speak to us now?"

"If it will help to avenge my husband's death, then I have all the strength I need," she said.

They sat around the bed, Oliver and Berenguer to one side, Raquel, Isaac, and Yusuf on the other. Oliver glanced at the Bishop and began. "Señora, I now realize that your husband was visiting you when he disappeared from time to time without any explanation. What I must ask you is whether he said anything in those few days before his death that might help us."

"Yes," she said firmly. "Before he came to the *finca* he was at an inn close by. The first time he tried to come home, he was followed. It didn't surprise him, my lord, because the two of you had been followed all the way from Castile, as you know."

"By Martin de Tudela?" asked Berenguer.

"Yes," said Oliver.

"Not that night," she said. "Not at first. There were two of them. Gil didn't know them and doubled back to find out."

"It must have been Martin and his master, Geraldo," said Oliver. "The two Castilians who followed us."

"Martin's master was no more Castilian than I am, my lord. He was born not far from here and his name is Gueralt."

"Gueralt!" said Oliver. "De Robau?"

"His mother is Castilian," said the Bishop.

"And so that is where he was schooled," said Oliver. "His father said he had just returned from completing his education."

"Where is he now?" said Berenguer.

"He disappeared in Valencia, Your Excellency," said Yusuf, looking stricken. "Even after His Majesty warned me about him, I had not thought him the traitor."

"He must have slipped across the border from Valencia to Castile," said Oliver.

"And then Gueralt left Martin to face your husband alone," said Isaac, ignoring Yusuf's discomfiture. "He could not allow himself to be recognized."

"No, Master Isaac. Gil knew both of them well enough," said Serena, with a touch of impatience, "and indeed, Martin was following him, discreetly, but so were a strange man and his servant—noisily and with little attempt at concealment."

"Gil didn't know who he was?" said the Bishop.

She shook her head. "No, Your Excellency. Nor did Martin."

"It was night," said Berenguer. "Too dark to see."

"The moon was full," observed Oliver. "Bright as day."

"It was, my lord," said Serena. "Martin told the stranger he was lost. He said that a drinking companion had promised him a bed if he came along with him, but that he had lost him in the dark. Martin asked the stranger if he had seen a man on a black horse and, if so, where he was going? The stranger said he'd give a hundred sous to the man who could find out where he lived. He and his servant were looking for him as well. Then Martin said he'd find the house gladly for a hundred sous."

"A hundred sous," said Isaac. "Luis."

"That was all that Gil heard of their conversation," said Serena wearily, "but it was enough. He decided that Martin was becoming too dangerous. He returned to the inn to lead them away from the *finca* for the time being, and the next night he set out again. Martin followed him once more. Only that time Gil lay in wait and attacked him. Then he came to see us for the weekend. He wasn't sure how badly he had injured him."

"He died a week or so later," said Berenguer. "He may have decided to avenge himself before he died—"

"Not likely, Your Excellency," said Isaac suddenly. "The wound was on his sword arm and would have weakened it. By Monday morning he must already have been feeling the effects of the increasing putrefaction. To stalk a man and make a swift thrust like that—a man who is on the lookout for enemies by habit and training—that is not likely."

"I have known badly wounded men to wreak terrible havoc on their enemies at the point of death," said Oliver.

"Indeed, my lord. Such feats by brave men do happen," said the physician. "But they do not creep from their beds, stiff with five-day-old wounds, far from the heat of battle, and ride out to seek vengeance. They wait until they are healed."

"Very true, Master Isaac. Then if not Martin, who?"

A long silence followed Oliver's question. "Who, indeed," said the Bishop.

"May I ask a question?" asked Serena.

"Of course, señora," said the Bishop. "Any question you like."

"How did you find me? We thought I could only be tracked by someone following my husband. Lord Oliver said

that Violant told you, but that is not possible. She knew nothing about the *finca*."

"You told the Lady Violant that if Clara could not sleep,
she was to think that soon she would be where she could
hear the sound of the water and see the pool with the fish
and the pear tree again. She wrote it down so that anyone
else caring for her would know as well."

"And you found it from that?"

"Only after I discovered that my superior officer had a
wife. He kept a letter from you and your picture. I had the
child who looked like you, the letter that talked about the
finca, and the description from the convent. In addition, a
notary's clerk told me it was between Hostalric and Girona.
Having all that, I guessed wildly and was lucky."

"Señora," said the Bishop, "I think we should take steps
as soon as possible to bring your daughter back from Sardinia."

"Your Excellency," said Serena, coldly, "I have heard of
these things, where there are rich estates to be claimed, and
missing heirs turn up by the dozens. I do not think you are
trying to impose on my grief and credulity, but I believe that
the child and whoever instructed her are."

"No, señora," said Yusuf. "I spent several days with Clara.
We talked a great deal. And no matter what we said, she
continued to insist that her mother is dead. And I, too, have
noticed that you look so like her that the resemblance is
amazing."

"I cannot believe it," she said.

"Señora," said Oliver. "Let me read news of her that arrived in the last bag of letters that came to the palace. You
can judge for yourself if she sounds at all like your daughter."

"From whom?" asked Berenguer.

"From my spy," he said. "I told you, did I not, that I had
a spy in the Queen's court. My sister—my half sister, Tomasa, who is in Sardinia, and to whom I wrote. I begged her
to watch out for Clara, and be kind to her, since I thought
she might need a friend after living as she has been living
for so long."

"What do you mean?" asked Serena.

"Please, señora," said Oliver. "Listen. 'My dear brother, your friend has arrived and charms us all. She was bewildered after the voyage and touchingly worried that she had nothing to do, and so she has been helping me with one of Her Majesty's gowns. I made a shift for her, since her underclothes are sadly wanting, and she brought no cloth with her. While I was working, she embroidered one of my wedding shifts for me. You have never seen anything like it. I must insist on having a husband at once who can appreciate such a beautiful and witty piece of work. You will understand me. She is now placing fanciful beasts all over a splendid gown for Her Majesty, and everyone is enchanted with her. She is such a beauty but terribly shy and won't talk to anyone about who she is. Who is she?' and the rest is family gossip," he said.

Serena stared at Oliver as if he had brought the news of a hundred deaths. "Fanciful beasts?" she whispered. She touched Raquel's arm. "Tell Joana to bring me the bundle," she said.

The maid brought in a dusty and mud-stained heap of rags and set it on the bed for Serena to open. Inside the tattered remnants of a shawl was a gown, a child's gown, in a light, summery fabric. "Look," she said. On the sleeves and on the skirt were embroidered elongated, fantastical beasts, that in spite of their small size managed to have expressions on their faces—sly or amused or in the case of one cat, puzzled. "She was so skilled at this," said her mother. "And I spent my time scolding her and trying to get her to mend rips and make shifts before she started to amuse herself by decorating her own clothing."

Raquel picked up the gown and studied it with great interest. "But you bought her the best of silks to work with, señora. You cannot have been very unkind about it," she said.

"This was all I had of her," she said. "The night we fled from the house, a band of drunken louts set it alight."

"Were many hurt?" asked Raquel.

"No," said Serena. "The servants were expecting it, I was told. They left an hour or two before the attack. No doubt carrying all they could hold."

"Then shall I request her return, señora?" asked Berenguer.

"Please," said Serena. "I must see her at once. And I must go back to the *finca*. She should be there with me."

"You cannot go there until we have found the man who killed your husband, señora," said Oliver.

"Then find him, my lord," she said. "Find him."

NINETEEN

"**B**ut are we any closer to finding who killed her husband?" said Oliver, as they all walked into Berenguer's study.

"Does the map have anything to do with Gil's death?" asked Isaac.

"The map? It's the road to the *finca*," said Oliver, picking it up and holding it up, first one way and then another.

Bernat was standing behind Oliver's chair and looking at it over the bigger man's shoulder. "It's a stretch of road near the *finca*," he said, "but not the property itself. That's the river, but you don't see the bend or the waterfall on this map. That, however," he pointed out, "is the road to Hostalric. And here is an inn."

"The inn we stayed at," said Oliver. "And the stranger was the mysterious Luis who was willing to pay a hundred sous for a map. Who must have killed Pasqual. I mean Gil."

"It doesn't make sense," said Berenguer. "If he already knew the inn where Gil de Finestres was staying and the direction he would head in each night, why buy the map?"

"That wasn't the map he bought," said Isaac quietly. "He bought the rest of the map. The part that shows which house belonged to Gil de Finestres."

"Then why not attack him in a quiet and private spot near

the house or on the road somewhere? Why wait until Monday morning and kill him on the outskirts of the city?"

"Perhaps he didn't get the map until Sunday," said Oliver. "And if he knew that Gil and I were heading off Monday morning, it seemed less complicated to let Gil come to him than for him to go out there."

"It seems that Señor Gil's whereabouts were known to everyone in the diocese by then," said the physician. "After all, he'd been followed from Castile to the inn. It was Señora Serena's whereabouts that were in doubt."

"But she has not been troubled since her husband's death," said Oliver.

"I wonder," said Isaac. "If Your Lordship and Your Excellency have no objections, I would like to offer a suggestion."

"Impossible," said Oliver firmly. "I won't have it."

"Let me consider it," said Berenguer. "It has its possibilities."

"Only if everyone in the city knows about it," said Isaac.

The following Tuesday, Serena de Finestres left the protection of the episcopal palace and rode slowly back to her *finca* several miles outside the city. She was alone, except for her maid, her small son, the physician, his daughter, and Yusuf. The physician and his assistants were there to ensure that she withstood the short journey in good health. They were to return the following day.

She arrived at the *finca* without incident and, according to a neighbor who was passing by, disappeared at once into the interior of the well-barricaded house.

Opinion in the city was divided over the wisdom and propriety of the move.

"I would have done the same. I wouldn't like to stay in the Bishop's palace at such a sorrowful time," said Pons Manet's wife, who was much attached to her husband. "I would rather be at home if I could."

"But they say her life is in danger," said her daughter-in-law, Francesca, a timid young woman. "And she has no husband to protect her now. I would stay in the palace as long as I could."

And in the square, the corn merchant said to Pons Manet, "They say the Bishop chased her out. I agree with him. She has a fine property and she needs a man to look after it. She won't find one by hiding in the palace."

"Give the poor creature time to mourn her loss," said the good-hearted Master Pons, thinking of his own affectionate wife. "Let her stay where she's safe for a while at least."

"Where who is safe?" asked Luis Mercer, coming up to them.

"Pasqual's wife," said the corn merchant. "The Bishop has sent her home. Tired of having her around the palace, I expect."

"Has he?" said Mercer. "That doesn't sound like him."

"It's true," said the corn merchant. "I had it on excellent authority."

"Whose? Bartolomeu the fishmonger? Surely you don't believe the market gossip and rumors."

"What rumors?" asked Luis Vidal, who had joined the group.

"That Mistress Serena has returned to her *finca*. And I heard it from Father Francesc," said the corn merchant indignantly. "I don't listen to market gossip."

"That proves my point. There's an old woman for you," said Luis Mercer and both men laughed.

"It's true," said Vidal. "I was up early this morning and I saw her leave."

"Well guarded, I hope," said Pons Manet.

"Not a single one, unless you consider the physician's lad a guard," said Vidal. "He and his master were the only men."

"Then I pray she arrives safely," said Pons.

Clara was putting the finishing stitches in the sea-green gown for Her Majesty when she received the summons to go to her.

"Doña Clara," said Her Majesty, "come over and sit here by me."

Clara did as she was told.

"I have received letters concerning you, Clara de Finestres," said Her Majesty. There was a long pause. Clara stared down at her hands. "That is your name, is it not?"

"It is, Your Majesty," Clara said.

"These letters bring news for you. Some of it is joyful, but some full of sorrow."

"Yes, Your Majesty?" said Clara, scarcely able to speak for trembling. "May I ask what is to happen to me?"

"That question will be answered in a moment, Doña Clara. It grieves me much to tell you that your father, a loyal and trusted servant to His Majesty, has died at the hand of an assassin."

It was as if time had disappeared and she was eleven years old again. "But Your Majesty, that happened—"

"A month ago," said Doña Eleanora. "Your mother, however, is well and impatient to see you."

"My mother? Your Majesty, my mother is dead."

"No, my child," said the Queen. "Your mother is alive and waiting your return. You will leave in the morning with a suitable escort. I am sending the Lady Tomasa with you since she would like to visit her brother. No doubt she will explain that. You will want to see to your things. The galley leaves at dawn."

Clara sat frozen, the Queen's last words echoing in her head.

"Do you understand what I am saying, Doña Clara?"

"Your Majesty is the most generous of monarchs," said Clara, her eyes filling with tears. "I do not know how, but you have rescued me and restored me to my family. I owe you my life and my honor. How am I to repay such a debt?"

"There is no debt, my child. I didn't find your mother," said the Queen. "Others did that. You will have the opportunity to thank them when you return home. I wish you a pleasant voyage," she said. The interview was over.

Clara was placing her possessions—a pitiful number, although more than she arrived with—in a box that had materialized from somewhere. They came nowhere close to the top. "Tomasa," she said. "Look at that. I could pack myself into the box, too, and there would still be room."

Doña Maria López de Herèdia pushed aside the flap of the tent. Both young women scrambled to their feet and dropped neat curtsies. "I have brought you something from Her Majesty," she said. "It is a wedding gift."

"A wedding gift," said Tomasa. "But neither of us—"

"It is for Doña Clara, for her father's sake and for hers," said Doña Maria, rather stiffly.

She stepped aside and the maid who followed her came in with the green gown that Clara had embroidered with circles of fantastic animals and flowers. "Shall I pack it for you?" asked the maid, and she began to settle it expertly into the box in a series of neat folds.

"You are most fortunate," said Doña Maria. "It is an extraordinary gift." She nodded and left.

"What she means by that," said Tomasa softly, "is that if it went to any one of us, it should have gone to Doña Maria. I thought it was for one of Her Majesty's nieces in Sicily."

The maid looked up, a grin flashed across her face and disappeared again, and she went back to packing it away.

TWENTY

On the second morning of his stay at the *finca,* Isaac awoke from a light sleep while the birds were still quarreling and singing their way into daybreak. He lay very still, listening to the sounds of someone rising quietly in a nearby room. At the creak of a door hinge, he rose, washed, arrayed his clothes as best he could, and said his morning prayers. Before picking up his staff and setting out on his own, he woke Yusuf, who was asleep in a makeshift cot in the same room.

He found the kitchen alive with activity. The fires had been lit, and he could hear at least two people moving about. "Good morning, Master Isaac," said the cook. "As soon as the oven's hot enough, I'll have today's bread in it. If you're hungry, I have a small loaf from yesterday."

"Many thanks, but I shall wait to break my fast, mistress," he said and headed toward the door.

"The señora will be in the near vineyard, Master Isaac," said the cook. "She sits there in the quiet of the morning. The lad will take you if you wish to join her."

"I can find my own way, mistress," said Isaac. "You are busy enough without worrying about me."

"That's true," said the cook, watching him go as she slapped pieces of dough into small, cylindrical shapes and put them to proof near the fire. "He's a wonder at finding his way around." But the boy was out tending to the oven fire and did not hear.

Isaac wandered around the outside of the house, sniffing the morning air and listening to the sounds of the countryside. At last he made his way along the path to the stream, located the footbridge, and crossed. From there he moved with confident steps toward the bench between the vines.

"Master Isaac," called Serena. "Come and join me here if you wish."

"I would be delighted, señora," he said.

"Sit here by me," she said. "This is where I come to find peace."

"It seems a place of great beauty," said the physician. "With sweetly scented flowers and fruit, birds singing and water splashing down."

"It is. I was here, looking over the grapes," she said, her voice controlled and tight, "when Lord Oliver brought me the news that Gil was dead." She paused to take a deep, gasping breath. "That was the second time I had endured that experience, Master Isaac. It was no easier for the practice," she added.

"The second time? How could that be?"

"The first time was in Barcelona," she said. "On his way to a meeting—an important and secret meeting—Gil was attacked. He barely escaped with his life. It seems one of my trusted servants was a spy. Someone decided it was best for the enemy to believe they had succeeded. They told me he was dead."

"Did they believe you were the spy?"

"No. But they wanted me to behave as if he were dead. For six terrible weeks, I tore my heart out before they told me that he was alive but we were in danger. They wished to keep him dead, officially, so that their enemies would no longer seek him out. I was told to live as any other new widow, preparing to move into my dower house. I did not need to pretend sorrow. I was separated from Gil and in the grip of such fear that no one could imagine me a happy woman," she added.

"A terrible sacrifice to pay, señora," said the physician.

"I thought so. But when I settled here, we were together often, more than some wives are with their husbands. And when I sit in the vineyard, I can almost believe those times have returned. For we were happy here when Gil was with us."

"Until they found you again."

"His Excellency believes that someone found me," said Serena. "Perhaps not the usual opponents."

"You are a brave woman, señora," said Isaac. "To come out here to face him, whoever he is."

"I am not brave, Master Isaac," said Serena. "I am angry. And I am not alone. Your presence is a great comfort to me. I trust that His Excellency will not be inconvenienced by your absence."

"Make no mistake. He will send for me quickly enough, señora, if he is," said the physician dryly.

"These are difficult days," said the widow in a low voice. "And I must take care of myself. For my daughter's sake, and my son's, and—because of my husband. It is a heavy burden."

"You are with child, señora?" he asked.

"How did you know?" she asked in a startled voice.

"I suspected it only. Did he know?"

"We rejoiced over it," said Serena, her voice rough with unshed tears. "Those last days. Like a newly wedded bride and groom."

"I am glad of that. And it explains why he said 'look after my little ones,' " said Isaac. "For as far as he knew at that moment, you had only one child, since your daughter had not been found–yet. That puzzled me."

"And you deduced it from that?"

"And other things. Perhaps your sorrow was of a different quality; of a mother as well as a wife. I cannot say, in truth, how I knew. It merely seemed to me that it was so. But, señora, you must try to eat, in spite of your sorrow," he said.

"I shall," she said. "I came out here with the intention of walking to the orchard for a sweet, ripe pear, but I sat down to listen to the birds and the water."

All this time, Blanqueta, the mastiff with the pale coat,

had been sleeping at Serena's feet. Suddenly, she raised her head and growled softly. "Hush, Blanqueta," said her mistress. "We have guests. Don't fret every time someone moves."

"Be very quiet, señora, please," whispered Isaac. "Keep a hand on the dog and listen."

But to Serena, the morning was as it always had been just before sunrise. In the barnyard a cock crowed. The birds' chatter and song died away; a breeze carried the smell of baking loaves toward them, accompanied by muted clatter from the open kitchen door. Then a twig cracked and her grip tightened on the nape of Blanqueta's neck.

"You're not as clever as you were," said a harsh voice.

Isaac stood and turned, holding his staff in front of him at a defensive angle.

"Who is that?" said Serena. "Creeping about at this hour?" Isaac could hear the slither of the material of her gown as she turned to look behind her. "You, sir, are on my property without my permission." Steely determination replaced the tremulous anguish in her voice. "Leave, or others will come to eject you."

"I am armed," he said. "And sitting in that oak is my bowman, who will put a bolt through your pretty dog's head if you move or do not keep her under control."

Isaac heard Serena rise to her feet. "And why should a stranger invade my peace?" she said. "What do you want of me, sir?"

"A stranger?" His voice rose in disbelief. "Me? I can't believe it, Serena. I foresaw so many problems. I expected you to be surrounded by armed men or locked in your fortress of a house. I was prepared for a mastiff. But not to find you alone, protected by a helpless blind man and armed in ignorance." He paused, as if in thought. "But you are pretending. You must be. You do know me."

"I have not the slightest idea who you are. Except that you must be mad."

"Who am I?" he said in anguished tones. "I am the man to whom all this property belongs, Serena. The man who has been cheated of his rights and has had his life destroyed because of your thieving, plotting ways."

"You *are* mad, sir," she said angrily. "This land is mine, given to me by my grandfather to hold as my own, and to dispose of as I will, by sale or testament."

"It was your dowry, Serena. He meant it for that. I should have had it. And you with it. You belong to me, and your children should have been mine. I have thought of little else since that day I stood and watched you come down the church steps on the arm of some other man—a nobody, an insignificant worm no one knew. Now he is dead, and only you and the boy stand in my way. When you die, it will all be mine, the way it should have been."

"Luis?" She shook her head in disbelief. "Only Luis could say that," she added, laughing. "It must really be you. I was told you were dead."

"You must forgive that slight untruth," he said stiffly. "It made my task easier. I hope the news did not distress you."

"It didn't, I assure you, my sweet cousin Luis. I recognize you now, but you look even worse than you did at thirteen. I cannot believe you ever thought I would marry you. Didn't I tell you I would rather take all my property into a convent? And I truly did not want to be a nun."

"You were promised to me!" he shrieked.

"By whom?" she asked. "Not Papa. Nor grandfather, who would not have given me this land if he had thought you would get it."

"Your mother promised my father—"

"Poor Mama," said Serena dismissively. "Papa took care of that. There was no more talk of it once he knew."

"You were promised!"

"There was no betrothal." She paused. The rustle of leaves and the low growl of the mastiff were the only sounds. "And you think that because Gil was killed that you can kill me and the baby and get it all? And after? What then? How will you leave my property? The way will be barred."

"By whom? A doddering old man, two boys, and some maids? The farm hands have left for the market, and there is no one else here. Who is to stop me? It will be easier to kill you than Gil, Serena. And I succeeded in that."

"Did you, Luis?" she asked softly. "Did you really kill my husband? I find it difficult to believe. Better men than you have tried to kill him in the past and discovered to their widows' sorrow that it was not easy. You lie, hoping to gain credit for a brave deed."

"I swear by the Holy Virgin I killed him, Serena. I told him who I was—his deadliest enemy—and like you, he laughed at me, saying I had no claim on him or his wife or her property. He turned his back to me, Serena, to ride away. I told him I would inherit everything when he was dead, and then I killed him."

"You killed the best man in the world and all for nothing," said Serena coldly. "Because if you kill me and Guillem, everything I own will go to Clara. She is alive. And safe."

"She *was* alive," he said. "That is true." He paused, and continued in a conversational tone, "I was suspicious of the story of her death, and so I looked for her. You hid her cleverly from me, Serena, but I found her, and I made sure she would be so far from this kingdom when I made my claim that no one else would ever discover she was still alive. If she is."

"When did you find her?" asked Serena.

"Only a month ago. It cost me five hundred sous to arrange to have her sold to slavers. But don't worry. I shall be well and truly compensated for my expenses," he said.

"You must have sold some other girl, Luis. Three days ago, Clara was living under Her Majesty's protection," said Serena. "I have proof of it. So leave my vineyard before I set my dog on you."

"I don't believe it," he said frantically. "She's in Egypt by now. He swore he was taking her to Egypt, where buyers pay top prices for a girl like her. You're lying to me."

"I am not lying. You may lie and cheat and stab unprepared men in the back, Luis, but I do not. I swear to you that what you have done has been done for nothing. She is alive and safe."

"Then I shall find her," he screamed, "and marry her myself."

Yusuf stumbled out of bed, dressed, and went barefooted down to the courtyard for cold water from the well. He washed his face and drank his fill before going to the kitchen, where the cook unceremoniously tossed him a loaf of yesterday's bread. Saluting her in thanks, he carried it out to the walled garden where the first rays of morning sun were already bathing the top of the western wall with light and warmth. He picked his way through the cabbages like a cat and reached the wall, climbed up, and began to observe with interest his master's wanderings around the house and over the meadow path almost as far as the stables. At one point Isaac lifted up his staff; Yusuf stuffed the remnant of the bread into his tunic and jumped down the far side of the wall.

He ran quickly and silently along the eastern edge of the meadow until he reached the line of trees that marked its southern limit. He paused for a while to listen, and then followed the line of trees toward the stables, stopping at the fourth one.

He had been told to cross the meadow without being seen, but there was no cover between him and the stream but a few grazing animals. Anyone in the near vineyard had an excellent view of the entire property down to the trees that flanked the road. Even crawling, he would be visible. But help can come from unexpected quarters. A nearby donkey was watching him with interest. He tore a piece from his loaf and held out his hand enticingly. She looked, considered, snatched up another mouthful of grass, and then drifted in his direction, her eye on the bread.

After one suspicious look, she delicately picked up the piece from his hand. He slipped the sash from his tunic over her neck. "Come along, sweetheart," he murmured, "let's go for a walk."

His plan was to make two diagonals across the meadow until he reached the stream, keeping the donkey between him and the vineyard. It succeeded wildly. Two horses and a mule, who had been observing their stablemate with vague curiosity, noticed the bread. In a moment, he was lost in a small herd. Judiciously doling out pieces as he went, he set out across the meadow.

He stopped in a slight hollow, protected by a bush; once again, slowly and methodically, his eyes searched the landscape. His followers waited for a few moments, and then, easily bored, began to wander off toward the stream. He freed the donkey, crouched down, and walked along beside them. At the bank, he jumped down; one splash into the cold water, and he was crouching, still and silent, listening. At last he began to pick his way quietly over stones, sharp gravel, and patches of mud. When he was close enough to the bench to hear, he settled down to wait.

Light creeping in through cracks in the shutters wakened Raquel. She eased herself out of bed, opened the door a crack, and listened. Except for sounds of muted activity from the kitchen, the household seemed to be asleep still. She threw a shawl over her shift, slipped into Guillem's chamber, and bent over to look at him. She laid a hand gently on his forehead. It was hot with fever. In the other bed, Joana the nursemaid was deep in slumber. Raquel was not surprised. Guillem had slept fitfully, tormented by bad dreams and a cough, keeping the nursemaid awake most of the night.

But sick or not, Guillem had to be moved. Gently, she draped him over her shoulder, his long legs dangling, and carried him down to the kitchen.

"What does he like in the morning?" she whispered. "He has a fever, I think, and slept badly."

"Bread and milk, the poor thing," whispered the cook. "With honey. Just a minute."

"I'll take him back to bed," she said, as soon as the cook put the dish in her half-free hand. "Thank you."

Instead of going back to the nursery, she found her way through narrow passages and up a steep stair to his mother's sitting room, a square tower in the southwest corner of the house. From its many windows, Serena had pointed out, one could see the road, the courtyard, the vineyards, and the hills rising behind them. This was where she sat at her needle and watched the road, looking for her husband's return while her son played at her feet. Guillem loved being in the room. He had a taste of bread and milk, sighed, and settled back to sleep on soft cushions piled up on a couch.

"Are the rest of them up?" asked the cook.

"I haven't heard them," said the kitchen lad.

"The mistress won't be pleased," she said, sitting down at the big table with a sigh. "Come and try the new loaves," she added. "We won't have many more spare moments to get off our feet once they start coming down." And the peace that comes before the raging tempest settled over the kitchen.

All that night, Oliver had been lying on a pair of rough boards up in the rafters of a shed in the vineyard, waiting. From up there, he had an excellent, if limited, view of the house, the stream, and the vineyard. He had seen Serena arrive and Isaac join her. He expected nothing in particular and was prepared for anything to happen.

When the stranger came through the vines and appeared suddenly in his field of vision, he gathered himself together, grasped the rafter beside him, and lowered himself down onto the hard dirt floor.

Unless Yusuf's eyes and ears had failed him or he was still asleep in his bed, Oliver felt moderately secure of the western approaches to the shed. He himself had had a good view of most of the land to the east. He concentrated on the man in the vineyard. This, he thought, must be Luis. He had a satisfactorily familiar air, even with his face turned away.

Somewhere, hiding in the vineyard, he must have left a few stout servants. If he was the Luis that Oliver thought he was, he would not have arrived alone. Cautiously, Oliver went down on his belly and crawled out of the shed, listening for the faintest rustle and searching the leafy rows for a sign of movement.

The attack was shocking in its unexpectedness. Suddenly, a massively heavy body landed on him, flattening him and rolling away. Then, during the split second in which he lay helpless, Oliver glimpsed the knife descending toward his back.

Oliver jerked over to one side, felt the steel strike his ribs, and snatched a long dagger out of his boot. He lashed out once, hit flesh, and bought a second in which to scramble upright.

He took another cut from the knife on his arm as he lunged for the hand holding it. Then he struck metal with metal and his opponent was disarmed. The attacker jumped away from Oliver, reached down for a long and heavy staff, and swung.

The sun was over the eastern hills, and the other servants were getting up when Joana cried out. Doors opened and slammed shut again and footsteps pounded along stone floors. Shouts echoed in the halls and confused cries for help.

Only the tower room was undisturbed. The heavy door at the foot of the stairs was barred; it would take ten men with a battering ram to budge it. Raquel leaned out the window to see what was going on, but except for her father standing in the vineyard, she could see nothing. Then she noticed Serena sitting in front of him. Something must have disturbed her, for she rose to her feet and turned to observe whatever it was.

As she made the turn, the rising sun caught the glint of the knife tucked into the bodice of her gown.

The chaos in the house increased in intensity as it moved down to the kitchen. "Guillem is gone and Mistress Raquel, too," shrieked Joana. "I searched all over the house. They are gone."

"Nonsense," said the cook. "Mistress Raquel brought him down for some bread and milk and then took him back up again."

"Dear God, how am I to tell the mistress?" said Joana. "Where is she?" She looked wildly around the kitchen as if she expected to find her tending the fire. "The mistress is gone, too," she cried out in panic.

"She's in the vineyard," said the cook. "Now get out of my kitchen, all of you. Out!"

And they all poured out, screaming and shouting, Dalmau, the nursemaid, and three maids, heading through the kitchen garden toward the vineyard.

At the sound of the uproar from the house, Luis Mercer drew his sword and whipped around, turning his back to Serena de Finestres and the physician in order to protect himself from the threat behind him.

Yusuf scrambled, damp and chilly, out of the streambed

and ran over to help his master. "Lord," he said, "once more I do not have my sword when I need it."

"Forget your sword, Yusuf," said Isaac. "Get his lordship."

"But I can't find him," said Yusuf. "I'll look again."

Serena de Finestres neither saw nor heard anything but Luis Mercer. "The maids and Dalmau might not be able to stop you," she said quietly to his back. "But I shall." Letting go of Blanqueta, she put a hand to her bosom. She took two steps after him. Then, firmly grasping a dagger held low in front of her and with all the force her rage could summon up, she thrust the weapon into his back.

Blanqueta, freed from her mistress's restraining hand and frantic with the smell of blood and rage, sprang up and sank her teeth into Luis's sword arm just above the wrist, knocking him down to the ground with her massive front paws.

Luis screamed in pain and astonishment. Hands grasped Serena's shoulders and pulled her to one side. "No, señora," said Oliver in a thick and groggy voice. "You must learn to place a knife correctly. You'll never kill a man that way."

Yusuf took Serena from Oliver and led her back to where his master stood. "I stabbed him, Master Isaac," she said without expression. "But he is not dead. Blanqueta has him on the ground, and Lord Oliver is watching him."

"Sit down, señora," said the physician. "Here next to me." She obeyed like a child. Isaac picked up her wrist and hand. The blood throbbed in her arm, but the hand was icy cold. He set it gently down again. "He killed my husband," she said, "and he was going to kill my baby. I stabbed him exactly as he stabbed my Gil." She began to shake violently.

Heavy footsteps on the wooden bridge over the stream heralded the approach of the nursemaid, trailed by the rest of the servants. "Señora," cried Joana. "I cannot find Guillem. I've looked everywhere, and I cannot find him. Or that Raquel."

Her mistress stared at her as if she were speaking in a strange and unknown tongue. "Did you look in my sitting room?" she said at last. "They were to go there and bar the door."

"Your sitting room," said Joana. "I didn't think to look there, señora," she muttered and turned away.

"Call off your dog, señora," said Oliver, who was kneeling by Luis.

"Well, go and look," she said to Joana. "Blanqueta, come. Leave him and come." She bent over, burying her face in the dog's neck. The kerchief she used to tie back her hair came loose; her heavy hair fell down over Blanqueta, hiding her from the world.

"Where is Master Luis?" asked Isaac, rising and reaching out his hand for his pupil.

"On the ground," murmured Yusuf, drawing him farther from Serena. "Lord Oliver is with him. He has turned him and taken the knife from his back, lord. He cleans it with a vine leaf."

"Take the knife from him, wash it in the stream, and give it to Dalmau. He will know where it belongs."

"At once, lord," he said and moved silently over to Oliver. "My master asks me to take the knife, wash it in the stream, and return it to its resting place, my lord. It is very bloody."

"She placed it well," said Oliver, catching his breath with difficulty. "But I gave him a wound in the front. It will serve for those who wish vermin to be killed in a fair fight."

"Is he dead?"

"Not yet. Take him to the house and bind up his wounds. Then if he lives they can hang him for killing His Majesty's officer."

"You are wounded as well, my lord," said Yusuf.

"Not by that creature," said Oliver. "By the wild man in the oak tree. Just a scratch," he added and crumpled in a swoon.

"The wild man in the oak tree?" said Yusuf.

Oliver de Centelles was carried to the house and taken to a chamber where Raquel, with the assistance of one of the maids, took care of his wounds in the arm, the ribs, and another on the scalp. She cleaned them, bound them up, gave him a draft for the pain, and told him his explanations could wait. "Sit with him," she told the maid. "Keep him from talking or moving about, and send for help if he gets difficult."

But Lord Oliver was drifting off to sleep as she spoke,

and she hurried down to help her father and Yusuf with the badly injured Luis Mercer.

"How is he, Papa?" she asked.

"We can do no more for him than we could for the man he killed," said Isaac in a voice that betrayed no emotion.

"I told him," said Serena, "to concern himself with the state of his soul. I sent the lad to fetch a priest, but he says over and over that he wants no priest, he only wants this land which is his and everything else of mine. The fool!" She shook her head. "How is Lord Oliver?"

"He has been in a fight," said Raquel. "He was wounded, and lost blood, but the wounds are stanched and he is asleep. I would not let him speak, and so I don't know who attacked him. This man?"

"Luis? No," said Serena. "Luis did not know Lord Oliver was here. But he said that he brought someone with him."

"He must have fled, señora," said Isaac.

"Why are we watching over this piece of carrion," she said bitterly, "as if his life had any value?"

"Peace, señora," said the physician softly. "He, too, is a man, made by the Lord. And he may have something useful to say."

The man on the bed seemed to have been reduced to a hollow face and sunken eyes, as if he were already without substance. He opened his eyes and blinked. "You speak as if I am not here," he whispered. "I can hear your every word. You will be sorry, my pretty cousin, that you married that worthless clerk when you could have had me. When my loyal Enrique carries out his final task for me." He coughed. Blood trickled out of his mouth and his eyes glazed over.

Isaac removed his hand from his chest. "It is sometimes useful to know who you must watch out for, señora," he said.

TWENTY-ONE

Three days later, Oliver de Centelles was sitting in a large chair, comfortably cushioned in pillows, enjoying the late-morning sun. Raquel sat nearby, at her needle, thinking her own thoughts. They were not of the burly man with the rough-hewn, pleasant features sitting near her, but of a tall, handsome man with a shy, sweet face who should, it seemed to her, have arrived back from Constantinople by now.

In her sitting room in the tower, Serena sat by a window at her work, half of her attention on Guillem, who was creating something complicated with blocks of wood, and the rest, as always, on the road.

She heard them before she saw them. Someone was singing, in a deep bass voice; the sound came from the direction of the highroad. Then a puff of wind blew a plume of dust in the direction of her house. She watched it scatter into the air and settle into nothingness. From the sheltering trees on either side of the narrow track that led to the *finca* she caught a glimpse of a horse, broad-chested and large. She went over to the window and looked out, by long habit shielding herself from the view of those looking up. Four men, riding chargers and armed with lances, were approaching her gates. Behind them rode four women, and after them came two grooms, baggage mules, and four more lancers, followed by an armed officer.

She snatched up Guillem and ran down the stairs, calling for Dalmau. "Open the door," she said. "The front door." As soon as he had struggled with the locks and the bar, she stepped outside, set Guillem on his feet, and waited.

The four lancers divided, leaving a space broad enough for the first two ladies to ride up to the steps. The grooms hurried over to assist them to dismount. The smaller of the two women jumped lightly down and ran forward. "Mama!" she cried and threw her arms around Serena, who bent to embrace her.

"Who is she?" asked the little boy, peering around from behind his mother, awestruck at the sight of so many strangers.

"Your sister," said Serena. "Clara. Clara has come home."

"From Heaven?" he asked skeptically.

"No, Guillem," said Clara. "From Sardinia. It's over the sea but not so far away as Heaven." She turned to the young lady beside her. "Doña Tomasa, I would like to present my mother. Mama, Doña Tomasa was very kind to me when I was in Sardinia."

"Doña Tomasa," said Serena. "I am honored. And if I am not mistaken, there is someone in the courtyard who is anxious to see you. Both of you."

She took them through the stone-flagged hall to a pair of heavy wooden doors. They led to a large courtyard formed by the main block of the house, its one wing, and two high, thick, stone walls. There was one gate to the outside, made of heavy wood and closed with a massive bar. In this secure retreat, a chair had been placed in the shade of a small tree, with its back to the house. "My lord," said Serena. "I have brought some friends to you. I will leave you to enjoy their company."

The man in the chair rose slowly and awkwardly, turning to face them. "Oliver!" cried Tomasa catching him affectionately by the hands. "What has happened to you?"

Clara stiffened as if she had been struck and then looked from one to the other. They both had tall frames, honey-colored curls, warm skin, and gray eyes. "My lord," said

Clara, curtsying. "You are somewhat alike," she added. "I had not seen the resemblance before."

"Poor Tomasa, if that is true. Did she fail to tell you that she is my sister?" said Oliver.

"Oliver," murmured Tomasa, "you asked me not to."

"Fortunately," said Oliver, "her father, Sant Climent, our mother's second husband, is better looking than my father was, so the likeness is not too powerful. I am happy to see you both," he added. "And as for me, I was caught unawares by a wild man with a staff and a knife, whose intent was to club me on the head and cut my throat, I believe."

"He didn't succeed," said Tomasa. "I'm glad. I would have been sorry to lose you. One needs a brother. Or at least I do."

"He surprised me," said Oliver in injured tones. "Falling like an extremely heavy nut out of a tree. Hence the wounds. But I marked him once or twice. I would have finished him off except for that staff."

"I am happy to be here," said Tomasa, "where there is real fighting. I was tiring of a peaceful life in a tent. Her Majesty talks of passing the winter in Sardinia. Or Sicily. How am I to find a husband if I am traveling constantly? And so I begged to accompany Clara, but now I see that my task will be to take you back to Mama. She will be pleased to see her wandering children, I hope. Do you recognize Clara, Oliver, now that she is no longer dressed like a boy? Or a friar?" asked Tomasa. "If so, you should speak to her. And nicely."

"You have not lost your skill at rapid speech in your time at court, Tomasa," said her brother, who was now swaying slightly and looking pale.

"It might be better if Lord Oliver sat down," said Clara. "And since I would like to talk to Mama, with your permission, my lady, I will leave you with your brother."

"Where is my mother?" Clara asked the first person she met. It was Dalmau.

"In her sitting room," he said. "Up those stairs, mistress."

Clara ran up them as lightly as if she had not been riding since dawn and burst into the room. "Mama," she said and fell on her knees, burying her head in her mother's lap. "I thought you were dead. Why didn't you come for me?" she said at last, raising her head. Her face was stained with tears. "I kept hoping, but you never came, and I knew you must be dead."

"I didn't know where you were, darling," said Serena, stroking her hair. "I searched and searched, but no one had seen or heard of you."

"I never told anyone who I was," said Clara.

"Why not?" asked her mother.

"You told me not to," she said, surprised. "You said not to mention Papa's name or none of us would be safe. So I didn't."

"I don't remember saying it," said her mother. "That terrible day. . . ." She stopped, her eyes full of tears, unable to continue. "If I hadn't," she said at last, "I might have found you. I searched all over the city. Then they told me that a bundle had been found in the arms of a little girl who died in that crowd. They gave it to me; it was yours."

"She stole it from me," said Clara. "She snatched it out of my hands. I tried to get it back, but the crowd was too thick."

"I buried her, Clara, thinking she was you. Poor little creature." She grasped her daughter tightly. "Where have you been? What have you been doing all this time?"

"Well," said Clara, unsure how much to say, "for a while I stayed at the convent, helping the sisters look after the younger children. They were very kind to me, Mama. Then I worked."

"Worked? What do you mean?" asked her mother.

"As a kitchen maid, Mama. You wouldn't believe how terrible a kitchen maid I was. And then I—well, I ran away, because the cook told me I wasn't safe where I was. She thought the mistress was going to send me away somewhere."

"I know about that," said her mother, looking stricken.

"And so the cook cut my hair, I put on the lad's old tunic, and I ran away, hoping to find our kin in Girona. Instead, I met Lord Oliver, Tomasa's brother. He sent me to the Queen."

"Thanks be to God," murmured her mother.

"And Her Majesty sent me to you. Mama, who is our cousin in Girona?"

"He was the man who killed your father and tried to sell you out of the country," she said bitterly. "He hated me, and he wanted our land and money."

"Then it's just as well I didn't get to the city. Although when I asked you about him, you might have told me what he was like," she said reproachfully.

"I never thought to see him again, darling. He was thirteen when we last met. I was seventeen and thought him loathsome. We had nothing to do with him after that. A while ago, I heard he had died in the plague. But he wasn't blood kin. He was the son of my grandfather's brother-in-law by a first marriage."

"Why would he hate you?"

"Because I told him I'd sooner lock myself away in a convent than marry him."

"Where is he now?"

"Dead. I watched him die. I tried to kill him myself, my love," Serena whispered. "In the vineyard. What must you think of your mama? And I was sure I had, but Lord Oliver swears not. He insists he ran Luis through in a fair fight when he attacked me."

"You are fierce and brave, Mama. I have always known it."

"Did you know that His Lordship and your father were in His Majesty's service together? But I must rest. We will have time together to talk of everything, my love. Go and join your guests in the courtyard. I am faint with too much joy."

"I will go in a moment, Mama. First tell me how you are."

"There is another person sitting here," observed Tomasa. "Does she not exist?"

"She most certainly does," said Oliver. "She and her father saved my life. Mistress Raquel," he said, in a louder voice. "I pray, excuse my discourtesy, but may I ask you to leave your comfortable seat and come here to meet my sister?"

"There was no need to raise your voice, my lord. I could hear you quite well," said Raquel, crossing the space and curtsying. "I am honored, Doña Tomasa. And may I remind you that you are here, my lord, to rest in the sweet air of Señora Serena's courtyard. Not to shout and walk about."

Tomasa laughed. "I am awed at your bravery, Mistress Raquel. Few people dare to speak so firmly to my brother."

"She is terrifying," said Oliver. "But she is also very skillful." A rustle of cloth behind him made him turn, pulling at the wound on his shoulder. He gasped once and Raquel leaned over with a soft cloth to pat dry the sweat on his forehead.

"You are quite safe here, my lord," said Raquel. "There is no need to look around constantly. It's not good for you."

"I am suitably chastened," he said. "Doña Clara, I thought I recognized your step, but I am forbidden by my physician from rising to greet you."

"Mistress Raquel," said Clara. "My mother is forever grateful for all you have done. Your presence here has been most comforting for her. And she tells me that without your help, she might never have been found by those seeking to reunite us."

"I did little," said Raquel. "And what I did, I did most gladly. Would you mind, Doña Clara, if we placed a chair for you here? Now Lord Oliver can talk to you without twisting about or raising his voice." Ignoring Clara's scarlet cheeks, she signaled to Dalmau to move the chair.

"My mother says she feels faint," said Clara. "Is she ill?"

"No," said Raquel with a sharp look. "But she has had grief as well as joy to deal with. I am sure she will tell you all that happened, but right now, she is exhausted. I will go to her."

"And I will take your comfortable seat, Mistress Raquel," said Tomasa, "since I, too, am weary from travel."

Tomasa seemed to be more restless than weary. After a few moments of quiet in the courtyard, in which the occasional chirp of a bird was the most conversation that could be heard, she jumped up energetically. "I have brought no work with me," she said. "I cannot sit here idly while you two chat. I have too much to do. I will just go up and see what has happened to my things." And without waiting for a response, she left.

Tomasa seemed to lose interest in her work somewhere between the courtyard and her chamber. She opened the door, looked in, saw everything laid out neatly, and closed the door again. "Where might I find the señora?" she asked Joana, who was passing by with an armload of clean linen.

"Up those stairs, Doña Tomasa," said Joana, managing a bobbing curtsy and to hold onto her load. "Do you want—"

"Don't trouble yourself," said Tomasa and ran up the narrow staircase.

"Please forgive this intrusion," said Tomasa. "Especially when you need to rest. But I decided that unless I left the courtyard, my poor brother would never be able to speak another word. I seem to act as a barrier as thick as any stone wall."

"A barrier, Doña Tomasa?"

"Yes, a barrier," said the young woman, pulling up a low stool close to the couch where Serena was lying down. "Oliver is usually as bold as a cage full of lions, and I know Clara is witty and charming. But señora, they are sitting as mute as two statues. And my brother has written to me about her in such terms that I cannot help wondering if he is taken with her."

"But Clara is just—"

"Clara is sixteen," said Tomasa.

"True," said her mother. "I haven't had a chance to think of her as almost a woman. It's a shock." She looked shrewdly at Tomasa. "And so, my lady, you are making up a match, are you?"

"I would like her as a sister," said Tomasa. "I enjoy her company. And looking at him down there, all unhappy and covered with confusion, I think I am right. It is amazing, señora," she added, "because women—great ladies with grand dowries—have been throwing themselves at him since he first sprouted a beard. But he didn't care enough for any of them to marry, much to my mother's distress. And he's very stubborn."

"I must consider this," said Serena. "And talk to Clara. My husband loved your brother dearly—as a son, or a younger brother. And trusted him absolutely. But she is young."

"Let us hear what others think of the match. Mistress Raquel? What do you say?"

"I like your brother, my lady," said Raquel. "But I think it should depend on the young lady's feelings."

"Ah, a believer in love matches! Excellent! Are you married, Mistress Raquel?"

"No, my lady, I am not," she said, burying her face in her work.

"Betrothed?"

"Yes, my lady."

"I wish I were," said Tomasa discontentedly. "Mama makes my life a misery over it."

"Would you like to be betrothed to someone in particular?" asked Serena. "Or do you simply want to have your own household?"

"If my brother married someone I liked," said Tomasa, as if she were answering the question, "I could live with him. His father's land is not far from here. A pretty *finca,* although not as grand as his father's estates were. But then he rebelled against His Majesty, which was neither loyal nor clever."

"Is it important?" asked Raquel. "To be not far from here?"

Tomasa's cheeks turned quite pink. "I have a distant cousin on my father's side who is charming and shy and courteous. He's also brave, except with women. My mother doesn't like him. He's not as rich as my father, and he cares nothing for advancement at court. She would rather I married a viscount, as she did. I point out that it does no good, because viscounts quarrel with the king, get banished, and die young, like Oliver's father."

"Surely not every viscount," said Serena, smothering a laugh. "What does your father think?"

"Papa likes him, but with Mama guarding the gate, he'll never have the courage to propose the match."

"And he lives near your brother's *finca?*" asked Raquel.

"How did you know that?"

"I guessed, my lady."

"Tell me about your betrothed," said Tomasa.

Raquel stumbled through the tale of her courtship, explaining with embarrassment how long it had taken her to see how wonderful Daniel was. "Now," she said, "his uncle has sent him to Constantinople, and I have such a feeling of dread when I think of the journey across the sea that I cannot bear it."

"Nonsense," said Tomasa. "I've been to Sardinia and back, and so has Clara, and we're both alive and well. Constantinople can't be that much farther away. When will he be back?"

"I don't know," said Raquel miserably. "Soon, I hope."

"Clara's poor mama is half dead with sleepiness, listening to our chatter," said Tomasa. "Let us return to my poor brother."

"Your sister has gone running out of the courtyard," said Clara. "I wonder what is wrong."

"Since it is my sister," said Oliver, "she remembered a tiny brooch she needs for her cloak or a silver pin for her hair."

"Doña Tomasa is not empty-headed," said Clara. "And I would have been lost and friendless in Sardinia without her. Not once did she ask me where I came from or who I was, unlike everyone else. She sensed that I did not want to talk about it."

Oliver reddened slightly. "She is good-hearted, but before you turn her into a saint, let me confess that one of the letters I sent with the ship was to Tomasa, saying you were coming and that she was not to ask about your name and family, since they involved the highest affairs of state."

"You should be ashamed, my lord," said Clara, "to tell me my kindest friend was good to me only because you asked her to be."

"No," said Oliver quietly. "She became attached to you as soon as you met. And no one, not even her brother, can force Tomasa to like someone against her will. Ask my mother. But if she refrained from questioning you, it might have been because she honored my request."

"Are you sure?"

"I am. I have a letter from her filled with your praises.

Someday I might show it to you," he said. "Or perhaps not. Clara, I have something to say to you." He stopped.

"Yes, my lord?"

"How long was your hair before the cook cut it off?"

Clara began to laugh. "What a strange question, my lord. But since you ask it, down to here," she said, indicating a place halfway down her back. "It will grow back, you know."

"You are—" He paused. "Extraordinary."

"That is it, my lord? I am extraordinary?"

"Yes. Brave and clever. You can madden me, but you also make me laugh." He leaned back in his chair, panting from effort. "I think if you were wearing a ragged tunic or a friar's robe, I could talk more easily to you. That silk gown and this charming courtyard make me tongue-tied and awkward."

"I make you laugh but you prefer me as a boy. A little brother?" she asked. There was a chill in her voice. "Or someone to help saddle the mules?"

"I never asked you to saddle the mules, Clara," he said.

"And now you see that I seem to be a rich young lady and must be treated courteously. And that troubles you, doesn't it? What did you think I was, my lord? Someone amusing to be tucked away in a pretty little house for when you were in the city?" She paused. "If I had wanted that, I could have solved my problems months ago and avoided much suffering. But I didn't."

"No," he said gravely. "That was far from my thoughts. I saw you were astonishing and knew I was in love with you."

"Love," said Clara bitterly. "My master spoke of love to me, too. And you're just as difficult to believe. The way you behaved is not how a man treats someone he loves."

"What do you know of how a man in love behaves?" he asked.

"I was poor, my lord, but I was not deprived of my sight, my hearing, or my wits. I observed."

"Perhaps you observed poor models, Doña Clara."

"And when did you fall in love with me?" she asked. "When you saw this, and realized that I would have a good dowry? Doña Tomasa used to talk about her brother who was too poor to marry."

"My sister has a habit of jesting about money to annoy

our mother," said Oliver. "No, Clara. I know many women with more land and bigger dowries. Mundina told me you were a girl, and I was in love with you from that moment. Although Sergeant Domingo accused me of it well before then and was mightily disturbed. After all, we thought you were an eleven-year-old boy."

She giggled suddenly. "Not a convincing boy, I'm afraid."

"You're wrong. You were an odd kitchen lad, but I was convinced you were a boy," he said. "It was your background you could not conceal. If you had been, as your appearance suggested, a child of the streets, would I have still loved you?" he asked. "I think so. And I would have done my best to keep you close by me so as not to lose you. As it was, knowing you must be a gentlewoman, I had to put you where you would be safe from your enemies and out of my reach."

"Mundina and then Sardinia," said Clara. "It did keep me out of reach. And I felt safe. But surely my reputation would have been safe somewhere closer than Sardinia."

"Not from me. I wanted to marry you, Clara. I still do."

"Marry me?" she said in horrified tones. "Now?"

"If not now, when?" he asked, his gray eyes turning chill in the sunny courtyard. "Will I seem more appealing in six months, or a year?"

"But how can I marry with hair this short?" she said in evident distress. "And I want to spend some time with Mama."

"Seeing your mother is reasonable, but I'm not waiting until your hair grows to your waist."

Clara folded her hands in her lap, looked up from under her lashes, and said, "In that case, you'll have to enter into negotiations with my mother. Unless she's changed in the past four years, I think you'll find her quite astute and ferocious."

"I shall," said Oliver. "She will find me as determined as she is astute."

"There's something you should tell Mama," said Clara.

"And what's that?"

"Her Majesty gave me a wedding present. A splendid gown."

"How did Her Majesty know?" asked Oliver.

"Perhaps you should ask your sister," said Clara. "I suspect her of more than one plot."

"I have one other thing to say to you," said Oliver. "When we leave here, whenever that is, I am taking you to the convent."

"Why?" said Clara.

"I promised the sister portress that you would come and see her. She will be happy to discover who you are."

TWENTY-TWO

"Master Isaac, I have called you here for a pleasant reason," said Berenguer.

"Your Excellency is not ill?"

"Not at all. I have word that Lord Oliver de Centelles is riding into the city, escorting your estimable daughter. They will come here first, because she wishes to ensure that he is well after the journey."

"It is only eight days since he received those wounds, and although he made light of them," said Isaac, "they could have killed a weaker man."

"I received a report from him saying, among other things, that he intends to secure the future safety of Señora Serena's daughter by marrying her himself. My good sergeant was convinced that no sooner did he see her, even dressed as she was, than he fell in love with her, so it is, perhaps, not surprising."

"He has put himself into danger for the family. I thought it was because of his affection for Pasqual Robert—or Gil de Finestres as he should be called," said the physician.

"I would like to think it was both," said the Bishop. "But Master Isaac, it troubles me that Luis Mercer should have embarked on such a course," said Berenguer. "He was not a pleasant man, and he had his strange side, but I would not have thought him mad."

"You think it madness, Your Excellency?" said Isaac. "I don't. These deeds spring from greed. So many have died and unwittingly enriched distant heirs with their lands and goods that our times have bred an army of liars and thieves. Now everyone casts about to find unclaimed riches in his family or beyond. It distresses me, but it has become part of ordinary life. Luis Mercer was not mad."

"But surely Luis Mercer was no kin to Gil."

"He wasn't, Your Excellency. He was distant kin to the señora. She told me that his father made approaches to her family when his son was a little boy. It seems that he raised the lad to believe he could mend his fortunes by marrying her. Mercer was furious when she married another."

"But a sane man does not nurse fury over so many years," said the Bishop.

"I don't suppose that he did," said Isaac. "After all, he married well, they say, but his wife and child both died. I think he spoke truth when he told me that he had been bothered with sleeplessness and melancholy for the past two years."

"He was said to be sorrowing over his wife's death," said Berenguer.

"I believe, Your Excellency, that he was brooding over the rich marriage he failed to secure. Consider this. Mercer was in Barcelona when his cousin married Gil de Finestres. He was waiting and saw them coming down the church steps. Pasqual Robert came here two years ago, and Mercer recognized him. Not as a valued servant of the King but as the man who married young Serena instead of him. He may have been the only person in the city to know who Pasqual Robert really was. And seeing him every day at the Exchange must have worked on him like a canker that grows worse every day."

"Are you saying, Master Isaac," said the Bishop, "that a man who was as secret as a tomb and as cautious as the wildest beast was recognized by someone who knew him only as the husband of the woman he had wanted to marry?"

"I am, Your Excellency. He thought she had given herself

and her wealth away to a clerk. Someone of inferior abilities and fortune to his own."

"And so he delivered the cruelest blow he could by killing him. Who knows . . . he may have hoped to marry her."

"She is with child, you know," observed the physician. "It has helped her to withstand the blow."

"Then there is joyful news in the midst of sorrow. And I think that bustle must be the arrival of your daughter and his lordship."

"What is the matter with you, Raquel?" said her mother impatiently. "In two days the High Holidays will be on us, there is much to do, and you sit there moping in the corner as if you were a grand lady with a hundred servants at your command."

"I'm tired, Mama," said Raquel. "I have been working hard."

"Nonsense," said her mother.

"For the last five days, Mama, I have either been consoling a widow who has lost a man she adored, or listening to the nonsense of two young ladies, both of whom think they are in love. Moving from grief that made me weep in sympathy to giving advice on what lovers mean when they say this or that or the other thing. And in between looking after a sick man who refused to do anything I told him. I'm tired."

"You're back now," said her mother.

"They moaned at me endlessly, Mama, and one of them had her lover right there and the other was not two hours' ride away." She burst into tears.

"He'll be back," said Judith, sitting down on the bench under the trees and putting her arm around her daughter.

"I shouldn't be so unkind," she said, sniffling. "Mistress Clara has suffered terribly, and Doña Tomasa's mother is trying to make her marry someone else. And she has been generous to me. She put a parcel wrapped in linen in my box just before it was closed up. I must look at it."

Leah was dispatched, grumbling, to fetch the parcel.

"She said it was from both of them," said Raquel, holding the parcel. "A token to thank us for saving Lord Oliver's life."

Judith was staring across the courtyard past Raquel's
shoulder. "Show it to me later," she said briskly. "I have to
see Naomi about—" and still talking, she was gone.

Raquel untied the knot on the ribbon that held the parcel
together and opened it. Inside was an exquisite shift of heavy
silk, embroidered in white and silver thread.

"Mama. Look at this," she said, holding it up. "It's lions,
playing." And then she remembered that she was alone.

"Of course, it's lions," said a deep voice behind her. "After
all, my name is Daniel."

"Daniel!" shrieked Raquel, jumping to her feet and dropping the shift down on its wrapping. "I thought you had been
lost at sea," she said, and threw her arms tightly around him.

"With you waiting for me?" he said. "Never."

"When did you return?" she asked, letting go and sitting
down demurely. "We heard nothing."

"I am still covered with the dust of the road," he said. "My
aunt does not know I am home, so I must go to her at once.
But I had to see you first. You are lovelier than ever," he
said. "But you've been crying."

"And you are dirty and as sunburnt as a sailor," said Raquel. "But as welcome as anyone could be."

"I cannot understand how a mother could lose a child like
that," said Judith. They were sitting in the courtyard after
supper. A breeze had blown out the candle, and Judith had
not called for another. "I could understand it in midst of war
or rioting. But she must have been careless."

"She blames herself, my dear," said Isaac. "But she loves
her children as passionately as any mother. We do not know
what was happening at that time in their lives, do we? Except
that there had been war and pestilence in the kingdom. These
things have unexpected effects that linger. She fled from danger, believing she had secured a safe place for her daughter."

"She was wrong, wasn't she?" said Judith. "Sending the
child off like that to the nuns. Not even to friends. It's not
like sending Miriam down the street to Dolça."

"Don't be too hard on her, Judith."

"I don't like to hear of the terrible things that can happen to children. I'm glad Daniel is back. I was beginning to be very worried about him."

"What is wrong, my love? You seem uneasy."

"Nothing. You were telling me about the señora, Isaac, and I interrupted you."

"I was trying to explain why it was important for Raquel to be there."

"She was looking after the great lord, wasn't she? He seemed a pleasant man, I thought, when no one knew he was a great lord."

"He still is, Judith. But from the time I first met her, I suspected that Serena de Finestres was with child, and so I was alarmed that her sorrow and distress kept her from eating or drinking," he said. "Raquel was there more to watch over her than over Lord Oliver who, injured as he was, seemed well able to care for himself. Her daughter has now taken over the task, and I gather they are looking after each other assiduously."

"How did you suspect?" asked Judith.

"I don't know. There's something about a woman with child . . . an air, a way of speech, it may even be a scent that seems to suggest it," he said.

"Then I wonder you haven't noticed it in me," she said. "Or does it only work if the woman is a stranger to you?"

There was a long silence, broken only by the chirping of insects in the warm night. Isaac took a deep breath. "Oh, my dearest love," he said at last. "Is that true? I cannot believe that after all this time—"

"The twins are only eight. And there was the baby I lost," she said. "It hasn't been that long. And I'm not all that old."

"You certainly are not, my love. A wedding and a child. I have been the most fortunate of men." And the blind physician ran his fingers lightly over Judith's well-remembered features.

"Don't say that," she said. "It's not lucky." And she began to laugh as he gathered her in his arms.